I0739544

PSY

www.psythebook.com

First edition

This is a work of fiction. Names, characters, businesses, places, events and incidents are either the product of the author's imagination or used in a fictitious manner. Any resemblance to actual persons, living or dead, or actual events, is purely coincidental.

ISBN: 978-0-9979619-1-1

PSY

JOEY SLATER-MILLIGAN

Our history is written, but our story is still being told...

7th November 1985

It never occurred to me that I was in a cult, but now I realise there's no other word for it. It's all over the papers. It's all over the news. Right now, I don't know what's real except this one thing: Silas is gone. They burned him alive.

I'm truly stunned. Only this afternoon was I telling him about the dissonance among the followers, and he just didn't believe me. I should have tried harder to make him see, to make him understand. I know I'm not to blame for his death, but perhaps I could have saved him.

As I write this, I'm hiding. It seems one of the followers has already divulged details to the press. I don't know who it was (although several people come to mind who I believe would be capable of such a thing).

The police are looking for the followers now, and they keep saying Silas was a murderer. I wish I could explain, but I know they won't be able to see it from our point of view. The truth is that the sacrifices volunteered themselves, they wanted to contribute their life to a greater entity. They weren't victims; they chose their path. I wish I could tell everyone this, but I'm sure the public would never believe it.

I can't get this word out of my head… cult. They say a cult is defined by its deviant behaviour. I can't deny our deviant beliefs, but it was our objective to inspire people to move away from the static mediocrity that seems to have taken hold in this country. That was our goal and, deviant or not, our intentions were good.

The one thing I do contest is that Silas was "disturbed." They're wrong. I'm certain he was a good man.

In our last conversation, Silas reminded me of his vision. He dreamed of making things better for parapsychs, and therefore the world. I truly believed he wanted to change the world for the better. And I honestly thought he was capable of doing so. If I tell anyone this now, I'll surely be arrested. I probably shouldn't even be writing this.

To protect my own life, I will no longer go by Lissy. I never felt a connection to the nickname anyway, but Silas took quite a liking to it. In his honour, Lissy dies here too.

I don't know what to do.

I suppose the only thing I can do is move on. I started this diary as a record of our enterprise, so that when the shift finally happened, we would be able to look back over our story. Instead, our tale has been prematurely and violently aborted.

This will be my last entry.

I know the world is not a bad place, but we wanted to make it even better. I suppose I will do my best to make positive changes in the small ways I can. Maybe one day, someone will change the world. Today is not that day.

1

Fear. Anxiety. Gel pens. Jessa Baxter cycled through her most recent thoughts. Friends. Telekinesis. Dread. She glanced at her phone to see a text message from her grandparents. Good luck, Jessamine. They never got to grips with the colloquialism of texting. She noticed a weather update: storms spreading from the west. Umbrella. Jacket. Boots. No—it was too early to try remembering things. She decided to focus first on the most urgent wrongs that needed righting. Emptiness. Hunger. Breakfast.

"Surprise!" Jessa's family yelled, far too loudly to be appropriate on an early Monday morning. Jessa stood in the doorway in her slippers and dressing gown. She rubbed her eyes and pushed the jumble of frizzy waves away from her face.

"What? What's going on?" she said. Her mother, father, and older sister Audrey sat around the pine table that lay adorned with the kind of breakfast feast usually reserved in the Baxter house for birthdays. Jessa ogled the bacon sandwiches, cut into small triangles just the way she liked them, and a towering plate of fluffy pancakes—a breakfast treat that the Baxter family had only recently discovered on holiday in America. Mrs Baxter had even brought out her 'special occasion' bowl, which she generally deemed too precious (and expensive) to use. But Mrs Baxter couldn't think of any occasion more special than the day her youngest daughter started at the most prestigious parapsych school in England.

"It's a surprise Fancy Breakfast!" Mrs Baxter clapped her hands together.

"You know how much Mum loves an excuse for Fancy Breakfast," said Audrey.

"Works for me," Jessa grabbed a sandwich and opened up the slices to dowse the bacon in ketchup, then hungrily scoffed the whole thing.

"We wanted to make sure you have a good start on your first day," said Mr Baxter.

"First day of high school," Mrs Baxter shook her head wistfully, "I just can't believe how fast you've grown up."

"Mum, don't get all soppy."

"I can't help it. It's very emotional for a parent to see their youngest child getting older. It just seems like yesterday that we found out you were a parapsych! What an exciting day that was."

"Remember Jessa's first day at PsychPlay?" said Audrey.

"I've never seen such a tantrum," Mr Baxter chuckled through his moustache.

"Can we please not re-live the train-set incident right now?" Jessa said.

"You were such a brat," said Audrey.

"You weren't even there!"

"Girls, girls. No hostility today, please."

"Fine, I'm sorry," said Audrey. "And to your credit, Jessa, you have matured a lot recently."

Jessa said nothing.

"I'm sorry for calling you a brat, all right?"

"All right," Jessa took an abnormally large bite of her sandwich and tiny ketchup blobs collected in the corners of her mouth.

"Maybe I can make it up to you with this," Audrey said, retrieving a gift from its hiding place under her chair.

"I get presents?" Jessa scrabbled at the impeccably wrapped box, tearing away the shimmering paper. "No way!"

Inside the box were the shoes Jessa had been fawning over for months. She'd never been especially into clothes, but after seeing members of her favourite bands wear them onstage, the blue and red high-tops had been at the top of Jessa's wish list.

"Thank you, they're amazing!"

"They'd better be amazing," Mr Baxter raised his wiry eyebrows. "Forty pounds for a pair of shoes!"

"Don't be a spoilsport, Daddy," said Audrey.

"They're very loud, though," said Mrs Baxter. "Will they go with many outfits?"

"Well, the lead singer of Since the Future wears them, *and* the guitarist of Falcon Draft wears them, so yeah, they go with everything." Jessa pulled up the legs of her pyjamas to more efficiently put on the shoes.

"I'm not quite sure what that means," said Mrs Baxter.

"Mum, they're two completely different genres," Jessa replied.

"Well, I'm glad you like them," Audrey smiled.

"I do, thank you," Jessa replied. "But wait, why are you still here? Don't you have classes on Mondays?"

"I told them I'd be late today so I could have breakfast at home. I'm so busy these days; I feel like I barely see all of you."

Jessa was too busy admiring the shoes to hear Audrey's response.

Mr Baxter pulled out something from a deep fleecy pocket of his dressing gown. "This is from your mum and me."

Jessa quietly opened the lid, to reveal a white gold pendant. It was a flat disc, with a smaller circle inscribed into the centre. Jessa's fingers gently turned over the charm. On the other side were three wavy lines.

"Oh," she said. "It's very pretty. But what is it?"

"I found it in Norway," Mrs Baxter said. "When I went over there to work at that big conference, I went to this little parapsych folklore shop in Oslo. The lady who owned the shop told me about her daughter, who's a telepath. Anyway, I mentioned that you'll be a telekinetic, so she showed me these pendants. Apparently, the waves are an ancient Scandinavian symbol for telekinetic powers, dating way back before humans really even knew what parapsych abilities were. She said the circle is a modern addition, and is meant to symbolise that, regardless of your powers, you are whole and beautiful."

Jessa removed the pendant from the box.

"Do you like it?" asked her father.

"I love it," she smiled.

Jessa held up her mess of bedhead hair so her mother could fasten the necklace clasp.

"And as we're feeling generous, we have a little something for Audrey, too." Mr Baxter handed a small box to his oldest daughter.

Mrs Baxter moved away from Jessa to rest her hands on Audrey's shoulders.

"Why does Audrey get a present? It's not her first day."

"We just like to spoil our girls sometimes, that's all."

"Oh my goodness, it's a Sheaffer," Audrey cooed.

"How exciting," Jessa muttered, "a *pen*."

"It's a Sheaffer fountain pen," Audrey corrected.

"That's what I said. A pen. Great," Jessa rolled her eyes.

"And it's engraved, look," Mrs Baxter pointed out the delicate calligraphy on the shaft.

"We know it's not your first day of university or anything, but it is a new term in your PhD, so we thought you deserved a little present too, just to show how proud of you we are."

"Thank you, Mum. Thank you, Daddy," Audrey kissed her parents.

"We're so proud of both of you. Our beautiful, intelligent girls," Mrs Baxter took her seat again and poured her daily bowl of Fit Flakes. "Oh, and I just remembered! You'll never guess what I heard about the people down at number 94."

Jessa tuned out of the conversation, choosing not to pay attention to her mother's neighbourhood gossip. She ketchuped another bacon sandwich and munched away, watching her parents and sister engage in idle chatter. She reached her hand into the fruit bowl to grab a particularly plump and juicy-looking pineapple chunk.

"Jessa, please," Mrs Baxter interjected, "not with your fingers. That's what the spoon is for. So anyway, the other man was appalled, of course..." Mrs Baxter continued her story.

"I guess we're done celebrating my big day, then," Jessa murmured.

"Jessa, please don't interrupt while I'm talking to your father."

Jessa left the table with a loud huff, stomping up the stairs in her new shoes.

"What's up with her?", said Mr Baxter.

"Hormones, probably," Mrs Baxter dismissed. "So anyway, you won't believe what they did next..."

2

To the casual observer, Winsbury Place might have seemed like any other residential block. On closer inspection of the modest facade of converted Georgian townhouses, however, the observer might just notice the simple brass plaque aside the front door that read "The Winsbury School of Parapsychology."

Jessa cautiously approached her new school, letting the quick-stepping and going-places adults zip past her with their newspapers and morning beverages in disposable cups. Older students took advantage of the remaining fifteen minutes before the first bell, lingering in groups on the pavement, or opposite the school in Winsbury Square Park.

Jessa felt a gross flutter in her stomach, and a brush of air as others hurried past her in the foyer. A middle-aged lady teetered over and thrust her round red face close to Jessa's.

"First year?" she squawked. Her breath smelled like coffee.

"Yes, miss."

"Wonderful! Welcome!" Her dangly earrings bobbed around as she spoke. "My name's Mrs Hoopey, and I'm the deputy headteacher. We're so very thrilled to welcome you to Winsbury. Here's your welcome pack. Trot along to the cafeteria, now. Help yourself to a snack and a drink, and settle down to make some wonderful new friends and some fabulous memories."

An involuntary gulp caught in Jessa's throat at the mention of new friends. She was the only parapsych from her middle school who had been accepted to Winsbury, and she was immediately envious of her old friends starting at high school together.

A long table in the cafeteria was already surrounded by about twenty students, each with a matching binder before them. The table was book-ended by decorative purple and gold balloon displays. Winsbury colours, Jessa had learned at the Open Evening, when she'd visited with her parents and been shown around by the captain of the Winsbury football team, who had thoroughly bored Jessa with his many tales of the inter-school football league final and "the power of purple and gold." Winsbury had won, 4-0.

Jessa eyed a seat next to a small blonde girl. Almost everyone else at the table was deeply engaged in the artless chatter of teenagers meeting each other for the first time, but the blonde girl had empty seats either side of her and her face bore down into a book.

"Do you mind if I sit here?" said Jessa.

The girl's face lit with a grateful and welcoming smile.

"No, please do. I'm Maggie. Nice to meet you," she offered her hand hesitantly.

"Jessa," she responded with a courteous shake. "What are you reading?"

"The Call of the Wild by Jack London. Have you read it?"

"Nope."

"What do you like to read?"

"Do you know a magazine called *Loud!*?"

"My brother reads it. It's about bands and stuff, right?"

"Yeah. That's mainly what I read."

"Cool. Well, I can lend this to you when I've finished, if you like."

Before Jessa had time to reply, a tall, pale, stern-faced woman entered the room and forced them all into silence without even saying a word. Jessa found herself sitting taut and upright, and noticed Maggie doing the same. Mrs Hoopey shuffled into the room alongside the other woman, and stood in front to announce her to the group, but Jessa remembered her from the welcome assembly at the Open Evening. She mostly remembered that she'd found the headteacher thoroughly frightening, and now, seeing her up close, even more so.

"Young ladies and gentlemen, please welcome the headteacher of Winsbury, Dr Mortlock." Mrs Hoopey pulled out a chair for Dr Mortlock, who came forward and stood before the first-years' staring faces.

"Good morning, students," she said without emotion.

"Good morning, Dr Mortlock," they responded together, polite, nervous and monotone.

Jessa wondered Dr Mortlock's age, but it was hard to tell. Her initial appearance was austere and cold. Militant, even. In her pristine black suit and turtle-neck, she was smart but categorically old-fashioned. It wasn't until a slight smile crept onto her face that a gentle softness came upon her.

"Welcome, and congratulations on your acceptance to the Winsbury School of Parapsychology. I'm sure you heard of Winsbury a long time ago and have known of our reputation, but now that you can see just how few first-years we admit, I hope you can fully appreciate how selective we are. Admittance to Winsbury is a great honour, and you should be very proud."

Jessa cast her mind back to the written test. She'd left the testing room feeling dismayed at her performance, so much so that she'd been convinced at first that her acceptance letter from Winsbury must have been a mistake.

"We analysed you all by your written exams, parapsychological aptitude tests, and your personal interviews, and in the twenty-six of you, we discovered something special that we'd like to nurture."

Jessa looked around the table and wondered how everyone else had done in the testing. Did she have the lowest grade of everyone there? Jessa Baxter was a mostly B or C student. She started racking her mind trying to remember if she'd ever been given an A in school. She did recall receiving some gold stars in playgroup, but she doubted that such high praise for correctly naming colours would be given at the Winsbury School of Parapsychology. Jessa suddenly felt very much out of her depth.

"We like to hold our first-year orientation here in the cafeteria to provide you with a more informal way in which to interact with your new classmates, and to help you relax into student life here. Please know that while we do hold you all to very high academic criteria, we want you to feel comfortable.

We've always maintained that students should enjoy their schooling, which is one of the reasons that we have no uniform code. You may use clothing to express yourself as you wish—within reason, of course," Dr Mortlock cast a critical glance around the table.

"You'll be split into two form groups, and each group will be assigned one of two tutors. Students with the following names, please pay attention, as you will be in Mr Fletcher's tutor group: Claire Adams, Sandra Allanberg, Jessamine Baxter, Elijah Cannon, Cecily Graves, Flynn Howard, Annora Huff, Phillip Jackson, Jodie O'Connor, Tonia Pitts, Thomas Stevens, Graham Townsend, and where is my number thirteen?" she trailed off, somehow lacking the final name for the group.

The students sat patiently as Dr Mortlock flipped through a couple of papers, scanning the page for the missing name.

"Aha. Margaret Turner, please make yourself known."

"Here, miss," Maggie croaked from Jessa's side.

"There you are. Number thirteen. Not going to be unlucky, are you?"

Maggie's face turned bright red under the gawp of everyone at the table.

"I...uh... hope not, miss."

"Very well. Though I would kindly request that you never again call me "miss." My name is Dr Mortlock, and I shan't respond otherwise."

Maggie looked like she might burst from embarrassment.

"Now," Dr Mortlock continued, "those of you whose names I didn't mention, you will be in Mrs Reid's tutor group. Your tutors will be with you shortly. Until then, feel free to spread out around the room and chat with your comrades. Share stories, and share your abilities. This is the beginning of a very special journey."

And with that, she stood up and strode from the room. Mrs Hoopey picked up the pile of papers and shuffled off in Dr Mortlock's wake.

The sound of chatter slowly returned to the room.

"I'm definitely a telekinetic, but I'd love to work on my telepath skills too," Jessa explained to Maggie as they moved to a quieter part of the cafeteria. "I know it's pretty rare to be really good at two parabilities, but I'd still like to improve both. There've been a few moments where I've had a sense connection with someone… what's that called again?"

"Sensoreading?"

"Maybe. Is that the one where you can feel someone's emotions?"

"Oh, no, sensoreading is a form of telepathy for actual senses, like smell or hearing. I think what you're describing is just empathism."

"Yes, that's it. Empathism. Thanks. So what about you?"

"I'm an empath too, though my skills are broad at the moment. I don't really score much higher in one area than another. But I want to be a vet someday, so I'm aiming to study telepathy and healing psychism so I can be a communicari."

"Awesome. Can you already communicate with animals at all?"

"Not really. I have a dog, but I can't read him."

"I heard communicariism is one of the rarest abilities."

"Yeah, very few people are born with it. But I've read that once you have the foundational skills like telepathy and empathism, then communicariism is pretty learnable. My older brother makes fun of me for it, though. He's a parapsych too but he wants to be an engineer. He thinks communicariism is silly. He calls it 'fairy science'."

"That's mean," said Jessa. "What do your parents think?"

"They're totally supportive. They said being a vet is a very respectable career. What do you want to be?"

"I don't really know," Jessa shrugged.

"No bother. You have plenty of time to decide."

"Excuse me," said a tentative voice. The girls looked up to see a boy standing before them. "Is it okay if I sit with you?"

He waited until they agreed before pulling out a chair for himself as if totally prepared to walk away if they declined his company.

"Yeah, 'course you can," said Jessa.

The boy slumped into the chair with a sideways smile. "Thanks. I'm Flynn, by the way. I was at that big table, but that group is, umm… not my kind of people."

They all looked over at a table where a girl wearing a lot of make-up was showing her classmates a hand-held device. Not only were the people at the table leaning to get a closer look, but other students were standing behind her, bending themselves to glimpse the desirable gadget.

"That's Cecily Graves," Flynn told them. "Apparently, her dad just gave her the new Folio smartphone. The one with the gold case."

"Wow," said Jessa. "I know they're cool phones and all, but that is so bloody gaudy. It looks like a disco ball."

"Spending that much money on a phone is what my mum calls having more money than sense," said Flynn.

"Most importantly, it's one hundred percent against the rules to have one in school," Maggie declared. "It says so right here in the welcome pack,' she flipped through the pages. "Here, on the 'Rules and Regulations' page. It very plainly says that students may bring a personal device to school but it must be handed in at reception in the morning."

"Yep," Flynn nodded. "She's been a student here for half an hour and she's already breaking the rules. That's ballsy."

"Or stupid," Jessa finished.

The loud clatter of desperate laughter sounded as Cecily played comedy videos on her phone. They looked over just in time to see Cecily mockingly holding her nose and wafting her hand. They couldn't hear what she was saying, but the girl standing next to Cecily promptly ran from the room, on the verge of tears.

"Yep. Definitely not my kind of people," Flynn reiterated.

"So Flynn," Maggie addressed him cordially. "I'm an empath and Jessa here is a telekin. What's your psych skill?"

"I think I'll be a telepath," he said, "though I have a little telekin ability that I'd love to improve."

"Nice," said Jessa, "I'm the opposite. When I was younger, all I wanted was to be a telepath, but telekinesis just came more naturally to me."

"It's pretty fun," said Flynn. "My mum helps me practice. Sometimes she'll think of a song and then I'll have to try and tune-in to her thoughts and guess the song. I have to be in the exact right mood to do it at all, but hopefully one day I'll be good. Maybe. I dunno."

"Wow, that's super advanced!" Maggie marvelled. "You're definitely above average for your age."

Mr Fletcher and Mrs Reid entered the cafeteria together.

"All right, everyone! I'm Mr Fletcher. All of you in my class, gather your things, follow me and get ready for the grand tour."

Mr Fletcher's thirteen students scuffled close to him in little steps into the main entrance hallway. Jessa was disappointed to see Cecily Graves in her tutor group.

"Over here we have Mrs Pacey, she's the school administrator and runs the reception. If you have any scheduling, technological, or attendance issues, she's the one to speak to."

Mrs Pacey waved at the students then quickly turned back to her devices. Her fingers ran swiftly and delicately between the glassy computer surfaces and the silvery matte trackpad on the desk in front of her.

Mr Fletcher walked the group down the main hallway and let them poke their heads into the library. Like most of the first-years, Jessa had toured Winsbury before applying, but the facilities seemed even more real and exciting now she was there as a real student. The library was so contemporary compared to the childish one at Jessa's middle school, which had cartoon animals painted on the walls and ragged, fading books on rickety shelves. Especially for such a small school, the Winsbury library was expansive and full of light streaming in through a wall of windows at the far end that looked out into the school gardens.

Mr Fletcher pointed down the hallway to the left of the library, explaining that this was the way to the gymnasium (a fact that Jessa dismissed somewhat, as she planned to spend as little time as possible in the gymnasium.)

The tour continued up the staircase, to the first floor. The stairway opened to a spacious landing area with a few clusters of squishy-looking beanbag chairs in front of big arched windows.

In the corner of the open space was a wall of ultramodern lockers, each with a small screen next to the handle notch. Every locker had a small light display on the screen, some showing yellow and some green.

"Everyone choose a locker with a green light," Mr Fletcher instructed, and the thirteen students each stood before the locker of their choice. Jessa, Maggie and Flynn all crouched to the lower, less popular row so they could secure neighbouring lockers.

"Tap the screen once until the light flashes, then hold your index finger on the middle of the screen until it stops flashing. This will be your locker, and only you can open it."

Each of the lockers flashed with recognition, welcoming their new keepers. Welcome, Baxter, J., Welcome, Turner, M., Welcome, Howard, F.

Mr Fletcher led them to the end of the East Wing corridor, to his personal classroom, their tutor group home for the next four years. The tables each had space for just two students, and Jessa and Maggie immediately chose a table together at the front of the class.

Flynn paused and looked around the room. He was the only one left without a seating partner.

"Here, Flynn, take this one," Jessa moved across to the next table.

"Are you sure?" he asked.

"Yeah, definitely. I'm left-handed anyway, so it's better for me if I sit on this side."

"Thanks," he slid into the seat Jessa had vacated.

Flynn copied Maggie and took out a pencil-case and notebook from his bag. The pencil-case was a worn brown leather that reminded Jessa of something her grandfather might have. In fact, many things about Flynn reminded her of someone a lot older; the large over-ear headphones that he clipped to his backpack, his well-worn trainers that looked like they might have been purchased in a supermarket.

Everything about Flynn was a little peculiar.

His dishevelled brown hair was mousy and unstylish by most teenagers' standards, and with a closer look at his yellow and blue striped polo shirt, Jessa noticed it was a little bobbly and dull around the collar. While everyone else in the class, herself included, was dressed up in the brand-spanking-new,

Flynn seemed a little faded among the technicolour.

Maggie and Flynn were both a little odd, Jessa thought, but one thing was certain, and Flynn's words came back into her mind. Her kind of people.

"Sorry the room is so bare right now," Mr Fletcher told the class. "I'm new here myself."

His dark blond hair looked crunchy with gel, and he was much more stylish than any of the other teachers. Plenty of the girls in the class were already swooning.

He handed out lesson schedules and talked through all the day's announcements, including details of extracurricular clubs and societies. Maggie urgently scribbled down notes, though Jessa couldn't tell what she could possibly be making notes about.

Mr Fletcher swiped through pages on his netpad, his eyes flitting back and forth over the screen, scanning for any other pertinent information.

"So I think that's everything I have to tell you. Does anyone have any questions for me?"

"Yeah," a tanned boy drawled. "Are you a parapsych?"

"Yes," said Mr Fletcher, "I'm a telekin. But perhaps more importantly, I consider my main attribute to be that I'm a massive Parapsych History nerd. Which means, aside from seeing you every morning for attendance and our PSE sessions on Mondays, you'll come to me for your weekly Parapsych History lessons, too. And further down the line, maybe we'll see each other more often if you decide to continue with me at P-Level!"

No response.

"No history buffs, eh?"

Apparently, even Maggie couldn't admit to being a history buff.

"Fine. Any other questions?"

"How old are you?" asked a girl from the back of the room.

"I don't think that's releva—"

"Are you single?" Cecily Graves interrupted him.

"That's definitely not relevant," he said quickly and turned around before the students noticed the blush in his cheeks.

Jessa was grateful when the bell rang for lunch. Despite her morning breakfast feast, she was starting to feel a grumble in her stomach.

By the time Jessa, Maggie, and Flynn arrived, the cafeteria was already quite full and loud with the hubbub of post-holiday catch-up, the clinking of cutlery on plates, and hands rustling in crisp packets.

The three of them took their place in the queue and surveyed the food options that shone under the yellow heat lamps.

"What can I get for you lovely young ladies?" said a blithe older woman behind the counter.

"Chicken pie and mash, please," said Jessa.

"Veggie pie and mash, please," added Maggie.

"And for you, kiddo?" the server looked over at Flynn.

His eyes searched from tray to tray and label to label. "Umm, nothing for me," he said, "I don't really fancy anything. I'll go and find us a table."

"Are you sure?" Jessa asked, but he was already walking away toward the cashier, where he quickly picked up just an apple and a bag of cheesy crackers.

"Excuse me," Jessa turned back to the lady behind the counter, "can I have a cheese and ham roll, too?"

"Looks like you've built up quite an appetite today!" she responded cheerfully, placing a roll on a plate for Jessa.

Jessa stabbed open the pastry lid of her pie to let the steam out. She noticed Flynn looking over at her plate.

"Is that going to be enough food for you, Flynn?" Maggie asked.

"Oh, yeah, I'm fine," he said loudly. "I'm not overly hungry."

He took another bite of his apple and chewed slowly.

"Well, if you change your mind," said Jessa, "I don't think I'll manage this sandwich."

"Oh," he hesitated. "Really?"

"Yeah. It looked really good, with this big thick cheddar slice in, and the roll looked nice and soft, but I had eyes bigger than my belly." She scooted the plate over towards him. "Here, why don't you take it? If you want it, I mean.

I'd hate for it to go to waste."

"Yeah. Okay," he said. "If you really don't want it."

Jessa and Maggie shared a subtle smile.

But it wasn't subtle enough. Flynn looked mortified.

Without a word, he took a bite, then pulled a textbook from his bag and put his head forward to read.

§

Jessa walked out of school with Maggie, whose entire family were waiting outside to take her to The Pizza Shack for a special first-day-of-school dinner. They said their goodbyes and then Jessa, too, headed off toward home.

A wave of tiredness crashed over her, and she suddenly regretted not training herself to wake up earlier each morning in preparation for the new term at school. "I'll try," she'd said to her mother. And for the past week, she *had* tried. Sort of. She had, at least, set her alarm for 6:45. And every day it went off at 6:45. And then again at 6:55, 7:05, and 7:15, at which point Jessa had, every day, given up on the snooze button and slept in until ten.

She trudged out of her daydream about bedtime and noticed up ahead a familiar yellow and blue polo shirt.

"Flynn!" she called out to him, but he couldn't hear her over the music in his headphones. She jogged to catch up with him and tapped his arm.

"Oh, hi, Jessa."

"Hi."

"How's it going?"

"Fine thanks. Look, I'm sorry if I embarrassed you at lunch."

"It was nothing," he shook his head.

"I really didn't mean to make you feel weird."

"I know you were just trying to be nice, but honestly? Yeah, it made me feel weird. I just don't want everyone to think that I'm like a…" he trailed off.

"Like a what?"

"I don't know. Everyone at Winsbury has loads of money. I don't want everyone to think I'm poor."

"Nobody thinks you're poor."

"'course they do. My clothes aren't new; my mum cuts my hair… I know what I look like. And usually it doesn't bother me because none of that stuff is important anyway, but sometimes it makes me feel rubbish. I especially don't want my friends to feel sorry for me."

"It's hard not to feel sorry for people, though."

"I guess," he shrugged. "But being treated like a charity case makes me feel really pathetic."

"I'm sorry, I didn't think of it that way. I never thought of you as a charity case. I actually think you're pretty cool. And I like your clothes. And I like your doofy haircut."

He laughed.

"I'm serious!" she said.

"Okay," he smiled.

"Friends?"

"Yeah, friends."

"Oh hey, this is where I turn off. I live down the road here."

"Cool. I live up that way," he pointed in the opposite direction.

"See you at school tomorrow, then."

"Yeah, see you!" he waved.

"Wait, Jessa!"

"Yeah?" she spun around.

"I forgot to say thanks. For the sandwich. I did appreciate it," he gave her a thumbs up of gratitude.

She smiled and gave him an exaggerated thumbs up in return.

3

It had been three weeks since the first day at Winsbury, and Cecily Graves had become the most popular—and the most feared—student in school. Even having her brand new Folio smartphone confiscated three times and getting a succession of demerits for inappropriate clothing hadn't knocked her spirits. Quite the opposite, in fact, she seemed to relish the notoriety, and it wasn't long before rumours began to take on lives of their own. Someone heard that Cecily Graves had a modelling contract at a big agency; someone else heard that Cecily Graves made a fourth-year cry; someone else heard that Cecily Graves owned an apartment in Mayfair. Nobody was sure where these rumours came from, but everybody knew about Cecily Graves.

"I heard her dad is one of the richest people in the country," Maggie said to Jessa and Flynn as they walked together up the stairs to the first floor.

"Me too," Jessa added. "Apparently, he just made billions more by building this mega hotel in the Middle East. That's where her family is going for the Christmas break. They're visiting one of their new resorts in Dubai."

"How do you know all this about her?" Flynn asked.

"I dunno. Just heard it."

"But where? Who says these things?"

"Everyone," Maggie stated.

"Yeah, just people," Jessa shrugged.

"Oh, right. Everyone and people. Sounds like a reliable source."

They made their way down the East Wing corridor. While the tutor groups at Winsbury were small, the whole class of twenty-six first years came together for subject classes. They entered room East 4, for Philosophy and Ethics, where Miss Farrell was waiting to greet them at the door.

"Come in, come in!" she invited. "Let's get settled and started."

Jessa, Maggie and Flynn took their usual seats in the front row of the classroom.

"So last week we were thinking about Law," Miss Farrell said. "Who remembers the name we give to the idea that there's an innate law inside all of us?"

Flynn raised his hand a little, and Miss Farrell looked at him inquiringly.

"Natural Law," he said.

"Exactly," Miss Farrell continued. "Natural Law, as we learned, is the theory of using reason to think about our moral behaviour." She glanced at Jessa, whose face was tense with concentration.

"Don't worry if this doesn't all make much sense yet. Philosophy is complicated. But I want you to have the concept of Natural Law at the back of your mind. Because as long as there have been people, there's been philosophy. And it was the earliest philosophers who paved the way to our current system of Parapsychological Law, which, I'm sure you know, is an incredibly interesting and constantly evolving area of research and legislation."

Jessa appreciated Miss Farrell's enthusiasm, but they were only just touching on entry-level philosophy, and she was already having difficulty understanding the concepts. She was reassured, though, to look back at her classmates to see that everyone else looked as apprehensive as she felt.

"Seriously," the teacher continued, "don't worry. I promise it's not as bad as it sounds. So let's open our textbooks to page 32."

Jessa opened the page to see a large heading:

FOUR LAWS OF PARAPSYCHOLOGICAL CONSTITUTION

"Even if you're not aware of the exact wording of the Laws, you've all been raised in accordance with them, even if your parents are lateral." Miss Farrell's subtle accent gave a pleasant softness and storytelling quality to her voice, though Jessa couldn't tell where she was from. Ireland, perhaps. Or Scotland. Or maybe Canada? Jessa had never been good at accents.

"The remarkable thing about Parapsychological Law is how it's been created as part of the whole judicial system, and our entire society has benefitted from it. Of course, there have been some, shall we say, dark moments, in our past, and you'll learn more about some of those in your history lessons. But it's crucial to remember that atrocities in the world have been committed by parapsychs and laterals alike. We all have the ability to destroy, just as much as we all have the choice to unify. When you look back far enough, you realise that as humans, we are all family."

Miss Farrell's words reminded Jessa of her mum. She was always talking about family. Jessa had never really thought about it before, but she was the only one in her immediate family to have parapsych abilities, and her best friends throughout primary and middle school were laterals, so she'd never felt any disconnect between herself and any lateral.

Jessa looked to her right and saw Flynn gazing at Miss Farrell in admiration, and she couldn't tell whether he was focussed on the teacher's words or her glossy red lips as she spoke. Miss Farrell was known for being the prettiest teacher in school, charming many of the male students with her good looks and gentle personality, while the girls marvelled at her dramatic style choices and swooned over the hefty diamond ring on her left hand that often glinted in the light as she gestured.

Miss Farrell turned her attention to the statements printed in the textbook and read them aloud.

It is a legal requirement for children with parapsychological abilities to

Register with the National Parapsychological Association (NPA) as a Person of Parapsychology Ability (PPA) within one calendar month of their 14th birthday.

Registered child citizens are required by law to enrol in a high school certified by the National Parapsychological Association's Education Institute.

It is a criminal offence to discriminate against or prosecute any member of society based on their parapsychological classification.

It is a criminal offence for any Person of Parapsychological Ability:

(i) to use their parapsychological abilities for personal gain if the act violates any other law, or:

(ii) to conceal their parapsychological abilities in order to gain an unfair advantage in any business-related or otherwise financial transaction.

§

"I'm glad I'm not a cat," said Jessa, "because that lesson would have cost me one of my nine lives."

"What are you talking about?" Maggie said. "I thought it was great! Miss Farrell is so good at making things interesting. Plus, I love when teachers make us do role-play, it makes the content so much easier to get to grips with."

"Ugh, no," Jessa pulled a face. "I hate role-play. I like Miss Farrell a lot, but I just don't get any of this philosophy stuff. It's too hard. What do you think, Flynn?"

"Hmm? What?"

"Uh oh, I think Flynn's busy thinking about a certain Philosophy and Ethics teacher."

"I am not!" he blushed. "I was thinking about the Four Laws, actually."

"Yeah, sure," Jessa nudged him. "The Four Laws of lo-o-ove!"

"Shut up!" he quickly walked ahead, leaving the girls laughing behind him.

They caught up with him at the lockers.

"Shoot," Maggie fumbled with an armful of possessions and her binder covered in dog stickers smacked to the ground. She crouched to pick it up and unwittingly putting herself in the path of Cecily Graves.

"Watch it!" Cecily snarled.

"Oh, I'm sorry," Maggie apologised, looking up as Cecily shadowed over her.

"What's wrong with you?" said Cecily. "Were you too busy daydreaming about puppies to watch where you were going?"

"No, I—" Maggie stammered, clutching the binder to her chest, trying to cover up the images on its outside. "I just—"

"You just what?" Cecily interrupted, stepping uncomfortably close to Maggie.

Jessa put her arm in between the two of them, shielding her friend from Cecily's intrusive lean.

"Calm down, Cecily, it was an accident. We were just chatting about the lesson and didn't hear you behind us, that's all."

"Yeah, that sounds about right. Blabbing away about Miss Farrell's nonsense laws. Typical."

"What?" Jessa said. "They're not nonsense laws, they're real laws that we all live by."

Cecily lowered her voice. "Without those laws, my father would be the richest man in the world."

"That would make your father a criminal," Jessa said plainly, narrowing her eyes into Cecily's glare.

"Not if the laws favoured parapsychs," Cecily sneered, "as they should."

"Is everything okay here?" came the familiar voice of Mr Fletcher behind them.

"Yes, Mr Fletcher!" Cecily said sweetly.

"Glad to hear it," he said, looking straight through her innocent ruse. "You should probably head downstairs for lunch."

"Yes, sir," she flashed a coquettish smile, but he didn't react. He waited until Cecily had disappeared down the staircase.

"You all right, Maggie?"

"Yeah I'm fine." She looked down. "It was nothing."

"It wasn't. But don't worry," said Mr Fletcher. "I heard everything."

§

"Do you think she meant that?" Flynn asked the girls once they'd found an empty picnic bench in the Winsbury garden. "I mean, do you think her family really believes that parapsychs should be treated differently?"

"Maybe," said Maggie, putting down the apple slice she was just about to bite into. "My mum's a primary school teacher in Hammersmith, and she told me a story about these parents who pulled their kid out of school and said they'd homeschool him until he was Registered and could go to a psych school. Apparently he was kind of a late bloomer, so at first, it didn't seem like he was a parapsych at all, even though both his parents were. Then once they found out he was, they took him out of school so he couldn't mix with the other kids."

"That seems excessive," said Flynn. "There still would have been other parapsych kids in that school for him to play with, right?"

"Yeah," Jessa joined in. "And if they wanted him to spend more time around parapsychs, what about like a Sunday school like PsychPlay? I went to one of those, and it was great."

"Me too," said Flynn.

"So did I," Maggie replied. "But I don't know. That's just what my mum said. They wanted him to spend less time around laterals because they thought that's what stunted his parapsychism. I suppose some people are just sensitive about that kind of thing."

"Wow, I can't imagine having that sort of reaction," Jessa pondered. "I'm the only psych in my family. I can't imagine someone feeling that way about them."

"Same," said Flynn. "Maggie, you have other parapsychs in your family, right?"

"Both of my brothers are, and so's my Mum, but Dad's a lateral, and so are most of my cousins. I agree with you. For someone to have that kind of thought is just so… I don't know…"

"Heartless," said Jessa.

§

Jessa and Flynn left school together. They walked through Winsbury Square Park and out the other side onto Gramercy Street, toward their homes. After a few moments of meandering in a comfortable silence, Jessa spoke.

"Do you think Cecily is pretty?"

"I haven't really thought about it. Why?"

"Because it's like everyone thinks she's amazing and wants to hang out with her."

"Do *you* think she's amazing?" he asked.

"Well, no."

"Do *you* want to hang out with her?"

"No, that sounds like a nightmare," she snickered.

"Well there you go," Flynn smiled. "People like her because she's rich and fashionable and loud. It's a status thing, isn't it? She acts like she's better than everyone else, and her confidence makes other people want to be with her.

But she's totally arrogant, and can also be really mean, so maybe they're just afraid of her."

"Yeah. You're probably right."

"I'm definitely right. In case you hadn't noticed, I'm always right." He flashed her a big grin.

"Oh yeah? Now who's the arrogant one?" Jessa laughed.

"Honestly, though, both you and Maggie are prettier than Cecily," he said without a hint of a blush on his cheeks.

"No way," Jessa scoffed. "Maggie is, but not me."

"What did I just say? I'm always right, remember? Cecily has a pretty face, but it's ruined by her mean expressions and all the terrible things she says. So yeah, I guess she's pretty on the outside, but underneath it, she's a really ugly person." He paused for a moment, then sighed. "You and Maggie are the only people in school who have been properly nice to me. Even in primary school, people were only friendly when they had to be."

Jessa's heart cramped at the thought of a young Flynn with no friends.

"Nobody wanted to play with me. They'd say that I smelled bad, or I had fleas. Stupid stuff, but it hurt. Before I started at Winsbury I was scared I'd spend the next four years eating my lunch alone, but you and Maggie sit with me every day. I'm just trying to say that it doesn't matter if people judge you or me, or if they think Cecily is great. Just be a good person and don't worry about anything else."

Jessa pulled Flynn's bony torso toward her own. Her arms awkwardly grasped around his backpack in a weird hug, then they said their goodbyes and walked away.

4

Jessa turned over the page on her calendar and unthinkingly clenched her fist in excitement as the highlighted box for October 31st came into view. Since she was very young, Halloween had been Jessa's second favourite time of year, closely following Christmas. As far as she was concerned, it was even better than collecting chocolate eggs at Easter, and even more fun than counting down to the New Year wearing silly glasses and hats. So, in honour of their youngest daughter's strange love for the holiday, Mr and Mrs Baxter had, every year, gone out of their way to make it an extra special occasion. Mrs Baxter, whose professional career was in events management, seemed never to tire of party planning, and this Halloween was no exception. It was to be the biggest Baxter party yet.

"Have you decided on your costume, Jessa?" Jean Baxter asked her daughter, handing her a box of Cinnamon Twist.

"Yes," Jessa replied matter-of-factly. "I think I want to be a zombie this year."

Audrey looked up from a large book and grimaced.

"Do you have a problem with that?" Jessa retorted.

"No..." Audrey rolled her eyes.

"Do you want a costume this year, too, Audrey?" their mother asked the oldest sister.

"No, thanks, I'll just be a doctor. I can bring my lab coat home and wear that."

"Again?!" Jessa exclaimed. "Doctor Bored-rey, paging Doctor Bored-rey to the operating room, stat!"

"Firstly," Audrey placed the book onto the table with a loud plop, "I wouldn't get paged verbally because that makes no sense. And secondly, some of us have work to do, Jessa, and we don't have time to worry about Halloween costumes."

"Whatever you say, Doctor Bored-rey."

"Jessa, please," Audrey glared at her younger sister. Jessa muttered something under her breath, but it was drowned out by the tinkling of cinnamon squares tumbling into her bowl.

"Oh, you girls," Mrs Baxter sighed. "Thirteen years and—"

"And worlds apart," Jessa finished. "We know."

"Well it's true, you two are so different, sometimes I still wonder if there was a mix—"

"A mixup at the hospital. We know. You need some new catchphrases, Mum."

Mrs Baxter playfully swatted her youngest daughter on the back of her head, then her face showed concern as she turned to Audrey.

"Sweetheart, maybe the university is putting too much pressure on you."

"It's what I need to do, Mum."

"I just worry about you."

"There's no need, I'm fine," Audrey assured her.

Despite always having an intelligence level above average for her age, Audrey was also introverted, shy, and an overachiever. She'd only ever scored the highest grades possible in every exam, a fact of which Jessa had been reminded throughout her whole life.

Jessa stared into her cereal bowl, swishing the little squares around in the milk. "I got an A on my parapsych physics project," she blurted out. Her face immediately heated up with shame at her lie. She had actually received a very respectable B- on the project, but she knew that wasn't enough to compete with Audrey.

"That's wonderful, Jessa!" her mother beamed proudly. "What did that entail, then?"

"Well, we've been learning about waves and frequency and stuff, so we're learning how that applies to telekinesis. Some of the others aren't very good because they're not good telekins, but I am."

"I'm so glad you're doing well," Mrs Baxter smiled. "So do you get to work on your abilities much in lessons?"

"Not really. Not yet, anyway. We have science lessons, but it's mostly theory at the moment, like how the sciencey stuff explains the parapsychey stuff."

"That all sounds very interesting. And do you think it's helping with your telekinesis?"

"I mean, my psych skills aren't strong yet, but yeah, I think I'm getting better."

"Gosh, it's so fascinating. Don't you think it's fascinating, Audrey?" Mrs Baxter asked. But before Audrey could reply, she was distracted by the sound of a loud buzz as her phone vibrated on the table. She swiped the screen up to reveal the message, and smiled cautiously to herself, before swiping away the message before her mother or Jessa could see.

"Was that you-know-who?" Mrs Baxter squeezed her hands around her mug.

"Mmhmm," Audrey giggled. Jessa raised her eyebrows at her sister's sudden girlishness. Audrey never giggled.

"What's going on? Who's the text from?" she asked.

"Audrey has a new boyfriend!" their mother jabbered.

"Mum!"

"I'm sorry, I couldn't help it! But it's all right, Jessa can keep a secret. We haven't had any Baxter girl talk in a while."

"Fine, yes, I'm seeing someone," Audrey said. "But I still don't want to say too much. He's very handsome, though, I can tell you that."

"What's his name?" Mrs Baxter prodded for more information.

"His name is Hugo."

"Hugo?" Jessa mocked. "Is he another Cambridge posh boy?"

"No, he didn't go to Cambridge," Audrey snapped. "But even if he did, there's nothing wrong with being well educated."

"Does he wear tweed? Does he have a monocle? Does he wear a top hat to dinner?"

"Come on, Jessa," Audrey rolled her eyes.

Jessa checked that their mother had turned away and then poked her tongue out at Audrey.

§

The final lesson of the day on Monday afternoon was art, which was always a really fun way to not do much work. And everyone liked Ms Storm, the art teacher, even when she thoroughly perplexed them with all her constant allusions to Mother Earth and artistic spirit guides. So, nobody was surprised that Ms Storm wanted to take advantage of an uncharacteristically warm October day by taking the students outside to draw leaves.

The Winsbury garden was small but elegantly maintained by Tony, the school's caretaker and groundskeeper. Formed by the Winsbury School building on one side, and a tall ivy-covered wall around the other sides, the garden was a sanctuary. The sound of Central London commotion faded into the background, hidden by the rippling whispers of trees and bushes, and the lazy burble of the miniature waterfall.

Jessa, Flynn, and Maggie rustled through the fallen foliage to find leaves with the best colour-to-shape ratio, then retired to their favourite corner of the garden, next to the old stone archway that they were convinced hardly anybody else knew about. Jessa sat cross-legged on the old wooden bench, with her sketchbook balanced between her knees. Flynn took the other end of the bench, and Maggie spread out her chunky cable-knit cardigan on the paving stones to use as a blanket.

"Do you mind if we sit with you?" a voice asked.

Tonia Pitts and Annora Huff stood before them, leaves in one hand, sketchbooks in the other.

"Not at all," Maggie was the first to welcome the pair.

Tonia took the place between Jessa and Flynn on the bench, while Annora simply plopped herself onto the ground, her skirt billowing like a little parachute on her way down.

"Thanks," said Tonia. "Cecily's back there talking about her Halloween party. It was driving me mad."

"And she's talking about it extra loud to make us feel bad," Annora added. "I think we're the only people who aren't invited."

Jessa had spoken to Tonia many times before, and found her to be very friendly, if a little blunt, but she realised that this was probably her first ever interaction with the usually shy and quiet Annora.

"Nah," Jessa replied. "We didn't get invited either. Do you want to come to my party instead? It's at my house, and it's going to be really fun. Here…" she scribbled down her address onto a blank sheet from her sketchbook and ripped it out for Annora and Tonia (on the assumption that the two of them were always together, so they probably wouldn't mind sharing the one invitation).

"Cool, thanks!" Tonia folded up the paper and slipped it into her bag.

"Sorry I didn't properly invite you," Jessa said sheepishly. "I honestly thought everyone was going to Cecily's party, so I didn't bother asking anyone else."

"Yeah right," Tonia said through teeth clamped around the pencil end she was chewing. "You'd have to pay me to go to that."

"I wouldn't go, even for a hundred pounds," Annora stated.

"A hundred?" Tonia thought about it. "Make it two, then I'll go to Cecily's. But don't worry, Jessa, I'll go to yours for free."

§

Jessa counted down the days. The party was set to have the best turnout of any Baxter gathering in recent history. Her four friends from school were coming, in addition to some of the neighbours who had children close to her age, and some aunts and uncles and cousins always came along. Audrey's best friend Sarah usually turned up for a little while, which Jessa always enjoyed because Sarah was a medical student and had plenty of gory stories about freak accidents and flesh-eating infections.

Everyone at school except Jessa and her friends was totally compelled by the unrelenting gossip about Cecily's party. Apparently, Cecily Graves' party was being held in the ballroom of her father's newly acquired hotel. Apparently, there would be a famous pop singer performing. Apparently, a world-renowned designer had personally created a series of dresses for Cecily to wear throughout the evening.

On the contrary, the most famous person invited to Jessa's party was probably her Uncle Morris, who lived up north and once won first prize in a pie-making contest. But Jessa kept her invitees interested every way she could, with mentions of her mother's best homemade spread of sandwiches, mini pizzas and cakes, and a family friend who was bringing a top-of-the-range FolioMax Hologram system with all the good party games. If they were lucky, Jessa's telekinetic Auntie Stella might even have one-too-many shandies and treat everyone to her infamous floating cups routine.

§

Saturday, October 31st finally arrived, and Jessa spent all afternoon making up her zombie face into a perfectly gruesome mess of fake bruises, dried blood and flaking skin. She rubbed baby powder into her long hair and brushed out the waves to make a grey frizzy mass that protruded from all over her head. She pulled on an old shirt of her father's that she'd purposefully dirtied with shoe polish and some strategic rips, and finished the look with a drizzling of fake blood over her chin and down the front of the shirt.

At exactly 5 pm, Flynn arrived at the door.

Jessa stared at his costume. "What are you?"

"Can't you tell? I'm a ghost!"

"Oh," she looked closer as Flynn stepped into the light of the house and she realised he was wearing a little makeup to lighten his skin and darken his eyes. "You look a lot like regular Flynn, though."

"Well yeah, just because I'm a ghost doesn't mean I'd look different. I'm Ghost Flynn."

"All right then, Ghost Flynn. Give me your coat. What do you think of my costume?"

"You look quite disgusting."

Flynn was greeted warmly by Mr and Mrs Baxter, dressed as a pirate and wench respectively, who immediately pulled him to the buffet table and handed him a paper plate. Just a few minutes later, the doorbell rang again. Jessa opened it to Maggie, wearing a hand-sewn cat costume, complete with collar, tail and ears, and a painted face with suitably cat-like eyes and whiskers.

"Meow," she presented a bottle of cola. "I brought fizzy pop. I know you have plenty, but it's polite to bring an offering for your host."

Tonia and Annora ran up the driveway just behind Maggie.

"You guys didn't dress up?!" Jessa exclaimed.

"Yeah, we did!" Tonia splayed out her arms under a colourful cape.

"We're each other!" Annora curtseyed in Tonia's denim skirt.

It wasn't long before the other guests had arrived, and the entire downstairs of 88 Duke Avenue was buzzing with the sound of friends and family and neighbours, some meeting for the first time, some reuniting after long whiles apart, and some who saw each other regularly but still found reason to celebrate. Even Annora, who Jessa suspected would be too timid to enjoy the party, had a great time and turned out to be a commendable guest, beating all the other players and defeating the hologram Dance King in the FolioMax DanceOff tournament. Everything was going perfectly until Jessa noticed Audrey take off her lab coat and remove the stethoscope from around her neck. Reduced to her regular clothing, Audrey said goodbye to a handful of people and walked toward the front door.

Jessa followed.

"Why are you leaving?" she asked as Audrey's hand unlatched the front door.

"Sorry Jess, I have plans with Hugo tonight."

"He can come here! Invite him to the party!"

"I don't think so. He hasn't met Mum and Dad yet, and I don't want to put too much pressure on him."

"So this is the perfect way for them to meet him. It's so casual."

"Yeah, but still no. Not tonight, Jessa. Maybe another time," she walked up the path towards the front gate. Her zombie sister still followed.

"Audrey, why are you being weird?"

"What do you mean?" she turned around. "I'm not doing anything, I just—"

"Yes you are," Jessa interrupted. "You're being weird with me. We met your old boyfriend, why can't we meet this one?"

Audrey resigned. "Fine, I'll tell you. I suppose you had to find out eventually."

"Find out what?"

"You kind of… already know him," she said quietly.

"What? What are you talking about? I don't know anyone called Hugo."

"No," Audrey paused. "You know him as Mr Fletcher."

5

"I still can't believe she would go out with my teacher."

"I can't believe this is still bugging you," Maggie replied.

"It's just weird!" Jessa exclaimed, en route to their Friday afternoon Parapsych Skills lesson. Maggie and Flynn had both been sympathetic towards Jessa's feelings, especially after hearing that Mr Fletcher had joined their family for dinner one evening during the week (and everyone agreed that seeing a teacher outside of school is weird anyway, let alone having them in the house for dinner) but Jessa's annoyance was starting to get old.

"Jessa," said Flynn, "I know this is strange for you, but think about it from Audrey's point of view."

"Like how?" Jessa snapped back. "From the point of view of someone who manages to make my life difficult without even realising it?"

"Exactly, she didn't realise it. She didn't do it on purpose. Didn't you say they met at a library? It's not like she came here and found a boyfriend deliberately to get on your nerves."

"Well no, but—"

"And then she kept it from you because she knew it would upset you. She was trying to protect you from that."

Jessa stayed quiet.

"Jessa…" Maggie said cautiously. "It sounds like Audrey really likes him. And we do too, remember? He's super nice, and helpful, and intelligent. He's total boyfriend material. Ask any of the girls in our school."

"Ugh," Jessa sighed. Maggie was right, she did like Mr Fletcher. Everyone did. "Fine, maybe I got a bit carried away. But it's still weird to be friendly with a teacher outside of school."

"Yes, we agree with you on that," said Maggie.

"I don't think it's that weird," said Flynn. "Teachers are just people."

"Still, I hope nobody else finds out apart from you two."

The first-years usually only went to the second floor for maths and science lessons, but once a week they ventured down the opposite corridor to 2nd Floor East, for Parapsych Skills with Ms Alzamora. Each of the five Parapsych labs was a base for the school's most renowned teachers—acclaimed parapsychs in their own right—and whose lessons were mostly reserved for the fourth and fifth-year students studying P-Levels.

Professor Winton, the oldest and wisest teacher in the school, taught Telekinesis, and he was known for training students so well that even those with very minimal ability would be able to easily levitate small-to-medium objects by the time they graduated. Dr Hoover was the Telepathy teacher. She was most known for her harrowing stare and for occasionally making students cry. Undoubtedly, the students' favourite parapsych teacher was the loud and rambunctious communicari, Mrs Tobias, whose Caribbean upbringing inspired her colourful personality and vibrant outfits. Her lessons in the animal communication parascience were highly anticipated by all the pet-loving students. The newest professor to the department was Dr Fish, who was relatively famous in the scholarly world for his work in the healing parasciences, which Jessa had discovered when Maggie emailed her a link to Dr Fish's most recent paper, 'Synaptic efficacy in post-surgery parapsychs', as soon as the latest quarterly edition of *The Journal of Parapsych Healing* was available. Maggie strongly urged Jessa to sign up for email alerts from the Journal. Jessa declined.

Finally, there was Ms Alzamora. She was not as bookish as the other Parapsych Lab teachers, nor as acclaimed. The students liked her, but there was something vaguely dishevelled about her that didn't command quite the same authority as the others. Her dark curly hair wound tightly to her head, and her handmade smocks always bilged out from her slim form, making her look shapeless and wide. She spoke with an ambiguous accent that made her seem worldly and well-traveled in a way that Jessa found particularly compelling.

She welcomed the first-years graciously into her lab and watched as they took their regular seats.

"Wait. What are we doing today?" she asked as a curtain of confusion fell over her face. "Oh yes, I remember. Today we'll be working on some open-mind practice, building on what you've begun investigating in both physics and biology lessons. What we call 'open-mind practice' is also used by advanced parapsychs as a basis for telepathic communication, clairvoyance and auto-writing, among other things, so if you can get really good at it, it can be extremely useful."

Jessa found the phrase 'open-mind' fascinating. While she'd always had some essence of a telekinetic mind ability, the idea of having an open mind captivated her.

"So!" Ms Alzamora announced loudly. "Find a partner!"

Jessa, Maggie and Flynn groaned. They hated when teachers told them to find a partner. Usually, it meant they'd get split up, and one of them would have to work with Gray Townsend, who was the third wheel to Eli and Cecily's pairing, since they'd recently started dating.

None of them disliked Gray, but he was a difficult partner because he was always too busy making jokes or gaseous sounds or saying "wait, man, you have to check out this song, it'll blow your mind." Jessa wasn't too bothered, but Maggie particularly hated working with him.

"It appears we're missing one of our classmates today," said the teacher. "So you three at the front can work as a group."

"Yessss," Jessa hissed quietly.

"Now, let's push the tables against the wall so we have some floor space. Then pick out a cushion or bolster from the storage cupboard, and settle down opposite your partner. Make sure you're comfortable but rigid. Sit strong! Strong posture brings a strong mind!"

She minced around the room and handed out cards, on which were printed a plain white circle on a black background.

Before making any further instruction, she pressed play on a sound system at the front of the classroom, and the tranquillising sound of ocean waves gently entered the room.

"Some people like to enjoy their open-mind practice in silence, but I find it helpful to have music or background noise. It's especially helpful when you're learning these skills so early in your parapsych career. It's important to be able to drown out enough distraction that you can find an inner focus."

Ms Alzamora flipped a switch and all the blinds in the room descended and fit themselves snugly inside the window frames, blocking out any fragment of light that could try to creep inside. Low-light sensors pulsated into action, feeding a gentle blue glow into the classroom.

When Ms Alzamora spoke again, she lowered her tone from its usual high pitch into a gentle, soothing, meditative voice.

"To have an open-mind, you need to be equally relaxed and aware. If you're too sleepy, you won't be able to concentrate. But if you're too awake and worried and thinking about lots of things, you won't be able to find a mindful state. Finding the perfect psychological position to awaken your mind is most of the battle. Some parapsychs take years, even decades to achieve the perfect state. It's a lifetime practice, so don't be upset if this doesn't come to you in your first year, or even during your entire time at Winsbury. Remember that we call it practice for a reason."

Jessa knew that Ms Alzamora was trying to reassure them, but she found the teacher's words frustrating. It sounded like she was proposing a challenge.

They sat as Ms Alzamora guided them through a relaxing meditation.

"Now, slowly open your eyes and take a look at your card." Every word came out as if she were reading a bedtime story. "Don't stare at it, and don't think about it. Just observe it and acknowledge your observations."

Whispers of boredom and puzzlement arose around the room.

"What is she on about?"

"I don't get it."

"What's supposed to happen?"

"If you've reached your capacity for practice today, please sit in quiet for a few more moments," said the teacher.

But Jessa's eyes lay unmoving from her card.

And she stayed there, still, quiet, and unaware of time.

"Now bring your attention away from the card and back into the room.

Jessa's eyes watered as she fluttered them fully open, and she realised she'd barely blinked during the whole practice. She wiped away the sudden excess moisture from around her eyes. Flynn and Maggie were staring at her.

"I've never seen you focus that hard on anything," said Maggie.

The blinds rose up and Jessa squinted in the light.

"Collect your things and you're free to leave at your leisure," the teacher invited.

"Wait, is the lesson over?" Jessa tried to gather herself among the hubbub of students hastening to leave the room. "I thought this was a double lesson?"

"It was. It's 3:40." Flynn took the girls' cushions and put them away with his own.

"What on earth was that all about?" Maggie whispered as they departed the lab. "I didn't understand it at all," she sighed. "And I was listening to what Ms Alzamora was saying, so it's not that I wasn't paying attention. I tried to do everything exactly how she said. So what did I do wrong?"

"Stop worrying," Jessa urged. "Remember, Ms Alzamora said that these things can take a long time to really get to grips with."

"Hmm," Maggie contemplated. "Maybe if I study really hard over the next week I'll be able to figure it out for the next lesson."

"Mags," Flynn said, "I don't think it's the kind of thing you can study for. We just need to practice, like she said."

"Yep," Jessa tried to smile at Maggie, who clearly doubted that progress in anything could be made without studying.

A Baxter Saturday morning was usually a leisurely affair. Jean would read the Guardian, and Michael would make a pot of coffee (coffee at 88 Duke Avenue was always the more recreational beverage, as opposed to the habitual and everyday partaking of tea). On a usual Saturday, the entire family would be in pyjamas until at least 11. That is, however, unless there was a party in the making.

It was Audrey's birthday, so Mrs Baxter had been preparing since 8 am, soaking the ladyfingers and marinating the chops and dyeing her hair.

Jessa was supposed to be helping but instead had found a series of videos online featuring hilarious clips of people falling off of trampolines, and was watching them on the netpad.

"Really, Jessa, must you always have your head craned over that thing?"

"Well, I could watch stuff on the big TV, but you wanted to keep UK Today on, even though you're not actually watching it."

"I'm listening to it, thank you very much! And I can choose whichever channel I want because I'm the one who pays the bill," Mrs Baxter playfully threw a pile of napkins at her daughter.

"Mum! You made me miss the good bit!" Jessa rewound the video by four seconds.

"I am so terribly sorry. Can you fold the napkins, please?"

"*...Prime Minister Linden has come under fire again for his potentially misleading and self-congratulatory declarations. In the studio, we have*

Hope4Humanity's director, Siobhan Duffy. What do you think of these accusations, Siobhan?"

"Well, Melissa, I think they're absolutely right to point out these flaws in the Prime Minister's statistics. He's making all these announcements about how he's building a better Britain, but when all his statements are based on his own privately-funded research, it brings about a very reasonable doubt.

"And, more specifically, what is Hope4Humanity's stance on the homelessness rates?"

"The Prime Minister seems to have latched on to homelessness as his key issue, but we've seen nothing to suggest that he's done any good at all. He has funded more shelters, which means there are more beds at night for the homeless. But this is very conflicting. Because, yes, technically there are fewer people sleeping rough, because now they have a place to go at night. But there's no follow-up, no infrastructure, nothing in place to help these people find real homes or jobs or to get them back into society. It's the humanitarian equivalent of sweeping dust under the rug."

"His opposition has suggested these fabrications are deliberate on the Prime Minister's part."

"I suppose I can't speak for that, but at best, it's a vast oversight of the basic needs of people…"

"Jessa, the napkins?"

"In a minute."

"Always in a minute…"

§

It was a small gathering. The girls' Nanny and Grandpa were away on the first of their 'winter sun' European holidays, as much as Jean Baxter protested that it was barely even autumn and there were plenty of sunny days left to enjoy in England. But they weren't having it, and had jetted off the Mediterranean.

Jessa had always been allowed to bring a friend to Audrey's birthday parties, because the sisters' age difference was vast enough that their parents wanted to make sure Jessa had somebody near her own age to talk to. Even as Jessa grew older and ever-more capable of conversation, so the tradition continued, and Maggie and Flynn had been invited to the dinner.

After Mrs Baxter's three course meal of prawn cocktail, followed by a pork roast, followed by a cheese and grape plate, the group retired to the living room for an evening of board games and dessert. And then, as is the case with any great party, it seemed to be over as soon as it began.

It was the first time that Jessa's friends had experienced Mr Fletcher outside of school, as Audrey's boyfriend, and while it was a little awkward at first when he insisted that, given the circumstances, they should call him Hugo, they quickly warmed up to him being around, and it turned out that he was great fun, and much to everyone's surprise, harboured a hidden talent for charades.

By 11 pm, Hugo was the only remaining guest. Mr and Mrs Baxter said goodnight and went upstairs to bed, leaving Hugo, Jessa and Audrey watching an old horror movie in the living room.

"Excuse me," Audrey stood up from the sofa. "Just popping to the facilities."

Hugo and Jessa listened as her footsteps dissolved up the carpeted staircase and into the bathroom.

"I hope this wasn't weird for you," Hugo said quietly in his girlfriend's absence.

"I thought it would be, but it was fine," Jessa smiled. "You're actually kind of cool, I suppose."

"Good," he replied. "Because I like Audrey a lot, so I'm glad I can hang out with you and your parents like this."

"What's your family like?" Jessa enquired.

"We're not a close a family."

"Do you have any brothers or sisters?"

"Nope. Just me."

"How old are you?"

"Twenty-eight."

"Where did you teach before Winsbury?"

Audrey's footsteps got closer as she came back down the stairs.

"Right before getting the Winsbury job I was based not too far away, elsewhere in London." He turned back to the television. "I just realised I've seen this film before."

And before Jessa could probe more into his personal life, Audrey was back in the room, and somehow it seemed inappropriate to continue questioning Hugo in front of her.

§

Jessa arrived at school on Monday morning at 8:30, as usual. But instead of the familiar bustle in the foyer and the everyday sight of students wandering around into the cafeteria or the library or their tutor rooms, there was an unfamiliar stillness. Mrs Pacey was away from her usual position at the reception desk and instead was meeting students at the door with an instruction to head straight to the hall.

Jessa felt a churn in her stomach. Something was wrong.

Some schools held daily assemblies in the morning before lessons began, which was the case at Jessa's middle school, but at Winsbury, the students had registration in the morning with their tutor, where they received any news bulletins or important updates. This made school-wide assemblies rare. So it was obvious to the students that if Dr Mortlock had summoned them to a full school assembly, it could only be in regards to something very good, or very bad.

Dr Mortlock sat, upright and prim, on the padded purple leather of her throne, looking out over the hall of students. Jessa shuffled sideways down the row to the seat that Maggie and Flynn had kept empty for her.

"What's going on? Did you hear anything before I got here?" she said.

"No, nobody's told us anything," Maggie replied. "We've noticed some of the teachers talking to each other, though. We couldn't hear what they said, but they all look really worried.

"I've never seen Dr Mortlock look like that before. Man, she's terrifying,"

Jessa whispered.

"She looks upset to me," said Maggie. "And, even weirder, I don't think she's moved an inch the whole time we've been here. She's been just up there watching everyone."

When Dr Mortlock stood to her feet, the scuffling and the muttering and the speculating ceased, and the hall fell into silence. When she spoke, her hushed voice commanded an even deeper quiet.

There was no "good morning." No "thank you for joining me."

"I'm afraid a tragedy has occurred," she began. "This weekend, our Head Girl, Emmeline Victor, was reported missing."

The hall burst into a hubbub. Many students gasped, and a couple of girls whimpered into tears.

Jessa didn't know Emmeline personally, but everyone knew of the Head Girl's stature in the school. Emmeline had been an impressive student since her first year. She consistently achieved top grades, partook in a record amount of clubs, and in her third year initiated and developed The Winsbury Times, an online newspaper that was not only one of the most notable and reliable youth news sources on the internet, but also provided an engaging and sometimes irreverent review of student life, enjoyed by students all over the United Kingdom, and possibly even further.

"Quiet please," Dr Mortlock continued. Again, the room hushed.

"Emmeline was last seen leaving school on Friday, but she never made it home. Her disappearance will be reported publicly later today, but we wanted you all to hear first so you can prepare yourselves for any potential backlash. Considering Emmeline's standing in this school and her notable online presence, we are anticipating an increased interest in Winsbury.

"If any member of the press approaches you, it is important that you do not engage them, but to direct them to contact the staff here. We are happy to cooperate by answering their questions.

I am imploring you to exercise extreme caution. We do not know the circumstances of Emmeline's disappearance, and the safety of our students is paramount. A security service is being implemented, who will be stationed outside the school. If you see anyone near the school that you do not recognise or who is not a uniformed officer, do not approach them, but come inside and report it to a member of staff immediately. Scheduled lessons will continue as normal."

Jessa had heard about missing children before, on the news, but it always happened so far away to people she didn't know. She'd seen footage of parents distraught over lost children, begging for their safe return. She looked around the hall to see students crying, comforting one another. Others in a desperate chatter about what could possibly have happened. This was not a distant news story. Winsbury had been shaken.

7

"And in local news, it's been two weeks since the disappearance of Emmeline Victor, head girl of the Winsbury School of Parapsychology. Police have confirmed that the body of a woman pulled from Regent's Canal yesterday is not that of Miss Victor, and the death is not being treated as suspicious. Any sightings of Emmeline Victor should be reported to the Missing Persons Hotline..."

"Terrible, just terrible," Mrs Baxter shook her head gently.

"Local bus services into Central London will be increased by 15% this month as we approach December and the biggest shopping season of the year..."

"Oh, well that's handy," she mused. "Any idea what you want for Christmas?"

"I don't know," Jessa looked up from her magazine. "Records. Download credit."

"We can't all give you download credit every year," her mother tutted.

"Why not? I use it all."

"It's not a very thoughtful present."

"It is for someone who likes downloading stuff."

"You kids, really... in my day we played with real toys. We went outside!"

"I go outside."

"Walking to and from school doesn't count."

Jessa shrugged and delved back into reading the month's best album reviews.

"Morning, all," said Hugo Fletcher, after letting himself in with Audrey's spare key.

"Morning, poppet," Jean Baxter embraced him. "Are you all right? You look exhausted."

"Yeah," he rubbed his face, "just had a lot going on."

"Of course. Still bogged down with all the Emmeline Victor stuff?"

He frowned down at his phone. "Hmm? What, sorry?"

"I said are you still caught up in all this Emmeline stuff?"

"Oh. Sorry, Jean. Yes, very much so."

"What do they want from you, though? Are the police bothering you?"

"No, they're not bothering me, it's just. . ." he shrugged, "considering I was the last person at school who had any contact with Emmeline, they want to make sure that they have all bases covered."

"You already gave them a statement, though, didn't you?" asked Jessa.

"Yeah, I did. I guess they just keep coming up with new questions."

"Like what?"

"I can't really divulge that, Jessa, it's confidential."

"But I mean, why do they keep having new questions for you?"

"Jessa, give the poor man a break!" her mother scolded.

"I was just asking!"

"It's all right, Jean, she's just curious. You're right, Jessa, I gave them my statement. I suppose they're just hoping I remember any other bits of information that might be helpful."

"Well, I do wish they'd leave you alone," said Jean. "You look like you haven't slept in a week."

"Yeah, it's been tough."

§

"Can I tell you guys something?" Jessa said quietly to Maggie and Flynn.

"'course," Flynn nodded.

"You'd better be quick, though," Maggie warned. "Mr Fletcher's probably going to arrive soon."

"Actually, he's the one I want to talk about."

"What about him?"

"Do you think he's been acting strange lately?"

"He's seemed a bit distant, but that's about it."

"He came over to see us yesterday, and he looked rough."

"How?"

"He was all tired and stressed. He said he's been involved with the Emmeline case."

"That's bound to be putting extra stress on him," Maggie said.

"Yes. But it made me think, why is *he* helping?"

"What do you mean?"

"I mean what does he have to contribute? He's new here, so he barely knew Emmeline."

"Well, we know he was the last person in school to see her," said Flynn.

"Right, but how can they be drawing that out for so long? He started acting funny the day Emmeline disappeared, and he's continued to be weird for the past two weeks. What's going on?"

Before Maggie or Flynn could reply, Mrs Sullivan, the English teacher from down the corridor, scuttled into the room.

"So sorry, everyone! I was supposed to take your register this morning, but I got held up in a meeting. Is everyone here? Good. Off you go, then!"

"Excuse me, Mrs Sullivan?" Jessa spoke up before the muddled young teacher had time to hurry out of the room again, "Where's Mr Fletcher?"

"He's stuck in traffic. Not to worry!" And with that, she left.

The rest of the class filtered out of the room and made their way down the hallway, but Jessa held Maggie and Flynn back.

"What's wrong?" Maggie asked.

"He's not stuck in traffic, he stayed over at our house last night," Jessa whispered. "There's no way there's traffic in between my house and here."

"Maybe he went somewhere else this morning?" Flynn suggested. "Don't he and Audrey go to the gym in the morning?"

"Yeah, they do, but… I don't know. It feels like something weird is happening."

"What is it you're worried about?" Flynn asked.

Jessa shrugged. "I don't know, it's just a feeling. I can't describe it."

"Come on," Maggie urged, "we're going to be late to French! I'm sure everything's fine. He'll probably be back soon."

Jessa couldn't concentrate at all during French. Maggie made a point of shooting Jessa her most disapproving of glares whenever she noticed Jessa didn't have her textbook open to the right page, or when she wasn't copying anything from the board. She remained preoccupied during break time and didn't even finish her bag of spicy tortilla chips.

When the bell rang at 11:10, the three friends packed away their refreshments and walked back up the stairs to the East Wing corridor, returning to their form room for a Parapsych History lesson.

Jessa looked over at Mr Fletcher's desk. He wasn't there. In his place was Mrs Reid, the other History teacher.

Jessa's stomach flopped.

"Mr Fletcher isn't able to make it in today, so I'll be covering him for your Parapsych History lesson, and we'll just carry on from where you were last week." Mrs Reid's grey curly hair bobbed as she spoke.

"I logged into Mr Fletcher's class notes, and I saw you've been learning about Medieval times and the Parapsych-hunts. Very gruesome stuff, wasn't it? Fascinating, though, don't you think? Anyway, please open your books to page 57, and start reading the section titled 'Heresy and Mind Control: Parapsychs vs. Witches.'"

Flynn grinned over at Jessa before diving in over his textbook. She admired how much he'd come to enjoy history, but she certainly didn't feel the same way. No amount of jazzed up titles could trick Jessa Baxter into enjoying reading about the late middle ages.

"So what have we learned so far in this chapter?" Mrs Reid asked the class.

Maggie raised her hand.

"Yes, Maggie."

"When the Christian Age took hold, there was an intense dissidence between the Catholic side and the Protestant side, so it was a very tumultuous time. Beliefs in witchcraft were thought of as superstition, which was a punishable offence. Unfortunately, they couldn't tell the difference between witchcraft and parapsychism at that point, so a lot of people who we now believe were actually parapsychs, were tried and even executed as witches."

"Very good, Maggie! Would anyone else like to share anything they've learned? What else was happening in Europe that contributed to this timeline events?"

Maggie's hand was in the air again.

"I suppose it started with the Romans…"

Jessa zoned out. Nothing they were discussing in the lesson seemed important. She couldn't shake the feeling of unease. The day seemed endless.

§

"Why are you in such a hurry to get home?" Flynn huffed. "I can barely keep up!"

"Sorry," she said but didn't slow down. "I just want to get home and see if he's there."

"What does it matter if he's there or not? He might just be sick; maybe he's at home in bed."

"I don't think so."

"Jessa, wait up, you know I'm not into exercising!" he trotted alongside her strides.

Jessa fumbled for keys in the bottom of her backpack and let herself and Flynn into the house. They heard the sound of voices coming from the kitchen.

"The family must be so grateful. And just in time for Christmas."

"Mmhmm," Audrey's voice agreed.

"What's going on?" Jessa and Flynn entered the kitchen, and there, drinking tea and eating biscuits with the Baxters, was the enigmatic Hugo

Fletcher.

"Hi, guys."

"Where were you today?"

"Sorry, Jessa, I was busy," he sighed. "They found Emmeline."

"Really? Where was she? Is she okay?" Jessa rattled off her thoughts.

"She's alive," Hugo responded, "but barely. She was found alone, wandering in the city, very early this morning."

"Did someone abduct her? Did she say anything?" asked Flynn.

"No," said Hugo, "she hasn't said anything at all."

His tired eyes stared down into his tea. He had clearly already told the others the details of Emmeline's disturbing reappearance, and they all mirrored his gaze, looking down, preparing themselves to hear it again.

"In short, the doctors seem to think that Emmeline was kept somewhere dark. She was tied up. It looks like she was hardly given any food or water. And her eyes… there's nothing there. She's like a ghost."

Hugo tried to shake the image from his mind.

"How do you know all this? How did you see her?" Jessa pressed.

"There was an urgent teachers' meeting this morning after Emmeline's parents contacted Dr Mortlock. Then I had to go answer a couple more questions, so they let me see her."

Jessa's family all nodded in acknowledgement of his answer.

But Jessa wasn't satisfied. He hadn't answered the question. An urgent teachers' meeting? None of the other teachers had shown any signs of distress. And even if Emmeline's parents had got in touch with Dr Mortlock to pass on the news, why would Dr Mortlock summon the newest teacher to visit the Head Girl? And why would his visit have taken all day?

Jessa stood there as the adults continued their conversation. She kept her eyes on Hugo, who didn't look back up at all. Was he deliberately avoiding eye contact? She wanted to ask him more questions, but it wasn't the right time.

"So I know the albums we're trading are Eels and The Cars, but do you have anything by The Talking Heads?" Flynn asked, walking up the stairs behind Jessa. "I want to hear the one with "Psycho Killer" on—"

Jessa made sure the door was closed. "I don't believe him."

"What?"

"Fletcher! Did you just see how sketchy he was acting?"

"Uh, no?"

"I asked him how he saw Emmeline, and he gave me some vague, indirect response. He was avoiding the question."

"So? He's probably distracted."

"Something's up."

"Um, Jess? Can I just get those records?"

"Yeah, help yourself," she gestured toward her shelves stocked with vinyl. "You don't think anything seemed strange about him?"

"Can't say I did, but I also wasn't paying that much attention to his personal state— What's this one, 'Lincoln'?"

"It's by a band called They Might Be Giants. It's weird, you'll like it. Take the one called 'Flood', too."

"Thanks. Like I said, I wasn't really noticing him, per se. I think you might be reading too much into it. Are you sure you're not still mad at him and Audrey for dating?"

"I wasn't mad at him. He can't help who he meets in public places. Although he has very questionable taste if he likes my snooty-arse sister. But I'm over that. This is something else."

"Well, please don't let it eat you up. We have that group presentation for Geography tomorrow."

"Oh yeah…"

"So you'd better get to work learning your parts. You know Maggie'll explode if you get it wrong."

"Yes. Exploding Maggie is my least favourite Maggie."

"So get to work, and stop worrying."

Jessa managed to reduce her share of the presentation to the permitted quantity of bullet-points, but she just couldn't concentrate enough to memorise the content further.

She decided it was worth practising the open-mind techniques that Ms Alzamora had been teaching them in Parapsych Skills.

She tried to recall the teacher's instruction. The stillness. The quiet. The acknowledgement and setting aside of thoughts as they arose. Jessa grabbed a sheet of notepaper and drew a circle onto it, the shape that Ms Alzamora had recommended they use as "the symbol of unwavering mindfulness."

But Jessa's mind was far from unwavering. In fact, it was very distinctly and plainly wavering.

She found that by holding her hand directly over the circle she was able to focus more fully, but it was as though the more open her mind became, the more thoughts came rushing in, like seawater into a freshly excavated sand pit.

Her brain was bogging under the weight of questions upon questions about Hugo Fletcher and lingering feelings of disquiet about Emmeline Victor's strange and worrisome trauma.

Jessa thought about the events and tried to piece together any connection Hugo might have to Emmeline, but as far as she could work out, they would scarcely have met. Did he really see her? Why would he be the one to visit? What could have happened that would require personal involvement from the Parapsych History teacher?

Jessa wriggled in under her duvet and pulled it up close around her face. With questions and a curious turbulence in her mind, she eventually fell to sleep.

"Why are you so late?" Jessa climbed into Audrey's car without a hello.

"Because I was in a seminar. You know, most people would just wait until the weekend."

"No way. We always put up the decorations exactly two weeks before Christmas. I can't help it if your seminars clash with family traditions."

Audrey rolled her eyes. "Where's Hugo?"

"He said he'd leave in a few minutes. He wanted to make sure nobody saw us getting in your car together. Where are Mum and Dad?"

"On their way to the garden centre. We'll just meet them there."

Hugo Fletcher opened the passenger side door and greeted Audrey with a kiss on the cheek.

"Ready for some Baxter family fun?" she said.

"I hope so! What's the big deal with decorations today, then?"

Jessa scooted into the centre of the back seat so she could lean forward between the two adults. "Today we're getting the tree because decorations go up two weeks before Christmas," she explained. "Dad should have already got the other stuff down from the attic, so when we get home, we'll eat mince pies and listen to Christmas music as we put up the decorations. And I always put the star on the top of the tree."

"Wow, so the Baxters go all out for Christmas. I feel like I should get something festive for my place."

"You don't have any decorations?" Jessa ridiculed.

"Well, I have a wreath on the front door. But only because my neighbour made them for everyone on my floor, so I had to put it up. It's made of paper."

Jessa slapped her hands on the leather car seats. "It's made of *what*? No. That's just wrong. We are definitely getting you some decorations."

For the few days after Emmeline's reappearance, Jessa had watched Hugo intently at any possible moment, trying to catch something, anything, that might give an insight into his character. Yet he seemed to quickly get back to his old self. He was still rather uncommunicative, but not in a way that seemed suspicious. He looked well-rested, and he hadn't had any more oddly-explained absences from school.

Jessa started to think it might just have been stress that had got to him, or perhaps that she had even imagined or exaggerated his irregular behaviour. Either way, here, looking at Christmas trees in the garden centre, he couldn't possibly have looked more normal.

It took a good deal of wrestling with the unwielding bushiness of the Douglas Fir, but Mr Baxter and Hugo eventually managed to secure it to the roof of the Baxters' car.

"We'll meet you back at the house, then," Jean Baxter said to Audrey. "Jessa, are you coming with Dad and me?"

"Nah," Jessa declined, climbing into the back seat of her sister's car.

"Jessa, please sit back properly," Audrey said sternly.

"I'm fine; I'm wearing a seatbelt!"

"It doesn't count if you're holding it loosely in your lap like that," the older sister chastened.

"It probably is safer for you to sit back, Jessa," Hugo said softly.

Jessa scooted back in her seat, letting the seatbelt pull taut over her thighs

"There," she huffed, leaning inward to rest her elbows on her knees

"Why do you always have to be so contentious?" Audrey scoffed.

"Why do you always have to be so annoying?" Jessa retorted.

Hugo said nothing.

The three of them sat quietly as the rumble of the car whiled away the time.

"Oh, so anyway, remember that girl I was telling you about in my lab group?" Audrey said to Hugo. "Apparently, she did turn down that placement, so it might be available after all." She paused, turning the car onto a smaller road to avoid the stopping-and-starting of the traffic-lighted section of the main road. "So I was thinking of asking Professor Mollings to write me a recommendation…"

Still, they drove.

"I know I said it's not essential for me to get a lab placement, but I just think it would be good, you know? And it would look great on my CV when it comes to applying for jobs. What do you think?"

No reply.

"Hugo?"

Still nothing.

Jessa leaned forward, craning her neck to look at him.

His eyes flew open from a clench and he grabbed Audrey's arm.

"Pull over!"

"What? Why?"

"Audrey, stop the car!"

But she was already turning into the intersection.

"No!" he bellowed.

That's when she finally saw the lights of the oncoming car, speeding up the road in the wrong direction. Directly towards them. Audrey screamed and grabbed onto the steering wheel, throwing the car into a ninety-degree turn until the front end smashed into a brick wall. The other car careered toward Audrey's side.

Hugo outstretched his palm toward the car and howled under the weight of pain.

The other car spun and crashed sideways into Audrey's side of the car. The seatbelt punched into Jessa's hips as the blow heaved her from the seat. The groan of metal on metal made every bone in her body ache. The other car, still heavy from momentum, pushed Audrey's car a few metres until the friction of the road ground them to a halt.

"Audrey," Hugo shook Audrey's limp body. She lay forward, slumped over the wheel. "Audrey," he shook her harder. "Jessa, are you okay?"

"Yeah," she managed to reply, eyes wide, mouth gaping, ears ringing.

"Okay. Audrey, can you hear me?" he shoved his hand to her neck, testing for her pulse. "Audrey, wake up! Shit. Shit!" he swore louder and louder, forcing his weight into the car door to push it open.

Jessa finally snapped back into the present. She clambered from the back seat and joined Hugo in pulling Audrey's feeble body from the car.

Onlookers began to swarm around them.

"Are you all okay?"

"Are you hurt?"

"Is she breathing?"

"Someone call an ambulance!"

Jessa heard them but couldn't answer; she couldn't release her attention from her sister's blood-covered face. She crouched over Audrey's head, gently stroking her hair and whispering. "You're gonna be fine. You're gonna be fine. Everything's gonna be fine."

Hugo grasped Audrey's hand in his and rocked back and forth, back and forth.

§

"Well, she's going to be sore for a while, but it looks like there's no permanent damage and no broken bones," the doctor told them. "She's very lucky."

"Thank goodness," Jean Baxter exhaled loudly and hugged her husband in relief.

"She's awake but groggy, so you can go in and see her but only for a little while. She needs to rest." The family nodded and entered the room quietly.

Mrs Baxter immediately burst into a flood of tears.

"My beautiful girl!" she wailed. "Thank all that's good. I'm so grateful for my beautiful girls. And you said Hugo's fine, didn't you?"

"Yes, Mrs Baxter," the doctor said. "They're probably almost finished putting on his cast. He has a few fractures, but fortunately, they're all quite clean, so they should heal nicely."

"Thank goodness, thank goodness," Mrs Baxter pulled Jessa into her bosom.

Still reeling from the shock of the accident, Jessa didn't even think to pull away like she often did. Instead, she just let herself be there, smothered with so much love that she was too bewildered to appreciate. She was completely flummoxed. The moment of impact played over and over in her mind. Slow motion and fast-forward. Rewind, and start again. Rewind, and start again. Rewind.

It was starting to come out of the fog and into focus. The hospital room became a distant blur as Jessa zeroed in on the recent memory.

Audrey's bleeding face. Before that, the crunch. Before that, the scream. The headlights. The turn.

Hugo Fletcher.

She remembered him reaching out his hand.

The car was heading right for us.

And then he… reached out.

The car hit us sideways.

The car had turned as he moved.

He… moved it?

Hugo Fletcher entered the room, his right forearm in a cast and held close to his chest in a sling.

"There you are!" Jean Baxter ran to him with a grateful embrace. "Are you in much pain?"

"They gave me plenty of painkillers, don't worry," he smiled. "Jessa, how are you feeling?"

She just looked at him.

"Jessa?" he said again.

Her eyes narrowed on his, and he saw in her face that his secret was out.

"I feel like some fresh air," Jessa said, not moving her eyes from Hugo.

"That sounds good," he replied. "Mind if I join you?"

Jessa stomped through the hospital until she was safely outside and away from unwanted eavesdroppers. He followed.

"Who *are* you?! *What* are you?!" she said. "I knew something about you was weird!"

"Jessa, please don't be angry. Just listen."

"I'm not angry; I'm one hundred percent confused! What's going on? How did you do that?"

He scratched his head with his good hand. "It's just something I can do."

"Do you have some kind of freaky superhuman strength or something?"

"No, it's not physical strength. It's a form of advanced telekinesis. I was able to use my parapsych ability to deflect the car enough that it wouldn't crash right into us."

"It broke your arm!"

"Well, yes, energy is energy. I'm honestly not very well versed in the physics of it. I knew it would hurt me, but it would have killed Audrey if it hit us head-on."

"I knew you were hiding something."

"Well, there you go. Now you know my secret."

"Do I?"

"What do you mean?"

"Is that it?"

"Jessa, what are you talking about?"

"I think there's something else. Something else you're keeping from us."

"I'm not sure what you're getting at."

"Tell me the truth. Are you really a teacher?"

"Yes, of course I am."

"There's something else, I know it. I can feel it. I can see it in you, there's more. If you don't tell me, I'll find out for myself. You know I will."

He closed his eyes for a second and opened them slowly.

"Fine. Yes, I am a teacher. But I'm also a little more than that. You see, there's a kind of investigation happening in a few schools at the moment. You know about school inspections, right? It's a lot like that, but instead of going in for just one day like they usually do, I'm on a long-term assignment"

Jessa squeezed her lips together in thought. "You're an inspector."

"Yes."

"So who do you work for?"

"I'm employed by the Department of Education. I'm a real teacher."

"But why would—" Jessa began, then bit her tongue. Something told her not to push the matter any further.

"Are we cool? Can you keep my secret?" He raised his eyebrows and his forehead crinkled. "Jessa? Please?"

Mr Fletcher's words were spoken earnestly enough, but looking deep and inquiringly into his eyes, she felt a knot in her stomach.

"Okay," Jessa nodded, with fingers crossed inside her jeans pocket.

9

"Oh, Jessa, I wish you hadn't told us that!" Maggie moaned. She nervously looked around to see if any other students in the Winsbury garden were close enough to overhear.

"Why?!" Jessa replied. "I thought you'd be dying to know!"

"Because Mr Fletcher kept that secret for a reason, and now we're responsible for it, too," Flynn answered her, sharing in Maggie's disapproval.

"Well, I couldn't *not* tell you, could I? We're best friends; I have to tell you everything."

"Ugh," they surrendered.

"But anyway," said Jessa, "do you believe his story?"

Maggie's face crumpled thoughtfully. "Of course," she said. "I can't see why it wouldn't be true."

"Me neither," added Flynn. "It seems like a reasonable explanation."

"Really?" Jessa huffed. "You think there's a secret group of teachers who are working for the government, inspecting schools? That seems *reasonable* to you?!

"Well," said Flynn, "when you say it in that tone you make it sound a bit ridiculous. But at face value, yeah, it sounds plausible."

"You don't think it seems like a lot of effort to go to?"

"I don't think there's such a thing as too much effort when it comes to regulating the quality of schooling," Maggie said honestly.

"Okay, then what about these weird super abilities? That's some superhero kind of crap, why would he be keeping that a secret? Even if this teaching-inspector thing is true—"

"Jessa," Flynn said, in the voice he always used when Jessa got carried away with her own thoughts. "Is it so hard for you to accept that there are some things we just don't know about? And why should we know about them? Mr Fletcher had a secret. You found out what his secret is, and he explained why he kept it quiet. He gave you an answer—"

"But he was so vague and weird about it. I mean, an undercover school inspector? Have you ever heard of that?"

"No, I'm fourteen! I'm not a teacher! And I don't work for the government! And neither do you, so why do you think you're some kind of expert? Why do you need to know everything? Why can't you just let it go and stop being so bloody nosy about it?"

Jessa shut her mouth tight and breathed heavily. Her face puckered and for a second it looked like her bottom lip wobbled. Without a word, Jessa flung her backpack over her shoulder and stormed off, disappearing through the cold and back into the school building.

"Uh oh," said Maggie. "You've done it now."

"I didn't mean to upset her," Flynn replied.

"I know," she replied through the muffling of scarf wrapped high around her face. "And you were right. You've never told her off like that before, though."

"Yeah. I'll apologise. She just gets so carried away."

"She'll be fine, don't worry."

§

Jessa had avoided Maggie and Flynn for the rest of the day. Even in the Physics lab when Mr Keeley told the first-years to get into groups of three or four, Jessa made a point of leaving her usual table with Maggie and Flynn to work with Ben Rivers and Emily Edwards on the other side of the room. She didn't even like Emily Edwards, but considering Emily was Maggie's rival for highest grades in the class, Jessa knew it would drive Maggie crazy.

She wanted to make up with Maggie and Flynn, but whenever she thought about their disagreement, it just reminded her of the very thing about which they'd been disagreeing, and she started getting frustrated all over again.

"Careful, Jessa!" Mrs Baxter blurted just in time to save Jessa's plate from overflowing with gravy.

"Save some for the rest of us!" her father jeered.

"Oh, sorry," she passed the jug to him. She simply couldn't stop her brain from thinking about the very thing she was trying so hard not to think about.

"You're quiet, today, Jessa. Everything all right at school?" Mrs Baxter asked.

"Mmhmm," Jessa shoved a roasted potato into her mouth and avoided looking at her mother.

"You know you can talk to us if something's bothering you..." Mrs Baxter was interrupted by the twittering chirp of a telephone on a side table. She reached to pick up the device.

"Jessa, Flynn's calling you. Be quick, though."

Jessa considered letting it go to voicemail but supposed she had to talk to him at some point. The rest of the day had been awfully lonely.

"Hi," she answered.

"Hey! It's Flynn."

"Yeah I know. I can't talk, I'm in the middle of dinner."

"Oh, sorry. Please can I just talk to you, though? Five minutes?"

"Okay," Jessa walked into the living room and closed the door so her parents couldn't hear the conversation. "What's up?"

"Come on, Jess, please don't give me that voice."

"I don't know what you mean," she said dispassionately.

"I'm sorry, okay? I didn't mean to call you nosy."

"Yes, you did! You knew what you were saying. I was trying to tell you something that I thought was really important, and both of you just sat there like you thought I was mental."

"Don't say that, Jess. No-one thinks you're mental. We didn't mean to make you feel that way."

"Well, you did. You made me feel rubbish."

"I'm really sorry. Please can we be friends again? Maggie and I felt horrible all afternoon."

Jessa chewed lightly on her bottom lip.

"Please, Jessa?"

"Okay," she said. "You're forgiven. But mostly because I can't stand Emily Edwards."

"Fair enough," said Flynn. "Gotta say, it was very surprising to see you go off with her and Ben."

"I know! I wanted Tonia and Annora, but Jodie and Claire got there first. You know, Emily is even worse than Maggie about following rules. I was writing down all of our results, and I rounded up 0.58 to 0.6. Emily flipped out like you wouldn't believe."

"Oh, I believe it," he laughed.

"I have to go, though, my dinner's getting cold."

"All right. Thanks for chatting."

"No problem. See you tomorrow."

She hung up the phone and joined her parents again at the table.

Jessa knew she shouldn't mention her doubts to Maggie and Flynn again, but she still couldn't get her mind off Hugo Fletcher's story. She'd have to keep it to herself. For now, anyway.

She wanted to believe Mr Fletcher, and she guessed that the story itself was plausible. But her suspicion was coming from somewhere else. When he'd told her, there was something in his eyes, that she'd never seen in someone before. She'd seen something in him, something deceitful that she couldn't explain but she could feel. A feeling coming from a deep place within herself of which she'd never been aware.

10

Jessa, Maggie and Flynn gazed up at the twenty-foot Christmas tree in the Winsbury school hall, surveying its bare and unadorned branches.

They had volunteered themselves as WinterFest reps so they could spend more time together before the two-week Christmas holiday. Mrs Hoopey wasn't lying when she promised being a rep would be fun, and Jessa and her friends quickly discovered why WinterFest had been talked about since the start of term. The best part about being a rep was that they could get involved in all the activities. Of course, there were some chores involved (which Jessa made very clear that she found incredibly dull), like taking tickets at the door for the Winsbury Concerts, and picking up rubbish in the park during the seasonal market (she particularly hated that job). Naturally, the task she was most pleased about was putting up the tree.

"My friend Hayley goes to a parapsych school in Lancashire and they don't have any parties or anything, not even at Christmas," Maggie said, taking lids off boxes to reveal all the different decorations inside.

"Oh yeah," Flynn replied. "Winsbury is well known for the social events. That's the main reason why most kids want to go here."

"Really?" Maggie hooted. "You think they care more about parties than academics?"

Jessa laughed. "Yes. Duh."

"So far, WinterFest is my favourite school event," Flynn stated.

"Mine too," Jessa agreed. "I want to go through the German market on the way home and get more of that Stollen bread."

"And hot apple cider!" Maggie chimed in.

"And bratwurst!" Flynn added cheerfully.

Jessa climbed midway up the stepladder to arrange a string of lights near the top of the tree. "I'm excited about the music stuff," she said.

"Me too!" Maggie swooned. "I can't wait to play in the concert on Sunday. You won't believe how good the wind band sounds right now. We've been practising like crazy. Stravinsky really knew his stuff."

"I was thinking more about the rock gig," said Jessa.

"Oh." Maggie pondered for a moment. "No, I'm not so excited about that. Rock music is too loud."

"I'm interested to see Parasyko," Jessa said. "But I'm sure they're not as good as everyone in school seems to think," she took a long piece of tinsel from Maggie and trailed it up and over the bristling arms of the tree. "Gray's a good guitar player, though, and I've heard Eli's a great singer, so hopefully they'll be decent."

"So you haven't actually heard any of Parasyko's songs?" Flynn asked the girls.

"Nope, I haven't," said Maggie. "When Cecily was handing out download cards she deliberately didn't give me one."

"That's mature," laughed Flynn. "I'd have thought she'd want as many people as possible to hear it. Isn't she supposed to be their manager?"

"Yeah right!" Jessa exclaimed. "She gives out a few download cards and calls herself a manager? No way. She's just doing it because she wants everyone to think she's cool."

"Everyone does think she's cool," Flynn said plainly.

Jessa moved around to the other side of the tree with a box of shining silver and gold ornaments tucked under her arm. "It won't last. Those people aren't her real friends." She climbed a few rungs of the ladder again to hang the ornaments higher up.

"She doesn't really seem to have many actual friends, does she?" Maggie mused. "She's always hanging out with Eli and Gray, but it's the two boys who are best friends, and she's just there. Cecily never hangs out with other girls, does she?"

"Do we have to talk about Cecily?" Flynn pulled a face.

Jessa and Maggie ignored him.

"I guess she's friends with Amelia and Devi from Mrs Reid's class," Maggie continued.

"Those two are sheep, they just follow her around," Jessa tutted. "And boys only like her because they think she's pretty."

"Which is different to actually liking someone," Maggie pointed out. "You can be good-looking, but if you're not nice to be around then people won't like you, it's as simple as that. I think it's quite sad. Everyone deserves to have friends," she said.

Flynn shrugged.

"I disagree," Jessa climbed down from the ladder. "Cecily doesn't deserve friends because she's horrible to everyone. Boys only want to hang out with her because of her looks, and girls only want to hang out with her because there are boys there. She not nice to be around. Let's face it, she's kind of a bitch."

"Oh really, Jessa?" a voice appeared behind Maggie and Flynn. "Well, why don't you come out here and say that to my face?"

"Cecily?" Jessa moved around the tree and into view. "What are you even doing here? Are you a volunteer?"

"Oh yeah," Cecily said sarcastically. "Like I'd be in school if I didn't have to be. So what's up, Jessa? If you've got a problem with me, why don't you say it to me, not behind my back!" she advanced toward Jessa.

"No, I was just, umm…"

"What? One minute you're saying how much of a bitch I am and next minute you're all quiet? That's not like you, Jessamine. Come on, why don't you tell me what you really think?"

"Fine," Jessa snapped. "You're mean and aggressive and arrogant. You act like you're so much better than everyone else, and you make people feel bad. You're a bully."

Cecily's eyes grew wild with resentment. "What gives you the right to judge me like that?" she snarled. Her face was so close that Jessa could smell her shampoo. "You'd better watch yourself."

"Why? You can't do anything to me!"

Cecily backed off with a smirk. "You have no idea what I could do."

"Try me."

"All right. For starters, maybe I'll tell everyone that Mr Fletcher is in a relationship with your sister and that you three get special treatment."

Jessa's chest heaved. "We don't get special treatment."

"Hmmm. Or maybe I'll be more creative. Like, maybe I'll tell them about the time I was alone with Mr Fletcher in his classroom…" she lowered her voice to a whisper, "and he touched me."

"Don't you dare," Jessa spat the words out.

"At first, I just thought he was being friendly!" Cecily mimicked the voice of an innocent storyteller. "He said how pretty I am, and that he always thought there was a connection between us. Then he locked the door…"

"Stop it." Jessa's hands shook.

"That's when he put his hand on my leg…"

"Don't you dare lie about that!" Maggie flew forward.

"I'll do whatever I want." Cecily stomped her right foot forward onto Maggie's toes, pressing down through the heavy sole of her black leather boots.

"Ow!" Maggie squealed.

Flynn stepped forward in front of the two girls and looked directly into Cecily's face.

"What are you gonna do, big man?" Cecily mocked.

"Just leave, Cecily. Leave us alone," he spoke very calmly.

"Or what?" She pushed her face uncomfortably close to his. She slowly put her hand on his shoulder and pushed gently.

He stumbled. "Cecily, don't push me!"

"You are all so pathetic!" she yelled and shoved him hard enough to knock him backwards. He fell just close enough to the tree to push it over, bringing down all the decorations that hit the ground with a smattering of clinks and clangs.

"ENOUGH!" a voice thundered from the doorway. Dr Mortlock entered the room. Her black patent shoes clip-clopped as she marched towards them. Maggie and Jessa helped Flynn to his feet, and the three of them tried to pull the tree back up.

"Leave it," Dr Mortlock glowered down at them. "My office. Now.'

§

Jessa realised that this was the first time she'd ever seen inside the headteacher's office. Based on Dr Mortlock's severe personality, Jessa had imagined that her office would be dark and mysterious, but in reality, it was quite the opposite. The walls were white and plain. There were bookshelves full of books and binders, all curiously unlabelled.

"I never want to see that kind of behaviour again, do you understand?"

"Yes, Dr Mortlock," the four of them responded.

"But can I just say something?" Jessa spoke up, to her friends' obvious disapproval.

"Please listen to me very carefully, Miss Baxter," the headteacher replied without answering Jessa's question. "I truly don't care for the topic of this disagreement. And I certainly don't care who started it. Frankly, there are plenty more pressing matters I could be attending to right now than having this discussion."

It's barely a discussion, Jessa thought to herself.

"The Winsbury School of Parapsychology is a place for young men and women such as yourselves to learn how to function as citizens of an adult society. For this reason, I will not baby you in these petty discrepancies I am leaving it to you to reconcile your differences. How you do that is your choice, but I will not accept aggression or violence in any capacity. So I suggest you find a way to end this like adults. Do you understand?"

"Yes, Dr Mortlock."

"You are all dismissed for today. Miss Graves, your detention-assigned WinterFest duties will continue tomorrow as planned. Now all of you, get out of my office and go home."

Jessa and Flynn waited in the school foyer for Maggie's dad to arrive and pick her up.

"I can't believe she got off so lightly," Jessa shook her head. "It's so unfair that we all got told off. It was *so* Cecily's fault."

"I'm not sure about that," Flynn murmured.

"What?" Jessa turned to him.

"It wasn't completely Cecily's fault."

Jessa's jaw fell.

"We were talking about her, and she overheard," said Flynn.

"Since when was it a crime to talk about someone?"

"Talking about someone is different to bitching about them."

"But I didn't say anything that wasn't true."

"Jessa," Flynn crossed his arms. "Cecily is a bully, you're right. But being mean about someone else who's mean is basically the pot calling the kettle black."

Jessa huffed. "Well, I still think she should have got in more trouble for pushing you like that."

"Dr Mortlock did choose a very progressive way to handle the situation," Maggie said.

"But it's not a punishment like Cecily deserves," replied Jessa.

"The thing that bugs me the most," said Maggie, "is that volunteering at WinterFest is her punishment. It's a little insulting that she's doing it for detention, and the rest of us actually wanted to contribute."

"For someone like Cecily, doing something selfless is probably just as good a punishment," said Flynn.

"Ugh, I hate her so much," said Jessa.

"Don't hate her," Flynn said gently. "She's not worth your emotion. She's just a bulldozer. She can throw her weight around now, but it won't get her very far in life."

"We should just avoid her," said Maggie. "We signed up to help, remember? And to see each other as much as possible before the holiday. So we can't let Cecily get in the way of that."

Jessa sighed. Maybe her friends were right. But despite their differing ideas, there were two things that were undeniable: Dr Mortlock was even more of a puzzle than they thought, and Cecily was much more capable of wickedness.

•73•

11

The final day of WinterFest was the last day of term, two days before Christmas, and the first-years had their final PSE lesson.

"Most of your holiday assignments can be found here on your student intranet accounts." Mr Fletcher's finger scanned through pages on his tablet. "And you have printed copies of the science questions, yes? I'm not sure why the science department avoids this technology. You'd think they'd be into it, wouldn't you?" he wondered aloud.

"Maybe it's that the science teachers are such old fogeys that they don't know how to upload to the intranet," Gray called out from the back of the room.

Graham Townsend knew how to make the class laugh. His shaggy highlighted hair flopped down in front of his face and he emphatically ran his hand through it to brush it away from his eyes.

He does that a lot, Jessa thought. She wondered if he did it deliberately.

"So how are you all feeling about your first semester at Winsbury, now that it's coming to an end?" Mr Fletcher said, casually leaning against his desk. "Was it more difficult than you anticipated? Is there more homework than you expected? Come on, anything you want to share?"

"Too much homework!" Gray called out.

"Yeah, bit too much," Eli agreed.

Maggie raised her hand. "I think we get a very appropriate amount of homework."

"Yeah but I have band practice, like, three times a week," Gray droned. "And I have an unlimited cinema pass so I have to go at least twice a week to make it worthwhile. It adds up, y'know?"

"That does sound tough, Gray," Maggie looked annoyed. "Maybe you should transfer to Northgate Comprehensive; I hear they get plenty of downtime—"

"All right!" Mr Fletcher clapped his hands together loudly. "Anyone else?"

"I've enjoyed it," said Jessa.

"Me too," said the wispy voice of Annora Huff. "I love Parapsych Skills lessons."

A wave of "mmhmms" and "yeahs" rippled throughout the room.

"Well, I personally don't think the parapsych labs have been very useful," Cecily sneered.

"Why do you say that, Cecily?" the teacher asked.

"It's all so basic," she drawled. "When do we learn the real stuff?"

"I'm sorry to disappoint you," Mr Fletcher began politely, "but this is "real stuff." It's just foundational. You have to start small and practice and get stronger. So actually, while we're thinking about this, let's review a few things. Here's a nice easy question: who can tell me what a Level 1 Parapsych is?"

"Children are Level 1," said Tonia.

"Correct," Mr Fletcher responded. "Children, or perhaps adults who went to a parapsych school that wasn't as involved as Winsbury, and as such didn't learn effectively how to utilise their skills. Or maybe an adult who just doesn't use their skills much and falls out of practice. Basically, it's when someone has a hint of parapsychological ability but lacks control over it. So what's Level 2?"

"A lot of people are Level 2, right?" said Eli Cannon. "Uni students, adult parapsychs who practice a lot." Cecily turned to shoot him a glare. It looked like she mouthed "teacher's pet" at him, but Jessa couldn't quite tell.

"You're exactly right, Eli," the teacher replied. "When you arrive at Winsbury, you're all Level 1, whether you like it or not. But by the time you leave, you'll almost definitely be Level 2. Our curriculum is more intensive than most schools, which I'm sure you've noticed. When you graduate from

Winsbury many of you might take places at a standard University or a workplace apprenticeship, but you might even be Level 2 Plus, which makes you a prime candidate for further parapsych study. So what's Level 3?"

"It's like when people have more than one parability," Flynn answered.

"Yes, exactly. It's also when people use their ability directly in their job in a way that requires a lot of precision. Sometimes we call Level 3s 'Professional Parapsychs.' For example, psychiatrists who use telepathy in treatments, or doctors who use advanced telekinesis in microsurgery. Or psych vets who read animals. Or professors of parapsychism, even. So to return to Cecily's concern," he said, turning back to face her, "I'd like to remind you all that a parapsych is only as good as their practice. You wouldn't run a marathon without training first, would you? This school is here to teach you a consistency and precision that you don't currently have."

"Who are you to say how consistent or precise I am?" Cecily raised her carefully preened eyebrows. "You're just a history teacher."

He didn't raise his voice even a little. "Cecily, I'd appreciate it if you wouldn't speak to me like that. I apologise if I offended you or if you interpreted my words as insulting. But the fact of the matter is, biologically and psychologically speaking, you and your classmates are low-level parapsychs. That's just how it is."

"What are you even talking about?" she retorted. "Who are you to question my parapsych skills? You don't know anything about me or what I'm capable of! Just because your parapsychism is so weak that you had to settle to be some crappy ponce history teacher doesn't mean the rest of us should. You don't even know me!"

The entire class looked at Cecily. She knew she'd gone too far.

Slowly, the students turned back to the teacher, anxious to see how he responded.

He waited.

She said nothing.

He picked up his tablet and pressed on the screen, in gentle taps and swirls that showed the students he was typing. The familiar ding of a sent message broke through the quiet tension in the room, followed shortly by the dong of a received reply.

"Miss Graves," he finally said, looking up from the device. "Please gather your things. Mrs Hoopey is on her way here. She will escort you to your locker and you will empty it."

The first-years looked at him, wide-eyed.

"But wait—" she tried to say.

"No," he interrupted.

Mrs Hoopey arrived at the door.

"Thank you, Miss Graves," said Mr Fletcher. "You are dismissed."

§

The usual purple and yellow of the cafeteria had been adorned with balloons and silver and gold streamers that hung down from the ceiling. At every place-setting was a Christmas cracker, which the students had great fun pulling open to reveal inside the silly toys, slips of paper with terrible jokes printed on, and the classic tissue-paper crowns that they all wore so proudly.

Of course, Cecily's suspension was the talk of the whole school.

"I remember when Sally Potters got expelled in third-year, it was so exciting."

"I've never heard of someone talking to a teacher like that," said someone else.

"And a first-year? Wow."

Jessa, Maggie and Flynn joined the line for the buffet and the mutterings continued around them.

"I wonder if she'll be back next semester."

"I bet she'll be expelled for good."

"What kind of school will she end up at, after something like this?"

"I'm glad she finally got her comeuppance," said Jessa. "She had no right to talk to him like that."

"I doubt she's even going to learn from a suspension, though," Flynn wondered. "Especially as it's the last day of term. She's probably just at home now enjoying an extra day of the Christmas holiday."

"Damn, I hadn't thought of it that way," Jessa replied. "The thought of Cecily just chilling at home right now makes me feel a bit sick."

"Well, I suppose we'll just have to wait and find out," said Maggie. "Hungry, Flynn?" she changed the subject as Flynn piled at least six roasted parsnips onto his plate.

"Oh yeah, Christmas dinner is my favourite!" he said, moving on to deposit a heaving dollop of stuffing onto the plate in the best way it would fit.

"Don't overdo it, though," Maggie warned. "You'll be having another Christmas dinner in two days, remember."

"Nah, I don't think we're having one this year," he said.

"How come?"

"My mum has to work late on Christmas Eve, and she won't have any time to go shopping for dinner stuff. It's fine, though. At least I get to have some here!" He tried to sound cheerful, but he avoided eye contact the way he always did when he was upset.

"Let's make sure this one counts, then. Excuse me, Agnes," Maggie addressed the server, "can we please have three pieces of Christmas pudding, three slices of chocolate log, and three bowls of trifle? This one's on me, guys."

Mrs Hoopey's voice came in through the PA system, quieting the festive music for a moment. "Good afternoon, students!" she chirped. "When the bell rings at 2 pm, please make your way to the main hall for an afternoon of festive fun! First, we'll have the Big Quiz, so get yourself organised into teams of five or six! And then we'll cheer on the fourth and fifth-year participants in our Parapsych Games! And of course—everybody's favourite—the staff performance!"

The whole cafeteria erupted into cheer. Jessa had not yet witnessed the annual staff performance, but she'd heard legendary tales of the teachers' song and dance numbers.

During lunch, some of Emmeline Victor's friends put on a charity bake sale where they sold homemade Christmassy treats like mince pies and fig rolls and Linzer tarts. As if their triple-pudding medley wasn't enough, Jessa couldn't resist buying a selection of treats to share with her friends.

At the end of the afternoon, the fifth-years announced that the bake sale had raised over £650, which would go to Emmeline and her family. Jessa looked around the room at the students as they cheered Emmeline's name in her honour, and for the first time, she felt genuinely proud to be a Winsbury student.

§

"How was your last day of term?" Mrs Baxter asked as her daughter wiggled out of her outdoor layers. Jessa regaled her mother with tales of Hugo Fletcher suspending Cecily, and the Christmas lunch, which she said was good but not as nearly as good as a home-cooked one, which Mrs Baxter was glad to hear. Jessa continued chatting away about how her team didn't do very well in the quiz, even though Tonia was surprisingly good in the sport round. How the fourth-year students were really good at parapsych skills and that Timothy Gregson won the trophy with his auto-writing performance and how he already has a scholarship to a top American university, and how the teacher's performance was amazing and how Mr Fletcher played a prince in the comedy play they put on, and how…

"It sounds like you've had a good day," said Mrs Baxter.

"It was so fun," Jessa beamed.

"Poor Flynn, though, not getting a real Christmas dinner," Mrs Baxter said thoughtfully.

"I know," Jessa replied. "He said he was all right with it, but I can tell he wasn't really."

"I have an idea. Let's invite him and his mum here."

"Seriously? You're the best, Mum." Jessa initiated a hug with her mother for the first time in a long while.

Jessa ran to the phone and activated the voice line to call him on their telephone, as he didn't have a videocom system. His mother gratefully accepted the invitation and offered to bring mince pies, which of course, the Baxters accepted, because they couldn't possibly turn down mince pies.

It would be the best Baxter Christmas yet.

12

Jessa stretched out the cramp from her fingers. 6:12am said the clock. Still plenty of time. And Physics wasn't until third period, so theoretically, finishing at break time was still an option. But then Maggie would know Jessa had lied about having completed all her homework during the holidays. 6:13am. She rubbed her eyes.

A gentle knock at the door took Jessa's attention away from her books. It opened, and Audrey peered in, looking perfectly awake and irritatingly well-rested.

"Jessa? Are you okay? I saw your light on."

"I'm fine," Jessa shrugged.

"Then why are you up so ea—" Audrey noticed the papers on Jessa's desk and stopped herself. "Oh, that's why. You're cramming homework. Of course. Didn't you just have two weeks off?"

"Yes. What's your point?"

"Typical. Well, good luck with that. I'm going to the gym. Have a good day at school. Maybe they'll teach you time management skills this year."

Jessa clenched her jaw and made a face behind Audrey's back as she left the room. Audrey had probably never finished homework so late. Everything Jessa had ever heard about her sister made it seem like she was some genius child prodigy. Their parents still had all Audrey's report cards from school, full of words that Jessa couldn't even imagine appearing on hers. Excelled. Applied. Partakes. Achievement.

More wrong answers. Jessa worked through the questions in her textbook one by one, knowing they weren't right. But she was running out of time, and she figured it was better to hand in something incorrect than blank paper. She briefly entertained the idea of pretending to have left her homework at home, but decided against it. She knew she'd inevitably leave her homework at home for real sometime soon, and wouldn't be able to get away with that excuse too many times.

Jessa washed away the grime from her face but still couldn't shake the annoying interaction with her sister from her mind. She leaned closer to the mirror and prodded her skin. Audrey's pores were so much smaller. And Audrey's skin didn't have red blotches.

Jessa opened the cabinet and inspected Audrey's bottles of beauty concoctions. Cleansing milk, cleansing oil, cleansing lotion. No wonder Audrey always looked so… *clean*. Jessa grabbed a little green tube labelled 'Pore Refining Mask' and squeezed a small glob onto the tip of her finger. It was cold and smelled like dirt. She grimaced and washed the goop from her hand but decided to try the cleansing milk, the most seemingly inoffensive of the strange aqueous substances.

She pulled back her wavy, untamed hair and looked into the dark, unstriking eyes of her reflection and wondered if she'd ever be as delicate and sleek as her older sister.

§

Jessa, Maggie, and Flynn settled back into their tutor room. Maggie, who had clearly arrived at school considerably early, happily munched away on the rest of her Marmite toast from the cafeteria while poring over a textbook that Jessa didn't recognise.

"What are you reading? Is that a French book? Did we have homework that—"

"Jessa, chill out, it's not a set text," Maggie rolled her eyes.

"What is it, then?"

"It's the third-year French textbook. Madame Bellerose let me borrow a copy."

"And you're just reading it, for fun?"

"Over the holiday I used it as a reference for our French homework. But now I'm reading it for pleasure, yes. Oh, and speaking of homework, did you bring all your assignments?"

"Yes," Jessa yawned.

As the rest of the class slowly filtered in, the topic on everybody's lips was Cecily Graves and whether she would return. Rumour had it she'd enrolled in some kind of special intensive education programme in order to catch up with the Winsbury curriculum. A different rumour had it that she'd spent the holiday in Costa Rica. The latter seemed more likely, but evidently nobody in the class had actually heard from Cecily during the break, not even Eli or Gray.

Mr Fletcher entered the room cheerfully and immediately started checking names on his tablet, newly adorned with a green suede cover that Jessa knew to have been one of his Christmas gifts from Audrey.

"Welcome back, guys and girls!" he smiled. "I trust you all had a great break, and I hope you're ready to get back to work. The first semester at Winsbury was something of an introduction to student life here, so hopefully you feel warmed up and ready to delve into your studies even deeper."

Everyone looked up upon hearing the click of the doorknob fidgeting in its socket. The teacher paused.

In walked Cecily Graves, dressed in an uncharacteristically simple outfit of plain black trousers and a smart sweater. An obvious tension clenched the room as she entered, her eyes down as she hurried to the back of the class to an empty seat.

"I'm glad you could join us, Cecily," said Mr Fletcher.

The students exchanged unsubtle whispers.

Mr Fletcher briskly brought the attention back to himself. "Shush, quiet, please. Where were we? Oh yes, I have some announcements for you! We're going on the history trip to the National Parapsychological Museum this Saturday. Don't forget! You need to meet in the school foyer at 9 am, do not be late!

Secondly, you've had some time to 'shop' your extracurriculars, but from this point, you're all required to be a member of at least one extracurricular activity. I know many of you have been attending a club already, and that's great, but those of you who haven't chosen one yet, you have until the end of next week to make a choice and officially sign up through your online accounts."

Jessa zoned out while the teacher continued with more announcements and tuned back in just in time to hear him say "chat amongst yourselves."

"What do you think happened to her?" Jessa quickly whispered to Maggie.

"It's not the time to talk about that," Maggie replied. "You should focus on school stuff. I mean, what club are you going to join?"

"Urgh."

"Come on, you have to pick one!"

"I don't know," she whined back. "I'm not good at any of these things."

"Don't be silly, of course you are." Maggie leaned in closer. "Let's look at the list. All right, what about something musical? You love music."

"Yeah but I don't play an instrument."

"What about your guitar?"

"I'm not nearly good enough."

"Okay, then how about choir?"

"Nah."

"You could join WriteSoc with me," said Flynn.

"I'm not into creative writing, though. What other clubs are you in, Flynn?"

"Just WriteSoc and Coding Club. I might join Chess Club, too."

"You could pick something at random," Maggie suggested. "Then just see how it goes. You can always change your mind next term. What about Community 1? You'd get to do all sorts of interesting things, and it would be great to help other people."

"Yeah but they have meetings at the weekend," Jessa shook her head. "It's okay, I'll pick something eventually. I still have some time."

"And how are you three getting on today?" Mr Fletcher approached and crouched slightly to lean on their desk. "Feeling good about the new semester?"

"Yes, sir!" Maggie nodded.

"You know you don't have to call me sir, right?"

"I know. It's just a habit. In my house, we grew up calling older people 'sir' and 'ma'am'."

"Ouch, how old do you think I am?" he joked.

"I didn't mean it like that!" Maggie replied.

"It's okay, I'm yanking your chain," he chuckled. "But hey, would you three mind coming back here at break time?"

"Are we in trouble?" Maggie asked quickly.

"Do you have any reason to be in trouble?" he asked playfully, with a raised-eyebrow glance to Jessa.

Jessa smiled sweetly. "Of course not," she said, "...sir."

"Well played, Baxter. But no, I just want to chat to you about something."

§

"Hi guys, come on in."

Flynn made sure the door was closed behind them.

"Pull up some chairs," he gestured, then opened his desk drawer and took out a plate on which were four large muffins, "help yourself."

"What's going on?" asked Jessa. "What do you want to talk to us about?"

"Cecily," he said. "She was issued a formal warning after her dismissal at the end of last term. I know there was talk around here of her suspension being an extended holiday, but I promise you that wasn't the case. It's a real black mark on her school record now, and in conjunction with some previous misdemeanours—"

"Like pushing Flynn into the Christmas tree?!" Jessa sprayed muffin crumbs as she spoke.

"Like a few things, the details of which are not important right now," he corrected. Jessa rolled her eyes. "My point is that she's on very thin ice, and she's aware of it."

"So if she keeps it up, she'll get expelled?" Maggie asked.

"In short, yes. Ultimately, the Board decided that, for now, it's more beneficial for Cecily to be in school than under a suspension, which is why she's back today. But she's been warned."

"But Mr Fletcher," said Flynn, "what does this have to do with us?"

"Well, I know the three of you have had a few incidents with Cecily—"

"She started it!" Jessa interrupted.

Mr Fletcher held up his hands. "I need you to rise above it. Some people can't help looking for a fight. But it's important not to engage those people and bring yourself into a violent situation. Just remember that not everyone is exactly how they portray themselves. Quite often, there's more that they're hiding, and acting out is their way of distancing themselves from deeper problems."

"What?" said Jessa. "Are you trying to tell us we should feel sorry for her?"

"No, I'm not trying to tell you how to feel. I'm just reminding you to look beyond the surface. But now I have work to do, so get out," he jokingly shooed them from the room.

They retired to the beanbag chairs on the second-floor landing before double physics.

"What does he mean by 'deeper problems'?" Jessa wondered aloud, wriggling deeper into the beans. "I mean, she's rich, beautiful, and has everything she could ever want."

"Well, we know there's one thing she doesn't have," Maggie replied. "Real friends. I know I'd go crazy if I didn't have friends."

"I just don't get what he meant," said Jessa.

"If Mr Fletcher wanted us to know something, he would have told us," Flynn said, matter-of-factly. "All we need to know is there's something we don't know."

13

The rest of the boys in the class cheered when Gray Townsend finally walked up with his bike.

"Nice of you to show up, Graham," Mr Fletcher said, looking at Gray's freshly slicked hair. "I can only assume the reason you're so late is that you didn't actually ride that bike of yours for fear of ruining that fancy hairdo. All right, does everyone have what they need? Let's go."

Hugo Fletcher had expressed privately to Jessa and her family that he was anxious about the prospect of taking his class on a trip to the museum, especially as he'd taken Mrs Reid's tutor group the week prior and had trouble keeping track of everyone on the Tube (and Mrs Reid's form didn't even have a joker like Gray Townsend). But fortunately for Mr Fletcher, his students were either feeling extra-responsible or just too slumberous on a Saturday morning to get up to too much mischief.

§

The museum itself was beautiful. First opened in the 1600s, it was founded by the incredibly wealthy Forbes family, who had such an obsession with Italy that they hired an Italian architect to design the museum in the style of Italian Renaissance architecture. The other museums around London were mostly Victorian, or styled with the Greek Revival in mind, with Parthenon-style columns on their facades. In comparison, the National Parapsychological

Museum stood apart not just as a unique museum, but as one of the most remarkable buildings in the whole of London, as its intricate white dome stood out majestically in the London skyline.

Inside, the museum functioned with its authentic mosaic flooring, and high ceilings that soared above, carefully painted with vibrant depictions of cherubs and open skies in a rich palate of colours and golden highlights.

Mr Fletcher handed out maps to everyone and prepped them for the day. "Everyone has a phone, correct?" he asked.

They all nodded.

"Great. If you haven't already, please go to the email I sent this morning and add me as a direct contact. I know you want to explore the museum without a teacher hovering around you, but I do ask that you stay in groups of at least two. And contact me if you need anything. Understand?"

They nodded again.

"You are not to leave the museum under any circumstances. Got it?"

More nods.

"Can I get a 'Yes, Mr Fletcher'?"

"Yes, Mr Fletcher," they mumbled.

"Perfect. And you all have the worksheet attached to that e-mail. Enter the information as you go around the exhibits. Have fun. If you want to meet for lunch, I'll be in the cafe at 1 pm. Otherwise, feel free to eat on your own schedule. I'm sure I'll be fine... all alone... friendless... hopeless..." he pretended to look sad.

The class looked at him blankly.

"You may go."

And with that, the students dispersed in different directions, leaving Hugo Fletcher standing by himself in the foyer, surrounded by tourists and families.

"All right, Team Maggie!" Maggie summoned Jessa and Flynn.

"I did not agree for that to be our team name," Jessa mocked.

Maggie ignored her. "I think we should start in the Prehistory section, because, duh, it's prehistory. Then we'll move around according to time periods, first to the Ancient Egypt section, the Ancient Orient, Ancient Greece and Rome, through to the Middle Ages," she continued without so much as a glance at the map. "Then we should probably go to the Parapsychology in Religion section, then to the Parafolklore exhibit, then to the Myth & Legend rooms, the Witchcraft Wing, then to Antiques and Curiosities, the Instruments and Medicinal Parapsychology special exhibit, and finally we'll check out the Modern History department and the Art Gallery."

"Been here before, have you, Mags?" Flynn retorted.

"I know you're being sarcastic but actually, yes. My family has an annual museum pass so I come here a lot. Luckily for you."

"Mmhmm. Lucky," Jessa nudged Flynn with a giggle. "My parents brought me once as a kid."

"Oh, did you like it? The museum was so magical to me as a child."

"I cried the entire time."

Maggie rolled her eyes. "Come on, let's go."

Jessa, Maggie and Flynn stopped at every artefact and statue to read the information placards, and occasionally scanned the info-codes on their phones to watch the educational videos.

"This is actually quite fun," Jessa admitted.

"It's interesting to me how many of the items from these early periods were not even related to parapsychs," Flynn wondered out loud to the girls. "A lot of this stuff is from a time before parapsychological abilities were understood, but you can see how the culture progressed."

"That's a very astute observation, Flynn," Mr Fletcher's voice said behind them. "It's very important to appreciate the development of a humanity that would grow to embrace and advocate these abilities in a modern environment."

"Mr Fletcher, do you want to walk around with us?" Flynn asked.

"Aw, thanks, Flynn," the teacher replied. "But you don't have to invite me to hang out with you."

"I'd actually love to ask you some questions," Maggie piped up.

Mr Fletcher smiled. "Well okay then, I'll stick with you for a little while."

Mr Fletcher and Flynn walked side by side through the rooms, with

Maggie dashing between them and the windows of exhibits, determined to make her own extensive notes but desperate not to miss anything important the teacher might say.

"How many people do you think who were tried as witches, were actually parapsychs?" Maggie asked Mr Fletcher.

"It's a good question, though I personally couldn't estimate," he replied. "There have been a good few studies into that, though. You should look them up later. The problem is that we don't have many accurate sources from that time. Of course, we know now that witchcraft isn't real, but in those days, there was a real fear that witches were Devil-worshippers and were threatening to Christianity. Back then, people were very easily scared."

"But parapsychological abilities were known way before the Middle Ages, right?" Jessa inquired.

"That's true, but times change, beliefs change, and sometimes that results in tragedy. Do you remember what put an end to people being tried as witches?"

"The Witchcraft Act!" Maggie said quickly.

"Oh hey, someone does pay attention in my lessons!" Mr Fletcher joshed.

As they walked around the airy spaces, their feet stepped slowly and mindlessly across the tiles and their gaze drifted over the artefacts behind polished windows. Jessa found herself quite engrossed in the detail of generations before her, of centuries past and lifetimes immortalised by the items on display.

She noticed a gold-rimmed hourglass and stopped to read the information card, and discovered it was believed to have been made in the 1300s. She briefly considered how such items come to be invented: how deliberate and ingenious it was to create such a simple and effective solution to a problem.

Jessa had been a very imaginative child. She loved to build things or dress up, always finding ways to create and connect with characters in her mind. As she developed into a teenager, she lost much of her inclination to feel like someone else, but still had a habit of getting lost in daydreams.

She'd once asked her mother a question. *Do you ever imagine what it'd be like to be someone else?*

You are a peculiar girl, her mother had replied.

It was a moment that had continued to stick in her mind, for reasons Jessa could never quite place.

Mr Fletcher walked off to check in with Annora and Tonia across the gallery, and Jessa, Maggie and Flynn made their way into the Antiques and Curiosities Burrow, a series of small, interconnected rooms full of weird and intriguing things previously owned by parapsychs from around the world.

There were globes and goblets, pipes and pictures, table lamps and taxidermy, and so many other items Jessa couldn't even try to define. She scrunched up her face as they approached a glass cabinet full of skulls and body parts preserved in yellowing liquid. The case beside it was smaller and filled with the corpses of butterflies and moths, their papery wings pinned roughly to the back board. The next case was smaller still, filled with old coins that each had a hand-written note next to it, labelled with blotted ink on crumbly paper.

"Can you imagine the kind of person who would own this stuff?" Flynn marvelled. He read aloud the signs at the bottom of each of the cases. "Previously owned by Aleksander Saloman, 1857-1926, Norway. Donated to the Museum in 1994; Owned by Arthur Meek in Cambridge, Massachusetts. Donated to the Museum in 1975. It's so weird to think how far this has all come just for us to look at it," he said, making a quick sketch of a decorative cutlery set.

They'd been given a few question prompts to consider during their visit to the Museum, and one of them instructed the students to consider a topic for a personal project that they would be working on for the remainder of the semester.

"I think this is going to be my project," he said. "Something about what people choose to own and what that says about us."

"Excellent idea," Maggie nodded. "I'm going to do my report on medical parapsychology. I'll make sure to get some good pictures in that exhibit. What's your project going to be, Jessa?"

"I'm not sure, yet," Jessa said, still looking around wistfully.

After lunch, Jessa, Maggie and Flynn spent (or "wasted," according to Maggie) a little time in the Hands-On History Hall, which, despite being clearly designed for children, was occupied by many of their high school peers. Gray and Eli seemed to be a particular source of nuisance.

"Clang!" "Clunk!" "Kapow!" they narrated their battle with tiny plastic weapons, much to the glee of onlooking children and to the annoyance of parents who stood nearby with furrowed brows and folded arms.

"Gentlemen, please! These are toys for the kiddies! Please! You have to stop!" an irritated museum employee yelled over the laughs and sounds of flimsy toy swords thwacking against each other. Gray and Eli cackled in fits of ridiculous giggles while the poor museum worker pleaded with them to settle down.

Jessa and her friends slunk out of the room, embarrassed by their classmates. They went straight to the special exhibit gallery where Maggie fawned over the range of medical instruments used throughout the development of parapsychological medicine. "Look at this!" "Oh, wow!" "My goodness!"

"How long have you been interested in medicine, Mags?" Jessa enquired.

"Forever, I think," Maggie replied. "I got a toy doctor's kit for Christmas one year and it was my favourite thing. I used to play vet hospital with my stuffed animals. Did you ever watch the show Animal Doctors? There was a communicari vet on that, and I thought she was the coolest. That's when I made up my mind that I wanted to work in animal healing."

She held up her phone to scan info-codes and voraciously tapped to download all the links from popups that said things like "further information" and "more about this."

The exhibit guided them through the gruesomest trials and tribulations of medical history, with Roman speculums and forceps and vague pointed devices and unwieldy rusted knives. There were instruments used for things like cutting out patients' tonsils and sawing through skulls. There was even a large, ungainly clamp for holding patients in place while the most ghastly procedures took place.

"These instruments were used in the earliest days of parapsychological investigation," Maggie read to Flynn and Jessa from the information card. "These tuning forks were originally used for musical training but were discovered to be useful in measuring brainwaves during parapsychological activity. And these are vision-restricting goggles. They were first used for eye tests but then developed into apparatus in telekinesis research." She turned to add a footnote of her own, "I read in a textbook once that they used goggles to direct a test subject's vision. It helped to increase their telekinetic concentration. Eventually, they were able to increase telekinetic strength by training the subject to interact with objects that were placed outside of their restricted field of vision. Those techniques are still used today sometimes."

When Maggie decided she'd recorded enough details from the medical exhibit, they made their way down the corridor into the newest part of the building, the Modern History wing. They slowed on the walk to read all the literary quotes painted in calligraphic fonts onto the fresh whitewash walls.

Jessa's eye caught one phrase in particular:

Our history is written, but our story is still being told...

She copied the phrase into her notebook, unthinkingly replacing the dotdotdot of irresolution with a full-stop.

They entered the Modern History gallery and Jessa's eyes adjusted to the dim light that hung all around, allowing the spotlights on the exhibits to punctuate the room.

Then she stopped.

"Wait," she said.

She felt something.

What is that?

Her heart quaked. Her chest felt cavernous. Her fingers and hands tingled. Her skin shuddered with the caustic chill of sweat.

What's happening?

Her eyes darted from person to person. Nobody else looked uneasy.

Am I the only one who feels this?

Somewhere deep inside herself, she felt dread.

"Jessa, you okay?" She barely heard Flynn's voice over the piercing ring in her ears.

Her eyebrows scrunched her face into a deep frown and something pulled her attention into a far corner of the room.

What the something was, she didn't know. But it wanted her to move. She needed to move.

Flynn's hand on her arm snapped her back into the present.

"Jessa." He squeezed his fingers into the flesh of her forearm.

"I have to look over here…" she trailed off toward the corner.

What is it?

What's here?

Questions to no-one.

Her skin turned cold and prickly, her breath became short and her eyes strained to look for something. For anything that made it all make sense.

The title placard for the display read:

"TROUBLED MINDS; TROUBLED TIMES."

It was credited as a quote from a newspaper. Around the display was a selection of other newspaper clippings and front pages reporting the actions of a cult from the 1980s.

Deja vu.

"Have you heard anything about this before?" she asked her friends.

"I don't think so," Flynn replied slowly.

"Vaguely," Maggie added. "It happened when we were babies, I think, or maybe before we were born. I don't know. Why?"

"I don't know either," Jessa said. She shook her head slightly. "I have this feeling…"

"What kind of feeling?"

"I'm not sure. I don't know what happened. I came in here and just felt really strange. Something made me come over here."

"What do you mean?"

"It pulled me."

"What pulled you?"

"The feeling."

Maggie and Flynn glanced at each other.

Jessa continued searching the exhibit.

"Silas Lynch," she read. "Born in the early 60s to a parapsych mother and a lateral father, who raised him in a small village in Bedfordshire... Remarkably strong parapsych from a young age... gifted child...

...Disturbed."

"It says he lost his immediate family at the age of seven, in a freak accident that burned their house to the ground," Maggie reported.

"The young boy was fortunate to escape the wreck alive, but with burn damage to most of his body that would leave him covered in scars for the rest of his life," Flynn read. "Ouch."

"Witnesses said Lynch became increasingly introverted and barely spoke," Maggie continued. "He started speaking to himself in Latin. In interactions with others, he would often refer to the 'purity' of parapsychological evolution."

Jessa, too, searched the display case for information.

"...Rest of his childhood in an orphanage... ran away at fourteen...

...Disappeared.

Showed up in the 80s and formed an activist group..."

"Wow," said Maggie. "It says he tried to establish the idea that parapsychs should be treated as superior to laterals. Supposedly he was responsible for the sacrificial killing of twenty parapsychs, believing he could absorb their power. What a psycho."

Jessa kept looking for clues. It was all there but she couldn't make sense of it. "His own cult members tied him up, locked him in a coffin, then burned him alive," she said.

"Yikes," Maggie said.

"Apparently, he thought there was some government conspiracy against parapsychs."

"Jess," Flynn said gently, "look at me."

She ignored him and looked closer at an item in the case. It was a book of fairytales, held in a stand that grasped the middle pages open for display. Across the pages were dozens of versions of the same scribbled symbol, some large, some small, but all violently etched into the paper by the hand of a disturbed child. Jessa thought it looked like a teepee; a triangle with two long sides that slightly crossed over each other at the top, leaving the bottom end wide and empty.

She touched her hand to the display cabinet and her sweat-soaked fingertips slid on the glass.

Oh no.

"I'm gonna be sick," her stomach lurched and her mouth watered with the taste of acid. She gagged, trying to hold back.

"Let's get her outside." Maggie and Flynn grabbed Jessa and burst through the nearest fire exit.

She leaned forward, resting her hands on her knees.

"Just take deep breaths," Maggie soothed.

Jessa formed a tight circle with her lips and slowly sucked the cool air in and out.

"What just happened?" Flynn said.

"I don't know. I just got this really weird feeling—"

"Well, look who came to the party," a familiar voice interrupted. Jessa looked round to see Cecily Graves leaning against the wall with a cigarette perched neatly between her fingers.

Eli and Gray stood nearby, distracted by a music video playing on a phone. Amelia Waters and Devi Kapoor hovered awkwardly, each holding their own less-smoked cigarettes.

"This is none of your business, Cecily," Maggie tried to wave their attention away.

Cecily stepped closer. "That's funny, because my business is anything I want it to be. And guess what, you dumb bitch? This is my business, now."

She pushed Maggie with her free hand.

"Hey!" Jessa yelled. She quickly felt Flynn holding the back of her shirt.

"What's your problem, Sweat Patches? Ever heard of a thing called antiperspirant?"

Amelia and Devi cackled. Eli and Gray looked on.

Cecily snatched Maggie's notebook from her hand. "Oh, perfect!" she sneered sarcastically. "Maggie, can I borrow your notes? I would just love to catch up on all the details from this super cool museum." She flapped the notebook open. "Wait, silly me. No, I wouldn't. Because I have a fucking life." She ripped out leaves from the notebook and let them fall to the ground.

"Cecily, cut it out," Eli stepped forward and picked up the sheets.

Cecily rolled her eyes. "Relax, Eli, I'm just having some fun." She took a big puff from the lip-glossed end of her cigarette and blew the smoke into Jessa's face. "We're all friends, here, aren't we?"

"Whatever, Cecily," Flynn motioned to his friends to walk away.

"What's wrong, Flynn, am I scaring you?"

"No, you're boring me."

Cecily fumed.

They waited to see if she had any response.

"Come on, let's go back inside," Jessa began to turn around.

"I don't think so," Cecily said. "You don't get to walk away from me. You think you can just leave when I'm talking to you? That's very disrespectful, Jessamine."

"Yeah, yeah," Jessa said without even looking back.

She and her friends reached the fire exit door that Flynn had propped open with his backpack. They were just about to enter when they were stopped by Cecily's awful shriek from behind them.

Before Jessa even had the chance to turn around, she felt a piercing burn on the side of her arm. Recoiling in pain and surprise, it took a second to register the secondary sensation of Cecily's hand gripping her, pushing the burn deeper into her skin. Eli and Gray quickly rushed to pull Cecily away from Jessa, and the mangled cigarette butt fell to the ground.

Jessa brushed away the ash from her reddened skin.

§

"You have to tell Mr Fletcher," Maggie urged Jessa on the walk home.

It had been a tense ride back from the museum to school, made worse by the fact that Cecily had made a point of standing right behind Flynn on the Tube so she could whisper insults to him for the entire journey.

"I don't care about ratting on Cecily," Jessa dismissed Maggie's concern.

"She could get expelled for what she did to you," Flynn added.

"It doesn't even hurt that much," Jessa lied.

"That's beside the point. Causing you physical harm on a school trip is terrible," Maggie stated. "And we didn't even get to talk about what happened before that. Are you all right? After that thing in the museum, I mean? What on earth happened? Did you have an anxiety attack?"

"I don't know."

"It was scary," Maggie said.

"My heart was racing and my hands and feet went tingly like they were falling asleep."

"That sounds a lot like anxiety, Jess," Flynn nodded.

"But the other part wasn't frightening."

"What other part?"

"I don't know how to describe it."

"At the museum you said it pulled you."

"The feeling," she nodded. "It was like when you know the answer to a question on a quiz show but you don't know how you know it. You don't ever remember knowing it but somehow your brain presented it to you at the right moment. It felt like that, only it didn't feel like it came from my brain, it came from an organ way deep inside me, one that takes up my whole body."

"There's no such organ, Jessa," said Maggie.

"Not a literal one. It was something else."

Maggie's face dove down toward her smartphone, a veritable cornucopia of information. Maggie wasn't one for texting much, nor did she have a notable social media presence. But she was more than happy to indulge herself in technology in the name of research.

"Hmm. This is interesting," she mused, as the three of them approached Jessa's house. "It could just be anxiety. But your description fits this phenomenon called Acute Intuition Syndrome."

"What's that?" Jessa opened the door and let them in.

"Seems it's quite rare, and especially rare in young people, though not unheard of. I'll email you the link. And you should probably tell your parents."

"No, I don't want them to know."

"Well, tell Mr Fletcher, then."

"Why do I have to tell anyone?"

"Because it's the smart thing to do," said Maggie.

Jessa looked to Flynn.

"You probably should tell someone," he nodded. "Just in case."

"All right," she sighed, "just in case."

14

"What can I do for you, folks?" Mr Fletcher smiled.

"Jessa has something she wants to tell you," Maggie said quickly.

"Oh? Is everything all right?"

Jessa took a deep breath. "You have to promise not to think I'm crazy."

"Cross my heart," he looked earnest.

Jessa explained exactly what had happened at the museum. Mr Fletcher listened intently. When Jessa finished her story, she and both her friends looked to the teacher for his opinion.

"I don't think you're crazy," he reassured. "It could be anxiety, though it's possible Maggie could be onto something with this intuition idea. It is possible you had an intuitive reaction to something. It's actually quite normal for many parapsychs, and it's nothing to be ashamed or scared of."

"It's normal? The website said it's rare," said Maggie.

"In the full form, it is. You were probably reading about Acute Intuition Syndrome, yes?"

Maggie nodded.

"Yeah, full-on AIS is rare and very powerful. But it's pretty common for parapsychs, especially young ones like yourselves, to experience some level of intuition. It seems to be caused by your body and brain reacting to your parapsych ability as it gets stronger. People tend to grow out of intuitive episodes in a few months to a year or so."

"But it's called a syndrome, so does that mean it's an illness?" Jessa tried not to sound worried.

"Don't worry," Hugo Fletcher replied. "It's only a syndrome when the symptoms happen outside of someone's control. However, some psychs can voluntarily induce this kind of intuition, and in those cases, it's considered a parapsychological skill, you know? It basically means having an intense intuit ability, which is a much sought-after skill among parapsychs. Intuition is very powerful, but when you're not expecting it, it can bring on the same sort of symptoms as an anxiety attack: increased heart rate, uneasiness, lightheadedness, that 'fight-or-flight' feeling."

"That sounds like what happened to me," Jessa said quietly. "So you don't think I have a disorder?"

"Not at all," the teacher insisted. "It's probably nothing. The important thing is not to worry or obsess about it, because that can make the symptoms worse. Your open-mind practice can help train the intuition into something you can control. If it does happen again, try and relax and find a sense of grounding, to bring yourself out of it." He paused. "It's going to be fine."

The three students were about to leave the room when Jessa turned to ask one more question.

"Mr Fletcher? If what I had was an actual intuition—and not just my brain reacting to my parapsychism, or whatever you said happens—does that mean I was sensing something real? I mean, I sensed some kind of danger."

He looked at her curiously. "In what way did it feel like danger?"

"It was like when you get a feeling that something bad is going to happen. Like when you realise you left your bank card somewhere. Or if you think you lost your phone. That "oh no" moment. That's what I felt in the museum. A really, really big "oh no" moment."

He smiled gently. "It was almost definitely nothing, Jessa. Like I said, many young parapsychs experience this. Just be sure to let me know if it happens again."

What was that?

For the splittest of seconds, it seemed like there was a flicker of concern in his face. As quickly as she noticed it, it was gone.

Is he trying to keep me calm? Is this something real?

The feeling was back. Not nearly as intensely as before, but something way down inside her told her not to entirely trust what Hugo Fletcher was saying.

He lied before…

"So, are you okay?"

She nodded, wondering if he could sense her distrust in him. If he could, he didn't show it.

The conversation with Mr Fletcher distracted Jessa for the rest of the day.

What was it he said, the night of the accident… The night we found out about his abilities…

He's part of an undercover teaching assessment?

Something like that.

Her stomach churned.

But wait, think about this logically. What happened at the museum doesn't have anything to do with Mr Fletcher. He wasn't even in the room when that thing happened.

But the feeling.

This feeling.

The intuition. Whatever it is. It's the same.

Isn't it?

Jessa couldn't believe how slowly the day seemed to pass, and she completely lost count of how many times Maggie had to jab her with the end of a pencil to bring her out of the daydream haze. But Jessa couldn't get her mind to quiet.

Fletcher… the museum… intuition… Lynch? Silas Lynch.

Whenever she came back to thinking about Silas Lynch, her stomach turned into a brick.

There's something about Silas Lynch. What could it be?

The feeling was so real.

Why would Mr Fletcher say this was nothing?

Hugo Fletcher wasn't a bad person, she knew that much. The feeling wasn't telling her that he was bad.

He said to try and bring myself out of it.
Why doesn't he want me to let it happen?
He's trying to protect me.
From what?
This.

29th October 1985

The Yield did not go well. Silas is very unhappy; the followers even more so.

It started at dawn. We all went down to the lake to prepare, while Silas set up his "pure" space. He hasn't properly explained to me how he achieves this, but as far as I can tell, it's some kind of cleansing ritual.

Several of the twenty volunteers seemed a little nervous but all in all, I couldn't believe how beautifully open and devoted they were. Part of the preparation process was what Silas called "observance of compassion." Either singly or in small groups, we were paired with volunteers, and then we dispersed throughout the woods. I was assigned to Ethan. My duty was to listen with kindness as he told me his sins and regrets. Silas told us listeners that all we had to do was find forgiveness, but I was so overcome with Ethan's honesty and contrition that I held him in a long embrace. It felt wonderful.

When it came to start the ceremony, it was the middle of the afternoon, I'm not sure exactly when, but it was sunny enough that we sent up a tent to shield Silas from the direct sunlight.

The volunteers were all bathed and cleansed from the lake and took their places in the circle around Silas.

Silas gave me a special job. It was my responsibility to hand out cupfuls of the special cordial (he said it was an herbal elixir, but I think that might've been a stretch of the truth. I know he has access to plenty of people who can obtain substances a lot stronger than herbs). Anyway, it was supposed to relax their nervous systems, which would increase their receptivity to his power. That part definitely worked, because they slowly became captivated by their surroundings, and just stared in awe at the sky. They looked relaxed. Elated, even. I'm not sure if any of the followers realised during the ceremony that something was wrong. If they did, they didn't say anything about it. I certainly didn't notice anything until the end, and it was only from Silas' reaction that I knew it hadn't gone as he planned.

The process of watching them die wasn't as bad as I'd expected, as they didn't seem to be in pain (I suppose the 'herbal elixir' helped with that). They mostly just shook and gurgled a little, before finally falling still. But the look on Silas's face at the end told us everything.

He was so upset that he left us there, and we had to dispose of the volunteers' bodies. I'm trying not to think about that part, so I can't write about it now. I will never forget the smell of burning flesh.

The others started talking. I couldn't think of anything to contribute, and I didn't want to say anything bad about Silas, so I just listened. They were saying things about their faith being shaken and how they were starting to think Silas isn't as strong as he says he is. I've heard murmurings like that before, but not to this extent. Sometimes I feel like I'm in the middle, stuck in-between Silas and them. They complain about him more than I'd care to admit. I keep telling them to give him time, but after his failing at the Yield today, I think they've run out of patience. Kyrie said to me that he thinks Silas is all talk. I know he isn't. But then Kyrie pointed out that the Yield was supposed to be when Silas became the most powerful parapsych in the world. What actually happened was that Silas stayed the same, and the rest of us were left with a pile of dead bodies. So I can see Kyrie's point.

I just hope Silas can find a way to change their minds. If he can't, I worry for his safety.

Lissy

15

Late nights of fruitless internet searches were starting to take their toll. Her mother had insisted that Jessa go to bed early, if for no other reason than to work on getting rid of the dark circles that were beginning to settle under her eyes.

She was tired but not sleepy, so she pulled a book up from the pile on the floor next to her bed and opened it into the pale lamplight, hoping that a little scholastic bedtime reading might bore her into a restful lull.

A few sentences in and her quiet thought was interrupted by Audrey knocking at the door.

"Can I come in?" she said, widening the crack in the door and stepping inside the room almost silently as her fluffy slippers cushioned every step on the carpet. "What are you up to? Homework?"

Jessa nodded.

"All right, then I won't keep you long. I just have something I want to tell you."

"What is it?" Jessa said, finally looking up at her sister.

"I'm moving in with Hugo!"

Jessa paused, unsure of how to react. "Isn't it a bit soon? You've only been together for a few months."

"I know, but it's going great, and we're getting serious. We both think it feels right. So I'll be moving out, probably by the end of February."

"Okay," said Jessa. "Congratulations, then."

"What, that's it? You can't be more excited for me?"

"It's not like you're getting married or anything, you're just moving in together," Jessa shrugged.

"It's a step, though, Jess," Audrey said, exasperated. "It's a big step, and we're really happy about it."

"Well good, as long as you're happy."

"What's that supposed to mean? Why wouldn't I be happy?" Audrey didn't often get angry, but when she did, she looked older.

Jessa knew Audrey wouldn't like her answer, so she stayed quiet, wondering if her sister would give up and leave the room. She didn't.

"What is it, Jessa? What's the problem here?"

"There's no problem!" the younger sister snapped.

"Clearly, you have something you want to say, so please just say it."

Jessa sighed. "Fine," she whined. "I like Hugo. I swear I do. But do you ever get the feeling that he's hiding something?"

Audrey looked like she might cry. "Why is it that you and I can never connect?" she sighed sadly. "Of course I don't feel like he's hiding anything, because he's not. And quite frankly, he's your teacher, so it's quite disrespectful of you to say that that about him. So fine, Jessa, you don't have to be happy for me. But maybe one day when you grow up and stop living in your weirdo imagination, then we'll finally be able to have a real conversation." She held her hands up in surrender. "Goodnight."

Audrey closed the door quietly behind herself.

Jessa listened closely to the sound outside her room. There were a few seconds of silence before she heard the sound of the floorboards creaking as Audrey walked the landing and back downstairs.

She settled in for another restless night.

§

Jessa, Maggie and Flynn sat at their table and shared some mini macaroons that Maggie's mum had made.

"I just keep thinking about it," said Jessa. "The intuition and the whole business with Silas Lynch."

"What in particular are you thinking about, though? I don't understand," Maggie replied, rummaging through the tupperware box to find one of the few remaining macaroons that were coated in chocolate.

"I feel like there's something there, that I have to find."

"What could there possibly be for you to find?" Maggie asked. "We saw it all at the museum. There's no question about Lynch."

"I have questions, though," Jessa urged. "They came to me. The feeling gave me these questions. I feel like I need to find out more about Lynch."

Flynn took a break from the box of treats and enjoyed a swig from his water bottle. "But Jessa—and please don't take this the wrong way—but what's the point of trying to find out more?" he asked her honestly. "You don't even know what you're looking for. You're just making yourself crazy."

There it is. They think I'm losing my mind.

"I'm not trying to be mean or anything, but you look exhausted, and it's upsetting for us to see you get so worked up over this."

They don't understand.

"Then help me figure out what's going on!"

"With what?" Maggie's voice rose slightly.

"Silas Lynch!" Jessa threw back.

"I don't get what there is to figure out!"

Jessa pressed her palms into her eye sockets and took a breath.

"I honestly don't know what I'm expecting to find. But I need to look for something, and whatever it is… I'll know it when I see it. The truth is, since that day at the museum, I haven't been able to get rid of this feeling that there's something more about Silas Lynch that I need to find out. You know that gut feeling you get sometimes, the kind that helps you make decisions like who to make friends with or when to say the right thing. It's like that, but even stronger. It's in my whole body. It keeps me awake at night. And it's telling me something. I'm not asking you to help me, but please don't try and put me off."

They waited. Maggie's lips pursed in thought. Flynn's eyes searched Jessa's.

"Of course we'll help you," said Flynn. "Right, Mags?"

She nodded her agreement but the frown lines remained firmly planted in her forehead.

"Really?" said Jessa.

"If it's that important to you, then yes," said Maggie. "We could use the school computers; there are some excellent resources in the library."

"Thanks," Jessa smiled. "But please don't tell anyone. It has to be our secret."

"Like a secret club?" Maggie suddenly looked a little excited.

"I suppose so, yeah," Jessa shrugged.

"Well, I do like the idea of that! And considering we'll be researching things from the past, can we call it our secret history club?"

"Actually, Mags, that's not a bad idea," said Jessa, reminded that she hadn't yet committed to her required extracurricular. "What if we combined it with some regular school stuff, and made it an actual club? Winsbury doesn't have a history club, does it?"

"Nope. I would be up for founding a history club," said Maggie, pulling out her notebook.

"Sounds good to me, too," Flynn agreed.

"If nothing else, starting an extracurricular society looks excellent on university applications," Maggie added. "Let's come up with some ideas for research topics. We should definitely look into World World One—it would be brilliant to get a head start on that for second-year."

"Uh, Mags," said Jessa, "we do have a topic already. Silas Lynch, remember?"

"Yes, yes, I'm just thinking about additional possibilities. There are so many options…"

"Oh boy," Jessa chortled.

§

"What a great idea!" Hugo Fletcher beamed. "To run a legitimate club you need to have regular meetings, be that weekly or fortnightly. You would also need to submit a proposal to Dr Mortlock detailing a plan for your club, for example where you want to hold your meetings and what kind of activities you'd want to do. And I'm sure she'd want a member of staff to oversee the club."

"Could you do it?" Jessa asked.

"I'd be happy to. Can you tell me more about it?"

"Oh. Hmm." Jessa thought for a moment. "It'd be like... umm."

Flynn stepped up. "It would be mostly research based," he said. "We were all quite inspired by the trip to the museum, so we'd like the opportunity to use the school facilities to find out more about parapsych history."

"Would we be allowed to use the time to research for our parapsych history class projects?" Maggie asked.

"Well, you can't use it explicitly for that, because that's a school project, and the whole point of an extracurricular activity is to do something different or that expands upon your school work. So you could use the time partially for additional research within the field of your project, as long as it's outside of the taught curriculum."

"I'm pretty sure we'll be researching outside of the curriculum," Flynn said.

Mr Fletcher looked at each of the three students. "You three had better not be up to anything. I'm happy to sign off on a history club, but keep in mind that it has to be serious. Extracurricular activities are held on school property and a teacher has to be involved. And as it's not a sport or a performance-based group, you'd probably have to submit a report at the end of the school year explaining what you've learned. Do you understand?"

He looked at Jessa and she shifted her weight from one foot to the other, trying to look casual.

When she'd first found out that Hugo Fletcher was dating her older sister, Jessa had worried that it would affect how they could interact at school. But as time went on she was increasingly able to differentiate between Mr Fletcher The Parapsych History Teacher and Audrey's Boyfriend Hugo.

At home, he was goofy and down-to-earth, and fortunately, his presence made Audrey more laid-back too. Jessa was convinced she and Audrey argued less when he was around, as his humour and playful attitude acted as a buffer between the two girls. Jessa's father was often vocal about how "nice it is to have another man in the house," and her mother continued to gush about what a "fine fellow" he was. In short, he was a welcome and warming presence in the Baxter household.

On the other hand, at school he was nothing but professional. He was always impartial in marking Jessa's homework, and whether or not they were in the presence of other students or teachers, he spoke to her with an authoritative respect that was anything but brotherly. Within the school walls, he was practically a different person.

"We'll be good," said Jessa, "I promise."

"Great," he replied. "Then, pending Dr Mortlock's approval, you have yourself a History Club."

Behind them, a small voice materialised from the doorway.

"Did you say you're making a History Club?" the voice said timidly. "Could I join?"

Jessa, Maggie, Flynn, and Mr Fletcher all looked toward the door to see Annora Huff and Tonia Pitts standing there, having arrived early for the first-year Parapsych History lesson.

"Me too, please," Tonia added.

"Yeah of course!" Flynn answered quickly and welcomingly. Jessa thought she even saw him blush as he answered directly to Tonia.

Jessa shot Flynn a wide-eyed glance. He didn't notice, and remained distracted by the two additions to the room.

§

Jessa slumped toward the flame of the bunsen burner. When Flynn left the room to go to the toilet, Jessa seized her chance.

"Why did he invite them to join?" she whispered angrily.

"What?" Maggie barely looked up from the litmus paper she was dunking into a test tube.

"The whole point of the club was so we could research Silas Lynch. It was a secret, and it was just the three of us. It'll be ruined if there are other people there. And Flynn only let them join because he fancies Tonia. It's so obvious." She leaned on her hand, smooshing the flesh of her cheek under her fingers.

"Jessa, as soon as you suggested making it a real club, you should have known there was a possibility of other people joining. It was your idea."

"Yeah, well, I wish we'd kept it secret, now."

"Look. At best, we have other people who can help you. At worst, you can choose not to tell Annora and Tonia anything about the secret stuff, and you're just a member of a regular old club."

Maggie was right, even though Jessa hated to admit it. Either way, she decided to sulk a little while longer.

16

The first-year class met in the library for their weekly private study period. It was supposed to be a quiet time, but their form tutor Mr Fletcher had left the group unattended to cover for Mrs Reid, who was away sick. So it was left to Mrs Wartridge, the school librarian, to watch over the first-years.

Mrs Wartridge's bird-like face peered out periodically from behind a stack of reference books. Her eyes squinted over the rim of her little glasses that balanced so low on her nose it was a wonder they were any use to her at all. Her perpetually tanned and wrinkled face scrunched even deeper as she pursed her lips together into a little circle, hissing out her shushes and grumbles of annoyance.

She seemed thoroughly out of place in the shiny and modern library. Considering the plethora of high-tech computer screens, the electronic information points, and the self-serve checkout station, many of the students had wondered why a librarian was necessary at all. Though if it weren't for Mrs Wartridge's continual shushing and scoffing at them, they'd probably have been lost in mindless chitchat within seconds of sitting down, so perhaps her most important library duty was that of peace-keeper.

Private study was a double period in which the students were supposed to take advantage of resources to help with any independent projects or homework assignments, and, as Mr Fletcher loved to describe it, "consolidate" their learning.

Naturally, Maggie relished the opportunity to make notes upon notes upon notes, and dominated the pages of her textbooks with legions of postits. But Jessa and Flynn had a more relaxing take on private study time. They had their books open and occasionally looked down at them to read a few sentences, but easily became engrossed in conversation again.

Annora and Tonia also proved to be something of a distraction at the table. Annora was particularly taken by Maggie's sticky notes. "What does that one say?" "Can I borrow a purple one?" "What's that diagram for? Can you draw one for me?" The questions poured, and Maggie was too kind to turn her down.

Tonia was a more subtle preoccupation.

Across the library, a sudden burst of obnoxious laughter erupted from Cecily Graves' table. Gray Townsend was using brightly coloured stickers to pull his face into contorted shapes for the entertainment of his table-mates, Eli, Cecily, and her cronies Amelia Waters and Devi Kapoor. Jessa noticed that the stickers were decorated in red, white and blue, and the words "VOTE GRAVES" were printed on them in big block letters. Cecily handed out strips of the stickers to her friends.

"So anyway!" Cecily's commanding voice cut through their laughter, calming down the hysterics and bringing the attention back to herself. "My dad just asks that you take home the information packet and have your parents look it over. His contact info is all on there. Daddy's incredibly committed to traditional values," she droned away at their disingenuously interested faces.

"I think my parents will be interested, they're always going on about that sort of thing," Amelia spluttered in her overly posh drawl.

"Perfect," Cecily responded, businesslike. "Daddy will be pleased. He just wants your parents to review his policies. And then, if they agree with him, to spread the word to their friends and business associates."

"Her father's in politics now?" said Jessa.

"Oh yes, you haven't heard? It's been going on for a while," Annora replied in a hushed voice. "My parents are quite outraged about the whole thing." Her naturally bulgy eyes honed in on them. "Mr Graves is running for the Parapsych Independence Party!"

"Is that a real party?" Jessa asked. "All I've heard about the PIP is that they're just a group of people with offensive beliefs about laterals. They've never actually been in government have they?"

"They've never won an election, if that's what you mean," said Flynn. "I think they're mostly ridiculed in politics."

"Mostly, yes. Or at least, they used to be," Annora replied. "But Jameson Graves wants to be nominated as the leader of the PIP, and he's trying to revamp the party to make it more modern and approachable. My parents said it's dangerous."

"I don't understand, though," said Tonia. "Isn't the whole point of a political party that they want to get as many votes as possible? Laterals would never vote for the PIP. The government is a mixture of parapsychs and laterals, right? So what are the PIP trying to do?"

"My mother said that they're trying to be less extreme and more like the conservative party, but just for parapsychs."

"That is extreme, though, isn't it?" Jessa said, a little too loudly. Flynn hushed for Jessa to keep her voice down.

"I know," Annora nodded. "But supposedly, it's different this time because he already has some rich and powerful people backing him."

"Ugh," Jessa groaned quietly, glancing over at Cecily, who had clearly moved on from the subject of politics but still managed to hold her place at the forefront of Jessa's irritation. "What do you think, Mags?"

"I think you should all stop with the silly gossip and do some work."

Jessa wondered if 'silly gossip'—curiously pronounced as though it were all one word—was a phrase that Maggie had picked up somewhere or if she had inadvertently chosen it as one of her own catchphrases. Whenever Jessa started getting tangled in a teenage grapevine reverie, Maggie was quick to cut her down with a swift scolding for engaging in silly gossip. You could always count on Maggie Turner to be quite the chatterbox at lunchtime or outside of school, but as soon as she was in a classroom and there was any potential threat of getting told off, she couldn't possibly let herself get caught up in idle sillygossip.

Before long, the class drew to an end, and Mr Fletcher burst in through the door and dismissed the students a few minutes early, thanking them for being so cooperative in his absence. Mrs Wartridge uttered a "humph!" of defiance and shook her hairsprayed head. As far as Mrs Wartridge was concerned, there was no bigger mischief than talking in the library.

§

"Now that we've done our open-mind practice, we are ready to introduce a new element! Today, students, we begin to investigate the fine art of pyrokinesis."

"Yessss!" some of the students hissed with glee. Gray made fists and punched the air in celebration.

Ms Alzamora brought down the chatter volume with her gentle hums and shushes and light touches to tensed shoulders. She pulled small candles from a wicker basket tucked under her arm and made a point of personally delivering a fresh white candle into the open palms of each student.

"Open textbooks to your circles, please."

They all flipped to the inside of the back cover.

"Place your candle inside the circle. Now, draw your visual focus to the candle wick, but keep your concentration on my voice," the teacher settled into her other-worldly drone. "Place your forearms on the table so your hands frame your candle. Hold your gaze. I will bring myself to each of you to light the flame. As your flame is born, take a smooth breath in, sit up straight and allow the feeling of inner peace and focus to flow up your spine and into your mindspace."

The students held their sight over the candle flames. Some of them crumpled their faces in concentration, while others simply stared, eyes wide and unblinking.

"Let your gaze travel down the wick to protect your eyes from the light, but keep your focus on the flame atop. Feel the motion of the flame as it moves. If you have the impulse to do so, lift your hands to either side of the flame and shield it from any flow of air that might impede the energy coming from you."

Ms Alzamora tip-toed around the room on her bare feet, holding her hands above the head of each student. A few of them broke their own focus to watch her curiously, lingering above each student mouthing words nobody could understand.

"When you're ready," she eventually spoke aloud, "envision the flame moving to one side, then summon your mind to push the energy out through your hand and into the flame."

Jessa consciously deepened her breathing and mentally visualised the energy filtering through her body, down her right arm and out through her fingertips. The candle flame bowed slightly to the left. She felt a pang of excitement jolt through her body, which completely stole her focus away from the flame, so she took a break and looked sideways to see how her friends were getting on. Maggie's flame was wobbling ever-so-slightly but wasn't quite leaning, while Flynn was easily holding his flame almost on its side. Flynn deliberately broke his concentration to look up at Jessa with a wide grin. But his smile quickly turned to something else, and he nodded toward the other side of the room.

Jessa followed his line of sight and turned her head to discover that it was Cecily Graves who had become the subject of his gaze. Jessa's mouth involuntarily fell open. She prodded Maggie, urging her to look up, as other students did to their neighbours and the nudge spread around the room. Even Ms Alzamora was dumbfounded.

Cecily's torso hunched toward her candle, undulating back and forth. Her hands were up from the table, with her fingers together in a tent-like formation directly above and around the flame. But her flame wasn't leaning to the side—it was growing upwards.

She rocked forward and back, pulsating her hands outward from the fingertips, stimulating the flame. It reached up at least three times the height of everyone else's flames, which had all lost the attention of their owners and just flickered silently to themselves.

Ms Alzamora shook her head to snap herself out of the daze and put an end to the spectacle with a few loud claps in quick succession. The whole class jumped as the sound brought them all back to a normal state of mind. Cecily flung her head up and her flame shrank back to its former self.

"Well well!" Ms Alzamora stammered. "It seems we have a very passionate pyrokin in our midst! Let's all give Cecily a round of applause for a remarkable display of… of… concentration!" she had trouble even getting the words out.

The class clapped, with the loudest applause coming from Amelia Waters and Devi Kapoor, while Eli emitted a generous "yeah!" and Gray hollered a loud whoop. But Cecily took the praise with a suspicious modesty, eliciting nothing but an arrogant sideways smile.

While the rest of the class began roaring with chatter about what they'd just witnessed, Cecily Graves remained in stillness and silence, deliberately locking eyes with Jessa from across the room. Cecily looked at her, steady and severe. The conceited smile fell away, leaving her face cold and cruel. Her lips parted to reveal the subtlest flash of teeth. And just for a second, Jessa felt a sensation in her empty hands. The undeniable sensation of burning.

17

The antiseptic cream cooled the raw blistering flesh on Jessa's upper arm. She wondered if it did indeed hurt a little less or if it was just her wishful thinking. It certainly didn't look much better. Jessa silently cursed Suzanne Daniels for a terrible pass in basketball the other day. Stupid Suzanne Daniels basically threw the ball directly at Jessa's arm. Stupid Suzanne Daniels should have known Jessa would not have caught the ball. Jessa never caught the ball. When the ball gets thrown at Jessa Baxter, Jessa Baxter turns away and the ball just bounces off her. Everyone should know that.

Bloody Suzanne Daniels. Bloody basketball.

The chemical scented cream slid under Jessa's fingertips in lazy circles. She hadn't shown the burn to anyone. A momentary pang of guilt flashed through her for not sharing it with Flynn or Maggie.

They'd only make a big deal out of it.

But it is a big deal, isn't it?

No, this is between me and Cecily.

Cecily. Jessa cast her mind back to the Parapsych Skills class earlier. Had she imagined the strange heat in her hands? She had been looking directly at Cecily when it happened. And Cecily had that… look. Maybe Jessa had simply been feeling the warmth from the candle. Yes, that must be it. That's the logical explanation. But it had felt so present and so strong. And, wait— had Jessa actually blown out her candle by then? She couldn't remember.

Could it really have been Cecily?

How?

Jessa sat on her bed for a moment and considered climbing under the covers. But she had more pressing matters, and pulled out her first-year Parapsych Skills textbook, laying it open to the back page and set one of her candles in the circle. It wasn't fresh and new and white like the one Ms Alzamora gave her, but it would do.

Relax.

Breathe.

Concentrate.

She worked, step by step, through her usual open-mind practice, then did her best to recall the teacher's instructions from the lesson in pyrokinesis.

To Jessa's frustration, she couldn't get the flame to lean even a little bit. She sat back in her chair and wondered what she was doing wrong. Thoughts began to climb into her brain. Thoughts of Cecily Graves, the candle, the museum, Silas Lynch, Hugo Fletcher, and the deep down something that was starting to give her the feeling that all these things were somehow connected.

Her eyes were sore with sleeplessness, but she felt so awake.

More thoughts, this time of Maggie, Flynn, Tonia and Annora. She wondered what Audrey was doing. Sleeping, probably. Audrey was so sensible; she'd probably be in bed, even though it was only—12:30 am?! How did it get so late?

Jessa lay down on her side. Her hair smelled bad.

Maybe I should go and shower.

No, her parents would definitely hear that, and then there would be too many follow-up questions. Jessa clicked on the television and muted it, then stared at the late night nonsense until the brightness fatigued her eyes so much that they forced themselves to rest.

"Welcome home, sweetheart. I'm afraid we have some sad news. Grandma died today."

"Oh," Jessa replied sadly.

"Come on, we're late for the funeral," her mother stepped into the backyard and took a seat at one of the pews.

"Our Jessa is going to say a few words now," she announced to the guests. *"Go on, love,"* she nudged Jessa down the aisle.

Everyone watched Jessa walk nervously between the rows, toward the pulpit at the other end of the garden. Puddles lined the aisle, and despite her best effort not to step in them, her feet landed with a splash every time. Guests tutted in shame, looking down at Jessa's bare, mud-covered feet.

"Jessa, I can't believe you forgot to wear shoes to your grandmother's funeral," Maggie looked dismayed.

Jessa finally arrived at the pulpit and looked out over the mass of guests looking at her expectantly. She glanced down at her speech and took a breath, preparing to read, but quickly realised her notes made no sense. The page was covered in gibberish.

"I... I can't..." she tried to speak but the words choked from her mouth.

Suddenly, everyone was running, screaming. Jessa noticed flames licking from inside her house.

"Jessa, do something!" Flynn yelled. *"Call the fire department!"*

Jessa pulled out her phone and frantically tried to dial 999 but the buttons weren't working. She jammed her finger onto the number 9 over and over. But nothing. Every other number appeared on the screen, but not a single 9.

Then nothing.

Everyone was gone. The flames were gone. She was alone. The garden shed door was wide open, beckoning her inside.

She was somewhere else. A young boy sat on the floor, surrounded by colourful picture books. He looked at her from the depths of his hollow eye sockets and let out a guttural moan as his small hand etched a symbol over and over into the pages. The boy stood to his feet and stared directly at her. His fleshy little fingers started picking at the skin on his face, and it fell away in chunks.

"Jessa," he said, pulling away a strip from his cheek. *"Jessa. Jessa,"* he said her name over and over, peeling away his skin with every syllable.

"No," Jessa managed to get out. *"Stop."*

He continued. His voice grew louder until it was so loud the entire room trembled under the resonance of her name. Louder still, and she screamed for it to stop. The floor beneath her began to crumble.

"Jessa, this way!" called a voice behind her.

Cecily Graves stood in a doorway, offering Jessa her hand. "Quick!"

Jessa reached and grabbed Cecily's hand, leaping to safety just in time before the aged wooden floor fell away into oblivion.

"Are you okay?" Cecily asked, closing the door, plunging them into almost complete darkness.

"Yes. Thank you," Jessa gasped, looking into Cecily's dark eyes.

Cecily dipped her face closer and rested her hands on Jessa's waist.

"What are you doing?" Jessa breathed.

Cecily answered with her lips, pressing them directly onto Jessa's. Jessa surrendered to Cecily's mouth. She received the warmth and let it spread through her whole body. She felt Cecily's lips and her tongue, and then her hands running through her hair then onto her neck.

The caress turned to a grasp.

"Cecily, no—"

Cecily's teeth gripped Jessa's lower lip. Her hands held tighter and Jessa flailed, trying to push Cecily away.

Jessa gasped for air.

Cecily spat out a hunk of Jessa's flesh and dove straight back in for more.

"No!" Jessa screamed. "No! No!"

Air. She gasped herself upright. Heart pounding, she kicked off the duvet and filled her lungs with unchoked air.

4:08am.

The bed sheet was thick with sweat and smelled like antiseptic cream. Jessa un-muted the television and watched, numb, as soap opera caricatures yammered in their imitation lives about nothing in particular.

18

Jessa cleared the spit from her throat. "Welcome to the first meeting of The History Club," she declared. "Mr Fletcher is here because he's going to oversee our activities, right, Mr Fletcher?"

"Yes, but don't worry, I won't be buzzing around too much. I'm not trying to babysit you; I just have to keep an eye out. You're in charge."

Jessa turned back to the others. "So I've planned out agendas for all our meetings for the rest of the school year." She handed out copies to everyone in the group.

The entire History Club comprised Jessa, Maggie, and Flynn as co-founding members, and Tonia Pitts and Annora Huff as regular members. They had to advertise the History Club around the school to attract any other potential interested parties, and had actually received replies from Kevin Xu, Lucy Adelman and Suzanne Daniels, all first-years from Mrs Reid's class. However, much to Jessa's relief, the Wednesday meet time for the History Club clashed with practice times for the athletics team of which all three of the other students were members. So the History Club ended up being just the five of them.

"I thought it would be fun for this month's meeting to be focused on family. In case you don't know, the study of family history is called "genealogy," and I thought we could go to the library and use the ancestry software to look into our family trees.

"Cool," Tonia nodded.

Maggie and Flynn had helped Jessa formulate the plans for each meeting, but it was new to Tonia and Annora, so Jessa was reassured to know they liked the idea she had for their first topic.

"You guys can head off to the library, then," said Mr Fletcher. "I'll be here marking some homework, so I'll log onto the chat network and you can give me a buzz if you need any help with anything. If not, I'll check in on you at the end."

Jessa noticed how quiet the halls were after school hours. Usually, when she wandered the corridors, it was in between lessons, which was when most of the other students were also milling around. But after school, there was an almost eerie stillness. The hallways seemed sad not to be filled with the banter of students and the clatter of feet traversing the floors. It was only a small school, but it seemed so bustling when filled with people. In the stillness of the late afternoon, it felt sterile and empty.

They settled into seats at the library computer corner and each signed into their school intranet accounts on the wide screens before them. Jessa described how to access the online genealogy software, giving them the log-in details Mr Fletcher had given to her.

Tonia and Annora each started exploring the options on the home page, pinching and swiping the digital buttons on the flat screen.

"Jessa," Maggie whispered, and Jessa rolled her desk chair closer. "Are you going to start looking for information about Silas Lynch?"

"Shhh!" Jessa hissed back, gesturing toward Tonia and Annora.

"Why are you shushing me?" Maggie said. "I thought that was the whole point."

"Are you all right?" Tonia folded her leg under her bottom and pushed herself up on the arms of her chair so she could see them.

"Yeah, we're fine," Jessa responded. "Don't worry about it."

"What's going on?" Annora's face poked out from behind her screen. "What's the big secret?"

"It's nothing!" Jessa exaggerated.

"I'm sure we can tell them, Jess," Flynn said. "They're in the club too. They probably deserve to know what they're getting themselves into."

Jessa sighed. She should have known that the History Club would not have been the covert operation that she'd hoped.

"Scoot your chairs over here."

§

"Woooooow!" Annora said, a little too loudly.

Jessa had told them everything. About the intuition she'd felt at the museum, about Silas Lynch, and then about how she'd wanted to set up a history club as a way to secretly research these things she'd found so intriguing.

"So it's really less of a history club, and more like a *mystery* club!" Annora giggled.

"Ha, yeah, I suppose it is," said Jessa. "Are you okay with that?"

"Definitely," Annora said before Jessa had barely finished the question. "I've never been in a secret club before."

"What about you, Tonia? I'm sorry if it was a real History Club you wanted."

"No offence, Jessa," she replied, "but I only wanted to be in your History Club because I hadn't joined any other club and I needed to fill the requirement. Mystery Club sounds way better."

They all swore themselves to secrecy that neither Mr Fletcher nor anyone else could find out what they were really doing. They also agreed that, so as to not arouse any kind of suspicion, they'd stick to Jessa's plan and actually partake in the regular activities. Fortunately, they all enjoyed history just enough that it wasn't too much of a misfortune to actually have to attend a History Club.

The five students decided they'd get the history part out of the way first, so they spent the best part of an hour exploring their own family trees. Jessa had secretly hoped that she would uncover some kind of great family conspiracy, perhaps an estranged cousin or a secret marriage or a famous relative. Her quiet fantasy was quickly brought to an end, however, when she saw her family tree digitally recreated on the screen before her, displaying every one of her known relatives, plain and clear and so very ordinary.

Jessa peered over at Flynn, whose face was rumpled in concentration. "Did you find anything good, Flynn?" She rolled her chair toward him to peer at his screen but he closed the page before she could see anything.

"No. Nothing really."

Jessa saw a sliver of embarrassment creep into his face and she knew not to ask any further questions. She'd always known that he lived with his mother, but she couldn't recall him ever mentioning his father, let alone any other family member. She left him to it.

On Jessa's other side, Maggie's head was wagging side to side, her eyes reading rapidly across the page.

"Interesting..." she said quietly.

"What is?" Jessa enquired.

"Well, I started searching for Silas Lynch."

"Oh! Already?"

"Yes, of course. I've researched my family tree in the past, so I didn't have to venture too far down the rabbit hole this time."

"Great, so what have you found then, boss?"

"Not much."

"So why is that interesting?" Flynn walked over to Maggie to lean on the back of her chair.

"Well, the birth records show he was born on the twelfth of June, 1961, and he was officially declared deceased in November 1985."

"Okay..." Jessa waited for Maggie to continue.

"But that's all there is. There's no place of birth, no address, no family members, none of that is listed here. It's like his whole record has been deleted."

"That is a bit weird," Flynn said curiously.

Tonia and Annora both moved to look at Maggie's screen, too.

"It gets weirder," Maggie added. "He's not in the parapsych database."

"What does that mean?" Jessa asked her.

"It means he was unregistered."

"Isn't that illegal?" Annora's soft voice questioned.

"Yep," said Maggie.

"But we know he was a parapsych." Jessa tried to understand what part of the puzzle was missing.

"What happens if you just do a regular search for his name? Does it bring up anything else?" Flynn asked.

Jessa shook her head. "Nope, I've been trying that since the trip. All that comes up are those newspaper articles, the same stuff we already know from the museum."

"Hmm," Maggie opened a new page and inputted the name Silas Lynch to see for herself. When the search returned exactly what Jessa described, Maggie seemed perplexed. "Well, that is curious."

"Why?" said Tonia, craning her neck to see what Maggie had found.

"Because there should be more on the net about a person than just archives of newspapers that mention them."

"What else should there be?" Jessa asked.

"I'll show you." She typed the name Reginald Turner into the search box. "This is my grandfather on my mother's side. He passed away when I was little. But here you can see pretty much everything about him: where he was born, his parents' names, where he went to school. He was a parapsych too, so you can see here is a record of his registration, and here we can see where he went to school, the jobs he had, how he died, the date of his funeral, et cetera."

"Whoa," Jessa said quietly, "I had no idea there was this much information available about people."

"Oh, yes," Maggie nodded. "Since the Community Information Act, basically every record that's ever been made is available digitally."

"That's a little creepy!" Tonia exclaimed.

"It's actually incredibly efficient," Maggie told her. "The records have always been accessible if you went to a library or county office, but this way they're available easily and for free to anyone who needs to access them."

"How do you know all this, Mags?" Jessa gushed.

"Computer Club! And my parents actually have this software on their home office computer, so I'm familiar with these search strings."

"All right, so we know there should be more information about Silas Lynch," Flynn said, getting back to the matter in hand. "But why isn't there?"

"That I don't know," Maggie shook her head.

"The articles said he was kind of a loner," Jessa postulated. "He was in a children's home until he was fourteen, so could it be possible that nobody cared about him enough to ever register him as a parapsych, or properly enrol him in school?"

"I'm sure a council-run children's home would require him to Register and go to school. I think it's more likely someone removed the data. What's really perplexing me is the absence of a death record, though."

"Why?"

"Because that's very highly controlled. When someone dies, their death has to be reported, and then verified, and then it's made available in this official database of Births and Deaths." She pointed to various parts of the screen as she explained. "So what we know from this is that someone reported Silas Lynch dead. But there's no official verification. The death wasn't formally logged in the system. Wait. Maybe if I look more into this..." she trailed off as she clicked and swiped and typed, delving deeper into the hoards of digital information.

"Yes... just what I'd have thought," she said, stretching out her fingers. "I just went a bit further into the Death Record Database. Look..." She pointed at the screen, and they all leaned closer to read the simple line of text she indicated.

"This record is incomplete," Jessa read aloud.

"What does that mean?" Flynn questioned. "Nobody verified his death?"

"Guys..." Maggie whispered, "I don't think he's dead."

A moment of quiet fell over the five teenagers as they pondered the implication of what Maggie had said.

"Is that even possible?" Tonia said incredulously. "Are you saying he faked his own death? This thing says he died in the 1980s. So you think he's been alive this whole time? Where could he have been hiding? It seems really unlikely that someone could just disappear like that."

"It does sound very implausible," Flynn agreed.

"But not impossible," Jessa said thoughtfully.

"I guess not. But okay then, here's a better question: Why? Why would someone pretend to die, and then hide for twenty years? It doesn't make sense."

Through the silence of the library came the nearing sound of footsteps.

"Shhh!" Maggie shooed her friends away from the huddle around her and Mr Fletcher entered the room with an exaggerated look of suspicion on his face.

"What's going on in here, then?" he said

"Nothing!" Jessa spoke with a forced nonchalance.

"Glad to hear it," Mr Fletcher responded plainly, still looking at Jessa intently. She squinted her eyes at the computer screen, trying to make it look like she was reading. She hoped that neither his general teacher-senses nor his parapsych abilities could see through her lie.

"Mr Fletcher, we've been researching our family phylogenies, in accordance with the plan Jessa made for our meetings," Maggie spoke in her classic talking-to-a-teacher voice. "So far I've found some very interesting details about my great-grandmother."

"That's great, Maggie. I researched my great-grandparents once too, and found out some pretty cool things about them."

"Is anyone else in your family a teacher, Mr Fletcher?" Annora asked him.

"Nope, just me," he walked to Jessa's chair. She felt the seat back move slightly under the weight of his lean.

"Have you found anything interesting, Jessa?"

"Umm, not really. My family's quite boring, I think," she could feel him reading her words for indirect information.

He noticed the pile of papers Maggie had printed, and picked them up to leaf through. Jessa's heart leapt in her chest, immediately assuming they were going to be found out so quickly, but breathed a sigh of relief when it turned out to be prints of Maggie's actual family tree.

"Well, I think it's probably time that you guys packed up and went home, don't you? It's almost half past five."

They hadn't noticed time going by so quickly, but did as he suggested, logging out of the computers and collecting up their belongings.

The students filed out of the library, but just before she walked through the doorway, Jessa heard Hugo Fletcher call her name. She spun round, trying to look chilled and aloof.

"Don't forget this!" he said, holding up her red pencil case.

She reached out her hand and clasped the pencil case tightly, expecting him to release his grip. But he held tight, and pulled it incrementally closer to himself.

She glanced up to his face where his deep eyes stared into her. And then she heard his voice. He didn't make a sound, and his lips didn't move, but she heard it as clear as anything.

"You'd better not be up to anything."

§

Jessa lay upon her bed, unable to fall asleep. Every time she came close to relaxing, her mind recharged with thoughts of school and friends and homework and mysteries. She swung her legs out of bed.

She was just about to stand up when she heard the sound of the front door opening downstairs. Her heart floundered for a second, in fear that someone was breaking into the house, but she quickly heard Audrey's voice talking to someone on the phone.

A glance at her alarm clock and Jessa wondered why Audrey was returning home at such an hour, and who she could possibly be on the phone with so late. Audrey walked up the staircase, trying and failing to avoid the creaks that whimpered out from beneath her feet. Jessa instinctively switched off her lamp so Audrey wouldn't see the light trickling out from under the door. She heard her sister's voice whisper into the phone as she entered her own room down the hall.

"Okay Sarah, I'm back. I'm in my room now," and the door clicked closed behind her.

Jessa couldn't resist. She pulled fuzzy slipper-socks over her feet and ever-so-gently opened her own bedroom door, straining her neck in the direction of Audrey's room. She took tiny steps, placing her heel slowly into the carpet and letting her weight reach the ball of her foot only after she was sure the step made no sound.

After what felt like far too long, she reached the outside of Audrey's room and placed her hands on either side of the frame, careful not to touch the actual door in case Audrey heard it. It was not Jessa's first time eavesdropping on her sister.

Audrey's voice became audible through the solid wood of the door.

"I thought we were going to get married!"

She was crying.

"We were supposed to move in together on Valentine's Day, and now he tells me all of this?!"

There was a long silence. Jessa waited to hear what her sister said next.

"I know... maybe I was starting to suspect something, but not this! I mean, he can be secretive sometimes but I thought he was just a bit shy about personal things, you know? I really can't believe it."

Another silence.

"Well yeah, obviously I'd rather know the truth than be kept in the dark about it. But I don't know if I can be with him now, Sarah. I really don't. It scares me. What if it puts my family and me in danger too? What if he goes out on a job and something happens to him? I couldn't bear it!"

Jessa's heart raced.

"Of course I love him. I just don't know anymore." She broke down again, sobbing heavily.

"I know. I'm so tired... You're right. I'll see how I feel tomorrow."

Audrey whispered goodnight and then the only sound Jessa heard was the thumping of her own pulse echoing in her head.

Afraid that Audrey would suddenly emerge from her room, Jessa tiptoed quickly back to her own bedroom and pushed the door closed.

19

Jessa got to Winsbury early enough to grab a bagel from the cafeteria, then ate it in the foyer while waiting for Maggie and Flynn to arrive. She paced up and down the hallway, still in her coat, scarf and woolly hat.

"Jessa?" said Flynn. "What's going on?"

"I need to talk to you," she said urgently.

"Okay, shall we go to the cafeteria?"

"No, let's go into the garden."

"But it's freezing outside!" Maggie exclaimed.

"I know, but I need to tell you something and I can't risk anyone else hearing. Come on—we have to hurry!" she turned quickly, zipped through the students loitering in the foyer and went out through the back door into the frosty Winsbury garden.

"I was right about Mr Fletcher. He's hiding something."

"Oh, Jessa, not this again!" Maggie whined.

"Shh! Just listen!" Jessa continued. "Something happened with him and Audrey. I overheard her on the phone last night. I think they broke up. Apparently, he told her some big secret."

"Like what?"

"I don't know. I couldn't hear much. But Audrey was crying, saying things about being in danger, and 'going out on a job'."

"Are you sure that's what she said?"

"Definitely. What do you think that means? What kind of danger could there be as a teacher?"

"Well, he can't be talking about teaching," Flynn said. "So he must have another job, right? Maybe it's related to that school inspector thing he told you about."

"There's no way being an inspector would be dangerous. I think he was lying about that. There was something funny about that explanation. I just don't believe it." She paused, unsure how her friends might react to her next idea. "Do you remember when Emmeline disappeared? Mr Fletcher was absent for a couple of days. And he was acting really weird."

"You don't think..." Maggie spoke slowly. "You don't think he had something to do with that, do you?"

"I don't know what I think, Mags. But something's going on, and I have a feeling it's connected somehow."

"He wouldn't hurt anyone."

"I'm not saying he abducted Emmeline or anything. But think; could there be a connection?"

"Maybe he's a police officer," Flynn suggested. "Like a detective, you know? He could have been investigating that case. And that would fit with Audrey saying something about dangerous jobs."

"That sounds plausible," said Maggie.

Jessa nodded her head thoughtfully. "Maybe," she muttered. "But then why would he be here?"

Flynn shrugged. "He could be a detective who's undercover as a teacher."

The sound of the morning bell put an end to their speculation. They ran back through the garden, up the stairs and along the corridor to Mr Fletcher's room. Their classmates looked up as the three of them entered, pink-faced and breathless.

"Sorry we're late," Maggie announced softly.

"Hurry up please, sit down," Mr Fletcher replied, barely acknowledging them. His demeanour was noticeably less cheerful than normal, and his dirty blond hair was unstyled, lacking its usual slick of gel.

He quickly took attendance, and read out the few announcements distractedly. "The, uh, Valentine's Day party is tomorrow night at 6 pm—

no, wait—7 pm, in the main hall. If you haven't returned your parental permission slip, please do so tomorrow morning, or you can get your parents to send an email confirming you're allowed to be there and who will pick you up. That's all. Off you go."

He waved his hand to dismiss them, and his other hand pinched the bridge of his nose. Jessa deliberately hung back in the class, picking up her bag extra slowly to see if he spoke to her or made any acknowledgement of what had transpired between him and her sister.

He didn't.

§

"I was thinking about it all morning, and I think you must be right, Flynn," Jessa said at break time. "He has to be a police officer. It's the only explanation, isn't it?"

"I can't think of anything else," said Maggie.

"So if that's the truth, then what is he here for? Does that mean he's not really a teacher at all? Do you think the other teachers know?" Jessa rattled off all the questions that poured from her mind.

"If his own girlfriend didn't know, I doubt the other teachers know. Except Dr Mortlock, maybe, because she knows everything," Flynn reasoned.

"My guess is that he isn't really a teacher," Maggie said. "But isn't that illegal? I mean, surely you can't be a teacher without all the qualifications. In fact, my parents would be very unhappy to know that there's a teacher here who isn't qualified. But on the other hand, I suppose a police officer is as good a person as any to protect us," her forehead wrinkled in apprehension. "But in that case, what is he here to protect us from?"

"Don't start getting scared," Jessa said sternly. "If we stay calm and be logical about everything, we can figure out what's going on."

The three of them sat quietly for a moment. It was Maggie who spoke up. "Wait, why do *we* have to figure out what's going on?"

"Mags, we just uncovered a huge secret. Don't you want to know more?" Jessa whispered.

"Well, yes, I suppose," she replied sheepishly. "What do you think, Flynn?"

"I think you're right to be a little worried. But I'm with Jessa; this is worth investigating."

Maggie sighed. "All right. But I have one rule."

Jessa rolled her eyes. Maggie saw but ignored it. "My rule is that there're no secrets from each other. If you have an idea about something, you share it with us."

"Deal," Jessa and Flynn both said. Maggie put her hand forward into the middle of the table, prompting Jessa and Flynn to do the same, sealing the pact.

"Did we miss something?" Tonia approached the table.

"Oh, hi, Tonia! Hi, Annora!" Jessa said, fake and cheerful.

"Jessa, I know you were just talking about something important. Why can't we be in on it too?"

"It's nothing, don't worry!"

"Jessa…" Flynn said quietly, "we can trust them. I think we should tell them everything."

Tonia reacted to the seriousness in Flynn's voice and pulled out the chair next to him. "What's going on? Did you find about something about Silas Lynch?"

"No, this is something else," said Maggie.

"Okay, I'll tell you," Jessa said. "But you have to swear—and I mean you really have to swear—to keep this a secret."

"I swear," Annora said instantly.

"Me too. Pinky swear," Tonia added seriously.

"All right. Where shall I start?"

It took the rest of break time and most of lunch time to do so, especially considering that every turn of the story prompted Jessa to launch into another round of what-ifs and wild speculations, but eventually, Jessa, Maggie and Flynn managed to fill in Tonia and Annora on every detail they could. The five students sat in the faraway corner of the garden, huddling in their winter coats, all clutching large paper cups of tea or hot chocolate that they sipped intermittently.

"So the big question is, what is he investigating? What's the crime?" Tonia stressed the last word with intensity. "Could it be one of the other teachers? I know you think it has something to do with what happened to Emmeline Victor, but we don't really know what happened to her, do we? Do you think one of the other teachers kidnapped her?"

They all gasped.

"No, that can't be it," said Flynn. "If the police suspected a teacher for that, I'm sure we would have heard about it. Let's think: has anything suspicious happened at all? Even something small?"

They sat quietly, deep in thought while the thick of bare bushes and trees rustled around them. Then, the sound of voices arising from the quiet pulled them all alert. The blustery wind carried cackling laughter closer, then footsteps became audible. From around the corner appeared Cecily Graves, flanked by Amelia Waters and Devi Kapoor.

"Oh, I'm so sorry!" Cecily wailed emphatically. "I had no idea the daily Geek Squad meeting was happening out here."

Amelia and Devi laughed.

"Yep, this is it," Jessa said defiantly. "Did you want to join? We always have room for a few more members!"

"As if!" Devi spluttered. Cecily's mouth just turned up at the sides into a disgusted sneer.

"What do you want?" Annora demanded.

"I want nothing from you, geek," Cecily spat her words with disdain.

"Come on, Cecily. Don't call her that," Flynn replied.

"What would you call her then? Freak? Loser?" Cecily paused. "Orphan?'

"That's enough, Cecily!" Jessa stood up, her fists clenched, ready.

"Ugh, you're such a bruiser," Cecily scorned. "I'm not going to fight you, Jessamine. I could, but I won't. This is a designer coat, and I wouldn't want to ruin it with the blood of a lateral."

"What are you even talking about? I'm a parapsych, stupid. This is a parapsych school!"

"Oh, please. I know all about your family of desperate laterals. You just got lucky."

"I think you should leave," Flynn said clearly and calmly, and Cecily moved toward him. He stood up to meet her, face-to-face. Ringlets of her dark hair spiralled down from underneath a black Russian fur hat that quivered in the breeze.

She brought her face close to his, while Devi and Amelia stared down the others.

When Cecily spoke again, it was almost a whisper, barely audible over the crackle of the twigs and the February wind in the air. "I will never, ever, care what you think, hobo. So why don't you go back to your box under the bridge and die."

"Bitch!" Jessa rushed toward Cecily angrily, but Flynn held her back.

"Oh look, girls! The beast has awoken!" Cecily called out to Devi and Amelia, who both quacked with laughter.

"Hey, this reminds me of a joke. It goes: 'A lateral, a hobo, and an orphan walk into a bar...'"

"Ha," Amelia snorted. "Good joke."

"Good one, Cecily!" Devi whinnied.

"Yeah, really great," Tonia stepped up. "It would be even better with a punchline, genius."

Cecily's arms folded across her chest. "Nobody asked you, you filthy mutt. What are you supposed to be, anyway? Are you black? Are you white? Are you some kind of mixed breed? I bet your parents say you're a precious cultural blend, right? You're the most revolting thing I've ever seen."

"Don't you dare talk to her like that!" Flynn said. "You can mock me all day long for not being rich like you, but insulting someone's race is unaccepta—"

Cecily slapped the back of her hand against Flynn's face.

Jessa couldn't help herself, and rushed forward before anyone had a chance to grab her.

"Hey!" Mr Fletcher's voice cut through the tension, startling them all. Dr Mortlock stood next to him.

"Cecily Graves. Over here, right now." Her voice was low and sincere.

"I don't know what happened, Dr Mortlock! She just tried to attack me! It was so frightening!"

"Drop the act, Miss Graves. It's in your best interest to join me in a visit to my office."

"But Dr Mortlock, you didn't see!"

"I see everything!" Dr Mortlock bellowed.

The students had never heard Dr Mortlock raise her voice before, and it was terrifying.

Even Cecily cowered.

"Come with me, Miss Graves. You two as well."

Cecily, Devi and Amelia bowed their heads and walked away with the headteacher.

"You kids all right?" Mr Fletcher asked the five students who remained in the garden.

"Yes, thanks," Annora replied.

"Jessa, you good?"

"Yeah, I'm fine. How did you know we were out here?"

"I was in the library with Dr Mortlock, and I saw you guys come out. When I noticed Cecily following, I figured something would go down."

"You were right about that," Tonia said.

"Bullies can be quite predictable."

"Yeah, we've noticed," Maggie sighed.

"Come on, lunch is almost over. Let's go back in," he waved them all back into the building. Annora, Maggie and Jessa followed quickly, while Flynn hung back a few paces and Tonia re-timed her pace to walk with him alone.

"Are you okay, Annora?" Jessa asked softly.

"Oh, I'm fine," her reply sounded sad and thoughtful. "Nobody's ever called me that before."

"That was out of order, she had no right," Maggie said reassuringly.

"She's not wrong, though. I am an orphan." Annora's gaze stayed on the ground.

"No you're not." Jessa stopped and looked at Annora intensely. "Your adoptive parents love you. That's what matters. You don't need to be directly related to someone for them to be your family."

"Thanks," Annora smiled.

Behind them, Flynn and Tonia remained in a gawky silence for the walk back to the main school building. The others went inside ahead of them, but Tonia stopped, letting the door close before her, sealing herself and Flynn outside in the stillness of the wintery garden.

"I just wanted to tell you, thanks for sticking up for me. It was really cool of you to stand up to her like that."

"Oh," he looked down at the patio, scuffing his shoe on the ground. "Thanks. I hope she apologises to you."

"You think she'd apologise?" Tonia asked.

"Probably not, but I can't forgive her unless she says sorry," he shrugged.

"Would you really forgive her if she apologised to you?" Tonia asked back.

"Of course," he looked up. "Forgiving someone is the kindest thing you can do."

Her gentle lips smiled at him. "Well, all right. If she says sorry, I'll forgive her, too. Eventually. Shall we go back inside?"

"Yes please, it's freezing!" he paused with his hand on the door. "But, um. Hey. Please don't listen to what Cecily said about the way you look. Because, um…" he grazed the sole of his shoe against the edge of the step. "I think you're really pretty, actually, so, um, yeah. That's it, really."

When he looked up again, Tonia was beaming at him.

"Are you going to the Valentine's party tomorrow night?" she said.

"Yeah. Are you?"

"Definitely," she smiled back and he breathed a sigh of relief.

§

"We just need to look for clues," Jessa said to Flynn on their shared walk home. "We should all pay attention to what Mr Fletcher says and does, and see if we can gather any hints."

"Are you worried about all this?" he replied.

"No. Are you?"

"No. But I get the feeling that I should be."

"Why?" she enquired.

"Because it's all so unknown."

"Yeah. But I've always felt like…" she drifted off, unsure how to place her words next.

"Like what?"

"Promise you won't make fun?"

"Cross my heart," he smiled his goofy smile.

"Honestly, I feel like we're on the verge of something. It's like when you're trying to think of a particular word, and you know it's in your mind but you can't quite get there."

"When it's on the tip of your tongue."

"Exactly. But I feel that inside my head. All these things are connected somehow. And I feel like I'm the one who has to connect them. Like *we* have to connect them."

"Why do you think we're responsible for it?"

"Because nobody else sees it. They will, eventually. But right now, it's us. We can do this. There's a mystery in here somewhere," she hung her head low and yanked on the straps of her backpack, pulling the weight of it close to her spine. "Do you think I'm weird?"

"Yes," he joked. "But I also think you might be right."

They reached the corner where they had to diverge toward their respective homes.

"Hey Flynn, before you go, can I ask you one thing?"

He nodded.

"When are you going to ask Tonia out?"

"Oh," he exclaimed softly, suddenly looking very awkward. "I don't know. Umm. I don't really know her well. Why, do you think, umm…" he scratched his head through his mousy brown hair. "Do you think she likes me?"

"Duh! Obviously." Jessa secretly enjoyed making him uncomfortable sometimes.

"Oh right, okay," his face blossomed into rosy pink, burning with bashfulness. "I don't know. She's going to the party tomorrow night."

"Perfect. As long as I have Maggie and Annora to hang out with, you can go off into a corner and get all smoochy with Tonia."

Flynn looked mortified.

"Sorry, sorry!" she laughed. "But seriously, she's really nice and super pretty, and I can tell she likes you. So if you want to ask her out, you should. And now I have to go because it's getting late and I don't want to miss dinner. It's spaghetti night."

"See you tomorrow," he said, offering her their daily goodbye high-five.

20

"Even the sleeves are five inches too long!" Flynn grimaced, holding his hands in fists so the sleeves engulfed his hands completely. "I can't wear this! I look like a child!"

Flynn apparently didn't have any smart shirts, but Maggie had borrowed a dark red one from her older brother Rowan. In her mind, Flynn and Rowan were about the same size, but in reality, Rowan's swimmer's physique gave him ample muscles to fill out his clothes, which Flynn lacked considerably.

"Wait, I'm sure we can fix it," Maggie purred, rolling up the sleeves loosely to his elbows. She motioned for him to tuck the flappy bottom part into his jeans.

"That looks much better, Flynn," Jessa said.

"You look so handsome!" Maggie cooed.

"Fine," he rolled his eyes. "But stop staring at me like that, it's making me feel weird."

Maggie herself was wearing the light pink chiffon gown her mother had bought for her to wear at Christmas, and Maggie was simply delighted to have another reason to wear it. She was, however, less enthused about Jessa's ensemble.

"I just think it's too casual," she said.

"It's the only dress I have," Jessa shrugged. "And it's red and white—that's Valentine's colours. It's perfect!"

"It's a stripy t-shirt dress and you're wearing it with high-tops and knee socks," Maggie said humourlessly.

"Mags," said Flynn, "just be glad she's not wearing a Since the Future t-shirt." He playfully elbowed Jessa's side.

"I have a three-part response to this," said Jessa, "A) Since the Future is a cutting-edge blend of new wave and alternative rock, and I'm proud to support their endeavours, B) I can wear whatever I want, and C) this outfit is killer. End of discussion."

§

Back at school, they couldn't believe the transformation of the main hall. The DJ had set up on stage, and his laser light show was already casting patterns and sequences around the room. One of the corners closest to the entrance was sectioned off as a lounge, with soft red sofas and a bubble machine. By the time Jessa and her friends arrived, the hall was already bustling with students, teachers, and catering staff in white jackets preparing the buffet table.

"This is so cool!" Jessa called out over the music.

Annora and Tonia bounded over to greet them.

"Wow, Annora, that dress is very, umm..." Maggie stuttered, "it's certainly unusual, isn't it?"

"I made it!" the redhead replied enthusiastically. "Well, I found the dress in a charity shop and then I sewed on all the other bits. Nobody else has a dress like it!"

Tonia, meanwhile, had opted for a more demure look, pairing a simple white denim skirt with a lacy white top. It emphasised her caramel skin, to which she'd applied a delicate sprinkling of gold body glitter.

"You look nice," Flynn said, looking at Tonia but then quickly addressing Annora as well. "Both of you, I mean. You both look really nice."

"Thanks," Tonia smiled. "I like your shirt!"

By 7:30 the hall was alive and buoyant. The guest-list also comprised students of Stanbrook—a neighbouring and equally prestigious lateral school—so the room practically swarmed with students dancing, posing for photos, dunking strawberries into chocolate fountains, and sloshing out servings of fruit punch and pink lemonade.

"Phew, it's hot," Jessa wiped the back of her hand against her moist hairline. "And I need to go to the toilet."

"Me too," Maggie added, taking a glance at Tonia and Flynn, who were standing noticeably close to one another. "Annora, do you want to come with us? We can touch up our makeup."

Annora nodded.

Flynn looked completely aghast as the three girls walked away.

"Oh boy, I hope he forgives us for that," Maggie joked.

"He'll be fine," Jessa laughed.

They walked up the stairs to the first-floor toilets because the queue was too long at the downstairs ones. They had to climb over the rope divider at the foot of the staircase that so prominently showed the words "No Students Past This Point," and Maggie stressed in advance that she would consider it Jessa's fault if they got in trouble. To Maggie's relief, they didn't run into any members of staff on their way up.

On the way down, however, they did.

They were about to descend to the ground floor again when Mr Fletcher suddenly appeared, rushing down the stairs from the second floor.

"Whoa!" Jessa blurted as he narrowly avoided smashing right into them.

"Sorry!" he said, barely even looking at them. "Didn't see you there!"

"Mr Fletcher? Are you okay?" Maggie said.

"Yes, thanks, Maggie. I just have something urgent to attend to. Have a good night, ladies!" he called out, hurrying down the corridor and disappearing into his classroom.

"That was weird," Jessa spoke quietly once the teacher was completely out of sight. Maggie and Annora both nodded. The three girls followed his steps along the darkened East Wing corridor, but couldn't hear anything through the door.

"Let's go tell the others," Jessa whispered, and they dashed back to the hall to inform their friends of the strange occurrence.

They all huddled in the foyer, quietly discussing the incident. Fortunately, a few other groups of students were hanging around, too, so it didn't look suspicious.

Their conversation was halted by the clump-clump-clump of heavy footsteps sounding down the stairs as Mr Fletcher's shiny shoes came into view, then the rest of him, all dressed up in his coat and scarf.

"Are you leaving the party, Mr Fletcher?" Annora asked innocently.

All of a sudden he appeared very calm and collected. "Yeah, unfortunately I'm not feeling too well," he said. "I think it's best that I head home. Enjoy the rest of the party!"

With a quick wave goodbye, he was gone.

"I bet he's going out on secret police business," Jessa whispered to her friends.

"What are we gonna do?" Tonia looked at Jessa.

"I say we follow him. And find out what's really going on." Jessa waited for reactions from her friends. She was expecting at least one of them to protest, but to her amazement, the excitement of the evening must have increased their adrenaline and sense for adventure, because they all agreed to it.

She formulated a plan quickly.

"Okay, we're not supposed to leave without a parent signing us out. But if we get our things from the coat check and then wait until Mrs Pacey is looking away, we can probably get out without her seeing."

They casually moseyed toward the cafeteria door and slinked in.

"You kids not enjoying the party?" asked one of the three ladies behind the coat check desk. Jessa vaguely recognised her as one of the school governors, whom she'd seen in the school newspaper. "Leaving early aren't you?"

Jessa made up an excuse. "Oh no, not yet! It's just a bit too loud and hot in there so we thought we'd sit in the garden for a few minutes to cool off."

"Good thinking," the lady said.

She took the numbered tickets and returned with their things.

Upon leaving the cafeteria, Jessa checked behind them and saw that the three chatty ladies were already too deep in gossip again to notice which direction they went, and Mrs Pacey was looking down at her puzzle book. The five friends seized their moment and slipped out through the front door before even putting their coats on.

"What now?" Annora asked quickly, shivering against the cold. They slithered into their warm attire.

"We should probably check the car park," Flynn noted. "What if he's driven off somewhere already?"

They walked to the end of the block and crossed the road to the private area where teachers parked their cars. It was more empty than usual, but Jessa quickly recognised Mr Fletcher's car.

"That's his over there, the little silver one. Wait, is that him in the car right now?"

They squinted around the corner, trying to focus their eyes on the darkened car, when the inside of it suddenly shone in a dim blue light that illuminated Mr Fletcher's face.

"What's he doing?"

"What is that?"

"Is it a torch?"

They whispered questions to each other as the light in the car turned into a white flicker.

"It's a video call," Maggie realised. "See, he's talking to someone."

He lifted the screen upwards in front of his face and they could clearly see him speaking. They watched as he nodded his head a lot, as if listening to instructions. The light went out and the car became dark.

The sound of the car door slam pierced the stillness. The sound of footsteps came closer.

"Quick, over here!" Flynn dashed in through the open gate of someone's front garden and the four girls followed quickly, ducking down behind a hedge. Jessa peered up through the twiggy branches.

"There he goes!" She stood up and her friends followed, while Maggie politely closed the gate behind them.

"He's walking so fast," Tonia huffed. "Must be in a real hurry."

"Everyone put your hood up," Jessa said quietly. "And we should walk on the other side of the road." She jutted out across the street when there was a break in the traffic.

"Why?" asked Maggie. "Why should we be on this side?"

"Because if he stops or turns around quickly, he's much less likely to notice us on this side. Geez, Maggie, haven't you ever followed someone before?"

"It might surprise you, but no. No I haven't."

They stayed back a safe distance and were glad that plenty of other people out helped disguise them into the London streets. After only ten or so minutes of walking, Mr Fletcher turned quickly into a dark passageway between two townhouses.

The students jogged to catch up.

Jessa crouched and peered her face around the corner, just enough to see down the eerie lane. "I can't see anything. He must have gone inside somewhere. I think I heard a gate closing."

"Let's go check it out," Flynn crept quietly down the dark passage.

"I'm pretty sure it sounded like a gate on a wooden fence, so it must be this one. It's the only one with a wood fence, right?" She looked up and counted up to the building. "It's the fourth house in this row. Let's try round the front and see if we can see anything."

The building looked out over a busy main road. Groups of well-dressed twenty-somethings walked by, on their way out to bars and pubs.

The five students looked at the front of the building and saw that it wasn't housing at all, but a row of little shops. The first one, right on the corner, was a hardware store that had been locked up for the night. Next was an Indian takeaway, and next to that was an off-license, with big signs in the window for a Valentine's Day sale on wine and cocktail mixers. But the fourth shop front was, surprisingly, nothing at all. It looked like it had once been a shop, but now stood very closed, with boarded-up windows and a chain across the front door.

"Are you sure it was this one?"

"It has to be."

"It doesn't look like anything," said Annora.

"Wait, look!" Maggie pointed.

A light flipped on inside the building.

They all cowered instinctively, but then realised the window glass had been painted over in white paint, so the light shone through but nobody could see in or out.

"This place is super creepy," Tonia said.

"What should we do now?" Annora said.

They crept round to the back of the disused shop once again.

"Flynn, can you hoist me up?" Jessa asked. He made a cradle with his hands for her to step into. She pulled against the top of the fence, lifting herself upwards.

"What can you see?" Maggie whispered through the darkness.

"Not much!"

He lowered her back down.

"There's a downstairs window, though. And it's not painted, just boarded up. But I can see there's little gaps in the boards. I bet I could see through them if I could get over there."

"But this gate is locked, right?"

"It is. But there are some bins on the other side of the fence. If I jump over, I'm sure I could climb back out."

"Do you really want to try?" Maggie said, seriously. "You don't have to do anything if you don't feel safe."

"I feel fine. I mean, there's five of us here. What's the worst that could happen?"

"We get caught?" Tonia whispered huskily.

"We don't even know what getting caught would mean. We're not at school; Mr Fletcher can't give us detention."

Flynn offered his hands once again to lift her up. She slipped off her shoes and stepped her socked foot into his hands, heaving herself up and over onto the other side. The only sound she made was a very delicate plop as one of her feet graced a bin lid.

"Jessa?" Maggie's voice whispered from the outer side of the fence. "You okay?"

"Yeah, I'm fine!" she whispered back into the air. "Going closer to the house now!"

"Be careful!"

Jessa stepped delicately over the potentially-noisy gravel path and tiptoed through the dewy grass. The cold frost seeped into her socks. She heard her heartbeat thumping loudly deep inside her ears. With every step she crept closer to the window, approaching from the side in case anybody inside could see out.

Jessa knelt down on the wet ground and rested her knees in the long sheathy grass and weeds that had grown near the wall. She drew her face closer to the window and looked inside, blinking into the light that emerged through the crack.

She saw a large table in the centre of an otherwise empty room, and counted eight people sitting around it, including Mr Fletcher. Everyone at the table was looking toward a man who stood, gesturing, making some kind of presentation, while those seated took notes on netpads or notebooks. Jessa looked closer at the people sitting down, and she realised she knew someone else at the table. Dr Mortlock.

As much as she tried to strain her ears, she couldn't hear anything they were saying.

She pulled away from the window and crawled along the grass toward the closed back door. She pressed the side of her face into the door but still couldn't hear a thing.

Scanning the door for possibilities, she noticed the letterbox. She placed two fingers on the chilled rusty brass of the letterbox flap and gradually applied light pressure until it began to open inward.

She paused, afraid that someone inside might see the letterbox opening. Holding the flap still and dipping a finger inside, she found that it was the kind of letterbox with draught-excluding bristles on the inside, which meant she could open the flap a good inch or so without disrupting the bristles and potentially alerting someone she was there.

She lowered her ear to the letterbox.

"Sue, have you had any insights at Harnbury?" a man's voice questioned. Jessa recognised the name Harnbury as another parapsych school in London.

"Nothing at all," Sue replied. "Nothing going on with the students or teachers."

"What about you, Hugo? Noticed anything at Winsbury?"

"No signs of activity, John," Mr Fletcher's voice responded clearly. "But let's be honest, we don't really know what we're looking for. And I'm sorry to say it, but whatever we're doing here just isn't enough. It's happened again, hasn't it? None of us saw any signs."

"Hugo has a point," said the voice called Sue. "Maybe we need more Agents in the schools?"

"We don't even have one Agent in every school in London. We don't have the manpower to increase our numbers."

"Even if we did, I don't think it would be effective," Mr Fletcher said. "We need to figure out if there's a method to how these kids are being chosen. Let's face it, we knew this was going to happen again, and we couldn't do anything because we didn't know when it would be, or who it would be."

"You're right, Hugo," said John. "But do you have any ideas how we can predict this? Our best clairvoyants aren't picking anything up, and until any kind of pattern emerges, parabilities are all we have."

"Are you honestly suggesting that we simply wait for a pattern to emerge?" said the stern drawl of Dr Mortlock. "How many times does this have to occur before you notice a pattern, Detective?" She spoke the last word with contempt.

"This is upsetting for all of us, Felicia," he replied. "And I'm sorry I don't have more information for you. But I can only give you as much information as my intel gives me."

Dr Mortlock scoffed.

Another lady spoke up. "John, where is Victim 2 now?"

"He's in the same ward that Victim 1 was held in after we found her. But you should all know we're choosing to present this one as a mugging. The media can't find out he has the same symptoms as Victim 1. People were shaken up the first time. If the public learns it's happened again, they'll start to panic, and we can't let that happen."

"Don't you think people have the right to know, John? Then maybe parents will be more vigilant," another unfamiliar voice said.

"Absolutely not," John spoke defiantly. "We can't let people ask questions until we have answers."

The room fell quiet.

Jessa's mind raced. Agents in schools? Victim 2? She became distracted enough for a second that she lost focus on her fingers keeping the letterbox pried open so delicately.

Her hand slipped, and the metallic flap slammed itself closed with a loud snap.

In that second she knew her position had been exposed.

She sprang up in an instant and ran back to the rubbish bins, clambering on top and hurling herself over the top of the fence so hard that she tumbled down over the other side where her fall was softened by Flynn. The two of them fell to the ground, and Maggie, Tonia and Annora all helped them up as quickly as possible. From the other side of the fence, they heard the back door creaking open and the sound of footsteps on the gravel pathway.

The students stared at each other in horror.

Jessa spoke one barely audible word, but it was all it took to bring them back into the moment and get them moving.

"Run."

21

Feet pounded on the hard London pavement. Cold February air bit at panicked young faces.

Flynn took the lead, still clutching Jessa's shoes. They made turns left and right and left and right again. Flat-out sprinting, desperate and electric with adrenaline.

A park.

They ran toward a decorative fountain with a little wall all around and threw themselves onto the ground behind it. In a huddle, they peered over, looking back across to the gate.

Nobody else entered.

They were alone.

"That was close," Maggie whispered breathlessly. "Do you think anyone saw us?"

"I don't think so," Flynn tried to catch his breath. "We got away quickly."

Jessa peeled off her sopping wet socks and shoved them into her coat pocket before wiggling bare feet back into her shoes.

"Did you see anything in there, Jess?"

"Yeah," a worried scowl contorted her face. "There were a bunch of people in there talking about… about… something that happened. They said it had happened again. There was a first victim and now there's a second one, but they're going to say the second victim got mugged so that people don't get scared."

"What does that mean?"

"Who was in there?"

"Did you see Mr Fletcher?"

"Whoa, slow down. Yeah, I saw him. Dr Mortlock was there too. And other teachers, I think. From other schools. But they're not really teachers. They said they're "Agents." There are Agents in all our schools, to protect us. But it's not working. Something's out there, and we're in danger."

"What is it?"

"I don't know. Neither do they."

Maggie put her arm around Jessa. "It's almost half-past nine. We should get back to school."

§

Some parents had already arrived for pick-ups. Their cars stood stationary in front of the school, hazard lights blinking with disapproval that the child to be collected wasn't ready and waiting outside as they'd promised.

Jessa and her friends entered the bright lights of the foyer, receiving odd glances from passers-by who noticed their pink cheeks, dishevelled hair and wet-patched coats. It wasn't long before Annora's mum pulled up to collect her and Tonia. They gave each other quiet goodbyes, and just before leaving, Tonia pulled Jessa into a tight, reassuring hug.

"You were really brave tonight," she said. "Good job."

"Thanks, Tonia."

"No problem. I'll see you all on Monday."

"Bye."

They noticed that many students were leaving the main hall with cups of hot chocolate, so Jessa, Maggie and Flynn went to investigate. The hall looked very different to how they left it. Mellow music played quietly in the background, students stood around in groups, chatting, but the dancing was over. The flashing lights had ceased, and the bright main lights were on.

The party was most definitely over.

"What do you think they were talking about in that place?" said Maggie.

"I don't know, Mags. Honestly, it sounded like they don't know much."

Jessa felt the familiar vibration of the phone ringing within her coat pocket. She pulled it out and confirmed the arrival of her mother, who was to give Maggie and Flynn rides home too.

"You all look knackered! Lots of dancing?" Mrs Baxter's joyful eyes questioned them through the rear-view mirror.

"Yeah," they all mumbled back.

"Wow, that much fun?" came the sarcastic reply.

"Sorry, Mrs Baxter, it was just a long day, and we're all a bit tired now. The party was really nice."

"Thank you, Flynn," she smiled at him from the driver's seat.

Mrs Baxter switched on the radio just in time to catch one of her favourite songs from the 90s, which she sang along to with an embarrassing gumption. The last few notes of the song faded out and were overridden by the familiar sound of Big Ben's chime, announcing the hourly news report.

"It's 10 pm on Friday the 12th of February. I'm Sandy Sanderson and this is NewsBullet. A bank in Wotheringham was raided today by masked bandits wielding knives. Fortunately, one of the employees pushed a panic button under the desk and the police arrived within minutes and arrested the wannabe bank robbers. In Frankerley Common, a road traffic accident has caused multiple injuries and slow moving traffic from Sentley Road all the way to the A879. And we are just getting reports that a teenage boy has been taken to hospital after being mugged near his home in Central London."

Jessa's spine straightened.

"Police say the fifteen-year-old boy, who has been named as Greg Sideman, a student at Field Lane, didn't arrive home from school. Later this evening, he was found, barely conscious, by a couple who called an ambulance. The boy was taken to a nearby hospital, where he remains at this time. The police are calling for any witnesses. That's all from me. Join us again at 11 for another NewsBullet. I'm Sandy Sanderson."

"How awful," Mrs Baxter tutted, turning down the radio so she didn't have to listen to the adverts that followed the news. "There are some rotten people in this world."

They dropped Maggie off at her house, then Flynn to his flat on the way back to 88 Duke Avenue, where Jessa exited the car and went inside without so much as a word to her mother.

"Is everything okay, love?"

"Mmm? Yeah, I'm just tired."

"Are you feeling a bit low because you don't have a boyfriend on Valentine's Day? I wouldn't blame you. It's very natural for girls your age to want a boyfriend."

"I'm really fine. It's nothing to do with that."

"Are you sure? Because you know you can talk to me about anything. What about Flynn? He's ever-such a nice boy."

"What are you talking about? Flynn's one of my best friends!"

"Well, I'm just saying… feelings can be tricky at your age."

"Mu-uum!" Jessa whined. "Please stop! I don't want a boyfriend, and I especially don't fancy Flynn, that would be so weird."

"All right. Get up to bed, then, you ragamuffin. And why are your feet so dirty? You kids… I don't know…" she trailed off as her youngest daughter plodded up the stairs to her room.

"Love you, poppet!"

"Love you too, Mum. G'night."

§

"Ugh, nobody should come to school this early," Jessa yawned. "It's not right."

"Dude, you're the one who called a breakfast meeting," said Tonia.

"Right. Hang on," Jessa took a hearty swig of tea. "I've been checking the news a lot, and there've been no other reports of a student getting mugged, so this Greg Sideman kid has to be the one they're talking about."

"Yep. The news this morning said the police are still asking around for witnesses. So I guess they still don't know what really happened to him,"

Maggie continued.

"Do we know exactly where he was found?"

"No, they haven't said," Maggie's gentle voice spoke again, "But they mentioned he's at Great Lambert Hospital, so it must have been near there."

"Didn't they say he goes to Field Lane, though?" asked Tonia. "If he was on his way home from school, then he wouldn't have been anywhere near Great Lambert Hospital. I grew up near Lambert and it's south of the river, quite a trek from Field Lane."

"Wait," Jessa dropped the spoon into her cereal bowl with a splash. She lowered her voice to continue. "When my sister was going out with Hugo… I mean, Mr Fletcher, he was round my house quite a lot. And when that whole thing with Emmeline Victor was happening, he said he went to Great Lambert Hospital to visit her."

"Oh no, do you think Emmeline was Victim 1 and now this Field Lane boy is Victim 2?" Maggie said aloud.

Jessa nodded. "Whatever happened to him is the same thing that happened to Emmeline, and they think it's going to keep happening."

Annora lifted a granola bar to her mouth and took a tiny bite but didn't really chew it so much as thoughtfully move her lips.

Flynn sipped his coffee, then cleared his throat. "We can't let this scare us. Obviously, whoever these Agents are, they're trying to protect us. And they're right, people will panic if they think there's something bad going on. So we have to keep this to ourselves. For now, anyway. Okay?" He looked around at each of them.

"But we also have to be alert in case anything happens here," said Jessa. "Even if Dr Mortlock and Mr Fletcher are the Agents at this school, they can't be everywhere all the time. So we can help. We can keep a look out for anyone acting strange. Right?"

"Right," they all agreed.

"So it's officially a new entry in the Mystery Club's 'Book of Secrets,' then?" Flynn joked.

He offered his hand into the centre of the circle to seal the pact with a group handshake. They all followed suit, with Tonia going last, placing her hand underneath Flynn's instead of on top of the pile.

"As long as we stick together, everything will be fine."

§

"Good morning, everyone," Mr Fletcher greeted his class. "We have our PSE session first thing, so let's just get straight on with it, shall we? The topic this week is 'Relationships'."

He noticed immediately when a couple of the students blushed or shifted awkwardly. Jessa felt her skin prickle.

"I don't want anyone to be embarrassed. Biologically speaking, at your age there's a lot of weird, new stuff happening inside your bodies as well as your minds, so it's only natural to be a little confused, or even scared."

Jessa was instantly reminded of the conversation she'd sort-of had with her mother just a couple of nights prior, and wished she could leave the classroom as easily as she'd departed the room at home and just gone to bed.

She'd always been private about her feelings, and never found herself with a crush on a boy. Even when Maggie swooned over the older boys at school, or her mother and sister saw famous actors on the TV and used words like "dreamy" or "hunky," Jessa usually ended up rolling her eyes and keeping quiet, or just uttering a casual "mmhmm" if asked for her opinion.

Fortunately, Mr Fletcher wasn't asking her opinion on the varying hunkiness of men, and Jessa was very pleased to find out that the lesson wasn't nearly as personal as she'd initially feared. It was actually more interesting than she'd expected, as Mr Fletcher shared with them some articles about the psychology of relationships and how people form attachments. Thinking about relationships, Jessa found herself staring at Cecily and Eli, who were giving each other sensual looks across the classroom.

What does he see in her?

Jessa remembered the dream.

Her lips… her teeth… her grip.

She shuddered. The whirlwind of daydreams kept her mind occupied for the remainder of the lesson. She kept replaying the events from Friday night over in her head. It almost seemed unreal, the fact that she and her friends had followed Mr Fletcher to the curious location and eavesdropped on something they couldn't even begin to fathom. It felt more like a dream. But it was completely real, and she had the churning knot in her stomach to prove it.

"Jessa—" Flynn tapped on her shoulder.

"Huh? What?"

"Lesson's over. Time to go."

Half the class had already left the classroom. She scooped up the line of pencils that she'd been mindlessly playing with on the desk, as Maggie and Flynn stood beside her and Tonia and Annora waited just outside the door. They all avoided looking at Mr Fletcher, whose burning eyes watched them from across the room.

Maggie, Jessa and Flynn were almost at the door when he spoke.

"Oh hey, guys?"

They turned around.

"I'm just wondering something…"

The three of them all tried hard to look as cool as possible.

He continued. "Is there anything you want to talk to me about?"

"You mean about the lesson today, Mr Fletcher?" Maggie asked innocently.

"Not what I was referring to, no, but is there anything about the lesson today that you'd like to discuss with me, Maggie?"

"No, I don't think so," she replied.

He just looked at them. Then he smiled. "No worries, then."

Jessa realised she was holding her breath as she stepped out of the doorway, noticing Tonia and Annora hiding just out of Mr Fletcher's sight.

"Actually, can you do me a favour?" he called out. "Jessa?"

She spun around slowly, trying hard to relax her face. "Of course. How can I help?" She tried to swallow away the lump in her throat.

"As you're on your way to Maths, would you mind taking this to Mr Tucker for me?" he held out a folder of papers.

Jessa sighed inwardly with relief. He held the folder out toward her and she looked up to smile as she took it from him. But the instant her fingers touched the cool surface of the binder she realised she'd been tricked.

Jessa immediately recognised the sensation she'd felt in the library when Mr Fletcher had handed her the pencil case and somehow incepted his spoken message voicelessly into her mind.

A jolt ran from her fingertips and zipped through her entire body in a second. She shrieked with surprise and jerked away as though she received a static shock. Mr Fletcher yanked the folder from her hand, shutting down their invisible connection.

Flynn, Maggie, Tonia and Annora all stood at the doorway, wide-eyed and watching. Jessa knew what Mr Fletcher had found out, and she looked up at him, waiting for a reaction. He leaned back on his desk again, his face low, rubbing his forehead. "I'm really sorry I had to do that, Jessa. But I needed to know."

"You already knew, though, didn't you?" she asked quietly.

"I had an inkling. All of you come in, please, and shut the door behind you." He picked up his tablet. "I'm sending a message to Mr Tucker to let him know you'll be late to Maths. We have some things to discuss."

Maggie closed the door and Mr Fletcher motioned for the five students to sit down.

"What you guys just saw was something called transmitting. It's a kind of telepathy, where you make a psychological connection with someone and gain an insight into a particular event or emotion."

"You read Jessa's mind?!" Annora gasped.

"Not exactly," he reassured. "The person sending the transmission usually has to be very focused and active in their thought which, of course, Jessa isn't because she's not trained in this. So I had to perform what's known as a transmission extraction. Don't worry—it's not painful, and it's not intrusive. But you all know why I had to do that, don't you? I knew you weren't going to say anything, and I couldn't let you go on without being able to talk to me about this. I mean, geez, I can't even imagine what you're thinking. I can't even believe you did that."

He paused. None of them could look at him.

"Do you have any idea how irresponsible that was? You snuck out of school during an official school event, and you didn't think twice about galavanting around the streets of London at night."

"It wasn't even that late, though!" Jessa immediately jumped to their defence. "And we were all together! We stayed safe!"

"It's not as simple as that, Jessa. What if something had happened to you? Your parents would be devastated. The school would be under a major investigation. There are so many consequences you didn't even stop to consider."

Jessa picked at her cuticles. Anything to not look at Hugo Fletcher's disapproving face.

"We're really sorry, Mr Fletcher," Maggie's voice wavered. "We're not going to get expelled, are we?" A big fat tear plopped out of her eye and rolled down her cheek. Jessa was sure this was the first time Maggie had ever been told off by a teacher.

"Don't cry, Maggie, it's okay." He took a long breath. "You're not getting expelled."

Maggie sniffed with relief.

"What I don't understand, though, is why were you following me in the first place?"

"Because we know your secret," Tonia said quietly.

"What's that, then?" he said.

"We know you're a police officer," Annora said. "But don't worry, we won't tell anyone."

"I heard Audrey on the phone one night," said Jessa. "She was crying to Sarah, saying that you'd told her that you have some kind of secret, and she was saying that it was dangerous and stuff, and we figured out that you were a detective or something, and we knew something was going on, and we wanted to find out why—"

"Jessa," he cut her off.

"You're right. My presence here is not entirely as it seems."

"Are you a spy? Like in the secret service?" Flynn asked.

"Something like that. I can't tell you exactly."

"Are you going to tell us what you're investigating, though?" Jessa asked.

"Absolutely not. You know too much already."

"Exactly, we already know it's something about people attacking kids or abducting them or something! So why can't you just tell us?"

"You're not in a place to understand, Jessa. Please believe me when I say I appreciate your interest, but you need to let this go."

"But—!"

"No buts! You're fourteen years old. You should be worrying about—I don't know—make-up, or boys, or homework, or heaven knows what else. This is bigger than you, Jessa, and I'm asking you to drop it. If you see or hear anything suspicious, you contact me immediately. Understood?"

They nodded dejectedly.

"All right, you'd better get to Maths. Make sure you apologise to Mr Tucker."

The five friends shuffled out of the room and silently headed toward the staircase. The hallways were quiet and from behind closed doors they heard the muffled sounds of teachers speaking.

They reached the open landing of the first floor, and Jessa pulled her friends into a huddle.

"Are we really going to drop it?" Maggie whispered.

"No way," Jessa replied. "If you guys want out, that's fine by me. But I'm not letting this go."

"Me neither," said Flynn. "I know Mr Fletcher's just trying to keep us safe, but I think if we're smart about it, we might even be able to help."

"I'm in," said Tonia.

"And me," chimed Annora.

"Mags?"

"Don't worry. I'm not going anywhere."

22

"I wish we could talk about all this at school. It would be so much easier," Jessa said to her four friends as they all lounged on the floor of her bedroom.

"It really would," Maggie agreed. "But we can't risk anyone else finding out Mr Fletcher's secret. Plus, anybody who heard us would think we're mad."

"To be fair," Tonia raised an eyebrow, "they already think we're a bit nuts. Flynn, pass the ball."

Flynn was thoughtfully squidging the tips of his fingers into the surface of the beach ball. He placed it firmly in front of his crossed legs and held his hand about seven inches behind it. On an exaggerated breath out, the ball moved away from his hand and toward Tonia across the circle.

"Gosh, Flynn, you're so good at this," said Maggie. "Your hand doesn't even move! I thought we weren't supposed to be able to do motionless telekinesis until second or third year."

"It's amazing how you've picked up telekinesis, Flynn," said Annora.

"Well, they do say it's easier for a telepath to learn telekinesis than the other way round," he said casually. "So it's really not that impressive."

"Of course it's impressive. You're great at both," Maggie sighed.

"You'll get there, Maggie, don't worry." Tonia took her turn passing the ball touchlessly across the carpet, moving her hand slightly to guide the motion as she manipulated it with her thought.

Maggie was the least competent telekin of her friendship group, and—to her dismay—one of the least competent in the whole class.

"Mags, don't forget that your telekinetic ability is still on par with what's expected of you as a first-year," Flynn tried to reassure her. "You're not below average."

"Doesn't make me feel any better, though," Maggie retorted. "Most of you are *above* average."

The ball rolled to Annora, who stopped it with her pointer finger and then poked it back to nobody in particular. She had barely developed her telekinetic skill but, unlike Maggie, was not the slightest bit bothered.

"Annora, you always choose this game," Jessa said, "but why do you want to play psychball if you're just going to pass it like a regular ball?"

"Because it's still fun! In primary school nobody ever wanted to play ball with me, except in PE lessons. And that's only because they had to."

"That's so mean," Maggie sympathised. "I'm sorry."

"It's all right. I'm just glad I finally found some real friends. I love being able to share things with you guys."

"Speaking of sharing," Tonia turned to Jessa, "did you tell your sister that we know about Mr Fletcher?"

"No way. She'd tell my parents what we did, and I'd be grounded for a million years. They got back together the other day, though. Even my mum doesn't know that they broke up, she thinks they had an argument and decided to wait a while before moving in together." Jessa paused. "Honestly, I wish he'd just tell us more about what's going on."

"He's trying to protect us," Flynn said sincerely.

"I know. But come on, we know this much. He should just tell us everything."

"Knock knock! Who's hungry?" the chirpy voice of Mrs Baxter said from outside the door. Jessa stood to open the door for her mother, knowing that if she verbally said the words "knock knock" instead of knocking, her hands must be full.

Jessa's mother entered the room with a large tea tray supporting a plate overflowing with sandwiches, a teapot and five mugs all with different decorations: a smiley face, a World's Best Dad, a Greetings from Cornwall!, a The name Audrey means…, and a brightly coloured, hand-painted JESSA, which was promptly grabbed by Jessa herself.

"Help yourselves, loves. And if you're still hungry, there's cake downstairs." Mrs Baxter left with a gigantic grin on her face.

"Your mum is so nice," Annora said. "You're really lucky to have such a nice family, Jessa."

"Thanks," Jessa smiled. My sister's kind of annoying, but I suppose she's all right most of the time. I don't see her much these days anyway."

"I always wanted a real sister," Annora continued. "My parents fostered a little girl once. That was a bit like having a sister, I think."

"Annora, if you don't mind me asking," Jessa began, "do you call your parents "mum" and "dad," or by their names?"

"I call them Mum and Dad."

"Do you miss your birth parents?" Maggie asked tentatively.

Annora held the beach ball close to her and rested her arms over it.

"I don't really remember them. Sometimes I think I remember the accident, but I told my therapist that once and he said I couldn't be remembering it for real, because I was too young. But Carol and Stanley adopted me when I was four, so I think of them as my parents, even though I know I wasn't their baby."

Jessa suddenly felt guilty for complaining about her sister, or for ever saying anything bad about her parents.

"You don't have to feel sad for me," Annora told them with a gentle smile. "I'm not sad. Sad things happen. I was given a second chance, and I'm very grateful."

A gentle moment fell over the five friends.

"So now I have a question for you, Jessa," Annora said.

"Yeah?"

"What's our next move?"

Jessa looked at each pair of eyes that awaited her response.

"Well," she began slowly, "we know Lynch is out there somewhere. I think our first step is to figure out where he is."

"How do we do that?" Annora enquired.

"I'm not sure."

"Should we tell Mr Fletcher?" Annora asked innocently. "Maybe he can help, you know?"

"I don't think we should risk it," said Tonia. "He's already suspicious of us right now. It's probably best if we act totally chill for a while. And we have a History Club meeting this week, so I think we should use it for regular stuff. You know, actual history stuff."

"I think so too," said Jessa. "Mr Fletcher's probably going to be watching us like a hawk."

"Even if he's not watching us," said Maggie, "he still might try and check up on what we've been doing. If he found out we're using school time to look into Lynch or the kidnapped children, I think he'd flip out."

"And anyway," said Jessa, "we still don't know exactly what Mr Fletcher is up to. Maybe he can't be trusted."

"That's harsh," Tonia said.

"But think about it, we found out his secret but he still won't tell us what's going on."

"Jessa, we've been through this," said Flynn, "he's doing it for our own good."

"But I feel like we're beyond that now. We're too far into it. He said it himself—we already know too much," she replied. "So in regards to *that* mystery, the question is: who is taking these kids? We need to find that out."

"We sure have a lot to figure out, don't we?" Annora said.

"Going back to what you overheard, Jessa," said Maggie. "They said something about other Agents in schools, right?"

Jessa nodded.

"So we know it's not specific to Winsbury," she thought aloud. "Hand me that netpad, please."

"What are you looking for, Mags?"

"I'm just searching general crime records."

"Let's think," Tonia stated. "What kind of thing could it be? Child trafficking?"

"I think we'd have heard about that," Jessa replied.

"If it were anything big, we'd have heard about it already," Flynn added.

"Which means it probably hasn't been in the news."

"Interesting," Maggie said quietly. "I just ran a search for crime records involving young people, and there's been a string of people under the age of sixteen reported missing."

"Like Emmeline?" Tonia asked.

"No, different to Emmeline. None of these were injured. They were all reported missing and then found the next day, so the cases were closed."

"How many?"

"At least thirty, and the activity dates back to almost a year ago. All over London."

"But they definitely all came back?" asked Jessa.

"Yep," Maggie replied. "All returned, with no explanation."

"That has to be related, right?" Jessa said.

"Maybe the Agents realised something suspicious was going on and sent Mr Fletcher to Winsbury to check up on it."

They sat for a moment.

"So what do you think we should do?" Jessa posed to the group. "We can't really go out looking for people who are kidnapping teenagers. But I feel like we're responsible for what we know. My dad always says "knowledge is power." But what do we do?"

None of them knew what to say next. The thoughtful silence was interrupted by a rapid knock at the door, then Mrs Baxter poked her head in.

"Sorry to bother you kids, but Annora's mum is here to pick up her and Tonia. And I'm going out to the supermarket now, so I'll be back in an hour or so. I just love doing the weekly shop in the evening, I get any parking space I want—what a treat! Okay, you all be good while I'm gone!" her voice trailed off as she walked away, and the teenagers heard the chitter chatter of the two mums jabbering away by the front door.

"Well, I suppose we should go," Tonia suggested to Annora, who pulled herself up from the floor and straightened out her skirt.

The group of friends hugged their hugs and said their goodbyes as Tonia and Annora climbed into the back of Annora's mum's little purple car.

Jessa closed the cold night away and she and Flynn and Maggie scuttled back up the stairs into the sanctuary of her room. Jessa promptly flopped herself down on the bed with a loud sigh.

"Oh, this is a pretty scarf," Maggie cooed from her seat on the rug.

"It's Annora's," Jessa said, resting her head on her hand to look in Maggie's direction.

"Ah, you're right. Do you want to hold onto it for her or shall I take it home with me?"

"I can do it," Jessa said, standing up from the bed. "I'll go and shove it in my bag so I remember to take it to school on Monday." She held out her hand and took the bunched up scarf from Maggie's hold.

"It's so soft!" Jessa wrapped the long scarf around her neck twice, snuggling into the chunky knit. She sauntered to the full-length mirror on the back of the door and looked into the reflection, striking a silly pose just for fun.

Then her eyes met those of her reflection, and she stopped.

No.

All Jessa saw was darkness.

Black as though she were asleep in the dark of midnight. But her eyes were wide and sleep was absent.

Panic.

Her heart quickly turned to a thumping drum inside her chest, keeping the time that her mind could no longer comprehend. The darkness took over all her senses.

Then, from the black hole came a ringing that pierced through her brain.

Out of the darkness came a scene from somewhere other than reality...

She was formless, watching two men in long coats exit a white van.

The sight before her shook with the disintegrity of a television screen with a wavering connection, flickering and shuddering.

With a loud whoosh, the scene skipped to the two men hurriedly walking down a London street. Jessa felt the pounding of their shiny shoes on the pavement.

"Excuse me, Miss?" one of their voices growled.

Annora.

Jessa saw the small girl's youthful face turn to view the two men. Her red mane of hair tumbled from her head and spilled out over the scarf tied firmly around her neck.

"Yes?" she replied so politely.

Whoosh.

Their hands grabbed at Annora's arms, trying to hold her from failing. One of them shoved a hand over her screaming mouth.

Her calls for help reverberated inside Jessa's head.

Jessa tried to yell but could make no sound from her shapeless embodiment floating in the scene.

Whoosh.

A dimly lit room. Annora stood silently, the two men behind her. Her pupils were wide and darkened, staring, unfocused. She didn't move.

"It didn't work, your Grace," spoke the same man's voice that addressed Annora on the street.

"What?" The tiny reply was spoken by another man. Jessa couldn't see him clearly. His form flickered more intensely; his long dark coat made him difficult to see in the darkened room.

"The tag didn't work, your Grace. We couldn't tag her."

"What are you saying? I taught you how to do it. I gave you the power to do it," the small but intense voice said. "You're supposed to be my aides. Do you know what that means, Woodrow?"

"Yes, your Grace."

"And what does it mean, Woodrow?"

"It means… uh… that we aid, you? Your Grace?"

"You are an imbecile. What's your excuse, Brooks?"

"I'm sorry, your Grace," the second man said with his head down.

"You're sorry about what, exactly?" the well-spoken, quiet man said.

"That, um, I'm an imbecile, your Grace?"

"Well, at least you have the enterprise to admit it," the small man snarled. "You should both feel incredibly ashamed of this unprosperous occurrence.

We've come too far and we can't afford to let mistakes like this happen. I have other things to concentrate on now—that's why I need you to take care of the gathering. The only other tag I wish to perform myself is the final one. So we will train again, and next time you will not fail me."

"Yes, your Grace," Woodrow and Brooks said quickly.

The man lowered himself gently to look directly at Annora, who still stood, unmoving.

Whoosh.

Jessa suddenly felt the sensation of having a body, but it wasn't her own.

With all her effort she tried to move, but to no avail. She was completely powerless. All she could do was watch through Annora's eyes as the man's face came level with hers.

His eyes had no colour. His skin was almost grey.

He reached his hand toward her face, in front of her eyes. His cold skin touched hers.

"Mmm, another parapsych," he said genially. "It is true that my grand vision is all-inclusive, and a lateral life force is just as useful to me as a parapsych's. But, oh," he shuddered, "there is something so deliciously sweet about a young parapsych mind."

His fingers gripped her skin. And then further.

Jessa felt his awful hand penetrate her head, reaching for thoughts and memories, breaching Annora's mind.

Jessa was trapped in Annora's body. The searing pain of white noise ached in her consciousness.

She felt flashing lights and the seething of time, and heard whispers through the blackout. The sound of voices in unison, hissing his name.

"Silas."

Whoosh.

A return to darkness, and she heard his voice roll from his pockmarked throat.

"Take her back," he said. "She's ours now."

"Jessa? Can you hear me?" a familiar voice faded in through space. "I think she's unconscious. Flynn, call an ambulance! Jessa!"

"Maggie?" Jessa groaned and fluttered her eyes open.

"Jessa!" Maggie touched the back of her hand to Jessa's forehead. "Oh my goodness, are you all right?"

"I—I think so," the words came out weak and forced.

"Can you see how many fingers I'm holding up?" Maggie asked.

"Yes, three," Jessa replied.

"Okay, now focus on the tip of my finger…" she pulled her index finger closer and away from Jessa's face, then side to side.

"I'm okay, Mags." Jessa pulled herself up to rest on her elbows. Flynn touched his hand to her arm.

"What just happened?" Flynn swept Jessa's hair out of her face. "We thought the scarf was choking you."

"The scarf…"

"Yeah, Annora's scarf, remember?"

Jessa scrunched up her face, trying hard to recall what now felt like a dream from which she'd awoken.

"I put it on. But then I saw her wearing it."

"What?"

Jessa sat up quickly, eyes wide and panicked. "We have to find Annora! He's going to take her."

"Slow down, take it easy!"

"I think I just saw the future!"

Maggie and Flynn looked at each other.

"Don't look like that! I swear I'm not hallucinating or remembering wrong or whatever you think is going on here." Jessa pointed to the scarf. "I put that on, and then I was… somewhere else. On a street, somewhere. And Annora was there, but then two men took her."

"What men?"

"They took her somewhere dark," Jessa interrupted, not even hearing Maggie's question. "They told him that they tried to do… something, to her I don't remember." Jessa stopped. "It was him. He read her mind, I felt it. I saw him. And he's going to keep her."

"Jessa, who are you talking about? Who's going to keep her?"

"It was Silas Lynch. He's the one who took the missing children, and he's going to take Annora."

Jessa recounted her story over and over until her friends knew every word. Mrs Baxter returned home and poked her head in to check on the three of them, but Jessa deliberately chose not to tell her mother anything.

"We should really tell someone about this," Maggie whispered after Mrs Baxter went back downstairs.

"Not my mum," Jessa replied. "She won't understand, and she'll worry."

"I think she has a right to be worried!" Maggie scolded. "If this is real, and you really saw the future, then we need to tell someone immediately."

"Jessa, could you tell from the vision, when this is going to happen?" Flynn asked.

She shook her head.

"I think we need to tell Mr Fletcher," said Flynn. "What if it's going to happen tomorrow? We have to protect Annora. Mr Fletcher told us to go to him if we had any information about the people who are attacking students, and if you think you saw them and that Annora's next, we have to tell him, right now."

"It's almost 10:30, though, my dad will be here soon to pick us up, Flynn," said Maggie.

"I'll try calling him," Jessa picked up the netpad from her bedside table.

"Dialling, HugoFletcher," the machine spoke in its vaguely inhuman way. The three teenagers waited.

"HugoFletcher unavailable."

"Try again."

"Dialling, HugoFletcher. HugoFletcher unavailable."

"VoiceDial Audrey Baxter"

"Dialling, AudreyBaxter. AudreyBaxter unavailable."

"Close VoiceDial!" Jessa said through gritted teeth and tossed the netpad onto her bed.

"We should just go there," Flynn picked up Annora's scarf. "And we should take this too so he can look at it. He doesn't live too far away, does he?

"No, it's about a ten-minute drive. But we don't have time to go there before Maggie's dad comes to take you both home."

"And I'm sure Jessa's mum wouldn't let us go out this late anyway, Flynn," Maggie reasoned.

"Jessa, what if you ask your mum if we can sleep over tonight?" Flynn proposed. "Do you think there's any way we can sneak out?"

"Mum will go to bed at about 11, and dad went to the pub with his work friends so he won't be back until about 1. So yeah, we could probably get out without being noticed. And I know Mum would say yes if I asked for you both to stay over. What do you think, Mags?"

"I can't believe I let you talk me into these things." She took a deep breath and reached for the netpad. "VoiceDial Celine Turner."

§

"So what now?" Maggie asked. "We just wait until your mum goes to bed and then we walk out?"

"Well, we can't just walk out," Jessa lowered her voice. "To get downstairs we'd have to go right past my parents' room. And my mum does fall asleep as soon as her head hits the pillow, but she's a light sleeper. She'll wake up for sure, if she hears us going downstairs late."

"So how do we get out?" asked Flynn.

"The window." Jessa pulled her curtains apart to show them the slanting roof right under her window.

"You can't be serious," said Maggie.

"It's totally safe, I've climbed down here before."

"Why?!" Maggie exclaimed.

"I don't know," Jessa shrugged. "Seemed like a good idea at the time."

"Sometimes I think you're a bad influence on me, Jessamine Baxter,' Maggie said, cupping her hands on the window to look out into the darkness.

"It's easy, I promise. We just climb down this little section of the roof, and then the garden fence is right there below, so we can easily hop down onto the patio. Then we just go out through the side entrance. We have to be quiet on the front drive because my parents' window looks out over the front of the house. Then once we get up to the main road, it'll be easy to get a taxi."

Jessa handed out hoodies for Maggie and Flynn to wear, as they couldn't return downstairs to get their coats without raising suspicion. Fortunately, they all had their own shoes, which Flynn was particularly pleased about, as Jessa had limited footwear in her bedroom and he "didn't fancy wearing slippers or flip-flops."

"We can pretend we're just watching a movie." Jessa flipped on the television. She dove onto the duvet and pulled a fluffy blanket over her legs. Maggie and Flynn did the same, wrapping themselves up cosily.

It wasn't long before Mrs Baxter knocked on the door, just as Jessa had predicted. "Have fun, kids," she blew kisses from the door, "and don't stay up too late. Audrey's room is made up ready for Flynn whenever you go to bed."

"Thanks, Mum!"

"Goodnight, Mrs Baxter!" they said, as coolly as possible.

The door closed and they all stared at the movie on the screen. Some ruggedly good-looking actor was fighting grubby bad guys.

They counted down the minutes until it was safe to leave.

11.15.

"Wait here," Jessa tiptoed out of her room toward the closed door of her parents' bedroom. She returned within seconds, with thumbs up, to see Maggie holding the netpad again.

"Just thought I'd try one more time," Maggie said. "It still says he's unavailable. And neither he nor Audrey has responded to the text messages. So I guess we're doing this?" Maggie glanced over at the window.

"You ready?" Jessa asked quietly. They both nodded.

Flynn stuffed Annora's scarf in a small yellow rucksack that he pulled from the wardrobe.

Jessa unlatched the window and pushed it open. They all tightened into their warm layers a little more as the cold March air rushed into the room.

"Climb down backwards, on your hands and knees," she instructed. "Just go slow, and you'll be fine. Then when you get to the edge, put your feet on the fence and jump down."

Flynn went first.

The two girls watched him make his way to the edge, where he gave them an 'OK' hand signal before jumping onto the patio beneath. Maggie took a deep breath and exhaled forcefully before copying him, slowly crawling her way down. Then Jessa too, backed out of the window, leaving the movie playing at a low volume to mask any unwanted sounds from their atypical exit.

As Jessa had predicted, there were plenty of London taxis available

"Bit late for you kids to be out, ennit?" the brusque taxi driver questioned, peering at them in his rear-view mirror.

"Bit late for you to be poking your nose into other people's business, ennit?" Jessa retorted.

"Oi," came his meagre response.

Maggie read from the piece of paper onto which she'd written Hugo Fletcher's address. "Please take us to Foxdown Court, Battersea."

"You got it."

And he drove.

§

It was easy to locate Mr Fletcher's apartment in the newly built Foxdown Court complex. They had wondered how they'd even get into the building if the main door were key-operated, but were fortunate enough to run into a group of elegantly-dressed but slightly inebriated women who held the door open for them.

"9F. Here it is," Jessa said. She knocked, to no answer. She knocked again, but still nothing. "I guess we'll just wait, then."

§

"Jessa?!" Audrey exclaimed.

"Where have you been?!" Jessa exclaimed.

"Excuse me? Where have I been? What on earth are you all doing here outside Hugo's apartment? It's the middle of the night! Mum and Dad will be worried sick!"

"It's all right; they don't know we left—"

"You snuck out of the house? What were you thinking?"

"Hey, ladies, let's just go inside," said Hugo. "I'm sure they have a reason for being here." He unlocked the door and motioned for them to enter. "They'd better have a reason for being here."

"We had to come to you, Mr Fletcher," Flynn began. "Jessa had another intuition, and we think Annora's going to be kidnapped next."

"We did try calling you first but neither of you picked up the phone," Maggie said apologetically. "We thought it was too important not to tell you immediately."

Mr Fletcher sighed. "Tell me what happened, Jessa, as detailed as you can remember."

She recounted the story, of putting on the scarf, of collapsing, of watching Annora being kidnapped by the dark-coated men.

"It was him, Mr Fletcher, it was Silas Lynch," she finished and waited anxiously for his response.

Jessa thought she was dropping a kind of bombshell, a fantastic piece of evidence into the mystery. But Mr Fletcher just looked at her, blinking in a moment of misapprehension.

"I'm not following," he said. "The only Silas Lynch I know of is the one from twentysomething years ago…"

"Yes, that one!" she said.

"I'm sorry Jessa; I'm still not getting it."

"What don't you get? You don't believe me?"

"Calm down, it's not that I don't believe you, I just don't understand. I need you to be a little more specific."

"Silas Lynch is back! He's alive!"

"O-kay…" he said slowly.

"Remember what I told you after our trip to the National Parapsychological Museum? In the Modern History exhibit…" she trailed off, imploring him to understand her.

"Yes, I remember you telling me that. But again, what's the connection?"

"It's him! It's Silas! He's the one who's kidnapping students!"

"I studied that story," Audrey interjected. "He was burned alive."

"No, they tried to burn him alive," Jessa held her hands out emphatically, stressing her words. "But he's not dead!"

"I don't know how you come up with this stuff, Jessa," Audrey shook her head.

"I'm not making it up!"

"We actually looked into it," Maggie did her best to sound reasonable. "We checked the database, and Silas Lynch's death record is incomplete. There is real evidence to suggest that he didn't die."

"So that's what you've been up to…" Mr Fletcher said quietly. He took a deep breath and smiled at the three teenagers gently. "All right, listen up. I appreciate you coming to me, and for looking out for your friend, but it's extremely unlikely that you saw the future. That kind of skill just doesn't happen out of nowhere."

"It must be some kind of object-reading! I know that's a real thing. I put on Annora's scarf and that's when I had the vision. I saw it, Mr Fletcher, I know it's going to happen. She's next."

"Futuresight isn't an object-based ability," Hugo Fletcher said calmly. "You see, there's no certainty that an object would be in use at any point in time in the future, so objects can't allow readers to see future events. Does that make sense?"

Maggie and Flynn nodded.

Jessa frowned. "I know what I saw."

"And I believe you saw something, though it couldn't have been futuresight. Please don't worry. I'll keep a close eye on Annora, as a precaution. But I'm sure she'll be fine. Now let's talk about getting you all home, shall we?" He suddenly looked very stern.

"We just need to go back to Jessa's house, our parents both agreed we could stay over tonight."

"I'll drive them back," Audrey tutted.

"Please don't tell Mum," Jessa whined. "Please please please?"

Audrey sighed. "Fine. I won't tell this time. But I swear, Jessa, if you ever pull anything like this again, you will be in so much trouble."

23

The looming architecture of the National Parapsychological Museum came closer as Audrey and Hugo bustled to get in from the whipping rain outside. Even in the harsh London weather, the majestic front steps swarmed with camera-handed tourists and impatient would-be ticket purchasers. With a flash of their IDs at the ticket booth, the couple were waved inside by a smiling older woman.

"What exactly are you hoping to find?" Audrey Baxter asked her boyfriend.

"I'm not sure. I just feel like I should check out this exhibit where Jessa experienced that intuition."

"So what do you actually mean by intuition? It's such a vague description. It's not strictly a parability, is it?"

"It is and it isn't. It's not taught on a parapsych curriculum, if that's what you mean. It's more a combination of aspects from different parabilities. It's sometimes described as a sixth sense. And unfortunately, it's not easy to study, because it's unpredictable and pretty rare."

"But you think Jessa has it?"

"It's hard to say."

"Why? Hugo, you can be honest with me. I know I'm a lateral, but I do study parapsychological fields."

"I know, and you probably know more about parapsychology than most parapsychs, I don't doubt that at all."

"What it is, then? Is it a bad thing? Do you think something's wrong with

Jessa?"

He stopped. "I can't say I know what's going on in Jessa's head, parapsych abilities or otherwise. I know she has great potential, but unfortunately, she's also probably the most stubborn and curious kid in the class, and those are traits that can get people in trouble. The only thing I know for sure is that Jessa's had two strange experiences, both apparently linked by this Silas Lynch.

What's making me wonder is this vision she had. She said she saw two men in dark coats take Annora. She doesn't even know it yet, but that part of her story correlates with some of our eyewitness accounts of suspicious activity. So even if her vision wasn't futuresight as I know it, she might actually be onto something."

They walked the rest of the way to the Silas Lynch exhibit in silence, looking around at all the statues, paintings, and artefacts being ogled by tourists' faces and camera lenses.

"Here it is," Hugo pointed to the display case detailing the story of Silas Lynch.

"I remember I was a kid when this was on the news," said Audrey. "My dad used to say he was a 'nasty piece of work'."

"Mmhmm," Hugo muttered, absentmindedly waving his hand gently in front of the glass.

Audrey sidled up to him. "Can you… feel anything?"

"No," he said, stepping back. "The window is probably preventing me from reading anything. If there's even anything to be read in these objects, that is."

He stepped back even further, looking broadly at the exhibit. "Nothing's jumping out at me. I don't know what I was expecting, honestly. I just thought maybe I'd see something," he sighed. "All right. I guess we can go."

They began to walk away when Audrey looked back one more time.

"Hugo," she pointed. "Look."

A museum worker was opening the window display case.

"Excuse me!" Hugo Fletcher rushed back. "Just wondering, what are you doing?"

"Doin' my job, mate," the man replied. "Gotta take one of these things out of the exhibit."

"Why?"

"Dunno, mate," the young Londoner said, pulling on protective gloves. "We move stuff around and take stuff away all the time. Usually, it's 'cause the piece is owned by a private collector, y'see, and sometimes they're movin' it to a different museum, or maybe they just want it back for their own collection, y'know?"

"I see." Hugo and Audrey watched as the man carefully picked up a book from the display, closed it and brought it to a trolley, where he placed it on a specially laid-out piece of fabric. "Do you know who owns this piece?" Hugo said.

"Wouldn't 'ave a clue, mate. You might be able to find out in the exhibit directory. Look up that number," he pointed to the tiny code at the bottom of the information plaque. "That might tell you summin'."

He folded the book in the fabric and placed it in a metal box, then locked the lid in place. "'ave a good one, mate," he uttered, then pushed the trolley away through the museum.

"Apparently, the book has been in the museum's possession since the early 90s," Hugo read aloud from a netpad at the information station in the museum foyer. "It's owned by someone called Francis Jackson. Ring any bells?"

Audrey shrugged.

"Me neither," he said. "And under 'current status' it says 'Returned to owner.' Interesting that the owner of this book in the Silas Lynch exhibit would want it back at basically the same time that Jessa would have this intuition about Lynch."

"It could just be coincidence," Audrey postulated. "How do we find out if there's a connection?"

"It might be worth looking into this Francis Jackson person. And just for the hell of it, let's check out the database and read up on Mr Silas Lynch."

"Hugo," Audrey lowered her tone, "do you really think that Silas Lynch could be alive, and have something to do with your investigation? I mean… the kidnappings? Really?"

"Well, when that guy took the book out of the case, I could sense the energy coming from it. That book has something to tell. Unfortunately, I wasn't close enough to object-read it. I don't know. This could all be nothing. It could be meaningless. But it's my duty as an Agent to treat any lead with sincerity."

"You're considering Jessa's vision-thing an actual lead, now?" Audrey said with disbelief. "Shouldn't you be following up with more, you know, substantial leads?"

"Audrey," he said gravely, "this is the only lead we have."

§

The high-speed trains of the London Underground echoed gently in the background as Hugo and Audrey waited at the platform. Their train arrived quickly, defying its own groaning gravitational pull on the electric rails. It slid into position at the platform, coming to a standstill with a light hiss.

"So where exactly are we going to execute this idea of yours?" Hugo asked.

"Have you been to the Humboldt Library?"

His response of a shrugged shoulder told her he had not.

"Well, it's incredible," she said.

The train doors closed silently, and the standing passengers took hold of the rails as the vehicle hummed into action and pulled into the tunnel.

"It's a huge block of a building, and there are no windows, so from the outside, it looks very bizarre."

"This is the Churchill Line express service to Dartford. The next stop will be Leicester Square."

"Oh yeah, I've seen that place," he said. "It's gigantic."

"It is, there are over a million volumes inside. Some of the most valuable and influential books in the world are stored there, first editions and such. There are rare books, manuscripts, ancient scriptures from when people were beginning to explore parapsychism. But it's also home to the Archives."

"What's that?"

"Well, as you know, all of the UK's social records are stored electronically, but for as long as we've been keeping records digitally, we've been continuing to store analogue records too."

"So the Births & Deaths records are there…"

"Exactly. Births, deaths, parapsych registrations, all the original paperwork is there. If the kids were right and someone removed data from the online database, we might be able to find something out from the hard copies."

"Is it easy to get into a place like that?"

"Actually no, it's quite difficult," she smiled proudly. "But I've already been fully vetted and given clearance access as a PhD student, and I can check in up to one guest with me when I visit."

"This is the Churchill Line express service to Dartford. The next stop will be Devon Place."

Audrey and Hugo walked the one block from Devon Place station to the Humboldt Library. It was every bit as impressive as Audrey had described. The intimidating concrete exterior stood out from the other surrounding buildings, in contrast with both the intricate old ones and the alien modernities.

"Wow. This might be the ugliest building in London," Hugo wrinkled his nose.

"It's windowless to protect the rare volumes that can be ruined by sunlight. Just wait until you see inside." She tugged his hand and urged him toward the entrance.

IDs shown, fingerprints scanned, cellular devices handed in and any metal items metal detected, and they proceeded to the central part of the special collections library.

The cube-like shape from the outside was mirrored on the inside, where a smaller yet still gigantic cube stood regally in the centre, storeys upon storeys of books behind a cage of windows, all bathed in a soft golden light.

"Whoa."

"I know," Audrey agreed. "It's the coolest place, and always super quiet and relaxing because nobody really comes here. But anyway, let's go. Over here," she lead him away from the cube and toward a nondescript door at the back of the room.

A simple sign on the door read "Archives." On the other side, they descended a flight of stairs to another set of doors, open this time, welcoming them inside.

"Audrey!" a delighted voice said from behind a desk.

"Mrs Mays, how are you?" Audrey kissed the older woman on the cheek.

"I'm well, dear, and yourself?"

"Very well, thanks. This is my colleague," she said, "Mr Hugo Fletcher."

He kindly shook the lady's hand.

"Just here to check a few records, if that's all right."

"Of course, dear! Go ahead—you know where everything is."

"Thanks, Mrs Mays."

Audrey led Hugo down a narrow corridor with a single keypad entry door at the end. She confidently entered the code and clicked the doorknob open.

"Access past this point with security escort only?" Hugo read aloud the sign. "And that lady just let you walk right in here?"

"I used to come here a lot when I was interning at the hospital. A lot of birth and death fact-checking, and that sort of thing. But there's also a computer lab down here in a pretty little reading room, so sometimes I like to come here to catch up on my books. Mrs Mays doesn't mind."

The cavernous Archives sprawled out before them. Rows of shelves followed rows of shelves, floor to ceiling, packed with binders and books and boxes labelled with categories that Hugo couldn't accurately read because Audrey was so swiftly directing them through the labyrinth. He quickly realised that they'd already made so many turns that if Audrey weren't there, he'd have trouble finding his way back to the entrance.

"It's a little claustrophobic, isn't it?" he said.

"I think it's quite cosy, actually," Audrey cooed in response.

"But I mean, isn't there a fire escape or anything?"

"Getting a little scared down here, are we, Mr Fletcher?" she mocked.

"Not scared," he mumbled. "Just, you know, concerned about safety precautions. For you, I mean. It's your safety I'm thinking about."

"Oh, sure," she laughed. "Well, thanks for looking out for me. Ah! Here we go, 'Lynch' starts here." She pulled three large leather-bound books from the shelf and plonked them into Hugo's arms. "I know how concerned you are with my safety, so I'm sure you won't mind carrying these big heavy books for me."

"Touché."

Several twists and turns later, they arrived at the reading room.

"Okay, do you know how to work the national databases?" Audrey asked. "If you can do that, I'll look up the Lynch family in the books and we can compare them."

He nodded and they got to work.

Hugo was eventually able to access the same database pages that Maggie had found many weeks before in the school library.

"Found it. They were right, the Silas Lynch death record is incomplete."

"All right..." Audrey muttered. She stretched across the three open volumes before her, looking from book to book, her fingers and her eyes quickly scanning and flipping the pages.

"I'm just checking... and cross-referencing... Hmmm," she said loudly, finally looking up from the page.

"What can you see?" Hugo asked.

"I found Silas Lynch's family. The cause of death is listed as 'burn injuries and suffocation,' which is concurrent with the fire that we read about happening at their home in 1968."

She placed her hand on the largest book of the three and read the facts as her fingertips traced them. Silas Lynch, born on the 12th of June, 1961, in the town of Woburn Vale, it says. But then if we look over here,' she moved to the second book, "his cause of death actually says 'unknown.' An official cause of death can only be logged when the death is verified by a recognised professional. So from that, we immediately know the verification process didn't happen. But there is a death entry that says he died on the 7th of November, 1985."

"I don't understand."

"His death entry was submitted but not verified. The reference here says the entry was logged a few days after he supposedly died. The rest is incomplete."

"Can we find out who submitted the entry?"

"Already checking…" she flipped through the final book. "I just have to find the matching reference number to the one assigned to Silas Lynch's death record. Aha, here it is. It says 'This entry was supplied by Mr F Jackson'." Audrey looked up at Hugo.

"Francis Jackson."

Hugo Fletcher spun round on his chair and rapidly began typing into the database. His fingers made the subtlest of taps as they fell quickly onto the touchpad keyboard.

"Found him. Doesn't seem like anything out of the ordinary, though. He's old. Had a wife who died fifteen years ago. Still lives in Woburn Vale."

"Where in Woburn Vale?" Audrey asked him, pulling her chair over to join him at the computer. "The book says the Lynch family lived on Lowe Road."

"He's at 10 Lowe Road."

"The Lynches were at number 13."

"Unlucky for some, eh?" Hugo muttered.

"So they were neighbours," Audrey stated. "Check out the satellite view for 10 Lowe Road."

He did as she suggested.

"That's where number 13 would be," Audrey said, pinching outwards on the screen to zoom in. "Looks like they just levelled it all to the ground after the fire destroyed it. And there's number 10, right across the road. But here's a question," she turned to face Hugo. "If there are no members of the Lynch family left in Woburn Vale, and Silas has been gone for all these years, what would make Francis Jackson suddenly—"

"Want his book back from the museum?" Hugo finished the question.

"Exactly."

They sat quietly, each thinking about the potential answers to their questions.

"What are you thinking?" she asked.

"Well, I thought Jessa and her friends were just grasping at straws with this Silas Lynch thing. Or at the very least just letting their imaginations get away with them. But now, after seeing all this, and the book being taken from the museum... I don't know. Maybe I'm just crazy, but it does seem to be a little too coincidental."

"It does. But it also raises so many other questions. If Silas is still alive, then where on Earth is he? How has he managed to remain undetected for all this time? And why hasn't anybody noticed this oversight in the paperwork? I can't imagine that nobody in database management thought it was strange that the death of a cult leader went unverified?" Audrey's speech became more and more exasperated. "It's a major blunder for the national database to leave a file incomplete! I mean, really! It's government-run after all, so it's very irresponsible of them to not keep the system as thorough as possible." She exhaled heavily.

"Tomorrow after school, I'll get the train out to Woburn Vale and have a look around."

"Shouldn't you tell the Agency about this first?" Audrey asked.

"Not yet. I don't have enough to go on."

She frowned.

"Don't worry! I'm just going to pay our friend Mr Jackson a visit, that's all."

24

"You're sure, Annora?" Jessa implored. "You're sure you haven't seen anything weird? Nobody's followed you, or spoken to you?"

"I told you, I haven't seen anything strange!" Annora sighed.

"Jessa, chill out, you're going to scare her," Maggie said.

"I just don't understand why someone would want to kidnap me," Annora said.

"I don't think he's putting that much thought into it," said Jessa. "It looked to me like he's taking people randomly."

"Jessa," Maggie glared. "What did I just say?"

"It is a bit scary," Annora mused. "But I feel better knowing that people are looking out for me. I mean, it's always better when we can predict bad things, isn't it?"

"I suppose so," Maggie conceded, but kept the scowl on her face. "I would feel better if I heard something positive from Mr Fletcher, though."

"Yeah right," Tonia scoffed. "He barely even looked at us in PSE this morning."

The five friends munched away on their lunch sandwiches.

"Mr Fletcher has a lot of pressure on him, remember?" said Flynn.

"Speak of the devil..." Maggie uttered quietly.

Mr Fletcher strode over to their table. He pulled up a chair and sat down. "Hey," he spoke quietly. "In your, uh, research sessions, have you come across the name Francis Jackson?"

They all shook their heads.

"Are you positive? You haven't seen or heard that name before?"

"Positive," said Jessa. "Never heard of him. Why?"

Mr Fletcher sighed. "Well, I guess…" he trailed off reluctantly. "I guess you may have been right about Lynch being alive. I did some research myself, and there's still a lot to look into, but maybe."

A flash of adrenaline shot through Jessa's brain. "I knew it," she whispered.

"What did you find?" Flynn asked.

"Mostly the same things you did, but a couple of results have turned up this name."

"So who is it?" Jessa questioned urgently.

"He was a neighbour of the Lynch family. I'm going to visit him after school today. He still lives in Woburn Vale, so he's pretty easy to get to."

"Can we come?" Jessa asked immediately.

"Absolutely not," Mr Fletcher answered without a split-second of hesitation.

"Why!" they all whined.

"Because I don't know what we're dealing with here! But I promise I'll check in with you tomorrow and let you know what I find out. Is that fair?"

"Fine."

"Great, I'll get back to you tomorrow morning." He left the table.

Jessa waited until he had completely exited the cafeteria before proceeding.

"Who wants to go to Woburn Vale after school, then?"

§

The five students followed a safe distance behind the teacher, travelling on the Underground all the way to Euston Station. A sea of commuters conveniently provided cover for them to remain unseen, and the teenagers held onto each other's hands to keep from being separated by the flow of foot traffic.

"I see him. He's going to the ticket machine," Annora noted. Jessa approached a different ticket machine on the opposite side of the concourse.

"I'll keep watch," Maggie said. "But hurry. These ticket booths are all so exposed. If he turns around, he'll see us."

"I have enough money for three tickets," Jessa said quickly. "Does anyone else have enough for two more?"

"I do," Tonia rummaged in her tote for a purse and thrust it into Jessa's hand to take the cash.

"All right, here you go," Jessa handed out a ticket to each of them.

"The next train to Woburn Vale leaves in seven minutes," Flynn announced, pointing to the departures board that dominated an entire wall of the station. "Mr Fletcher's going through the barrier now."

They watched from afar to see which carriage he entered, then chose seats in the carriage down from his.

The five of them spread out over two tables on either side of the train aisle, and took the opportunity to do some homework. Jessa opened her physics books but kept looking up and out the window, distracted by the blur of suburban London as it whizzed past them at ninety miles per hour. The moving landscape view transformed from suburbia to the quiet English countryside, dreary under a gloaming sky.

The train stopped periodically at curiously named places, letting off a few people here and there in villages like Wobbly Lake, Little Hambly, and Valley Crows. Jessa remained dissolved in her own thoughts, staring blankly out the window at the places and people, until something suddenly grabbed her attention.

"Wait!" She pressed her face against the glass to look at someone who had just exited the train. "There!"

"What is it?" Maggie craned her neck to see. "Oh my goodness, is that Mr Fletcher?!" She pointed toward the back of a young man in dark khakis and a brown jacket who looked an awful lot like Mr Fletcher.

"What?!" Annora, Tonia and Flynn looked over in concern. "He got off already?" said Flynn. "Where are we?"

"We're not in Woburn Vale," Maggie said, "but that really looks like him."

"Shit. Should we get off now?" Tonia said, quickly stuffing her books into her bag.

"Too late. Damn," Jessa said as the train began to pull away from the station. "Maybe we can get off at the next stop and get the next train back.'

"Before we panic too much, we should check that he's definitely not here," Flynn suggested.

They walked up the aisle of the train in single file, holding the backs of seats to keep their balance on the carriage as it swayed in motion.

Jessa halted the group at the glass door at the carriage entry. "I can't see him, but there are a few people with their backs to us. What should we do?"

"I think we should go in," Annora said.

"What if he is in there, though?" Maggie said. "He'll see us."

"He had to find out sometime that we were going to Woburn Vale with him," said Tonia. "So if he's there and he sees us, well, it was going to happen at some point."

"Tonia's right," said Flynn.

"Here we go, then." Jessa waved her hand in front of the motion sensor at the door slid open.

They made their way cautiously through the carriage, checking every seat until they ended up at the other end of the car, next to the little WC cubicle in the vestibule between the carriages. Mr Fletcher was nowhere to be seen. Just to be sure, Jessa peered through the glass, checking the next carriage.

She shook her head.

"Damn!" Tonia exclaimed.

"Why would he get off the train back there! Where was that?!" Maggie remarked.

"It's fine," said Jessa. "We'll just get off at the next stop and go back."

They were waiting by the door when the airy hum of a hand-dryer sounded from inside the cubicle. The door slid open, and a young, blond man in dark khakis and a brown jacket stepped out.

"You have to be kidding me..."

"Oh, hi, Mr Fletcher," they all mumbled sheepishly.

One hand braced himself on a rail, and the other ran through his hair. He shook his head slowly. "Unbelievable. What did I tell you?!"

They said nothing.

"I promised I'd keep you updated. You deliberately disobeyed me."

"Technically it's after school hours, so you're not in charge of us anymore."

"Jessa, don't be smart with me. You're in big trouble."

"Ugh, you sound like my sister."

He scrunched his hair. "I don't know what I'm going to do with you."

"You can't do anything, Mr Fletch," Tonia smirked. "We're here now, aren't we?"

"I did not sign up for this," he said under his breath. "Fine, you can come with me, but you are never to call me Mr Fletch again."

"How about just Fletch?"

He blinked. "Definitely not. Now shut up and sit down."

§

"Here it is," Mr Fletcher said as they reached 10 Lowe Road. He looked over the hedge at the old detached house, already locked up for the evening, curtains closed with artificial light shining out. "Please behave yourselves. I don't want this poor old man calling the police on us for harassing him."

The others nodded their approval, but Jessa was distracted. She walked out across the quiet road to the opposite side, gazing into the space between two houses where another once stood.

"This is where he lived, wasn't it," she said absentmindedly. "I can feel it."

"What can you feel, Jessa?" Mr Fletcher moved to stand right behind her.

The space was unkempt. Grass had clearly grown and died there many times, and the ground was dry from winter.

"It feels…" she drifted into quietness, and crouched to place her hands on the ground. "Warm. Warm and sad."

"It feels warm to you? Physically?"

"Yes. Why, is that strange?"

"No," he smiled kindly, though Jessa suspected his response was not completely truthful. "Come on, let's go."

Knock, knock, knock.

No answer.

Harder, knock, knock. They could hear the sound of a television blasting from inside.

Harder still, knock kno—

"Quit your yammering, I'm coming!" a wavering voice rattled from the other side of a door. Eventually, it opened, slowly, and still with the chain lock across. A wrinkled man peeked his head into the ajar space and peeped out through his bifocals.

"Good evening, Mr Jackson, my name's Hugo Fletch—"

"No thank you! No cold-calling!" He began to close the door on them, but Jessa stepped forward.

"Wait! Mr Jackson?"

Hearing the young girl, the man opened the door again curiously and peered again over the tense chain.

"My name's Jessa. This is Maggie, and Flynn, and Tonia, Annora and Hugo. We just came here from London. We were hoping to talk to you about the Lynch family. You knew them, didn't you? You knew Silas Lynch?"

The door closed. A few seconds and some jangling sounds later, it reopened wider.

"Wipe your feet." Francis Jackson hobbled back to his armchair, allowing his visitors to see themselves in.

Francis Jackson's living room walls were cluttered with a lifetime of photographs. Upon the walls were shelves that bowed under too many books and tchotchkes, vases and figurines, mismatched and dusty. The wallpaper, probably once a vibrant marigold, had faded to a dry wheatsheaf brown.

Francis pointed his clunky remote control at the even-clunkier television, silencing the soap opera shenanigans that were left dancing across the screen soundlessly.

"Get on with it then, I don't have all night," he urged his visitors, who perched themselves on the sofa across from his chair.

"You knew Silas Lynch, didn't you?" Jessa began.

The old man nodded gravely in return.

"What can you tell us about him?"

"You'll have to be more specific, missy. I knew the Lynch family well. Such a tragedy."

"Well…" Jessa spoke slowly, figuring out her own line of questioning as she spoke. "Did… did you always know… no, let me start again. Did Silas always seem… well… different?"

"He was always a strange child, but he wasn't the monster that the newspapers made him out to be. They wrote some horrible things about him." Francis' voice rose in volume. "It was disrespectful to his family, may they rest in peace, to say those things about him."

"But Sir," Maggie chirped gently, "the newspapers were just reporting his activities, weren't they? He did some terrible things."

"Pah!" he exclaimed. "Silas was the product of a society that couldn't care less about him. He lost his whole family in that fire, for cripes' sake. Then he was shipped off to the orphanage like some sort of throwaway. I'm not defending the things he did, but the boy needed mental help. Help that nobody wanted to give him. In those days nobody cared about that sort of thing. Labelled him crazy and never gave him a chance."

"What was he like as a child?" Jessa asked.

"He was a good boy—very intelligent, and an excellent parapsych. I always thought he was destined for greatness. I remember when he was very young, my wife and I would babysit Silas and his sisters from time to time. Those girls were the loveliest children, very playful, and they'd always want to be outside playing in the garden, picking flowers and whatnot. But Silas was always an old soul; he preferred to stay inside and read. And then, after the accident, he became a mute. Never spoke at all. He even lost his parapsychism for a while; the boy was in such shock."

"Mr Jackson, if you don't mind my asking, why didn't you take Silas in after the fire?" Hugo Fletcher asked.

"Well," the older man spoke quietly, looking down at his wavering hand as it gripped a mug of weak tea. "I asked myself that for a long time. Silas even asked if he could live here, but we were already getting on a bit, and my wife had some health problems, so we thought it would be better for him to be placed into a real family. At that point, we couldn't have foreseen that no family would take him. Nobody wanted to adopt such a forlorn child, and especially one with such disfigurement… the fire took so much from him, in so many ways."

"Then what happened to him?" Jessa enquired further.

"Once he was old enough to leave the children's home, he did just that. He simply walked out and then the next time I heard from him was when he started his campaigning."

"And you had no idea he had those beliefs?" Jessa pushed.

Mr Jackson paused, staring into space. He let out a long 'hmmm' and pushed his glasses higher onto the bridge of his nose.

"There were signs," he admitted. "Even at his young age, he said he didn't like school because it wasn't doing right by his abilities. His older sister was in high school, and he heard tales from her that made him think the school wasn't teaching children how to really use their abilities."

"That's some serious talk." Mr Fletcher raised his eyebrows.

"Silas Lynch was a serious child," Mr Jackson offered in response. "What's made you so curious about Silas all of a sudden, anyway?"

"No particular reason," Mr Fletcher smiled. "We were just trying to fill in some blanks. Mr Jackson, do you know anything about a book at the Parapsychological Museum?"

"You mean my book?"

"Your book, yes. Did you ask for it back?"

Francis Jackson's eyes narrowed. "Why yes, I did."

"What made you ask for it back, Mr Jackson?"

"Someone wanted it."

"Who?"

"Men came and took it away. Two of them."

Two men. Jessa's mind flashed back to her intuition. The two men she saw taking Annora. It's him.

"I don't know why they wanted it," the old man continued. "But anyway, it was in London, so I had to phone the big museum and ask for it back, and then the men came to collect it."

"Mr Jackson, do you recall the names of those men?" Mr Fletcher implored.

"Gosh, no, I don't believe I do. Come to think of it, I don't think they told me their names."

"Do you remember what they looked like?" Jessa asked.

"Very normal, hard to say."

"Do you remember anything distinctive? Anything at all? What were they wearing?" Mr Fletcher pressed him.

"They were most unremarkable, I'd say. Just two normal-looking men in normal-looking coats."

Jessa opened her mouth as if to speak but Mr Fletcher's look told her not to. He pulled back the sleeve of his jacket to check the time. "I'm afraid we have to go."

"All righty then," Mr Jackson said, almost sounding disappointed to lose the company. "I hope you don't mind to see yourselves out. It's awfully difficult to get up and down from this chair, you see."

"Oh, Mr Jackson, before I go, I have one more question," Mr Fletcher said. "Why were you the one to register Silas' death? In the database the record has your name attached."

"It just felt like the right thing to do. I knew nobody else would, and when I read in the paper about the night his so-called followers turned on him, well, I thought I owed it to the boy to put him to rest in the only way I could. I would have wanted to hold a funeral, but as you can imagine, there was no way to recover a body from that mess. Tragic. Poor boy."

25

Poor boy.

Poor boy?

Jessa replayed Francis Jackson's words over and over.

How could he say that? Lynch believed laterals were scum.

She thought about everyone she knew who was a lateral. Her parents. Her sister. Her friends from primary school. So many people.

What kind of person would be so hateful to an entire population?

An evil one.

Disturbed, they said.

But he was in so much pain.

Sad people do terrible things. Sadness is never an excuse.

He needed help, Francis had said.

Nobody wanted to help him.

Nobody gave him a chance.

The creaking of the stairs told Jessa her parents were going to bed. She turned her pillow over and smooshed her face into the cool side.

Her eyes gazed into the darkness.

The two men came to get the book.

She tried to call up the rational side of her brain.

They could have been anyone.

No, you know it's him. He's still alive. You saw him. You felt him.

Annora's in danger.

Mr Fletcher said he'll protect her. That's what he's here for.

Is it? He's still keeping secrets from us. We need to find out what he's hiding.

Could this really all be connected?

Yes. Listen.

26

"Jessa, could I see you for a moment?" Mr Fletcher asked as his class filed out for their first lesson of the day.

Flynn, Maggie, Tonia and Annora also all hung back.

"Sorry, guys, I just need to talk to Jessa alone."

They hesitated before leaving.

"We'll wait outside," said Tonia.

"I need to ask you something alone, because I want you to reply without the influence of your friends." he judged her expression carefully.

"Okay."

"Jessa, based on some new information that we've learned recently, I want to pay another visit to Emmeline Victor. Do you remember who that is?"

"Of course, she was the Head Girl. And she was the first victim."

"That's right. So I'd like to go and see her again, and I'd like you to consider joining me—"

"Definitely," she replied before he'd barely finished speaking.

"Before you make any decision, please just think about it. Because Emmeline isn't in a healthy state. She's been thoroughly changed by her experience, and it's very sad, and potentially scary, and I don't want to put you in a position—"

"I want to go. I don't need to think about it—I want to help."

"All right," he saw the determination on her young face. "I got my car back from the mechanic this morning, so I'll drive us there at lunch time."

§

The car slowly trundled up a narrow lane with a five mile-per-hour speed limit and a noticeable abundance of SLOW signs. A mile or so later, they came across a barrier where a security guard emerged from a small booth and greeted Mr Fletcher at the driver's window.

"Name?"

"Fletcher and Baxter."

The security guard peered into the car and looked over at Jessa.

"How old is she?"

"Fourteen. We've been authorised."

"I can see that," the security guard nodded at his netpad. He opened the barrier and waved them forward.

They pulled up to the imposing building of the Morelands Hospital. If Jessa hadn't known any better, she might have guessed from its high walls and advanced security that it was less a hospital and more a prison.

"Why is Emmeline still in hospital? I thought she'd be home by now. It's been a long time since her accident."

Mr Fletcher turned to her and spoke very quietly. "Jessa, Emmeline hasn't been home since the incident. This is a high-security psychiatric hospital. As far as any doctors can tell, something happened to Emmeline's brain in her attack, and while most of the time she doesn't speak or move at all, she's had a couple of episodes that were nothing short of, well, 'mentally disturbed' is how the nurse described it. So Emmeline has to stay here. For her own protection."

"Oh."

"We don't have to go inside. If this is too much, we can turn around right now."

"No," Jessa said. "I want to do this."

The halls of Morelands Hospital were decorated with some artwork and photographs, but the injections of colour did little to detract from the clinical interior, and nothing could override the vague smell of disinfectant and latex in the air.

A young nurse in white scrubs led them through the corridors, scanning her ID card at every door point for access. "Most days now she just stares out the window," she said. "She used to be in a room without windows, but since we moved her to this one, she seems to be making a little progress.

Please remember, the door must stay open at all times while you're in there. If you need assistance, you can call for help by pressing either of the emergency buttons: one is by the door, and the other is by the side of the bed.

Mr Fletcher, you've accepted responsibility for bringing a minor into the facility," she gestured toward Jessa. "Her safety is of primary importance. For this reason, we strongly recommend that you do not make any physical contact with the patient."

They stopped, and the nurse scanned her ID at a door once again.

"Good afternoon, Emmeline!" the young nurse's voice brightened.

Jessa swallowed hard and stepped into the room, her eyes fixed on the back of Emmeline's head as she stared, motionless, through the bars in front of the window.

The room was sparse.

A small headboardless bed protruded into the room, its thin, cheap blankets made up neatly and pulled tight under the sides of the mattress. A small table sat to the side of the bed, with nothing upon it but an untouched paper cup of water. The only other item of furniture in the room was the chair in which Emmeline sat, with her bony bare feet flat on the ground and her arms resting rigidly on each of the side arms.

The nurse bent forward in front of Emmeline so they were face to face. "You have some visitors today, sweetheart. It's Mr Fletcher and Jessa from school. Do you remember them? Mr Fletcher and Jessa?" She took a step away from Emmeline, allowing the visitors to come forward.

"I'll leave you to it. If you need me at all, I'll be in the office just down the hall." And with that, she left the three of them in the room.

"Hi, Emmeline. I visited you before, do you remember? And I brought Jessa with me today because I think the two of you could get on well. Jessa, do you want to come and say hi?"

The closer she stepped towards Emmeline, the harder her heart pounded.

She'd never met Emmeline Victor at school, only seen her in passing, but she knew her face from the photograph in the school foyer, and she knew her reputation.

The person sitting before her in the hospital room was barely recognisable as the beautiful and accomplished student who had once proudly reigned as head girl of Winsbury. Her skin was colourless and thin, pulled severely over her gaunt form. She was draped in a beige hospital gown that sagged from her frame and spilled over her thighs. Her long reddish brown hair hung, lifeless and greasy, a few tendrils dangling by her jutting cheekbones.

Jessa's memory suddenly threw her back to when Mr Fletcher told them Emmeline had been found. His words echoed in Jessa's mind. *A ghost.*

The girl sitting before her in the hospital was as ghostly as Jessa could have possibly imagined a living person to be.

Whether it was curiosity, or a desire to help in the investigation, or even just the stubbornness of not wanting to let Hugo Fletcher see how nervous she was, Jessa took a deep breath and came forward, in the same manner as the nurse had done.

She brought her eyes level with Emmeline's, staring right into the emptiness that glazed over them.

She remembered the vision in which she'd seen Annora staring into Silas' black eyes.

When Jessa finally spoke, the words came out in a whisper. "He did this to you."

She focused on Emmeline's pupils. Was that indeed a flicker of recognition?

She whispered again, "I've seen him too."

Every inch of her skin stung with sensation. She felt a deep compulsion to touch Emmeline, but a recollection of the nurse's warning pinged in Jessa's mind and she held her hands back, resting them instead on the ends of the arms right in front of Emmeline's.

Close but untouching.

Then, before Jessa had time to move, Emmeline flinched. She grabbed hold of Jessa's hands and pinned them to the arms of the chair.

Emmeline locked her eyes on Jessa's, and that's when Jessa felt it.

The energy rushing through her entire body. The ringing sound reverberating through her skull. The fading to black in her vision, and the returning clarity as she appeared in a different, reconstructed reality.

Everything was blurry, like she'd been hit on the head. She could tell that people were moving around her, but she couldn't see them. All she could see were shadows across her faltering vision, fading in and out of sight. Hands gripped her skull, torturously pulling at her consciousness.

The vision broke, and Jessa was back in the hospital room, gasping. Emmeline's fingers dug into the backs of Jessa's hands.

Emmeline whispered one word.

"Shadows."

Jessa froze.

"Shadows," Emmeline uttered again, the word barely a wisp from her mouth.

"Yes. I saw them, Emmeline. I saw the shadows. Is that what happened to you? Did you just show me what happened?" Jessa's words tumbled out of her mouth desperately.

"Shadows," Emmeline said, louder.

Emmeline's head jerked from side to side.

Jessa recoiled and cowered toward Hugo Fletcher, who protectively pulled her in toward his own body.

Emmeline's head tilted back and her mouth threw itself open, letting out air as though a scream should emerge, but only a ghostly wheeze came out. Mr Fletcher tore back and pressed the emergency button by the side of the bed, and a screeching alarm wailed into the room. Three male nurses in white scrubs ran into the room. Two of them picked up Emmeline and moved her onto the bed while the third nurse ushered Mr Fletcher and Jessa from the room.

Jessa gripped his hand tightly, her face stuck in a horrified gawp as she watched the scene unfold before her.

Mr Fletcher pulled Jessa to the door and led her briskly by the hand back through the corridors as the nurse walked ahead of them, scanning his ID card at every door to aid their departure.

He didn't stop until they reached the car. He immediately wrapped his arms tightly around her, pulling Jessa's shaking body into his chest.

"It's okay," he spoke, breathlessly. "It's okay…"

"I'm taking you home. Don't worry about the rest of the school day; I'll sign a medical slip for your parents. Just tell them you weren't feeling well. Is that all right?"

Jessa nodded. The rumbles from the car soothed her tense body.

"Jessa, I am so, so sorry."

She turned to him and smiled weakly. The smile didn't reach her eyes. "I know," she said. "I just didn't know what to expect. Why did you want me to go there? Did you know she would do that?"

"If I knew it would be like that I wouldn't have taken you, I swear," he said. "Are you able to describe it?"

"I think I saw what happened to her. Or rather, I felt what happened to her." Jessa's voice cracked. "It was like someone was sucking my brain out through my skin. Sucking my mind out. It felt like I was losing my…" her voice trembled as the lump swelled in her throat. "My whole identity, my thoughts, my emotions, my parabilities, everything… it was all being torn away. That's what he did to her. He took away everything that made her a person." Jessa paused. "If a ghost is a soul without a body, then he made her the opposite. She's empty. And he's a monster."

"Well, we don't know for sure that it's Si—"

"Yes, I do. It's him. I know it's him."

§

Jessa lay on her bed, already cosied up in her pyjamas and dressing gown by 4 pm. The whole afternoon had been occupied by reliving her experience with Emmeline, again and again, cycling through anger, fear, and upset. Her thoughts were interrupted by a gentle tapping at the door.

"Yeah?"

"Can I come in?" Flynn poked his head into the room. "Your mum said it was okay for me to come up, I hope you don't mind."

"I'm so glad you're here!" Jessa climbed from her foetal position and greeted him with a hug.

"First things first," he said. "I told your mum I came here to give you your homework from the rest of the day. And I'm a man of my word, so here you go," he handed her a selection of printed homework assignments.

"What! We got homework for Music *and* Religious Theory?"

"You missed a thrilling afternoon," he said dryly.

Jessa slapped the papers down onto her desk and slumped herself back onto the duvet, tapping it to welcome Flynn to lie down next to her. He pushed off his shoes and slid onto the bed, facing her.

"Mr Fletcher told us what happened."

Jessa burst into tears. She'd been holding it back all day, telling herself that she was brave and strong, but in the kind and gentle presence of Flynn Howard, Jessa's true feelings came pouring out.

"Hey…" he said, and stroked her back soothingly as she bawled, face down into her pillow. He said nothing else. He just let her cry.

"I'm sorry," she sniffed and blinked away the last of the tears from her red eyes.

"Don't be."

"Flynn, it was awful."

"I can only imagine. Do you want to talk about it more?"

"No, not really. Mr Fletcher told you the whole thing?"

"Pretty much. Maggie got all the details from him."

"Of course she did."

"Mr Fletcher spoke very highly of you."

"What do you mean?"

"He said your intuition is something he's never seen before. Apparently, he's never heard of someone being able to connect and share a memory like that. He told me that privately, though."

"Why?" Jessa propped up her head on her hand. Flynn mirrored her.

"Because he wanted me to talk to you about something."

"Okay?"

"He thinks you could be an asset to the investigation."

"Aren't I already an asset to the investigation? He already took me out on a... I don't know, whatever you want to call it. A mission? A meeting? And he took us all to see that man. Well, he didn't take us exactly, but he let us help when we were there."

"His idea is for us to join the Agency."

"Are you kidding?"

Flynn shook his head.

"Why did he want you to talk to me about this? Why wouldn't he ask me himself?"

"Because he thought you'd be more honest with me. And because you need to take some time and think about it." She tried to interrupt but he continued, "Jess, it happened again. Another kid got attacked last night. It's getting worse and the Agency is desperate. Mr Fletcher believes that somehow we can help. But it's potentially dangerous, and has to be kept completely secret. We'd all be keeping it from our families, from everyone at school. It's a big commitment. So yeah, the others don't know about this yet, but if you're in, it's offered to all of us. But without you, we're all out and this conversation stays between the two of us. Think about it."

Flynn said his goodbye and Jessa's ears followed the sound of his departure from the house.

You have to join the Agency.
You have to stop this.

But how do you stop something when you can't even make sense of it? Why are they attacking school children? Who are these men? What do they want?

You can find out.

Why me?

Someone has to figure it out. Why not you? Your friends are on your side. Mr Fletcher is on your side. Join the Agency and help them bring him down.

Do you feel that burning deep down inside of you? Let it show you what you can do.

Join the Agency.

Get Lynch.

15th September 1985

I'm thrilled. I recruited two new followers this week. Silas is very pleased.

A few of the followers are "squatters." I hadn't heard of this term before, but apparently, it's when people live in places they don't own, and they don't pay for it. It's quite revolutionary. Frog and Marx took Silas and me to stay at the warehouse they squat in. I think it'll get cold in winter, but it's fine for the time being. They asked if Silas and I were romantically linked. I said no, of course, but Silas said nothing at all. It was awkward. In some way I find him alluring, but I don't think we'd ever be in a position to go steady. He's not that type of man.

I've been helping him train. We found an old cart with wheels, and I helped him practice his telekinesis by putting different weighted objects on it. He's strong enough to push me on it! He spends a lot of his time in open-mind, however. Some days he completely forgets to eat. At least I'm here to help him with things like that.

We've also begun preparations for the Yield. There are eleven volunteers so far, so he only needs nine more. I did ask him how he'd feel if I volunteered, and he said he'd prefer if I didn't. I would be lying if I said I wasn't frightened at the prospect, but Silas insists that when the ceremony takes place and the volunteers donate their life to him, they will feel the most enthralling ecstasy, and a part of me is intrigued by that prospect.

I'm also happy to report that the plant project is going swimmingly.

I've continued to keep detailed notes, so I'll make sure to do some official write-ups in my next few entries. In short, however, all of the seed types subjected to Silas' influences have sprouted and grown faster than the control seeds. After the Yield, Silas says he's planning to train us and teach us those skills. He's convinced that growth influence is one of the things that the public will be most interested in.

Anyway, I have to go now because some of the other female followers and I have formed a clairvoyance group and we have a meeting scheduled for this evening.

I'll write more soon.

Lissy

27

It felt like a lifetime before Saturday finally arrived and the five students were able to attend their first meeting with the Agency. Jessa thought the room seemed quite different from the inside. It was definitely more cramped, although that might have been down to the addition of the five teenagers, squeezed together in a row on one end of the table.

"I can say with certainty, that Jessa has a level of parapsychological ability that I've never seen before," Hugo Fletcher addressed the group, who mostly continued staring at Jessa. "In fact, I've been monitoring the parabilities of all these kids, and they're all above-average in their respective skills."

None of the students knew quite what he was referring to at this point, but they all remained still and quiet, letting him speak.

"Not only that, but their interest in this investigation is unparalleled, and I think that could be a huge benefit to us."

"Hugo, are you really suggesting," a shiny-headed man began, "that the person behind these acts is someone who has, in a manner of speaking, risen from the dead, and now because some kid had an "intuition," that we should actually consider it an actual line of enquiry?" Ridicule oozed from his every word.

"Actually, Howard," Mr Fletcher responded forcefully, "I'm not suggesting that Silas Lynch has, in any manner of speaking, 'risen from the dead.' What I am suggesting is that he's alive and never died at all, a theory which you can see in the report that I've printed for you, has a lot of solid evidence. Furthermore, yes, a "kid" had an intuition, but I've also just told you that she has an incredible level of ability. We use other Agency members' parabilities to our advantage, so I don't see why we should treat these people any differently based on their age."

Jessa felt her mouth turning up into a smug smile at Mr Fletcher's rebuttal. The bald man called Howard was still contorting his face into an almost comical crumple of stubbornness, but he did turn his gaze to the little folder in front of him.

Dr Mortlock sat stock still, looking at the front of her folder. At school it was difficult to read anything of the headteacher's expression; she was usually so impassive and stoic. But in the stark strangeness of the Agency meeting, she was a picture of emotion. Sadness, confusion and worry painted across her face, subtle as watercolour but definitely there.

"Silas Lynch," she said quietly as she opened the folder to the first page.

"Yes, Felicia," Hugo Fletcher nodded. "I know it sounds farfetched, but there really is a good amount of evidence to suggest that he escaped death. I haven't quite worked out how, but if we look into it more, I think we can figure it out. "

The skin on Dr Mortlock's forehead puckered. She cleared her throat and turned her gaze downward to read the material Hugo Fletcher had provided for them.

"So what exactly are you proposing here, Hugo?" said Howard.

"A full-scale investigation into Silas Lynch," he replied calmly.

"Won't happen," said the smooth voice of an older man. "I trust your judgment on this, Hugo, and your suggestion is worth looking into. But unfortunately, this isn't enough tangible evidence to use as the basis for a full investigation."

"John's right, Hugo," said an older lady with long curly hair, gesturing to the man who just spoke. Jessa recognised her voice. "This just isn't enough to use all our resources on. John and Matt have been using their intel to compare official investigations with ours, and—"

"And they haven't found anything, Sue!" Hugo Fletcher said strongly. "The authorities don't know anything! I fully appreciate the risks John and

Matt take to aid our investigation, but whatever results we've had so far just haven't been enough!"

"No disrespect, Hugo," said a forty-something-year-old man wearing a too-old-for-him jumper, "but how can we trust these kids not to go blabbering around."

"Because these are Winsbury students, Special Agent Allerton," Dr Mortlock said sternly. "Winsbury students do not simply blabber around. If Mr Fletcher is proposing the students as legitimate Agents in this investigation, then he has my support."

"With or without the student Agents, I still can't devote all our time and energy to Silas Lynch as a suspect. And that's final." John placed his palms down onto the table.

"Well then I request permission for a sub-team," Hugo Fletcher proposed. "I'll lead the students in our own self-directed research, and anyone else who wants to join, is welcome to do so."

"I'd be interested to join a sub-team on this," said a lady with a cropped hairstyle. She hadn't yet spoken in the meeting, but it turned out that she had a soft voice with a northern accent. Jessa thought her rather pretty, in a tomboyish sort of way.

"Thank you, Rachel," Hugo smiled.

"And I, too, stand with Winsbury," said Dr Mortlock.

John scrutinised Jessa through his squinched eyes. "I recognise the interest of a sub-team, but I still have my concerns." He looked at each of the teenagers, one by one. "Even with Felicia vouching for the sincerity of her students, how can we definitively know they're trustworthy enough to be involved?"

"John, if I may—"

"Hear me out, please, Hugo. Because it's not just a case of them— accidentally or otherwise—giving away information about the Agency's existence; my concern lies in the personal repercussions that might occur in that instance. We can't risk the reputations of our high profile members, or those of us who work in public services, for example. If those members get found out, it could mean losing everything."

"John, please," Hugo leaned forward in his seat, his hands clasped together on the table. "I'd like all of you to consider for a moment how long we've known each other. The newest member of this branch is Rachel, and even she has been involved for a year now, so I'd like to think we know each other quite well. Have I ever done anything—and I mean, anything—to make you doubt my allegiance or my passion for our service?"

John pursed his lips.

"So on what basis do you think I would invite anyone to the Agency if I thought their involvement would have any negative impact?"

The man called Howard shook his head. The fluorescent light bounced off his scalp. "It's not you, Hugo, it's just—"

"Come on!" Hugo slammed his fist lightly on the table. "You know full well that the nature of Agency membership is by invitation. These five people—"

"—children."

"Give it a rest, Howard. These people are here at my request because I solemnly believe they would be an asset to the Agency."

"Your belief isn't based on anything!" Howard sprayed a light sprinkling of saliva onto the table. He wiped his mouth with the back of his hand. "In the history of the Agency, we've never invited someone under the age of 18."

Hugo leaned into his backrest and rubbed his face.

"There is a first time for everything, Howard," said the apparently most subdued member of the group, a man with bright white hair, whose age was impossible to tell.

"Exactly, Henrik," said Hugo. "Thank you."

"Are you finished in your proposal, Hugo?" asked John.

Hugo responded with an exasperated shrug. "There's probably nothing else I can say to convince anyone who disagrees with me. It's all in the folder."

"Then I advise everyone to take a moment to look over the document Hugo has prepared for us."

The seven other adults flipped through the pages before them. Dr Mortlock finished with her paperwork first and placed it neatly back onto the table. Jessa kept her eyes on Howard, who read each page noisily, his lips making balmy smacks as he mouthed the words. He had fingermarks on his glasses and coffee stains on his teeth. He tutted again.

"Is everyone finished?" John asked the group.

They all returned their papers to the table.

"Then, by Agency tradition, it's my duty as branch director to request of you all your vote: in favour of, or in opposition to, the invitation of membership to the following: Jessamine Baxter, Flynn Howard, Annora Huff, Margaret Turner, and Tonia Pitts.

Felicia, your response?"

"Unquestionably in favour."

"Rachel?"

"In favour."

"Matt?"

"In favour."

"Howard?"

"Strongly opposed."

"Henrik?"

"I have my doubts, but I trust Hugo. In favour."

"Sue?"

"In favour."

"And I, John Cane, vote in favour. So by a vote of seven to one, the invitation is extended to all of you.

By the end of this meeting, we request that you submit to us your decision. If you decide you don't wish to partake, you'll be free to go, and our only request is that you keep all of your involvement so far to yourself and never speak of it again, to anyone. We hope that in the event of your parting ways with us that you respect the other members enough to protect them with your silence.

If you agree to membership, you'll be fully welcomed into the Agency and will be welcome at all branch meetings. I ask of your petitioner Hugo Fletcher and your headteacher Dr Mortlock, to take responsibility for keeping in contact with you regarding any relevant updates.

Now we turn our attention to you and we ask, do you have any questions?"

28

"What *is* the Agency?" said Maggie.

"The Agency is an independent security service," replied Detective John Cane.

"Independent from what?" said Flynn.

"From any other security service," said Hugo Fletcher. "When you think of national security, you usually think of the police or MI5. The Agency operates outside of any of those."

"So who runs it?" said Tonia.

"It was designed to be a self-maintaining organisation," said Rachel. "Do you know the term 'grassroots'? Because that's how I think of the Agency. It's a collection of individuals using their own experience and influence, coming together for a greater cause."

"But there has to be someone in charge?" Tonia asked again.

"Well, each branch has a director. Ours is John, here. Overseeing the whole thing is the Founder, but nobody knows who that is."

"What do you mean you don't know?"

"For the safety of the Founder and the Agency, the Founder remains anonymous. One of the rules of the Agency is that members are forbidden to speak of any contact the Founder makes with them."

"So the Founder chose the first members, and now you can all invite people?" Annora said thoughtfully.

"In a manner of speaking, yes," nodded Dr Mortlock. "But someone must be a participating member for years before their Request to Invitation is granted."

"Who are the members?" asked Flynn. "I mean, what does everyone do for a living?"

"Many work in government and national security," said Matt. "But we have plenty of doctors, teachers, computer scientists, engineers, artists; I could go on. Members are from all walks of life."

"And it's not just in London?" said Annora.

"Certainly not," replied Dr Mortlock. "There are branches across the whole United Kingdom. We have regular contact with the European division, the USA division. The Agency is worldwide, because security is a ubiquitous concern."

"I'm not quite following what you mean by 'security'," said Maggie.

"We specialise in parapsych security," said Hugo. "The government has protocols in place that aim to protect all of the population from criminal activity, without regard for whether the perpetrators or the victims are parapsychs or laterals. And it's a great theory, that everybody should be treated equally, but unfortunately, there are instances where parapsychs have used their abilities for ill, and that's where we come in."

"One aim of the Agency is to find and bring to justice parapsych felons," said Matt.

"But one of the Four Laws says that parapsychs cannot use their abilities if the action violates legislation," Maggie pointed out.

"The Laws do say that, Maggie, but some people do violate those rules," said Mr Fletcher. "Unfortunately, it's come to light in modern history that the Laws are inherently flawed. Not just the main Four Laws that everyone knows, but all the sub-sections and additional parts that contribute to the legislation. There's a lot of problems, and some people figured out how to use those problems to their own advantage."

"What happens to those people?" asked Tonia. "Do they go to jail?"

"Sometimes," he said. "But it's important to realise that there's no easy way to prove when someone uses their abilities. The Agency is constantly utilising the skills and advanced parabilities of its members, to find new ways to monitor illegal behaviours."

"Jessa, you've been very quiet," he said gently. "Is there anything you'd like to say?" She looked at him and he smiled sympathetically. "I know it's a lot to take in, but please feel free to ask anything. This is a safe place for your questions."

"I'm just…" she cleared her throat, "thinking."

"I don't understand," Annora said sweetly. "So there are parapsychs out there who are using their abilities to do bad things? They're criminals?"

"In short, yes," said Dr Mortlock.

"Why can't the police catch them?"

"Sometimes they do."

"But sometimes they don't?"

"I'm sorry to say, but yes, sometimes they don't. And that's what we're here for," Hugo Fletcher continued. "The majority of parapsychs stick to the law. In fact, most parapsychs' abilities aren't even strong enough to harm someone. Statistically speaking, more violent crimes are committed by laterals, and the parapsychs who do commit crimes don't do it using their abilities. Still, there are exceptions to the rule. And it pains me to have to tell you this, but those are the ones that can create the most harm. That's what we at the Agency try to combat."

"So the Agency is here to protect people from bad parapsychs," said Jessa.

"And to protect the name of good parapsychs," he added.

"But wait," Maggie said. "Why doesn't anyone know about this? If it's possible to use parapsychism to do horrible things, then why aren't people being educated differently? Why isn't anyone changing the law? Why is it a secret?"

Mr Fletcher frowned as though reluctant to speak. "Parapsychism is accepted all over the world, but we are still the minority. Can you imagine what could happen if laterals knew that parapsychs were able to use their abilities to hurt them? And then, that it might be possible for the criminal to go undiscovered? People fear what they don't understand. And laterals may accept parapsychs now, but if it got out that there are already parapsychs out there taking advantage of laterals… what do you think would happen?"

The silence in the room answered for them.

The Agency

Agent Contract

In becoming a Member of the Agency, you agree to keep undisclosed:

1. Your status as Member.
2. The status of other Members.
3. Previous, present or past Agency activity.
4. Any objectives of Agents.

You agree to:

Join in the Agency's ongoing enterprise in protecting innocents from parapsychs who would abuse their abilities.

Commit to the Agency's view that parapsychs who consciously use their parapsychological abilities unlawfully will be brought to prosecution.

Remain true to the Agency's belief that Members may use their parapsychological ability extralegally in the name of the greater good.

You acknowledge that you may submit written resignation from Membership at any time.

In the event of your resignation, you agree for the Agency to permanently keep a record of your involvement. Under Agency rules, evidence of your Membership will never be disclosed.

As we, the Agency, hold our trust in you, your signature is your bond that you hereby subscribe to Membership.

Signed:

....

29

"Morning, love!"

"Mrgh," came Jessa's grumpy reply.

"Audrey's here, and we're going shopping! Thought you might want to come along for a girls' day out."

Jessa rolled over onto her back and opened her mouth wide in the kind of gigantic yawn that sent a ringing sound through her ears.

"All right," she said, realising that her mother must have been pretty excited about a shopping day to be up, dressed and made-up at 10 am on a Sunday. "Gimme a few minutes to get dressed."

"Woo!" Mrs Baxter danced out of the room.

Jessa pushed herself into a seat, letting her legs dangle over the edge of the bed, and blinked away the blur from her tired eyes. As she became more awake, the events from the previous day trickled in and filled the pit of her stomach with a heavy dread. She suddenly wished she'd declined the offer to go shopping.

"Are you ready, Jessa?" Mrs Baxter called from downstairs.

"Uhhh, almost…" she lied, looking down at her pyjamas.

§

Her mother had always had an affinity with commercialism, but the shopping bug had never really taken a hold in Jessa. Even Audrey, who was the most sensible—and the most boring—person Jessa could think of, would get excited about spending money on something new and fabulous.

"Okie dokie!" Mrs Baxter clasped her hands together excitedly. "We should start in the department stores, because I have some brilliant vouchers I can spend at Selfridges. Then we can stop for some lunch, and then hit the shoe shops and smaller clothes shops. Oh perfect, here's the air shuttle."

The familiar beep of the mall shuttle cleared the distracted shoppers from their meandering on the track marks on the ground. The gently hovering fifteen-foot pod lowered itself flush against the ground, and the entire side walls lifted up and into the ceiling, allowing passengers in and out from both sides. A young couple bustled out, loaded up with a surprising bulk of shopping bags considering the mall had only been open for about two hours.

Mrs Baxter led Jessa and Audrey into the front row of the shuttle. A few moments later, the cautionary announcement informed the passengers of the doors closing, and the air shuttle lifted a few inches from the ground once more and continued on its way, following the track on the ground below that lit up to remind any absent-minded shoppers to clear the route.

"Shall we ride just to the other end or to the top floor as well?" Audrey asked.

"To the top!" Mrs Baxter replied without a thought. Jessa drowsed next to her, clutching a to-go cup of tea that she insisted on getting from the cafe on the way in.

The hovering air shuttle travelled the one and a half miles smoothly down the centre of the mall, passing on the left the other air shuttle zipping in the opposite direction. Upon reaching the end, it opened up and let off two passengers, then closed again.

The pod turned 90 degrees so its longest side was against the wall, then zoomed upwards like an elevator, journeying up the five storeys of the mall before coming to rest at the top floor.

"Oh perfect, the teen section is up here. What do you think, Jessa? Shall we look for some new school clothes?" Mrs Baxter nudged her youngest daughter.

"Okay," Jessa smiled, trying not to seem disinterested. "But maybe not here, this shop's a bit expensive."

"It's a little on the pricier side, but that's okay. To be honest, I got a little bonus at work recently, and Daddy agrees it would be nice to spend it by spoiling my girls." She wrapped each of her arms around her daughters and entered the store.

"This is perfect for Jessa!" Audrey held up a blue and white sun dress.

Jessa's eyes widened. "Are you kidding?"

"No, it would look adorable on you!" her older sister defended. Jessa shook her head, then grabbed the dress from her sister to put it back on the rack.

"What about this one?" Audrey tried a second dress. "It's got this gorgeous sunflower print on the front."

"Yeah and if you bring that thing near me it'll have my vomit on the front."

"Jessa, please don't be vulgar," said Mrs Baxter. "Why don't you just try something on?" Her left arm bulged with a slew of clothing while her right hand flipped and skipped from rack to rack.

Jessa shrugged. Despite the enthusiasm from her mother and sister and their exclamations of items that would look "adorable" or "lovely" or "flattering," Jessa just couldn't get excited about clothes.

Three stores later, and Jessa had picked out one item just to placate her family.

"Are you sure you wouldn't prefer something more feminine?" her mother asked when Jessa selected the dark red sweatshirt with a white old-fashioned bicycle printed on the print. "Or would you at least like to get one that's not so baggy?"

"I want it baggy," she replied.

"I don't understand you young girls these days," Mrs Baxter said.

Jessa sat cross-legged on the large beanbag stool in the centre of the dressing room while her mother and sister disappeared into adjacent cubicles to try things on. She waited quietly, vacantly picking at the frayed edge of the bottom of her jeans, when a very familiar voice yelled from another cubicle

"Ugh, this is hideous!" the voice said. "Bring me another!"

"Yes, Miss Graves!" a nervous shop assistant said before scurrying off.

"What's taking so long?" the impatient voice of Cecily Graves berated to no-one, just seconds after she had dismissed her apparent helper.

The pink-cheeked young woman returned with two black dresses.

"H-here you go, Miss Graves," she stammered. The door opened a crack and Cecily's outstretched hand grabbed the dresses and snatched them inside.

"Really, Elaine," Cecily sneered loudly over the walls of her cubicle, "I sincerely hope my father isn't paying you extra for this, considering all the atrocities you've been bringing me today."

The woman called Elaine stared at the ground.

"Ohhh," Cecily swooned. "Oh yes, now this is more like it. All right, I'm coming out."

Jessa panicked. She couldn't think of anything less enjoyable than running into Cecily Graves in a clothing store. Jumping up, Jessa looked around for an open cubicle to hide in, but it was a small dressing room, and they all appeared to be taken.

Her mother and Audrey were chatting away over their shared cubicle wall, giving each other a second-by-second rundown of the clothes they were trying on.

Jessa pressed her face up against her mother's cubicle door and whispered as inconspicuously as she could.

"Mum! Mum, let me in! Mum! Hello?"

Unfortunately, Mrs Baxter was preoccupied with her positively Byzantine chronicle of some beige Capris that she couldn't fasten, and she couldn't hear her daughter's plea for help.

Jessa darted toward the exit, but it was a moment too late.

"Jessa Baxter?"

"Hi, Cecily…" Jessa turned back around slowly.

"What are you doing in here?"

"Just here with my mum and sister," Jessa gestured toward the other end of the dressing room.

"That's a surprise. I didn't know your family could afford to shop somewhere like this."

Jessa rolled her eyes. "Yep. Shocker."

Cecily caught a glimpse of herself in the large mirror on the dressing room wall and quickly lost interest in taunting Jessa.

The bandage-style dress hugged her body provocatively. She paraded up and down the dressing room like a model in a fashion show, teetering on her tiptoes, her hips swinging, ample and pendulumlike.

An older woman exited her cubicle to look at herself in the large mirror too, and Cecily immediately took advantage of her potential new viewer.

"I'm just not sure," she hammed. "I feel like it makes my waist look big. Does it make my waist look big? Do I look fat?"

"Not at all," the woman took the bait. "You look like a celebrity!"

"Oh, really!" Cecily schmaltzed. "That is so kind. And same to you. That long skirt is really slimming on you. And I find it totally cool that you're comfortable enough at your age to wear a top that revealing."

The lady quickly withdrew back into her cubicle.

"I'll take it," Cecily said. "Elaine, charge this to Daddy's card. In fact, I want to wear it home."

Elaine nodded and stepped forward to remove the electronic tag from the back of the dress. Cecily pulled on some very expensive-looking boots and a leather jacket and sauntered out of the dressing room.

Jessa breathed a sigh of relief.

Mrs Baxter and Audrey approached and handed to the assistant everything they had tried on.

"No good?" the tired-looking shop worker asked.

"Not today, thanks," Mrs Baxter smiled back at her.

"Oh my goodness, Jessa! Hi!" Cecily flittered over to the Baxter ladies and leaned in to give Jessa a hug. "It's so nice to see you!" she said exaggeratedly. Jessa stood with her arms planted by her sides, refusing to return the hug.

She wondered if Cecily had deliberately waited for them to exit the changing room.

"Hi, I'm Cecily!" she said loudly, shaking hands with Mrs Baxter and Audrey. "I'm one of Jessa's school friends—we're in the same class."

"How lovely," Mrs Baxter beamed. "I'm surprised we haven't met before. Jessa, you should invite Cecily over for dinner sometime."

"Mmhmm," Jessa squinted a glare at Cecily.

"Mrs Baxter, I would simply love to come over for dinner," she smiled a big, gleaming, toothy smile.

"Wonderful, I'll let you and Jessa arrange that, but honestly dear, feel free to come over any day. Are you here alone? Would you like to shop with us? We're having a girls' day out."

"You know what, that does sound super," Cecily squeezed the top of Jessa's arm, "but I'm actually here with two of my father's staff."

"His staff?" Mrs Baxter enquired.

"Yes, Daddy has a full-time driver and personal assistant on staff, so they're with me today while I enjoy a little retail therapy. Don't get me wrong—we're not that privileged. This is a rare treat. It's Daddy's way of rewarding me for getting good grades this year." She flashed her bleach-white smile again.

"Well, I say…" an embarrassed pink flushed over Mrs Baxter's face.

"Anyway, I'd better be off. Glen and Mark are waiting for me outside. Jessa, again, it was so good to see you," she embraced Jessa once more. She smelled like vanilla and smoke. "And it was lovely to meet both of you."

She shook the hands of Jessa's family once more before strolling confidently from the store. Jessa waited until Cecily was out of sight and out of earshot.

"She is not coming over for dinner."

"What's wrong, I thought she's your friend?" said Mrs Baxter, tidying a wayward curl from Jessa's head and tucking it gently in among the others.

"Yeah right! She's an evil witch, is what she is."

"Jessa, come on."

"I'm not kidding, Mum. If I never saw Cecily Graves again, it wouldn't be the worst thing."

"Jessa, be nice!" Audrey criticised.

"No way. She's the worst. The *worst.*"

"You girls these days," Mrs Baxter rolled her eyes.

As they walked back toward the car, Jessa couldn't shake the prickling feeling that she was being watched. She tried to casually look from side to side, scanning for anyone looking in their direction.

Then suddenly came the sensation that she'd felt once before. The feeling of burning in the tips of her fingers.

She turned back and saw Cecily standing on the other side of the car park. She stood perfectly still, the tails of her long black hair whipping against her jacket, and in her hand was a lighter, its flame lightly flickering in the wind.

Cecily turned away, summoning two men to join her. And as the three of them walked toward a very shiny black car with tinted windows, Jessa's eyes widened as she looked closer at Cecily's companions: two men in long dark coats.

30

"Jessa?! What are you doing here?" said Flynn. Jessa propped herself up on the door frame and tried to catch her breath. "Did you run here? What's wrong?"

"Cecily…" She exhaled deep and slow. "I saw her with the two men. I think she's involved with Silas Lynch."

"Come inside."

In the stairway up to Flynn's flat, Jessa could smell grease from the chip shop on the ground floor, but as soon as she entered the living room, the fatty smell was overridden by a very pleasant herbal one.

"Sorry for the mess, I was just doing some ironing." There were bundles of clothes along the sofa seat. He quickly pulled them into one large pile and loaded them back into the basket. "Here, sit down."

"I can't believe I've never been to your flat before."

He looked embarrassed. "It's not that nice, so I don't really invite people over."

"Is your mum at work?"

"Yeah."

Jessa sank much further into the sofa than she expected but found it perfectly comfortable. She looked around at walls that were covered in photographs of Flynn throughout his life. It reminded her of Francis Jackson's house, pictures upon pictures, memories upon paper, old-fashioned and warm.

She gratefully took from him a chipped ceramic mug steaming with hot coffee. She hadn't even realised how cold her hands were until her fingers began to tingle from being warmed up.

"You have so many photographs."

"Oh, yeah. My mum couldn't afford a regular camera so when I was a baby she got one of those old ones where you have to put a film in and then get them printed. We still have it, actually. I told her we should save up for a normal one and just use the little chip to put in the digital frames, but she says she likes doing it this way. The photos don't look as clear, though."

"I think they look great. My grandparents had a camera like that when I was little. But now, whenever we take photos, we always take a few shots and then choose the best one. These pictures look different. You can tell they capture really special moments." Her gaze stopped on what appeared to be the most recent image. It showed Flynn's mum with her arm around her son and a huge smile on her face, as Flynn held up his acceptance letter to the Winsbury School of Parapsychology.

"So tell me about these men that you saw," said Flynn.

"They were tall, wearing dark coats, just like Mr Jackson said, and just like I saw in the vision of Annora." She ended her sentence definitively. Flynn waited for more, but it didn't come.

"Is that it?" he said.

"Well, yeah."

"So you didn't see their faces?"

"No."

"And they weren't doing anything suspicious?"

"They were with Cecily Graves."

"Jess."

"What? We know her family is rich and elitist, and it's totally reasonable to imagine they could be involved with a crazy guy who thinks parapsychs are superior to laterals. Remember what she said to Maggie that time?"

"Jessa, do you remember what the detective at the Agency said? Evidence has to be real and tangible. Those men could be anyone."

"I am just remembering, she did say she was with two of her dad's staff.

But maybe…"

"No. You need to stop. You have to be careful about these things."

"What do you mean?"

"I mean you have to take care of yourself."

"What are you talking about?"

"Since all this started, you've just been a bit different, that's all."

"Different how?"

"I don't know. Tired. Distracted."

She thought nobody had noticed.

"I've been finding it hard to sleep, but other than that I'm fine."

"Well, I know you got in trouble with Mrs Dusto for not handing in your geography homework, and I noticed on your French test you got a D—"

"Okay, wait a minute," she interrupted. "Firstly, Mrs Dusto can shut up because geography is rubbish anyway, and secondly, I'm just not very good at French. It has nothing to do with all of this."

"Really? Because you used to get mostly Bs and even a few As. Look, I'm not judging."

"It sounds like you are," she sulked.

"I promise I'm not. I just want you to be all right. We're in this Silas Lynch business together, so I don't want you to feel like you're taking on more than you have to. And if you need help with school stuff, you just need to ask."

"I'm sorry."

"It's okay," his mouth turned up gently. "Where did you see Cecily, anyway?"

"At the mall."

"What were you doing at the mall?"

"My mum and sister wanted a girls' day out shopping."

"Oh yay, you love shopping!"

"Shut up!" she playfully pushed his leg with her foot.

"So anyway," he said, changing the subject. "I've been thinking. I'm not sure how this stuff works, but there has to be footage from surveillance cameras on the streets. So maybe if there's a way we can get video from the night any of the three victims went missing, maybe we can find the moment they were attacked and see exactly what happened."

"That's a good idea! We should ask Maggie tomorrow. She's good at the computer stuff, so maybe she'll know of a way to do that."

Flynn clicked on the television and flipped through some of the channels.

"Do you watch much TV?" he asked Jessa.

"Not regular TV. Mostly just subs. You?"

"Not a lot. But we don't have any subs. Mum doesn't think we have enough spare time to make it worth paying the subscriptions."

"Yeah, it's not cheap. My dad's obsessed with all those detective dramas, and he reckons he has to get his money's worth. So basically he just watches TV every second he's home."

"That's the thing, isn't it? If you pay for the subscription, then you feel like you have to make the most of it. So we just have normal telly and barely watch it because it's all adverts."

"Oh wait, go back! That was Cecily's dad."

"His moustache looks weird."

"He's so gross. Unmute it, let's see what he's saying."

"*...the sheer volume of donations that the party has received tells me that people are indeed ready for a new way of thinking. It's my view that Prime Minister Linden has been somewhat indoctrinated by these so-called liberals, enough so that he's not truly following through with the ideals he originally set out to pursue. My vision is for the PIP to bring those values to the forefront of society. Our goal is a modern Britain. One that strives for economic stability, true justice, and of course, one that gives a much more appropriate application of commendation to the parapsych population. Parapsychism is the evolution of humanity, and the PIP is the evolution of politics—*"

"Shall we see what else is on?"

"Please."

31

Maggie's face lit up.

"I've never used Public Access Surveillance before, but I'm sure I could figure it out," she gabbed. "I'm surprised you two even know about the P.A.S Act!"

"Oh, yeah… of course." Jessa shrugged at Flynn, who had clearly never heard of it either. Jessa was just relieved that Maggie knew a way to make Flynn's idea a reality.

"I can investigate on the computer tonight. I'll get back to you tomorrow. But perhaps more importantly, did you all get the email notification about end-of-year exams?"

"I'm sorry, did you just say that exams are more important?" Jessa gibed.

"Jessa, some of us still want to get good grades," Maggie said pointedly.

"I haven't checked my email for a few days, so I didn't see anything," Annora reached into the bag of crisps that she and Tonia were sharing. "But I thought exams aren't until May?"

"Yes, and it's already March!" Maggie exclaimed. "Don't tell me none of you have started revising yet?" She looked around the lunch table at her four friends, who all said nothing. "Have you even made a revision schedule?" Maggie's eyebrows practically relocated two inches north of her eyes.

Jessa looked sideways at Flynn, who was trying not to laugh, but his sideways smile was creeping further and further up his lips. Jessa couldn't save herself from doing the same, which tipped Flynn over the edge as he and Jessa snorted with laughter at Maggie's expense.

"Having fun in our geek squad meeting today, are we?" Cecily sneered, framed by Devi Kapoor and Amelia Waters.

"Yes, thanks for your concern," Annora retorted.

Cecily kept her eyes locked on Jessa. Her thumb flicked at the top of a lighter, inviting the flame to lick upward seductively. After a few seconds, Jessa felt the familiar heat taunting the skin of her palms.

Cecily turned, swishing her long black hair over her shoulders.

"Come on, ladies," she instructed, and the other two followed.

"Ugh," Jessa shuddered noticeably.

"You okay?" said Flynn.

"Yeah," said Jessa. "She just… keeps doing this thing to me."

"What do you mean?" Maggie leaned forward. Her eyebrows had migrated back down south.

"She does this thing where she makes my hands burn."

"Are you serious?" asked Tonia. "She's been flame-trolling you?"

"Yeah," Jessa said sheepishly, noticing Maggie's eyes gleaming with concern.

"Man, that's a dirty trick," Tonia shook her head.

"I cannot believe you kept that from us!" Maggie tried and failed to keep her voice down. "And I can't believe you'd let her get away with that, Jessa! That behaviour is completely unacceptable!"

"How long has it been happening?" Flynn said calmly.

"A few times. The first was in that parapsych skills lesson with the candles."

"We should tell Mr Fletcher immediately," Maggie folded her arms. "I can't imagine why you kept this to yourself."

"I didn't think it was that big a deal—I just thought she was being a bitch. And I don't want to tell Mr Fletcher."

Maggie frowned. "Cecily shouldn't be allowed to get away with this. Why don't you want to tell?"

"I was hoping to just keep it between us and Cecily."

Maggie's face tightened. "Why is your instinct always to fight alone? Teachers have authority here, Jessa, not you. Why can't you let them handle it?"

Jessa's eyes narrowed at Maggie.

She doesn't understand.

"I mean, really, Jessa," Maggie continued. "This is a prime example of bullying, and it's not up to you to teach Cecily a lesson. Especially after what she did to you at the museum."

She thinks she knows.

She has no idea.

"We could easily go to Mr Fletcher or Dr Mortlock and get Cecily expelled for the things she's done and said to you."

I don't care how irrational they think I am. I know what I saw.

If Cecily is involved with Silas Lynch, it's better to keep her around.

Keep your enemies close, they say.

Jessa looked at Flynn and remembered their conversation at his flat. How quickly he'd dismissed her idea that Cecily could be connected to Silas. How he'd told her to stop.

Stop what? Stop trying to help? Stop trying to solve a crime? Do they just have no faith in me whatsoever?

Wait. Just breathe.

Keep quiet.

Be cool.

"You're right, Mags," Jessa said. "I'll think about telling a teacher."

Maggie's hands visibly relaxed.

"But I'll do it by myself. Don't worry."

32

Jessa hurried into the cafeteria to see Maggie's books sprawled across the table as she fit in some early morning revision between spoonfuls of shredded wheat and sips of orange juice. Annora bustled in next, cheeks flushed with pink and her gentle mouth exclaiming apologies for her tardiness. Then Tonia and Flynn walked in casually, trying much too hard to make it look like them walking in together was merely a coincidence.

"Thanks for coming in early, everyone. I wanted to talk to you about the video surveillance idea that Jessa and Flynn had yesterday. I've been looking into it, and it's definitely possible to access all the footage. But the problem is, there are roughly half a million CCTV cameras in London. There's also no eye-witness accounts of Emmeline on her way home, which is usually what the police use to start a search like this.

I checked Emmeline Victor's address, and it seems that her walk home from school was about a mile or so. And we don't know which route she would take, so we'd have to just take a chance on different files to view. I narrowed the results down to within a ten-mile radius of the school, but that still leaves us with close to a couple of thousand video files."

They all waited for a solution, but it didn't come. Maggie handed out a wad of paperwork to each of them.

"What's this?" Flynn asked, thumbing through the pile handed to him.

"I divided the number of video files by five, which gives us about 370 each. In these papers are instructions on how to access the selection of files that I've allocated to you. You just type the web address, then find the day we need. Then you just hit the play button and fast forward to the time we think Emmeline would have been walking home. Each viewing should be about twenty minutes. I don't recommend watching it on fast-forward, because we need to be diligent about this. By my calculation, if we each work through all of these in our spare time, it's possible to be done in about a month."

"A month?!" Jessa exploded.

"If we're lucky," Maggie said, handing out another sheet of paper to everyone. "I also printed out copies of my revision schedule for everyone. In case you didn't already have one."

"How does she have time to do all this?" Flynn muttered under his breath.

"Is there really no way to do this quicker?" Jessa griped.

"Not that I can see," Maggie answered. "If we're going try and find out exactly what happened to Emmeline, this is the only way that makes any logical sense. It might even turn out that none of the cameras managed to capture the moment she was attacked."

"But we won't know until we look," said Annora.

"Exactly. It's all we have right now."

§

The quiet murmur of chitchat pervaded Mrs Sullivan's English room.

"We're allowed to discuss, you know," Maggie said quietly to Jessa, setting her poetry book face down on the table to hold its place.

"I know," she didn't look up.

"What's wrong?"

"Nothing, I'm just working."

"Jessa."

"What?"

"Are you mad at me?"

"No."

"You've barely spoken to me since this morning. You look really annoyed."

"I'm not annoyed at you, I'm just annoyed. I can't believe it's going to take us so long to look at all those videos."

"Oh. Yeah. I'm sorry about that. It's a huge project, though, and we spend so much of our time with school and homework, I just don't see any way we can get it done quicker."

Jessa checked Mrs Sullivan wasn't behind her. "What if I took some days off school?" she whispered.

"Are you crazy? You can't do that!"

"It wouldn't be that bad."

"Of course it would. We're two months away from end-of-year exams; you can't go skiving now."

"It's not skiving."

"Yes, it is. Taking time off when you're not sick is skiving."

"Do you have any better ideas?"

"Yes, my idea is to work through at a reasonable pace that doesn't have the possibility of you getting suspended. But evidently, you don't like my idea. As usual, you want to do it your way."

Jessa clenched her fists under the table. Her face rushed with heat. Her eyes suddenly felt like she hadn't blinked in an hour.

"Excuse me, Mrs Sullivan, I have to go to the toilet," Jessa's chair screeched on the linoleum in her haste to exit the room.

She leaned against the mirror and tried to breathe deeply. The air escaped her nostrils and fogged up the glass. With every inhale the metallic remnants of body spray stuck in her throat. Through the walls, the sound of lessons continued to rumble away like distant traffic. The whitish glow of neon light mocked her with its uncaring electric flicker.

Jessa gripped the edges of the cold ceramic sink and desperately tried to calm herself, but her tongue was already wet with briny phlegm, and she barely made it into a cubicle before the contents of her stomach retched up through her lips.

The next thing she knew, she was curled around the toilet. A group of gawping students gossiped above her.

"Jessa? Oh my goodness, are you all right?" Tonia and Annora pushed through the onlookers and helped her up.

"What happened?" said Jessa. "Why are all these people here? What's going on?" She blinked hard through the blurry film on her eyeballs.

"It's break time—English is over."

"What? How long have I been here?"

"She looks really bad," Annora said to Tonia indiscreetly.

"Come on, we're taking you to the school nurse. Maggie's packing up your books and stuff."

§

"My poor baby," Jean Baxter cooed as she delivered a mug of hot water and lemon despite Jessa's protesting that she hated hot water and lemon.

"Mum, stop fussing, I feel fine."

And she did. She felt totally fine.

Jessa grimaced into the mug. She watched the lemon wedges swim around in the cloudy water. A rogue pip pulsated on the liquid skin.

She breathed a sigh of relief when her mother left the room, and put the cup down without taking a sip.

Her mind flew back to Mrs Sullivan's English lesson. She remembered sitting next to Maggie. She remembered the semicolons on the board. She remembered hearing Claire Adams and Jodie O'Connor talking about the latest episode of Teen Digs. She remembered the faint smell of eggs that wafted across the room when Thomas Stevens' lunchbox had accidentally come undone. She remembered everything more clearly than she'd lived it.

She had wanted to take time off school. She remembered Maggie's outrage.

She remembered the storm that started to brew inside her veins. She remembered having no control.

She remembered it taking over her body.

The lights that became brighter. The quivering in her muscles. The bitter heat that spewed out from her oesophagus.

And she was home by lunch time.

Jessa pulled out the batch of papers Maggie had given her earlier. On top of the pile was Maggie's revision timetable, which Jessa quickly pulled off and discarded onto her bedside table.

She flipped through pages upon pages of the printed information. It was a mammoth list of web addresses, varying only by the sequence of numbers at the end. She pulled the netpad off its charger and began typing the one at the very top of the page.

33

Jessa: You guys awake?

Tonia: I am. How are you feeling?

Jessa: Better!

Flynn: Glad to hear it

Jessa: Just wondering if any of you managed to get through any of the videos yet?

Maggie: Not yet, loads of homework today. I emailed you about an assignment.

Jessa: I got it. Anyone else?

Flynn: I watched one.

Tonia: None for me, sorry

Annora: Me neither

Jessa: OK fine

Annora: ???

Jessa: What?

Annora: You sound mad

Jessa: I'm not mad! Why does everyone keep thinking I'm angry all the time???!

Flynn: Because that's how it seems. Even if you don't mean to, that's how it's coming across.

Jessa: I have to go to bed

Flynn: alright

Maggie: Sleep well x

Tonia: Night Jessa, see you soon hopefully

Flynn: gnight

Annora: byeeeee

Jessa has left the group conversation

Tonia: Is it me or she's been super weird lately?

Maggie: I wasn't sure if everyone else had noticed it too…

Flynn: I think she's just stressed

Maggie: But why? We're all here to help

Flynn: I know, but she feels more responsibility because it's like HER thing

Maggie: Her thing? I thought it was OUR thing

Flynn: Yeah but she was the one who had the intuition in the first place. She was the one Mr Fletcher wanted to take to see Emmeline. It was her that he wanted to join the Agency.

Annora: But we're helping!

Flynn: I know. I think Jessa knows that too, even though she's not really showing it right now. Please don't be too hard on her. She's having this whole intuition thing, but she doesn't really understand it. That's gotta be frustrating.

Tonia: Yeah OK.

Flynn: I should go to bed too. See you all on Monday.

§

The whites of Jessa's eyes reflected the greeny glow of the netpad. Her unplugged alarm clock couldn't show her the time, but her drooping eyelids told her they were ready for rest. She tried to watch to the end of the video but her body betrayed her, and slipped into a daze of sleep.

Jessa heard the sound of her friends laughing somewhere from the darkness. She tried to sit upright but her arms were weighed down as if her hands were

made of stone. Drops of water fell onto her from somewhere above.

More laughter.

"Jessa, what's wrong with you?" Maggie called out. "Come and join us."

"Yeah, Jessa!" the others said.

She still couldn't move.

The bare skin on her legs began to tickle with the baleful steps of unseen creatures. Creeping and crawling, they came in their hoards, all over her body, finally reaching her shoulders and head.

Wherever her friends were, they finally noticed her distress.

"Oh shit, quick!" Tonia yelled. "Do something!"

Jessa's body writhed as the creatures grovelled into her mouth.

"Drown them!" Annora screamed from the blackness.

A cold stream of water hit Jessa's face abruptly. She felt relief for a moment as the insects fell away from her skin. But the water started to fill around her body. Faster and faster it inched up, over her ribs, her arms, her neck, her chin.

"Jessa, get up!" She could barely make out Flynn's voice through the sound of water rushing into her ears.

"Jessa!"

The sounds became more muffled as the water rose higher and higher, covering her eyes and surging into her nostrils.

She pulled harder, trying to sit up, but her leadened hands held her down under the water.

She couldn't hold her breath any longer and opened her mouth, gasping an unending current of water into her surrendering lungs.

Jessa Baxter jolted herself awake into the safe darkness of her room In a puddle of sweat and on the verge of tears, she graciously gulped the dry air into her heaving chest.

34

It had been three weeks before Jessa and her friends found anything at all notable in the surveillance footage. By the four-week mark, they had six different files that showed Emmeline Victor at some point on her walk home the day she was attacked. And by the fifth week, it seemed that everybody except Jessa had lost some element of interest in the process, although they were all happy to hang out at her house while she stared at the netpad screen, making her way through the video files.

It was a particularly lovely late April day and the five teenagers sprawled themselves around Jessa's bedroom, despite Mrs Baxter's repeated suggestions that they go out and enjoy the sunshine.

"Are there any other Lynch-y things we can research in the meantime?" Annora said.

"I think we've exhausted all our resources on that," Maggie replied. "And although it's History stuff, not Mystery stuff, I've genuinely enjoyed the biography project we've been doing for the last couple of meetings."

"Yeah that's been cool," said Tonia. "You did FDR, right, Mags?"

"Yep. I wish we studied more American history in lessons."

"Maybe we can work that into History Club next year," said Flynn. "What do you think, Jess?"

No reply.

"Never mind, then," Flynn shook his head and passed the ball to Annora.

They'd been intensively practising telekinesis at lunch time by playing psychball at the table, and even Maggie and Annora were at a point where they could comfortably hover a light ball above their hand and submit it to another player.

"Turn your hand a little as you pass it, that'll help," said Flynn, who was trying to teach the girls how to put a spin on the ball when moving it.

"It's too hard!" Maggie slapped her hands down. "Jessa, can you do this spin thing?"

"Mmm?" Jessa didn't look up from the screen.

"Flynn's spinning thing with the ball, can you do that?"

"I, umm…"

"Jess, maybe you should take a break from—"

"Holy crap." Jessa froze.

"What is it?" they all turned to look at her.

"Holy CRAP," she said again. "Get up here right now."

Her four friends piled around her on the bed so they could all see the netpad. Jessa pulled back on the bar at the bottom of the screen to rewind. She tapped the centre, and it began to play again.

It was a pretty empty residential London street. A couple of cars drove down the road. Nothing of note, it seemed. A lady holding a baby emerged from a doorway and climbed into a Ford Focus.

From the angle of the camera they could see her strapping the baby into a car seat, before fastening her own seatbelt and pulling away.

"What are we supposed t—"

"Shhh," Jessa interrupted urgently, "just watch."

Thirty seconds later, a figure emerged and walked into view. Clothed in a heavy winter coat with the hood up, Emmeline was barely recognisable if not for her trademark auburn curls that escaped around the sides of her hood, and the Winsbury school logo emblazoned on the front of the binder she held in her arm.

"There she is… now watch…" Jessa's voice dried in her throat.

Emmeline walked toward the bottom of the screen, and then stopped.

She stood perfectly still except for the strands of hair flapping around her face in the wind.

And then she vanished.

"Wait, what?" Jessa's four friends looked up at her, shocked and confused. "Rewind it."

"She just… disappeared…" said Maggie.

"She literally disappeared… I mean… for real?" said Tonia. "I don't get it."

"That's not possible. Right?" Maggie tried to process what she was seeing. "I mean, that's not *possible.*"

They watched the video again and again, but it never became any more than perfectly clear. There was no mistaking that the video plainly showed Emmeline Victor disappearing into thin air.

"We need to get this to Mr Fletcher," Jessa said, handing the netpad to Maggie. "Can you send this to him?"

"Not directly, but I can send a link. Hold on."

The familiar -dink- of a sent message followed shortly. The five students sat quietly, waiting for a response, and sure enough, an incoming call from Mr Hugo Fletcher came very quickly.

"Meet me at the Agency."

§

They crunched up the gravel pathway to the door that Mr Fletcher had left unbolted for them. Accompanying him was the young northern lady who had attended the previous Agency meeting.

"You remember Rachel," Mr Fletcher said, and she gave them a gentle wave of hello.

Any semblance of a welcome smile instantly disappeared from Hugo Fletcher's face. "I need to know, has anybody else seen this video?"

"No, we saw it and sent you the link right away," said Jessa.

"Good. Well, we just watched it a few times, and Rachel noticed something interesting." He rewound the video projection onto the whitewashed wall and played it again from the moment right before Emmeline vanished.

"See here, how Emmeline stops next to this white van. She's in between the house and the van. And notice how she's level with the front door, not the window of the house. That means nobody inside would be able to see her. She's hidden. Now watch what happens a couple of minutes after she disappears."

They all watched intently as the scene continued to play before them. If not for the time stamp in the corner of the screen that counted away the seconds, it would have seemed like an unmoving picture, as everything in the frame remained stoic and motionless for almost seventy seconds, at which point the van pulled away from the kerb and out of sight.

"The van drove away," said Jessa. "What does that mean?"

Rachel and Mr Fletcher shared a knowing glance.

"I think Emmeline was in the van," Rachel said softly, and the teenagers responded with blank faces. "My guess is that this is an example of telelocation. It's an extremely advanced form of telekinesis that can actually move an object from one location to another."

"Are you serious?" Maggie said, wide-eyed. Rachel nodded.

"My speciality is Psychokinetics, which is centred on studies of parapsychology and telekinesis. And I've heard of some literature, mostly ancient, that speculates on some advanced parapsych abilities, for instance, telelocation."

"Ancient parapsych literature?" Maggie's bottom jaw dropped slightly.

"Yes," Mr Fletcher said. "And naturally, you're all much too young for me to feel comfortable sharing all this with you, but it's too late now, you're already in it. And to be honest, we need all the help we can get. So we'll start at the beginning."

"Felix Aurelius was an ancient parapsych," Rachel spoke in her gentle accent. "Diviner, astrologer, future-seer, and healer, he was very widely regarded in his time, although that was mostly because people put a lot more faith in prophecy back then. His first major publication was something called the Hundred Quatrains, which were a series of short verses that each stood as a prophecy for the future. But then, as history tells it, he started getting some ideas that led him to be taken over by some supposedly darker powers. Then he started writing these manuals about increased abilities, much of it theoretical, of course, but there were some supposedly first-hand accounts of things he'd learned to do."

"What kind of things?" asked Flynn.

Another glance between the two adults.

"For starters, he wrote that he could telelocate. He also said he could directly communicate with the dead," Rachel said. "In one of his manuals he detailed ways in which he believed a parapsych could separate their consciousness from their body and move around undetected by other people."

"That can't possibly be real," Tonia derided.

"It does sound unlikely," Flynn agreed.

"It sounds like magic," said Annora.

"It's not," Mr Fletcher said, scratching the side of his face through a light layer of stubble. "It's just parapsychism. But unfortunately, we don't know what the limits of parapsychism are."

"Do you think Silas has those kinds of abilities?" Jessa looked directly at Mr Fletcher.

"I'm not sure. Research has shown that telelocation is possible, although it takes a very powerful parapsych to be able to perform it. And to perform it on a person? Well, that's a whole other level of power. I've never heard of someone actually doing that before."

Rachel adjusted the black hairband that reached around her crown. "I think you guys are right about Silas Lynch, and based on my own research I've come up with another theory about him."

"What is it?" Jessa asked.

"I looked into him a little, and I started thinking about the circumstances of Lynch's death. Throughout his childhood, it seems he had an affinity with fire. I can't tell if his interest was driven by his inherent pyrokinetic ability, or the other way round. But I know for sure that he had a strong connection to fire energy. I began to think that if he was really that powerful a pyrokinetic, it could account for his survival of the fire as a child. Perhaps he was able to use his abilities to protect himself."

"So based on that, you think that when his cult turned on him and tried to burn him alive, that he was able to keep the flames at bay?" Jessa finished the thought.

"Exactly."

"And if he could telelocate…" added Flynn.

"That's how he was able to escape," Tonia said.

"And that's why his death wasn't verified…" Maggie said thoughtfully.

"Because he didn't die," Annora finished.

Jessa nodded. "See, we knew he didn't die, we just couldn't figure out what did happen to him."

Jessa blinked her gaze away from Mr Fletcher and into space, feeling her brain grow heavy with questions. Her eyebrows drooped, cinching in close to one another as a deep furrow dug into her forehead.

"But," she said, translating her worry into words, "if Silas Lynch is capable of these parapsych abilities that we didn't even know were real… what else can he do?"

35

"What's the latest on the campaign posters?"

"I sent the final design to the printer yesterday, and they should be with us by the end of the week."

"Perfect. And has everyone RSVPed to the dinner?"

"Yes, sir, every table is full."

"Wonderful, wonderful."

Mr Graves tented his hand, delicately placing his fingertips on the window pane. The prints of his fingers squelched under the pressure.

"Goodness me, the rose bushes do need a good pruning, don't they? Maybe we ought to find a more competent gardener."

"Daddy?" a cautious voice said from outside the office door.

"What do you want, Cecily?" Mr Graves sighed.

"Oh, I was just wondering if you wanted to watch a film with me." She pushed the door open and poked her head in through the crack. "NetFilms just released some new stuff, and I thought you might like to see—"

"Cecily, do you remember the rule? If the office door is closed, it means—"

"…you're working, I know. Never mind then. Sorry."

"I don't understand why you're thinking about films anyway, you should be concentrating on revision. Do you know how many cheques I've had to send to that school to keep you from getting suspended after all your outrageous behaviour recently? If you fail these exams, who knows how much I'll have to plump up to save you from getting kicked out or held back a year.

So go and revise, please."

"Yes, Daddy," Cecily said quietly, closing the door behind her.

"Where were we, Jones?"

"The dinner, sir."

"Ah yes. So the event organiser confirmed that we'll have a PA system, microphones, screens for my presentation, et cetera?"

"Yes sir, it's all sorted."

"Wonderful. Simply wonderful." He turned to lean gently onto the pane, pressing the pads of his chubby hands onto the surface.

"I'm going to head out now, sir. I have that meeting with the investors this evening."

"Excellent. Thank you, Jones. You may see yourself out."

"Thank you, sir. See you tomorrow."

Jones collected his briefcase and blazer.

"Oh, and Jones?"

"Yes, Mr Graves?"

"Tell one of the housekeeping staff to give these windows some attention. They're filthy."

§

Cecily sat, pyjamaed and cross-legged on her bed, mindlessly flicking the screen of her netpad, barely even looking at the images and articles that appeared from one side of the screen and disappeared into the other. She sighed audibly, and leaned back into the symmetrical arrangement of hard pillows that spanned the top end of her double bed.

Without warning, Mrs Graves burst into the room, holding a bundle of evening dresses in plastic sheaths. "Why are you already in pyjamas? It's only 7 pm."

"Just felt like being comfy."

"Bedclothes before bedtime is awfully slobbish, Cece, you know that. It's hardly surprising Eli dumped you. Boys don't like lazy girls, you know. Come and stand over here, please." She hung up all the gowns on a rack that

Cecily hadn't even noticed had been placed in the room. "All right, try this one," she handed her daughter a deep red prom dress with an oversized bow on the back. Without a word, Cecily stripped to her underwear and stepped into the dress.

Mrs Graves grimaced. "Oh no, not a good length for you. Cuts off your calves completely, makes you look chunky."

She held out the next dress.

"No. I forgot you don't look good in navy. Never mind, let's try the next one."

Her mother unwrapped the next dress from its protective jacket, and Cecily wriggled into it with a grunt.

"It's too small."

"Darn, so it is. Have you gained weight? The tailor can probably let out the sides a little, though if you're gaining weight, we should really get that in check. That said, I think this is the dress."

"Isn't it a bit much?" Cecily frowned at herself in the mirror. "It's bright gold."

"It's not gold, darling—it's bronze. And it's Daddy's big night, remember? We have to look our best. There's going to be a lot of very influential young men there too, so it's in your best interest to look as good as possible."

"Okay," Cecily mumbled, pulling her teddy bear pyjamas back on.

"Let's see if we can't tone up those thighs a little, hmm? And, really, Cecily," Mrs Graves pinched the underside of her daughter's arm, "you're too young for bingo-wings like this. Sort it out, please. We have a gym here; it's ridiculous for you to be letting yourself get like this. I'll arrange a personal training session for you tomorrow morning, so be in the gym at 8 am. Don't be late."

Mrs Graves bundled up the dresses and stomped out of her daughter's bedroom, leaving the door wide open and the hanging rack empty once again.

Cecily collapsed onto the heavy oak chair at her desk. She folded her legs in the seat that was just wide enough for her knees to graze the antique scroll arms. The top of the desk was bare except for a row of barely-touched schoolbooks.

She thumbed through the shiny leaves of Parapsych Skills in Theory and Practice, stopping at the chapter on flame-control, then reached for one of the scented candles on the shelf above her desk.

She traced the embossed lettering of the word 'serenity' on the side of the thick sunset yellow candle before striking a match and torching the virgin wick.

She rested her gaze just above the flame and positioned her hands in front of it, copying the finger formation printed in the textbook.

A sudden thump in the house broke Cecily's concentration before she had even found it.

Another thump.

Cecily straightened.

A woman's shriek sounded from somewhere nearby.

Cecily jerked herself up and without thinking raced from her bedroom. The voices of her parents became louder as she hurried down the landing. Cecily stopped outside her father's home office and listened from outside the ajar door.

"Why won't you tell me what's going on?" her mother shouted.

"Because it's none of your business!"

"I think it is my business if there's a stranger lurking around my house! What are you up to, Jameson? And you! Who the fuck are you?"

"Don't speak to him that way."

"How am I supposed to speak? This is my house!"

"I paid for this house, Elise."

"Don't you dare throw that in my face, Jameson. I have a right to know who you're fraternising with. I mean, here I was, thinking you were just working alone, and then I come in, and suddenly you're pushing me out of the room so you can be alone with this freak of an old man! And now he's just standing there looking at me? Hey you! What's your problem?"

"Elise, step away from him. Elise!"

The loud slap of skin on skin cut through the stillness in Cecily's ears and she burst into the room.

"Stop!"

"Go to your room, Cecily," her father warned.

Cecily looked down at her mother, who picked herself up off the floor, her bloody nose dripping onto her white silk blouse.

"Mummy, are you all right?" Cecily stammered.

"I'm fine, Cece, let's go."

The door slammed itself shut as Cecily and her mother approached it.

"Don't leave like this, Elise. Let me explain," Mr Graves said with a shake of his head. "This is my associate—"

She spat on the ground in front of him. "I don't care. I've had enough of this shit."

Cecily stood, paralysed by the scene before her. Her mother plugged the back of her hand against the dribble of blood from her nostril. Her father's fists shook with rage.

She took a step toward her father. "Daddy, please just—"

"Shut up, Cecily!" he shoved his daughter so hard that she fell into a sideboard. A clatter of shattering ornaments rained down over Cecily's body as she cowered on the ground. Her father didn't even look at her.

"Listen to me, Elise, he's on our side!"

"I don't even know what you're talking about, Jameson."

Cecily whimpered on the ground as her parents continued their exchange. The strange silent man stepped toward her and looked down curiously. He lifted his arm and Cecily winced, but then realised he was offering his hand to help her to her feet. She reached out and grasped the black leather of his glove, and he took hold of her.

"He's helping me realise the full extent of my abilities. And eventually, when we win the election, we'll help others realise their power too."

"What power? What are you talking about?"

"Parapsychism, Elise. He's shown me things—amazing things—you wouldn't even believe it. And when everyone else sees it too, they'll know."

"They'll know what?!"

"That parapsychs will reign." Mr Graves spoke earnestly and gently.

Cecily stood to her feet with the help of the dark-clothed man. He said nothing but looked into her eyes. She couldn't look away from his frightful face.

"You're scaring me, Jameson," Mrs Graves blubbed. "What about the things you used to talk about? Better education for parapsych kids, and support for adults who want to better their abilities." She gulped out her words between sniffles. "It was all so positive! But recently you've become so closed and morose, and now this? What happened to you?"

"I saw truth, Elise!" he screamed. "He showed me the truth and he showed me what it's like to feel power coursing through my whole body. I felt airless and electric. Just for a moment, I was invincible. He shared his power with me and showed me what I could cultivate. It's my duty, Elise! It's my duty to show them all."

"You're crazy."

"I'm alive!"

"I'm leaving. I'm taking our daughter right now and we are leaving."

"No."

"Let go."

"No." He gripped tightly on her upper arm.

"Let me go, Jameson!"

"I can't let you walk out. That's not part of the plan. You can't leave me," Jameson Graves spoke calmly into her face.

"So what, you'll just keep us here forever?" his wife threw back.

"No, I wouldn't dream of that," he smiled. "You see, Elise, you can either be with me and support me, or you just won't be at all. So I'm going to let you out of this room. But please believe it, the second you try and run away, I will be on you before you even know it. After all, nothing is more sympathetic than a widow. The voters would find me irresistible. I do love you, my darlings. I'm doing this for you, and for us, and for our people. But the plan is in motion now, and I'm afraid there's no going back."

36

Mrs Baxter paced back and forth in front of the kitchen table.

"What are you working on, Mum?" Jessa said, peering over at the sheets of paper spread all over the table.

"My company got an offer to organise an event. The event hosts were already working with one of our competitors, but something went wrong, and they got fired very suddenly. So it's a bit last minute but a huge event for us!"

"Cool, what is it?"

"A campaign dinner for someone trying to become the leader of a political party. Surprisingly fancy, too. He's apparently running for the PIP. Complete nonsense of course, but you should see how much they offered us to run the event."

"Is it Mr Graves? He's Cecily's dad. They're super rich."

"That's the one. Funny what people choose to spend their money on. Well, if he wants to try and buy his way into politics, fair play to him. They're all nuts, these political types. And I've just been on the phone with the catering company, and they have another event that night too, so they're hiring more temporary waiting staff for my event. So if you fancy earning some pocket money, I can get you a little job waitressing."

"Ugh, that means I'd have to see Cecily."

"I'm sure she'll be too busy to talk to you."

"I suppose."

"It's good money."

"Oh, all right, then. I think Flynn would be interested too."

"Lovely."

"At least that way I can keep an eye on Cecily," Jessa mumbled under her breath.

"What's that?"

"Oh, nothing," Jessa fiddled with a piece of her hair, twirling it around her fingers. "Mum, can I ask you something?"

"Of course, love."

"Have you ever been afraid of a parapsych?"

Her mother stopped fussing with the spreadsheets and looked at her daughter with concern. "Why would you ask that?"

"Well, have you?"

"Afraid? No, definitely not. Perhaps annoyed or angry, but never because of their parapsychism. A person isn't defined by their psych abilities, you know that. Why are you asking?"

"No reason. Just a project for school. I should probably get back to my revision."

Jessa's bed creaked as she jumped onto it and made herself comfortable in the corner. She flopped down with her older edition copy Mind Over Matter: Introduction to Telepathy and fingered through the pages quickly, reviewing her highlights and margin notes.

She gently closed the book and turned her gaze to the dimmer switch on the opposite wall, around which she'd placed a circle of card (as per Ms Alzamora's recommendation). Jessa softened her eyes in the centre of the circle, and let out her breath. She held her hand gently in space and imitated the motion of turning the dimmer switch.

The little knob turned.

The light dimmed.

"Yes," Jessa said under her breath.

She settled back into a comfortable reclined position, closed her eyes and began her open-mind practice.

"Hey Annora, you're here late," Jessa said, taking a seat next to her friend in the library.

"So are you!" Annora replied brightly. "I'm just here getting in some revision time. I find the library so relaxing after school hours." Her bushy red hair tumbled down over the exercise book on the table. "I'm working on my parapsych history project, what about you?"

"Also doing my project. And my English essay. And my chemistry homework. I'm, uh, not too good at keeping up with homework. Don't tell Maggie, though."

"My lips are sealed," said Annora, gesturing the motion of a key in a lock on her mouth.

"Oh hey, I think you have a bug in your hair."

"Ew, can you get it out?" Annora shuddered.

"Yeah, hang on." Jessa stood behind Annora and looked where she thought she had just seen the insect. She gently picked apart the bushy ginger wisps, separating a section of hair and pushing it over Annora's shoulder. "Maybe it fell out; I don't see it now. I think it was one of those tiny little spid— Whoa."

"What?" Annora said quickly.

"What happened to your head?"

"What do you mean?"

"These scars… Did something happen to you?"

"I don't know what you're talking about. Where are the scars?"

Jessa gently touched the scorched-looking skin on Annora's scalp.

"Ow!"

"Sorry!"

"Ow!" Annora yelled, louder. "Stop it!"

"Annora, I'm not touching you now," Jessa said, moving in front of her friend.

Annora threw her hands to her head, scraping her nails against her lesioned flesh. Tears streamed from her reddening face, and her yelps and shrieks turned to tortured screams and cries for help.

"Annora, stop!" Jessa called out as Annora tore at her own head, ripping out threads of hair in her fingers that were rapidly becoming coated with the red wetness of fresh blood. Two other students looked on, horrified.

"Go get help!" Jessa shouted to them, and one of them jumped into action, sprinting from the library with frenzied shouts for assistance.

Annora calmed and stared into space, then down at her bloody fingers. When she spoke, she spoke a crooked voice as well as her own. She choked the words as though trying to fight for air, through deep gasps. She pained through the rattle in her throat.

"I stand with Him, His Grace, His Lordship."

"Annora...?" Jessa spoke quietly, staring at the girl who had just turned from a friend into something else entirely.

"His time has come," Annora growled. "We have been chosen. We mark the path for his mighty resurrection."

The third-year boy raced back into the library, quickly followed by Mr Fletcher, who immediately went to Annora and placed his hands gently on hers.

"Annora? It's me, Mr Fletcher. Can you hear me?"

"We have been chosen. We mark the path for his mighty resurrection." Her black eyes didn't blink.

"Annora, I know you're in there."

"We have been chosen. We mark the path for his mighty resurrection." She pulled her hands away from his and pushed her chair back away from the table without touching it. The chair legs screeched as they pulled back on the floor. She stood and ran from the room.

Mr Fletcher and Jessa followed, but Annora was already running up the stairs. Her footsteps were quiet but the maniacal voice reverberated through the quiet hallways—an audible trail of crumbs up the staircase.

Suddenly, an alarm screamed an electronic wail of warning.

"The roof," Mr Fletcher ran along the top floor corridor toward the fire exit. He and Jessa reached the open door and were met by the cool evening air.

Annora stood on the wall at the edge of the building.

"No!" Jessa yelled and went to rush forward, but Mr Fletcher held her back. He shoved his phone into her hand.

"Call Rachel, tell her to contact everyone at the Agency, and tell her we'll be there as soon as possible."

He slowly approached the figure of Annora Huff that stood with her toes inched over the edge of the wall. Her blood-matted head glistened in the early evening sunlight.

"Hey, Annora. Why don't you come down?"

"You cannot change the path," a myriad of voices spoke through her vocal chords. "We mark the path for his mighty resurrection."

"Whose resurrection? Silas?"

"His lordship!" she growled without turning around. "He has come! Now we who have been chosen will commit ourselves to him. We mark the path for his mighty resurrection."

She stepped off the ledge.

Hugo Fletcher's arms reached up, forcing every volt of his telekinetic energy to channel through his body and the air, holding Annora's body in mid-air with her arms and legs splayed to the sides. Jessa gaped, frozen at the sight of his body shaking with the tension, and a long, involuntary groan escaping through his gritted teeth. With one final strain, he was able to pull her backwards enough and let her go. She fell, unconscious, but alive, onto the surface of the roof.

Jessa gasped herself awake. Her clothes were drenched in sweat, and she had to take slow, deliberate breaths to calm her racing heartbeat. Another nightmare. She shook her head in disbelief. The clock read 1:43 am.

She had barely fallen asleep again before her alarm rang for school.

37

"Hey, you got your cast off!" Jessa said to Mr Fletcher as she bumped into him on her way into school. "How does it feel?"

"Feels great!" he said, wiggling his arm proudly. "I can finally reach the itchy spots, which I'm very happy about."

"That's good," she replied.

"Are you okay?" he said. "You look exhausted."

"I'm all right, but this stuff is driving me crazy. You still haven't heard back from Rachel about the video?"

"Not yet, she's still working on the analysis. And we ran searches on the licence plates but found no record. Is anything else bothering you? Anything going on with Cecily?"

"Nope, she's been minding her own business lately. Other than that, I'm doing fine I guess, just haven't been sleeping well."

"Stressed about exams?"

"Maybe. I've been having these nightmares for a while, though. I've tried doing some open-mind practice before bed, to relax, you know? But apparently it relaxes me so much that I end up having these weird, vivid dreams that wake me up. Last night I had a horrible nightmare about Annora. It was different to the others, too. It wasn't a regular scary dream, though. It felt really real, but also totally surreal. Actually, it felt similar to the intuitions I had before. When I woke up, it felt more like a memory than a dream."

"That sounds intense," he said.

"Yeah. Those kind of dreams haven't all been nightmares, though. I mean, the other night I dreamed that we were in a parapsych history exam, and Maggie finished early but didn't realise there were two more questions on the back page so she failed."

"Sounds like a nightmare for Maggie," he chuckled. "Well, I hope in your dream you had time to revise for the test beforehand, because I am springing a mock exam on your class today."

"Noooooo!" she playfully feigned her horror as the two of them entered the classroom.

"Good morning, everyone!"

"G'morning, Mr Fletcher," the awaiting class replied.

"I have a nice change of pace for you this morning, as we had a slight schedule reshuffle. Madame Bellerose is away today, so you'll be staying in here for the first two lessons instead of going to French. And instead of a normal lesson, you will have not one, but two mock exams. French and Parapsych History. How does that sound?"

The room volume increased with whinges and whines.

"It's okay, this is what we've been preparing for," Maggie said, directing it at Flynn but seemingly more for her own benefit. "You've studied for this; you know the material."

"Mags, chill out, it's just a mock exam," Flynn soothed. Maggie responded with a glare.

"Mr Fletcher, I don't feel very well. May I be excused?" Cecily Graves uttered through her fingers as she held her head in her hands. He went to her and put a hand on her back.

"Yeah, you don't look very well at all. Want me to call your parents?"

"No," she shot back quickly. "Can I just go to the nurse's room?"

"Of course. I'll send her a message and let her know to expect you."

Cecily left the room quickly, keeping her head down so her hair could hide her face from the discerning looks of her classmates.

"She looks rough," said someone at the back of the class.

"I think breaking up with you is taking its toll on her, Eli," said someone else.

"That's enough," Mr Fletcher swiftly ended the teenage banter.

Every member of Jessa's first-year class watched the second hand of the clock making its way round to the 12. Pens in hand. Maggie breathed heavily in and out through her nose.

"You can begin," Mr Fletcher said as the second hand met its big hand associate at the 12. A papery woosh washed over the room with the turning over of the first page, followed by the scratching of nibs scrawling answers in French.

Forty minutes seemed to pass in moments, and Jessa didn't even have time to check over her answers before Mr Fletcher was asking them to put down their pens.

A quick break ended much too soon, as students tried to just as quickly switch their thinking mode from French to English in preparation for the next test, and then it was time to write again.

Jessa hunched over her paper, scribbling and scrabbling the blue ink across the pages, handwriting becoming progressively more illegible with every sentence. She took a moment to stretch and think about her next answer.

Fifteen minutes to go. Maggie was already sitting with her arms crossed.

Mr Fletcher leaned back in his chair, surveying the room of mostly hunkered students, manically getting answers out of their heads and onto the page.

Jessa followed his gaze around the room and felt a strange deja vu. Mr Fletcher stopped his focus on Maggie's desk, noticing that her papers were all tidily closed and positioned in front of her neatly folded arms. He stood. The deja vu continued.

He took a stroll around the room. "Ten minutes remaining," he informed them gently, and the writing became louder and quicker. Jessa knew she should return to her own paper but was still watching the teacher with a curious familiarity. As he passed Maggie, he gently touched his hand to her shoulder, and held it there for a second, in a motion unseen to any of the other scrambling students.

Maggie suddenly burst into action, swishing her paper over to look at the back page, where there were two additional questions lurking at the back.

It seemed like only seconds until Mr Fletcher announced the end of testing time and dismissed the class for break.

"Jessa, can I see you for a minute, please?" he asked, and she hung back near his desk as the rest of the class filed out, already chattering about the test and comparing answers.

"Do you realise what just happened?" he asked quietly.

"I'm not sure."

"Jessa, Maggie missed the last questions. She didn't look on the back page. That's the dream you told me about, isn't it?"

"Yeah, but what does that mean?"

"It means I need to know what you dreamed about Annora."

She told him everything. Break-time ended but still Mr Fletcher pried Jessa for as much detail as she could remember about her dream, and sent a message to the chemistry teacher to excuse Jessa from her next lesson. He marched her out of the classroom and toward the staircase.

"So what, you think my dreams were real?" Jessa asked in disbelief.

"I think they might be predictions," he replied quietly, hurrying down the West Wing corridor. He knocked loudly on Dr Mortlock's office, and she opened the door quickly enough that Jessa wondered if she'd sensed their arrival.

"Hugo. Miss Baxter. Come in." Her words welcomed them, but her cold eyes didn't.

"Felicia," Mr Fletcher began, "are we safe to talk here?" he glanced around the room, though Jessa couldn't tell what he was looking for.

"Of course," Dr Mortlock replied with derision.

"We've had an interesting development. I'm beginning to suspect that Jessa has some element of future-sight."

Dr Mortlock stared into Jessa with what could have been curiosity or ridicule.

"She's apparently been having some alarming dreams, one of which foreshadowed something that happened in my class today. Another one is more concerning, and regards Annora Huff."

He relayed the details of Jessa's dream to the headteacher, who simply nodded along with most minuscule of head jerks and occasionally squinted down to Jessa.

"And what do you think, Miss Baxter? What do you make of these dreams?" Dr Mortlock finally said to her.

"Well. Umm," Jessa cleared the dryness from her throat, "they've all been very vivid, and when the thing with Maggie's test happened today I did feel a weird deja vu thing… umm…" Jessa faltered, unsure whether Dr Mortlock was truly asking for her opinion or if she was being asked to justify herself.

"Felicia, apparently Jessa had done some open-mind practice right before going to bed."

Dr Mortlock craned her birdlike neck back toward Jessa. "Is this true?"

"Yes," Jessa replied. "Should I not have done that? Ms Alzamora said it could help us relax."

"It does for most people," said Mr Fletcher. "But the few parapsyche with futuresight do find that open-mind practice is what starts bringing out the skill. It often begins revealing itself through dreams."

"It certainly could be the beginning of a futuresight ability," Dr Mortlock said, more to Mr Fletcher than to Jessa. The two adults looked at one another for a moment.

"I told you I was having future visions, though, and you didn't believe me, you said it couldn't possibly be futuresight, remember? When we came to you that night and told you about the strange thing that happened to me when I put on Annora's scarf."

The look on Dr Mortlock's face was one of acute disdain. "Futuresight isn't relative to objects, Miss Baxter. Whatever you experienced then was certainly not futuresight. And children do not simply have conscious futuresight visions."

"I'm hardly a child," Jessa snapped.

"You're a fourteen-year-old student, Miss Baxter. By all accounts, you are most definitely a child."

"Child or not, Felicia, Jessa is onto something," said Mr Fletcher. "Now, Jessa, what you described in your first vision about Annora, really doesn't sound like futuresight. Are you absolutely sure it coincided with the moment you put on Annora's scarf?"

"Positive. I remember it. Annora had left her scarf at my house, and I put it on. And that's when I heard these whooshing noises, then I was sort of in the vision. It was like I was Annora. And in the vision, she was wearing the scarf too."

Mr Fletcher's face was frozen in concern. "You didn't mention the noises before."

"Oh. I didn't know that part was important. What do the noises mean?"

"Tell me, in the vision, when the noises happened, did it feel like your body was being whizzed from one scene into another?"

"I don't know what you mean."

"All right… You know how in a TV show, what you see on the screen is edited from different cameras and different angles, and from your perspective as the watcher you can see those switches between scenes?"

"Yeah…"

"Was it like that in the vision you had, with the changing of scenes and perspectives?

"Oh. Yes, just like that."

"And the whooshing sounds accompanied those transitions?"

"Yes."

He gently wetted his lips with his tongue, then rubbed his chin. Jessa watched the adults again.

They stood in silence but moment to moment their expressions changed slightly as though they were having a conversation. Out of nowhere, Dr Mortlock's body language changed from stern to worry. She touched her fingertips to her temples and massaged gently.

"Why?" Jessa said, growing frustrated. "What does this all mean?"

"I think what you experienced in that first vision wasn't a prediction, Jessa," said Mr Fletcher. "It was object-reading. I didn't think it was possible for someone to object-read without intensive training."

"Nor I," Dr Mortlock added. "Though in this case, it appears we have been let down by our own knowledge, Hugo. Or lack thereof."

"In that vision, I saw Annora with Silas Lynch."

"Yes," Mr Fletcher continued. "Based on the quality of your apparent futuresight and the accuracy in your description of object-reading, it looks like—"

"Like Annora is the next one to get taken?" Jessa answered.

"No, Miss Baxter," said Dr Mortlock, "object-reading is contingent on events that have already transpired. It would appear that Silas Lynch has already found Annora Huff."

"Hugo," Dr Mortlock continued, "I would find it prudent to call an urgent Agency meeting. I suggest you and Miss Baxter go ahead to the usual meeting place, and I will bring Miss Huff and our other young Agents shortly.

38

"What, why?"

"Just come over here please, Miss Huff," Dr Mortlock motioned with her fingertips for Annora to join her.

Three other members of the Agency had been able to arrive on short notice, so the Winsbury group was joined by Henrik Olsen, the tall white-haired Scandinavian; Special Agent Matt Allerton, wearing a patterned jumper that was far too chunky to be appropriate for springtime; and Rachel Malone, who looked especially concerned.

"Miss Huff," Dr Mortlock addressed Annora again.

"Felicia, I think she's fine where she is," Mr Fletcher sounded slightly annoyed as he spoke to the headteacher.

"Mr Fletcher, I would prefer for Miss Huff to join me on this side of the table."

Reluctantly, the red-haired young girl did as she was told, and looked very anxious to be the centre of attention of everyone in the room.

"The others are almost here," said Rachel, reading a message from the screen of her phone.

"We should wait for them," said Mr Fletcher.

"Agreed," Rachel added, ignoring the resulting scowl from Dr Mortlock.

"Are we allowed to know what's going on?" said Maggie.

"You'll find out, Maggie," Mr Fletcher assured. "It's just easier if we wait until they're here so we can explain to everyone at the same time."

They were all relieved when the remaining three members arrived. Sue, the teacher from Harnbury School, Detective John Cane, and Howard each pulled up a seat and shuffled themselves into place around the table.

"What's up, Hugo?" Detective Cane enquired. "Your message sounded serious."

"We wouldn't have called an urgent meeting for anything less than a serious matter, Detective," Dr Mortlock replied and John Cane snapped his mouth shut.

"My friends," Dr Mortlock addressed the room. "We have reason to suspect that our group has been infiltrated."

Eyes widened around the table.

"Infiltrated is a strong word—" Hugo Fletcher tried to ease the tension.

"It is an appropriate word, Mr Fletcher."

"But we don't know yet what we're dealing with, Felicia."

"Exactly," she snapped, "which is why we should exercise extreme diligence and not be blindsided by emotion, Mr Fletcher."

"Would one of you please explain what's going on, here?" Sue said, her huge head of tight curls shaking as she spoke.

"We believe Miss Huff has been compromised," Dr Mortlock cut right to the heart of the matter.

"What?" gasped Annora. Her shocked face looked directly to Jessa for help.

"What do you mean?" Tonia questioned forcefully. "Annora hasn't done anything!"

"Do you have any evidence?" Detective Cane jeered. "Or are we simply basing this on the hunches of a hormonal teenager again?"

Jessa felt her face burning in a rising panic. She wanted to say something—anything—to ease the increasing tension in the room, but she couldn't justify putting into words any of the thoughts that were jumbling themselves in her mind.

Oh no.

He's right. I don't have proof.

But Dr Mortlock and Mr Fletcher believe it this time. They were the ones who put the pieces together.

It's their theory, not mine.

She forced her concentration back into the room, where everyone was trying not to look too imploringly at Annora.

"Felicia," Matt Allerton started, "where is this idea coming from?"

"We received some… intuition… leading both Mr Fletcher and myself to conclude—"

"Intuition, eh?" Howard scoffed. "So it's Baxter again."

He doesn't believe me.

"What of it, Howard?" said Dr Mortlock. "We've already established that Miss Baxter is a highly skilled parapsych, so what does it matter if she was the source?"

"Because there's no evidence, dammit! This kid could be leading us on a wild horse chase, and we're expected just to go along with it? Nonsense!" He rose from the table.

Say something.

"I might expect this from Fletcher, as soft as he is, but come on, Felicia, let's be real."

"Sit down, please, Howard. I'd like Miss Baxter to detail her experiences to the group."

Howard crossed his arms over his bloated belly but made no move to return to his seat at the table. Everyone cast their gaze to Jessa.

Say. Something.

"Miss Baxter, would you please tell everyone about the dream you had?" Dr Mortlock proposed.

Say anything.

Jessa looked at Flynn. Everyone at the table was looking at her with either concern or fear or confusion. But Flynn simply looked on with kindness.

"I— I…" Jessa's voice cracked, and she cleared her throat more loudly than she intended. "I had a dream about Annora. I'd fallen asleep after my open-mind practice. I dreamed that she had these scars on the back of her head. But when I touched them she started, I don't know—she wasn't herself anymore." Jessa made the mistake of looking at Annora, who was quaking in silent tears. Jessa looked down and focused on the fingernail she was picking at. "She was possessed or something. And then she ran to the roof. I think she was going to…" she lowered her voice, "she was going to jump. She kept saying something about 'his mighty resurrection.' And that's it, really."

The room was quiet.

"Hugo, what makes you think this was futuresight?" Rachel asked reasonably.

"Jessa told me about another dream that I subsequently witnessed becoming something of a reality," he replied.

"So you've just had two of these dreams, Jessa?" Rachel questioned further.

"They're the only two I can remember."

"What was the second one, the one that Mr Fletcher knew about?"

"I dreamed Maggie failed a test because she missed some questions on the back page of an exam paper."

"So in real life, has Annora done anything to suggest this dream was futuresight?" Henrik asked rationally. "Because, no offence intended, but any futuresight, and especially one of this detail and magnitude, would be incredibly unlikely at Jessa's age."

"We couldn't take any chances, Henrik," said Mr Fletcher. "So no, I suppose Annora hasn't done anything, but we called this meeting immediately to decide how to proceed from here."

Everyone turned to Annora. The small girl seemed to have shrunk into her chair and disappeared into herself even further under everyone's scrutiny.

"I didn't do it," she said in a small voice. "I don't even know what you think I did, but I swear I didn't." Her eyes bulged with wetness.

"Miss Huff," Dr Mortlock said. "Pardon my directness, but, to your knowledge, have you ever met or had any interaction with Silas Lynch?"

"No! Of course not!" Annora wept.

"It's all right, Annora," Mr Fletcher said gently. "But think really hard, is there anything that's happened to you that might be linked to Silas Lynch? Or maybe you've seen the two men wearing long coats, like Jessa described to you once. Remember?"

"I remember Jessa saying it, but I've never seen them!" Annora implored.

"This is ridiculous," Detective Cane said. "She doesn't know anything; she's just a kid. This is a waste of time."

"Wait," said Rachel. "Before we get too carried away, has anyone checked Annora for the scars like Jessa's dream predicted?"

"I don't have any scars!" Annora said defensively.

"Maybe not," Rachel replied very calmly, "but would you mind if I just look?"

Jessa admired the soft quality to Rachel's voice. It also seemed to placate Annora, who nodded her approval. Rachel paused, then moved toward Annora.

The room and its occupants watched on in a curious and nervous silence. Rachel placed her hands on Annora's shoulders and squeezed gently to massage some of her tension away. "Don't worry, I'm not going to hurt you," she said softly, smoothing Annora's hair back into a ponytail. Annora closed her eyes and took a deep breath. Jessa stopped picking at her fingernails and paused with one nail indenting her own flesh.

Rachel parted Annora's hair down the centre of her scalp, exposing a white line of skin in between the two sides of taut gingery curls. She let out a light breath.

"Looks fine to me."

Annora also let out a sigh of relief.

Rachel lifted up the ponytail in her hand and leafed through the soft hair right at the back of Annora's skull. "Wait, what's…" her face scrunched for a second and then unscrunched into a blank look that the onlookers could only understand as horror.

"Oh shit."

39

"What?!" Annora screeched, throwing her hands to her head. Rachel looked like she was about to vomit. Mr Fletcher quickly ran to Rachel's side.

"Hey, Annora," he said calmly, "I just need to you keep really still for minute, all right?"

"What is it? What is it?" Annora panicked.

"Annora, love, please just keep still," as much as she tried, Rachel could not make her voice sound calm.

At the base of Annora's skull was an open wound. The flesh surrounding it was black and bruised and burnt. Fresh tissue had begun to grow back in shiny red leaves and flakes that tried to snake their way across Annora's exposed milky skull.

"Sue, you're a healer, right? Can you try and fix this?"

"Oh my," Sue uttered quietly when she saw Annora's head. "I don't know if I can," she whispered.

Annora wept harder, taking large gulps of air between her heavy sobs.

Maggie and Tonia crouched on either side of Annora, holding her hands. Jessa simply watched on with a hand over her mouth, until Flynn joined her and put his arm around her shoulder.

"It's not working, I'm not strong enough by myself," Sue said, inspecting the wound again. She moved her hands a little closer to Annora's head and closed her eyes again, using all the power she could to begin the healing process.

"Maybe I can help," Matt Allerton joined Sue. He clasped one of his hands around hers, and they each held their free hands over Annora's head.

A low gurgle came out of Annora's mouth. Her body stopped shuddering with tears and became very still. Her head drooped forward.

Suddenly, her mouth opened painfully wide and let out a disturbing roar. Everyone jumped back as Annora rose from the ground, her head forced back. She hovered, stuck in mid-air, vibrating as a translucent grey mist vaporised from her body.

"I think it's working! Keep going!" Jessa yelled over Annora's bellowing.

Sue and Matt bounded back into action, joining hands again and transmitting all the healing energy they could muster into Annora's quivering form. Her deep howl started to form words, slurred and exaggerated like a recording playing in slow motion. Jessa knew the phrase well.

"We mark the path for his mighty resurrection."

"We can't hold it much longer—we need more energy!" Sue begged of the other parapsychs. Hugo Fletcher, Rachel, Henrik and Detective Cane rushed out of their astonished, frozen states and to the sides of the healers. They all lay their hands on Matt and Sue and leaned in, pulsing their own psych energy into their Agency counterparts. Howard stayed across the room with his back pressed against the wall, frigid in terror.

Annora's friends watched on helplessly as the grey smog continued to escape her body and the words slowed even further, dribbling like slugs from her mouth. Jessa glanced over at Dr Mortlock, who had deliberately not aided the others but instead stood near the four other teenagers, arms outstretched, poised to protect them if required.

With one final spit, the last psychotic words drained from Annora Huff's vocal chords and she slumped onto the ground below as the last wisps of the dark haze seeped from her body and into the room, slowly dissipating into nothingness.

The adult parapsychs broke their connection and caught their breath. Rachel keeled forward, resting her hands on her knees, finding her strength again. Sue's legs buckled and she was caught by Hugo Fletcher, who helped her to a seat on the ground.

§

"Annora, can you hear me?" Tonia cradled Annora's skinny body in the back of Mr Fletcher's car. She hugged Annora's torso closer to her own, stroking her bushy red hair soothingly. "Why aren't we there yet?" Tonia urged Mr Fletcher, who tapped his fingers, rhythmic and impatient, on the steering wheel of the car as they waited at a red light.

"We're going to Morelands Hospital. It's a little further away."

"Can't we just take her to the closest one?"

"Morelands has more experience with… this kind of thing," he said.

"You mean parapsych-related things?"

"Well, not specifically. It's a psychiatric hospital, but given the recent circumstances, they have had more experience with parapsych patients."

"You mean Emmeline Victor?" asked Flynn.

"Exactly," the teacher nodded.

They pulled up to the hospital's emergency entrance. Hugo Fletcher disregarded the parking lines entirely, stopping the car diagonally across them, as close to the entrance as possible.

He pulled Annora's still unconscious body from Tonia in the backseat and rushed inside.

Within seconds, a team of nurses in white scrubs were pushing a wheeled bed over to them.

Jessa was quickly overwhelmed by the brightness of hospital lights and the clinical smell in the air that wasn't quite overpowered by synthetic lavender air fresheners. She sat down next to Maggie on the hard waiting room seats. The clunky roll of the bed and the hastened chatter of adults faded as they pushed Annora away down a corridor.

Tonia tried to follow them, but Flynn held her back.

She sighed loudly and stared into his eyes. He stared back, taking in everything about her; her shoulders drooping, her face distraught, the dark wisps escaping her ponytail. Her bottom lip trembled as she held back tears.

Flynn threw both of his arms around her and pulled her into him, and there, just standing in the centre of the hospital waiting room, he held her until her eyes dried up.

Mr Fletcher finally came back out to the waiting room. "They have a lot of tests and scans to do."

"She's going to be okay, though, isn't she?" Tonia asked.

"I really don't know, Tonia. Her state right now is… unprecedented, I suppose."

"What about Annora's parents, Mr Fletcher?" Flynn asked.

"The doctors are calling them right now."

"Can we stay until she's awake?" Tonia asked.

"Even if she wakes up soon, she's been through a lot, so we won't be able to see her for a while."

Tonia nodded sadly.

"Would you guys mind if Audrey comes to pick you up? I'd like to be here when Annora's parents arrive."

"What are you going to tell them?"

Mr Fletcher took a deep breath. "The truth. They deserve that much."

On the ride home, Audrey didn't try to distract the kids from their racing thoughts. Instead, she let the rumble of the road speak for itself. Jessa, in the passenger seat, rested her head back on the headrest and stared, unfocused, at the road ahead. Maggie, behind her in the back seat, closed her eyes.

Flynn looked down at Tonia's hands in her lap. He took his nervous hand and placed it gently atop hers, and she took it graciously, clasping her fingers around his. For the rest of the journey they remained. Overwrought, overtired, and intertwined.

40

"So how are you feeling about your progress?" asked the reporter.

"I'm thrilled," Mr Graves beamed. "I've put my heart and soul into this campaign, and I've been receiving so many positive responses. It was always going to be tough—I mean, we're practically trying to reinvent the party. But we've done our research, and we're staying true to our mission statement, and I'm confident about our future."

"You initially had a great deal of backlash for wanting to relaunch the Parapsych Independence Party, didn't you? For trying to appeal to only a portion of the population."

"Well, one could argue that every political party only appeals to a portion of the population. You can't please everyone, as the saying goes. Parapsychism is at the forefront of my politics, but I do believe having PIP representatives in government would be of immense benefit to everyone." He stroked out the bristles of his moustache. "I do understand the concern, of course I do. Highlighting parapsychs in politics is a radical idea, but I think when everyone sees how beneficial it is, they'll come around. You know, even my wife Elise wasn't sure at first!" He bellowed an exaggerated laugh. "But she saw how passionate I was about making positive changes to everyone's life, and since then she's been nothing but supportive. Isn't that right, darling?"

He hugged his wife closer and squeezed her shoulder a little harder than necessary.

"Mmhmm," she forced a smile, "yes."

"That is lovely," the reporter typed quickly on a netpad. "You do have a beautiful family. And your daughter goes to the Winsbury School of Parapsychology, I hear?" She turned to Cecily.

Cecily looked up from fiddling with her thumbs. "What was that, sorry?"

"Pay attention, angel!" her father urged.

"I was just confirming that you go to Winsbury. Is that right?"

"Oh, yeah that's right."

"Cecily is among the top students in her class, you know," her father added. "She's hoping to be Head Girl one day!"

"Really!" the reporter smiled a gummy smile. "Very impressive. And do you think business or politics is in your future like it was your father's?"

"Oh, I'm sure of it," Mr Graves interrupted. "She practically begged me to set up an internship for her at one of my hotels this summer."

Cecily sat back in the lush padded armchair and looked up at the chandelier on the living room ceiling. The family rarely used the living room, but Mr Graves had insisted on hosting the interview in there. He even had more family photos printed and framed. Forced smiles and stiff poses adorned the mantelpiece.

"Well, Mr Graves, I think I have everything I need. If my editor approves everything in the article, I'm hoping for it to be in print and online tomorrow," she stood, offering her hand to Mr Graves, his wife, and Cecily in turn.

"I'll walk you out," he smiled courteously, leading the reporter out of the living room and into the beflowered hallway of his London mansion.

"Really, Mr Graves (and this is off the record now), I'm very impressed with your campaign. At first, I wasn't sure. But I've been following you closely, and I'm thoroughly impressed at how your campaign is gaining momentum. You've really done all this independently of a campaign manager?"

"This is off the record?" he clarified. The reporter nodded.

"You're right, I didn't have a campaign manager. But I have been working with an associate of sorts."

"Oh?" the reporter's curiosity piqued.

"I can't say much at this stage, but he's been very much a part of my policy design. And I'm planning to announce him as my political partner at the PIP event this weekend."

"This is most intriguing, Mr Graves!"

"I should hope so!" Mr Graves trumpeted his forced laugh once again. "It's very exciting. The truth is, he has some political history of his own that we wanted to omit from this campaign. I wanted my policies to be the spearhead of the party, and for my own candidateship to stand for itself."

"Very wise. Well, I'm excited to cover the event, and I think readers of The London Citizen will be interested to learn more about your new take on politics."

"Just as I'm interested to share my views and continue my campaign for a fairer and more prosperous city."

"Thank you for your time, Mr Graves," the reporter offered her hand once more and he took it, shaking it a little too long and a little too tight for comfort.

41

Jessa's eyes were heavy with three days of disturbed sleep, and her mind lagged with the knowledge that Annora was still in a critical condition in hospital. Next to her, her desk was littered with un-started homework assignments and exam schedules. She lay on her bed, staring up at the ceiling, unblinking.

"Jessa, love? Mr Fletcher is on the phone for you."

"I'll take it on the netpad," she called quickly, hoping he was calling with good news.

The screen glimmered into life, alerting her with a call waiting signal. She waited for the icon to disable that signified her mother hanging up the other line, then pulled on a set of headphones.

"Hello?"

"Jessa? It's Hugo Fletcher."

"Hi."

"I just got back from the hospital."

"Is she okay?"

There was a long pause before he spoke. "She's been coming in and out of consciousness."

"But she's going to be all right." Jessa meant it as a question, but it came out more like a statement. One that she'd been trying to convince herself of for the past three days.

"I don't know, Jess," he sounded tired. "She's in really bad shape."

"I don't understand. Why can't they make her better? That's what healers are for! That's what medicine is for!"

"I know. Right now she's in what you could call a vegetative state. She's technically alive, and has some basic physical functions, but she has severe brain damage. Whatever he did to her… I don't know if she can come back from that."

"So you're saying Annora might die? You're calling me to tell me my friend might be dying right now?"

"I'm sorry, I didn't mean to. I just wanted to talk to you about it."

"Why?"

"…"

"Hugo?"

"I feel so terrible. I feel like I let the Agency down. I let you down. All of you. My responsibility at Winsbury was to protect people and to figure out what was happening. To help find out who was taking all those kids away."

"…"

"And then I developed this relationship with you and your friends, and you were so annoying but I knew I could trust you. I knew you were worth it to the investigation."

"…"

"And still, this happened. He got her. And I couldn't do anything about it."

"It's not your fault."

"I should have stopped it. But instead, I had no idea it was even happening."

"Of course you didn't. Nobody saw this coming."

"Except you."

"…"

"You saw it. You told me you saw it and I didn't believe you."

"Not really. I told you I thought I read the future. You were right not to believe I could do that."

"Sure, you didn't exactly read the future, but your intuition was right all along. You knew something was going on with Annora. You knew it was Lynch. You came to me and trusted me and I let you down."

"…"

"…"

"I don't know what to say now."

"You don't have to say anything. I just want you to know that I'm sorry. I'm sorry that I didn't help, and I'm sorry about Annora. I'm sorry for all of it. But I hope you know I'm on your side."

"I know," she whispered. "I should go to bed."

"Okay. See you tomorrow."

"See you tomorrow. Goodnight."

Jessa only slept when the sheer exhaustion took over her body and forced her into a slumber. Whenever she managed to drift into rest, she was swiftly awoken by nightmares or the uncomfortable soaking of night sweats.

The sunlight of dawn slowly crept in through her window, teasing her, mocking her. She gave up; sleep was too elusive. She opened her curtains and mindlessly watched the sky turning from dark through sunrise shades and finally into a springtime blue. She found herself asking questions upon questions. Questions that mumbled into her mind and hovered there, becoming dull and incomprehensible as even more questions forced their way in. But there was one that she kept coming back to, and still couldn't answer.

How does he do it?

Mr Fletcher said something about a philosopher who knew advanced parapsychism.

What was his name?

Aulious? Something like that. Autreous? Francis Au… something. No. Felix?

Jessa grabbed the netpad and opened a new page. She typed "Felix Autreous."

Did you mean 'Felix Aurelius?'

That's it.

She skimmed the results, but they were less than detailed, mostly giving the same information that Mr Fletcher and Rachel had already mentioned. She clicked a link to find out more about his Hundred Quatrains.

She whispered aloud as she read from the screen.

"It is believed that Aurelius originally hand-wrote three copies of Hundred Quatrains. None of the originals have survived to this day. The only remaining copy is a second-edition which is estimated to be over 1200 years old. It is kept in a high-protection environment in the Special Collections department of London's Humboldt Library, along with original copies of Aurelius' Manuals I, II and III, his infamous compendia of advanced parapsychism."

Manuals.

I need to go there.

I need to see what he saw.

I need to know what he knows.

42

"Audrey!" Jessa slumped up the steps, lopsided under the weight of her backpack, slung low over just one shoulder.

"Hey!" Audrey thumbed her book so she could greet her sister with a hug before organising a better bookmark. Jessa noticed the hug was closer and longer than the sisters had shared for a long time.

"How are you doing?" Audrey asked earnestly.

"I'm all right."

"You look a bit peaky."

"Yeah, well…" Jessa shrugged.

"Do you want to talk about it?"

"No."

"Well, you know you can, right? You can call me any time, or you—"

"I know. It's fine," Jessa smiled weakly. "Really, I'm fine. It was just a long day at school, that's all."

"What did you want to do here?" Audrey changed the subject. She packed away her reading book and took the final swig from her coffee flask before putting it away.

"There's something I want to look at, and I remember you said you could use your student membership to look at the special books here."

"Depending on what it is, of course."

"Ancient books by someone called Felix Aurelius. He has one called Hundred Quatrains and another set called Manuals."

"Hmm, I've never heard him. You're sure those are here?"

The younger sister nodded.

"All right," Audrey conceded, leading her younger sister through the revolving door of the Humboldt Library.

Jessa was surprised and impressed at the security measures required to enter the library. The grumpy frown on the security attendant's brow also did nothing to ease Jessa's tension about the walk-through metal detecting scanner, and she was left wondering just how much of her he was able to see on the screen. When Audrey explained they were hoping to look at something in the special collections, the cantankerous man issued them with a little pager and the instruction to push the button if they needed help accessing a book.

"So what now?" Jessa asked, looking up at the massive structure before her. Multiple storeys of books on shelves, tomes upon tomes of knowledge. The air smelled like leather and must.

Audrey beckoned for Jessa to follow her, and together they approached the cube. They entered into a narrow spiral staircase, and their hands made a tinkling brassy sound on the bannister as they went higher and higher.

"I'm assuming this is about the obvious," Audrey said, "so we'll start at the levels specifically dedicated to parapsych works."

"How much further is that?" Jessa huffed, stepping harder on each step to force herself up.

"Here we are, level six."

"Phew," Jessa breathed heavily and let her eyes adjust to the distinctly dimmer light.

Where the outside of the glass cube had seemed effortlessly beautiful, the inside was cloying and sickly. Each level was overpacked with bookshelves. At the end of the row was a doorway that Jessa presumed led to the outer walkways that had been visible from the ground floor. She considered the number of steps they'd just climbed and felt a pre-emptive vertigo thinking how high up they were. She hoped the books they were looking for would be on one of the inner shelves and not on the outer gallery.

"Aurelius, here it is," Audrey finally said, pushing her finger against a little glass door with the shelf behind it. The copy of Hundred Quatrains itself was larger than Jessa had expected, and it was too large to stand upright in the case, so was lain flat, where they could easily see the front cover. It looked as though it was once beautiful, but time had let it fade and decay to something homely and quite forgotten. Nothing about it jumped out to Jessa's interest.

"Where are the Manuals?"

"They're not here. I guess they're in a different section," Audrey replied, pressing the call button on the pager.

A strangely robotic voice suddenly sounded through speakers they didn't even realise were there.

"Please stand by. Someone will assist you shortly," it said militarily.

Jessa and Audrey waited somewhat impatiently at the behest of the robot voice. A balding man shuffled into the room through the doorway from the outer landing, holding a stack of books so high that he had to rest his chin on the top of the pile to help balance it. He wound his way over to them, the sides of his white lab coat billowing with his gait.

"Hullo hullo, what can I help you with?" he asked in an unusual accent.

"We're looking for something else by this author. Something called 'Manuals'," Audrey said politely.

"Vury good, vury nice. Over here," he disappeared out of sight with his stack. A moment later he returned and began unlocking the glass window of the next shelf over.

From his pocket, he pulled out a pair of stretchy gloves and made a point of putting them on with finesse, showoffingly stretching out all his fingers as the latex encased them. His gloved hands caressed the cover of one book and then another.

Jessa's heartbeat stumbled and a breath caught in her throat. A familiar knot formed in her stomach.

"Come wuth me, please," he trotted ahead, clack-clack-clacking in his brogues.

He pulled down a piece of fabric over an angled reading table and propped the books delicately upon it. Then he offered the Baxter sisters a box from which they were each to pull a set of gloves.

"These are some of our oldest editions!" he beamed. "I am honoured for you to see them, but please, no food, no drink, and absolutely no bare hands. Turn pages one at a time, lifting gently frum the corner of the page. I wull be working over here, so please call for me if you need assistance."

"Where's the other one?" Jessa looked at him.

"Whut?"

"The other one. There's supposed to be three."

"You're mistaken, missy. We have Manuals I and II."

"I can see you have them, but there's supposed to be three of them."

"Uncorrect!" And with that, he snapped around and went to the other desk, where his hefty pile of books was waiting for him.

Jessa frowned at Audrey. "He's wrong. There's one missing." She turned her attention to the first of the two books before her. "Oh," Jessa's heart sank as she turned to the first page, "it's in Latin."

Audrey rolled her eyes. "What were you expecting? It's an ancient text, it's not likely to be written in modern English, is it?"

"Well I don't know, I didn't think about that!"

Audrey sighed loudly.

"Hmm, there are pictures, though," Jessa said, mostly to herself, as she inspected some of the images on the decrepit beige pages.

"They look more like diagrams."

"What's the difference?"

"A diagram is instructional or technical. See here, for example, there's this main image that's repeated across three separate pages. And there are these lines underneath which change direction. My guess would be that they're showing movement."

Jessa bowed her head closer, trying to read the calligraphic writing.

"Gravis… Elevationis?"

"Sounds like it's about lifting up something heavy."

"Wait, do you speak Latin?"

Audrey shook her head. "No, but think about those words. 'Gravis' is like 'grave', or perhaps 'grand' as we might say now. And 'Elevationis' has 'elevation' in it. A lot of our words now come from Latin roots, remember?"

Jessa nodded, and turned more pages.

"Reliquum… adspecto. Vis… pelluceeo," Jessa tried to sound out the headings to see if any more of the words sounded familiar to English. "I was so sure something would be in here."

"What is it you're looking for?" Audrey whispered, moving closer to her sister. Jessa glanced over at the man, who was humming happily, inspecting some parchment with a magnifying glass.

"I had a feeling that Lynch had some connection to these books. I even felt something when the man took it off the shelf, but now, nothing. Maybe I was wrong."

Audrey paused, remembering Hugo's words. She might actually be onto something. "Let's keep looking," she encouraged.

The two sisters hunched over the large book, trying to make sense of the black ink etched into the sandy-coloured pages. Jessa huffed audibly through her nose. "Come on," she said under her breath. "I know there's something here… where are you…" Her voice became quieter and quieter, to a whisper and then to barely anything. "Show me… show me…"

Jessa squidged the thin rubbery layer of the gloves between her thumb and forefinger. She glanced over her shoulder to check the library attendant wasn't watching, then pulled off the sheath, freeing her slightly damp hand into the warm air.

Audrey moved to block the man's view in case he turned around.

Jessa felt the thickness of the page between her thumb and forefinger, gently rubbing her skin over the wovenesque papery leaves. Then she reached out and placed her clammy hand onto the cover of Manual II.

There it was, the moment she was hoping for and dreading.

Whoosh.

Darkness. The piercing ring seemed to come from inside her own skull. Then the scene came into focus.

She was hovering above the same table at which her bodily counterpart had been standing just moments ago. He was beneath her. Even from above, she knew it was Silas Lynch. His hair was pinguid and flat, black but greying.

The two men Jessa had seen before were standing back against the wall.

"Here we are," the frizzy head of the white-coated library man walked into view, carrying the Manuals, just as he had done for Jessa and Audrey. But he had three books, not two. He offered Silas gloves.

"No."

"Sur, it is the rule that gloves must be worn when reading these books. They are vury old and vury dulicate."

"Tell me what this says," his voice was quiet and sour.

"Please sur, you must put on the gloves before you touch the artefact!" he shoved the box in front of Silas's face.

"Listen to me, idiot," Silas put his hands around the man's neck and squeezed.

The man gasped for air. His fingers pulled at Silas', trying to release his grip. But Silas kept his hold and lifted him so that the toes of his maroon shoes were just barely scraping the ground.

Silas slowly took his hands away from physically touching the man, but by the sheer force of Silas' will, the man remained suspended.

"Please!" he begged.

"Tell me what this says," Silas said again, holding one of the books open and holding it in the man's red face.

"I don't know! It's advanced Latin!"

"Tell me."

"I swear I don't know!"

Silas swooped his hand through the air and the man's body followed, slamming into a bookcase and slumping to the ground where he sniffled for reprieve.

A growl of irritation escaped Silas's throat, and he turned his attention to the book. Jessa watched him flip through the pages. He closed Manual III and gripped it under his arm.

Silas moved to the snivelling man on the ground, and crouched lower.

"Face me," he instructed, and the blubbering man looked directly at him.

"Please don't hurt me, I promise I won't call the police."

Silas reached his sinewy hand toward the whimpering man's face and touched his skin.

Whoosh.

Jessa's floating consciousness transported from above the scene to inside the man's perspective as he looked into Silas's dark, vacant eyes.

"Of course you won't call the police. You won't call anyone. You won't remember any of this," the words slithered from his thin lips as he placed his cold fingertips around the man's head, pressing divots into his flesh.

A low gurgle escaped through the mouth that Jessa felt but was not her own. She felt the man's eyes roll back into his head as his consciousness faded. Finally, she felt the heavy and aching sensation in the man's brain as his memory was sucked out, violently and violated, until he collapsed into an exhausted heap.

Whoosh.

She saw the room from a different pair of eyes. Slightly dulled and everything greyish, she looked around through Silas's vision. He reached out his scarred hand and lightly touched the front cover of Manual II.

"We have what we need."

And he walked away.

Whoosh.

Jessa was pulled out of the scene by the grasp of a hand on her shoulder.

"What are you doing! I said no touching!" the man cawed, frantically blinking through his little round glasses. He pulled her bare hand away from the paper. "You cunnot touch the books, young lady!"

"Sorry… sorry," Jessa managed to say.

"I thunk you'd better go," he said, exasperated and frazzled, inspecting the page with the magnifying glass where Jessa had touched it.

"We're leaving," Audrey hurried her dazed sister out.

"You can't just come in here and disobey the rules… you have to ruspect the rules, ruspect the rules… no ruspect, these kids… grubby fingers…" his voice faded behind them into the warm upstairs with every step of their descent of the spiral staircase.

43

"It's inhumane," Jessa said, shaking her head vigorously.

"I agree completely," Maggie sighed. "It's practically cannibalistic. I mean, it's a deliberate separation of the weak from the strong."

"I think you might be exaggerating," Tonia shrugged. "I quite like dodgeball."

"Yeah, because you're good at it!" Maggie exclaimed.

"That's true," Tonia neatly tied up the laces on her white pumps.

"How are we doing in here?" Ms Jordan poked her head into the changing room.

"Ms Jordan, we really don't want to play dodgeball," said Maggie. "Please can we do something else? Tennis maybe?"

"Sure, if you want to go out to the courts in Winsbury Square Park, that's fine with me," the young teacher smiled. "I'll come out and check on you in a little while."

As soon as she'd walked away, Flynn appeared in the doorway with his hands over his eyes. "Are you decent?"

"We don't just get naked in here, you know," said Jessa.

"I don't know what you all get up to in your own time," he peered through a parting in his fingers, "girls are weird."

§

"I'm pretty sure lounging on the court isn't legal in official tennis rules," Tonia said as Jessa splayed out on the ground before even making one serve.

"I'm too tired for sports," Jessa replied.

The rest of them joined her on the ground.

"Do you think it's possible for us to learn the kind of powers he has?" she said thoughtfully.

"You mean evil powers?" said Tonia.

"Parapsych power is neither good nor evil," said Flynn. "It's up to the individual to decide how they want to use their abilities."

"Any power can make people do horrible things," said Maggie. "For instance political or financial power."

"It might not be that the power made them that way," said Flynn. "They might have already been inclined to do bad things, and that's what made them seek out the power."

"Silas is both," said Jessa. She plucked at the square holes of her tennis racket. "He was powerful, but nobody believed it, which made him want to do evil things, so he got more powerful and now wants to do even more evil things."

She positioned the tennis ball above her palm and let go. It levitated two inches above her skin. Flynn walked on his knees to get closer to Jessa. He moved his face close to the ball and made a gentle twisting motion with his hand. The ball began to spin on its axis.

"Do you think everyone at the Agency has those super-abilities?" Maggie asked.

"Probably," Jessa broke her concentration to answer, and the ball dropped onto the ground. "If Fletcher's anything to go by, that is. He still won't tell me anything about his psych abilities, though. He keeps saying it's not important that I know."

"He's right," said Maggie. "It's not really any of your business."

"I think it is my business; we're supposed to be on the same team. We're working together to bring Silas down."

"Silas aside," said Tonia, "it would be cool if we learned how to do some of the things they've told us about. Imagine if we could combine our abilities like they do. We'd be much stronger."

"Well, why can't we?" Flynn looked at them. "Nobody ever told us it was possible, so we never tried. But we should try."

Jessa pushed herself into a cross-legged position.

"I don't know," Maggie looked concerned, "what if something goes wrong?"

"Like what?" said Tonia. "We could just try something simple."

"What about this," said Jessa. "My telekinesis is strong enough to hover the ball if I physically place it in the air and let go. But if the ball starts on the ground, I can't lift it upwards. So why don't we try just lifting it up into the air?"

The four of them sat facing inward. Knees touching knees, hands connected. Jessa placed the tennis ball into the middle of the space and re-joined hands with Maggie beside her. They all breathed gently and deeply. Eyes relaxed, gaze softened, concentration focused on the fuzzy yellow ball.

It didn't move.

"It's not working," said Tonia. "Maybe we're not strong enough to do this after all."

"Wait," said Flynn. "At the Agency, when the others combined their powers to try and heal Annora, they didn't all touch hands. Sue was the main healer, and the others, sort of, gave her their power, remember? Maybe we should try that."

"Matt helped, he must be a healer too," Maggie said.

"Flynn and Jessa are the best telekins, so let's have the two of them try," said Tonia. "And Maggie and I will be the... I don't know, the givers? Whatever you want to call it."

Jessa and Flynn nodded and took hold of each other's hands. Maggie and Tonia moved behind them just as the Agency members had done. Again, Jessa and Flynn focused their attention on the ball while Maggie and Tonia closed their eyes in deep contemplation.

The ball started to move. Not upwards, but shivered slightly from side to side as though it were trying to carry out their wish but just couldn't make it happen.

Flynn turned his attention from the ball and onto Jessa, joining Maggie and Tonia in their assist. He placed both of his hands onto her shoulder. Tonia took his lead, and moved her hands from their position on Flynn's back to Jessa's.

Jessa inhaled sharply. The other three of them opened their eyes to see the ball moving upward through the air, higher and higher. One foot, two feet, three feet up, above their heads.

"Stop," Jessa said.

The ball stopped.

"Spin."

The ball spun.

"And what are you dumb fucks up to, then?" The ball dropped and incrementally bounced to a halt as Cecily stepped in front of them. "Wow, guys. Lifting up a tennis ball… I'm impressed. That's going to really gonna help you in life."

"I don't know, Cecily," Jessa stood up, "it's probably more useful than your tingly-finger fire trick, and you seem to have found plenty of uses for that."

"If you must know, Jessamine, I now have a few more tricks up my sleeve."

"Oh, really?" Tonia said. "Please demonstrate, because we'd just love to see that."

"Don't worry, mongrel, you'll all see exactly what I can do."

"Presumably one of the things you can do is 'play truant'," Maggie said, looking up and down at Cecily's outfit.

"No, Mags," said Jessa, "one of the things she does is 'do P.E. in prostitute boots'."

"You all think you're so funny," Cecily sneered.

"We're pretty funny," Tonia said.

"I wish I could see all your faces when it happens," Cecily said quietly. "Did you know that it's possible to kill someone and actually take their parapsych power from them? I read that recently. Interesting, don't you think?"

"Wait, Cecily. Hold up," Jessa said. "*You* read a book? Are you feeling okay?"

"Oh, Jessamine, you have no idea how good I feel," Cecily swooped back her mane of silken hair. "I feel strong, and rested, and positive. And I've found someone who understands me, you know? I'm just so done with these pathetic boys. I'm only interested in real men, now. Not that any of you will ever know what a relationship is like, unless, I don't know, maybe you'll get lucky and the adult retard club will have speed-dating nights or something.'

"What do you want, Cecily? Why don't you just leave us alone?" Flynn crossed his arms.

"Chill out, hobo, I'm on my way out. I have more important business to attend to than to stay at this ridiculous excuse for a school."

"Great. Have fun with that," he waved sarcastically. "See you around."

"See me around? Yeah," she said, "you will."

"Always a pleasure, Cecily!" Tonia called out as Cecily walked away.

"What a nutjob," Jessa tutted.

"Do you think she's really been reading about that sort of thing?" asked Maggie.

"Of course not," said Jessa. "It's all an act with her. Look, we can't get sidetracked by Cecily. We have more important things to concentrate on right now. Let's try this thing again, but this time we'll do the racket."

44

"Morning, petal!" Mrs Baxter chirped from behind the morning newspaper. "Are you all right?"

Jessa was bundled up in her fluffy dressing gown.

"I don't feel well," she groaned, holding her head low to let her bedraggled hair hang limply down over her unwashed face.

"You poor thing! Well, you should probably stay home from school today."

"I think you're right," Jessa said pathetically, looking at her mother with big, sad eyes.

"I'll call the school in a minute. I'd stay home and take care of you but you know we have this big event tomorrow night, and I really need to go into the office."

"I know, don't worry about it. I'm probably going to stay in bed all day anyway. I think I just need to rest."

"All right, poppet. Do you want me to bring you up some breakfast?"

"No it's okay, I'll just get a drink," Jessa poured herself a large mug of tea and poured the milk in slowly, watching the brown and white liquids intertwining.

"Feel better, love," Mrs Baxter said sympathetically, watching her youngest daughter shuffle her slippered feet out of the kitchen.

Jessa sat, fully clothed on the edge of her bed, supping at her tea and listening to her mother's morning routine about the house. She listened for the familiar click of the front door key turning in the lock, followed by the slam of the car door, and the car pulling out of the driveway.

She gave it fifteen minutes, on the off chance that her mother would have to return home to pick up something she'd forgotten, which gave Jessa plenty of time in which to splash some water on her face, brush her teeth and run a comb quickly through her hair.

Less than an hour later, and Jessamine Baxter was on the train to Woburn Vale.

She stared out the window at the whirr of English countryside green, and her mind began to wander.

He taught himself those powers. He didn't even go to school.

So far, Jessa's parapsychological abilities had become considerably stronger thanks to the Winsbury curriculum.

But could they be stronger?

We only have one parapsych skills class a week.

What if we had more?

She thought about how parapsych students are taught the broad curriculum in lower school, which is supposed to help hone the ability that comes most naturally to them, and those are the parapsych skills they are encouraged to continue in upper school P-Levels.

But what if we could study them all?

One question led to another, until Jessa's train of thought was interrupted by a very bored-sounding announcement.

"This station is Woburn Vale."

Jessa stepped onto the platform, pausing for a moment at the still-open doors, suddenly questioning her own actions. But the doors slid shut, and the train accelerated away.

§

"Who goes there?" Mr Jackson's old voice wavered.

"Hello, Mr Jackson. I visited once before, with my friends, do you remember?"

He studied her closely. "Yes, I remember. A young boy and some girls. With a tall blond man, correct?"

"That's right," Jessa smiled.

"You came to ask about Silas."

"Yes. Would you mind if I ask you some more questions?"

"You're by yourself this time?"

"Yes, sir."

"I suppose my crossword can wait," he hobbled back to the living room.

The room was just as she remembered. The fading snapshots of memories, the fusty paraphernalia. It felt cluttered and welcoming.

"D'ya want tea? I have Earl Grey."

"Earl Grey would be lovely, thank you."

"Humph," he shuffled from the room.

She took the time alone to inspect the room closer. She peered into all the shining photographs. The house felt old fashioned and homey, a place where happy people lived. She couldn't tell if the old man was happy anymore, but by the images of smiling adults and giddy children, it appeared he'd experienced many happy moments.

Jessa found herself drawn to one photograph in particular, of a dashing young man, clearly a youthful Mr Jackson, with three children. Two young girls in flowery dresses perched on his knees, and a very young-looking dark-haired boy sat cross-legged on the grass in front of them. The boy's inky eyes stared into the camera, unlit and ghoulish.

"That's him," Francis said, carefully carrying two over-full porcelain mugs back into the living room. Jessa graciously took the one offered to her.

"I hope you like it milky," he said gruffly.

He plopped his tired body down into his armchair. "That was taken at a garden party we had one summer. All the neighbours came over; it was quite the bash. So what do you want to know, lassy?"

Jessa thought for a moment, then decided to be honest. She'd come too far and seen too much to continue withholding information.

"Sir, what would you say if I told you Silas was still alive, and had been in hiding this whole time?"

He didn't look nearly as shocked as she'd expected. "If he'd been hiding for twenty-or-so years? Well, I'd be mad at him for not ever visiting me!"

"Really? Would you still want him to visit, after everything that happened?"

"Of course I would. I always considered that boy family."

"Why do you still care about him? I mean, he did such terrible things. And if he's been alive all this time and deliberately didn't let you know—even though he probably knew how much you loved him—wouldn't you just be angry and not want to see him?"

"Pah. I'm too old for grudges. He did some questionable things back then, but you have to understand, he truly believed he was doing them for the right reason. And despite his actions, he's still human, and I subscribe to the much-outdated belief of forgiving all others."

"But… what if…" Jessa stuttered, "what if he was still doing those things? Things that you didn't even know were possible?"

"I'm not sure what you're getting at, missy."

"I've seen him," her voice came out weak and crackly, like she might have been getting over a cold. But there was no illness, just the harsh reality of telling a complete outsider her theory. "Not in real life. Not yet, anyway. But I have these… visions. It's a type of intuition. I just learned I have some kind of futuresight, and I can also read objects that show me information about what happened around them. And I've seen him, and I've seen the kind of things he's doing. He's still alive, and he's preparing…"

Francis blinked. He looked sad, and confused, and curious. "What do you think he's preparing for?"

"I don't know. But I know he's learned how to enhance his parapsych abilities, and he's using them to hurt people. He… ummm… he hurt one of my best friends. The red-haired girl who was here with me last time."

"Oh goodness, is she all right?"

"She's in the hospital. It's bad. He brainwashed her."

"Really?"

"It looks as though he made her want to commit suicide."

"Hmm…" he uttered, quietly enough that she barely heard it. A gentle softness came over his wrinkled face.

"Fortunately, we were able to get to Annora before she actually… you know… but yeah, it's grim."

"I'm very sorry to hear that."

The two of them sat in silence for a moment, feeling the glassy heat from the outside of their mugs.

Jessa finally spoke. "Can I tell you something?"

"Mmhmm."

"I know I should probably be terrified, but really," she hesitated, "I'm fascinated by him." She finished her sentence quietly, as though she was saying something she might be judged for. "Is that wrong?"

"No, it's not wrong, kid," Francis sighed. "I always have been. He was such an intriguing child. What kind of four-or-five-year-old disapproves of the school system? What kind of child has so much disdain for other humans? He was such a unique youngster—it's no wonder he was more powerful than anyone knew, because nobody believed that he could be that powerful. The warning signs were there, and nobody cared to see them."

"I think he's planning something big. I've seen the sort of parabilities he has. You know him better than most—do you think he can be stopped?"

"Well, I suppose that if he could remain alive all this time, getting stronger and planning some kind of big display, I'd say there's no chance of stopping him."

Jessa stared into her half-drunk Earl Grey. "Can I use your toilet?"

"Upstairs. It'll be the door right ahead of you."

Jessa exited the bathroom and wiped her damp hands on her jeans. Her hand reached for the bannister, and she was just about to take the first step when she noticed something. A door to her right, closed. And where the light shone in through a small window and hit the surface of the faded door paint, she could see the outline of where childish block letters once were. "Silas."

She paused, dangling her foot over the step, considering her options.

Then, with a short exhale, she pulled back her foot and moved to the door.

The handle moved easily and quietly.

Jessa hadn't known exactly what she expected from Silas' old bedroom, but what she saw inside was not it.

Clean, not a speck of dust anywhere, with walls and floor painted brilliant white. Not at all faded. A single bed, topped with contemporary bedding, a divot on the edge where someone had recently sat. A bookcase too small for all its books, as some of them stood in stacks on the top and on the floor next to it. Jessa's attention was attracted to a large wooden screen blocking the furthest corner from view.

She approached the screen and saw the edge of it wasn't completely flush against the wall. A conveniently person-sized gap, she noticed.

She gently blew out the breath she hadn't realised she was holding. Then stepped through the space.

"What the…?" she whispered to no-one.

The reverse of the screen was also painted crisp white. On the floor lay the black outline of a circle. And right in the corner, an old church pulpit, painted in layers upon layers of white paint until every inch of grain was smothered in a smooth disguise.

And there, atop the stand, was the book. Jessa recognised it immediately. The same yellowing pages, the same occultish storybook images, the same lurch in her stomach. But this time, unlike the copy she'd seen in the museum, the book had not been defaced with symbols etched into the pages.

Jessa peeled over a page.

"You shouldn't be in here."

She spun around with a gasp. Francis Jackson stood in the gap between the screen and the wall, blocking her into the corner.

"Oh… I was just…" Jessa stammered.

"You can't be in here. He'll be very upset."

"What?"

"He doesn't like strangers going in his room."

"Who? Silas?"

"Nobody is supposed to see this."

"I didn't see anything, though. We can pretend nothing happened. I'll just go."

"I don't think I can let you go now. He'll need to make sure you can't tell anyone."

"I won't tell, I swear. You can let me go. Please, let's just go back downstairs—"

"No."

"Mr Jackson, please—"

"Young people these days have no respect."

"I'm sorry, I just— What is that? Is that a knife? What are you doing?"

"He said someone would find it eventually, and I said 'no no no, nobody will find us here. Nobody will find out our secret', but as usual, he was right."

"Please don't come any closer. Put it down, please. Can we talk about this?"

He stepped toward her.

"No! Please!"

Her back was against the wall with nowhere else to go.

"Stop!"

Jessa summoned every inch of her body and in one forceful movement, pushed her weight into the old man. He stumbled backwards, knocking the screen flat onto the floor with a loud thwack, and the weapon disengaged from his hand and flew across the room.

Jessa leapt forward and made a break for the door, but the man reached out his hand with an unforeseen dexterity and grabbed around her ankle.

She tripped and fell forward, just barely avoiding a head-on collision with the wall. His fingers gripped tighter as her legs thrashed and kicked. And then.

Whoosh.

"There you go. Happy now?"

" … "

"Of course not."

" … "

"It still has all your scribbles on it. Why did you want it back?"

"For the same reason I have the other copy in this room. It's much easier for me to transport when I use the book. Takes a lot less energy. Now I can keep this one with me."

"Fair enough. Though I still think it would be easier to use the door."

"I can't risk being seen, and you know I don't like to be outside. The sunlight hurts my skin."

"Get an umbrella! Or a hat! The transporting thing seems like such a lot of effort."

"It's not. Not in here, anyway. I told you I can teach you how to do it."

"Ha. At my age?"

"A parapsych is never too old to enhance their ability, Francis. I keep telling you that."

"Pish posh. I'm too old."

"You're—"

"Fine, I'm not too old, I just can't be bothered."

"…"

"Don't give me that look."

"…"

"Oh, Silas, while you're here, I need some help getting a step ladder from the shed. I know you can't do it, with your back and all, but maybe when you go, you can send in one of your boys."

"Yes."

"I'd be so grateful."

"…"

"You seem so down today. More-so than usual, anyway."

"I'm tired. I've been transporting a lot, and doing maintenance on my tag connections… You know how it is."

"I don't really know what that means, but I can imagine it takes a lot out of you. I wish you'd take better care of yourself, though. You know, you can still move in here."

"You say that every time I visit."

"And I mean it every time!"

"Francis, you know I can't. I have too much to do. It's all right; I have someone looking out for me."

"Whoever it is, I don't trust them."

"You don't have to."

"Hmm."

"I don't know why you always look so worried."

"Because I'm always worried about you."

"You needn't be.

"There's plenty of need. You look paler than ever, skinny as a rake, and knowing where you live and who you surround yourself with, I'm going to worry and you can't stop me."

"You're a good man, Francis."

Whoosh.

Jessa's foot wriggled free from the old man's grasp and she forced herself to stand. She ran down the stairs so fast she had to cling desperately to the handrail to avoid falling completely. Francis Jackson's shouts turned to cries for help.

"You can't leave an old man lying on the ground!"

Jessa paused at the bottom of the stairs, heart pummelling around in her chest. She expected to see her attacker come flying after her, but it never happened.

"Help me, please!" came his hysterical lament.

Jessa scrunched her eyes closed. She couldn't go back. She grabbed her jacket from the living room and departed the house with as much composure as she could muster.

Closing the gate behind her, Jessa felt a wave of nausea. She leaned her body onto a van parked next to the curb, feeling the cool white metal chill her forehead. She took a deep breath and sprinted back to the train station.

§

"Jessa?"

"Mr Fletcher! Thank goodness you picked up. I was worried you'd be in a lesson."

"I have a free period right now—I'm just doing some marking. Where are you?"

"I just… I'm really sorry…"

"Why? What happened?"

"I just… I went…"

"Jessa?"

"I went to see Francis Jackson."

"You what?!"

"…"

"Are you kidding me?"

"No…"

"Son of a… Ugh! Are you alone? Where are you right now?"

"I'm alone, yeah. I'm on the train back to London."

"Why on earth would you go there by yourself?"

"I don't know, I just had this compulsion to go. I kept thinking about all this stuff, and I wanted to ask him more about Lynch."

"Well, did you get to do that, at least?"

"Sort of. I found out that Lynch has been visiting Francis. He goes there regularly."

"Okay, well that's something."

"Yeah but I have to tell you something else."

"Go on."

"I was sort of, snooping, and I went in Silas' room. And then Francis Jackson caught me and tried to attack me."

"Bloody hell, are you serious? Are you hurt?"

"No, I'm fine. I got away. But, umm… he was still on the floor when I left."

"Oh no… was he conscious?"

"Yes, I didn't hurt him or anything like that. But he couldn't get up, so I ran away and went straight back to the train station. What should I do?"

"Nothing. You do absolutely nothing. I'll handle it."

"Are you sure?"

"Of course."

"I'm really sorry. I didn't mean to put more stress on you."

"Don't worry, I'll take care of everything. Please just promise me that you're going straight home."

"I am, I swear."

"And no more skiving."

"Okay."

"All right. I'll see you soon."

"Yeah. Bye."

•306•

45

Hugo Fletcher stared out his kitchen window, looking down upon the London street lights. His feet were cold against the ceramic tiles, and his leg hairs bristled against the chill from the inoperative radiator. He wished he'd put on his dressing gown.

Usually, through the walls of his flat he could hear the neighbours to the right yelling about something or other, and the neighbour to the left practising violin. On occasion, he could even hear the neighbour to the left of the violin player yelling at the violin player to shut the f—k up. But in the starkness of the night, there were no neighbours, no violins, no cursing, and as far as Hugo Fletcher himself was involved, no sleeping.

"Babe?"

"Audrey, I thought you were asleep. Did I disturb you?"

"No, I just woke up and panicked when you weren't there."

"Sorry," he sighed and took a seat on one of the kitchen island bar stools.

"What's going on?" she ran a compassionate hand through his hair.

"Can't sleep."

"You really should go to the doctor. Maybe they can give you something for it."

"I know it's just stress."

"But if you don't sort out the insomnia, you won't be able to handle the stress."

He reached his hands away from him and rested his forehead on the island.

"I feel like I'm going crazy," he said.

"About what? This Agency thing?"

"Lynch, the Agency, all of it. I'm so anxious all the time."

"Really? You've never said that before."

"I know. I wanted to keep it to myself."

"Well, you shouldn't. You know I'm here for you."

"I know."

"Can you tell me what's on your mind?"

He placed the palms of his hands into his eye sockets.

"Ugh," he grunted.

She waited.

"I keep reliving some memories. Things that haven't come up in a while. I thought I'd processed them and moved on. But now, it's all coming back."

"Like what?"

"My sister."

"What?"

"I had a sister. Imogen. She died."

"Oh, sweetheart. I'm sorry. I had no idea."

"I know, I don't talk about her. I find it too difficult to even think about her most of the time."

"Do you want to tell me what happened?"

He leaned on his elbows. His fingers palpated his forehead. His eyes glazed in reflection.

"We were on holiday in Ireland. It was our first family holiday since we were kids, because Immy had finished her P-Levels and we were celebrating that she accepted a place at St Andrew's. She was so excited; you wouldn't believe it. She'd always wanted to go to Ireland, so my parents thought it would be a good idea for all of us to go together, as I was home from uni for the summer, too.

We rented this little fishing boat, the two of us, and went out on the water. We were both experienced with boats, because my dad used to have one when we lived in Sussex. So we went out, and it was this perfect August afternoon. The sea was perfect. The temperature was perfect. And then she got all weird and said she had a bad feeling. Like a deja vu, she said. She had this feeling there was a storm coming.

And I told her I'd checked the weather, and it was forecast to be sunny all day. And again, she told me she had a really strong feeling that we should go back to shore. And I made fun of her for thinking she could predict something like that."

Hugo's face ached with the memory. His lips drew tightly together; his nostrils flared with every exaggerated breath. He swallowed hard.

"She was right. Of course."

"Sweetheart…" Audrey rubbed loose circles on his back.

"She was such a funny kid. She'd always be putting on these ridiculous shows for us, where she would play all these different characters. There'd be songs and dances. She was quite the musician. She barely needed piano lessons, she was so naturally good at it. She wanted to study music and art history."

"She sounds like a lovely sister."

"She was," he nodded vacantly. "She was perfect. And I couldn't save her."

"It wasn't your fault."

"Of course it was. I convinced her that her intuition was wrong. And I lay there with her as the black clouds came in. And still, I kept saying 'I'm sure it'll be fine' instead of heading back to shore immediately. And then once the rain started, we had no chance. We were trapped out there on a psychotic sea. The waves were knocking the boat in every direction. And she just held on to me so tight, and she was crying and begging me to tell her everything would be all right. And I did, I kept telling her that same fucking lie. I didn't know anything. I just kept saying it. Empty words that didn't mean anything. I couldn't protect her. The water got so deep into the top of the boat that it capsized and tipped us out. I managed to grab on to part of the boat as it floated, but she got swept further away. I couldn't reach her."

His bottom lip shook. His voice began to choke and strain through the desperate tears that he tried to hold back.

"The last thing she said was my name. She just kept screaming my name."

"Babe, there was nothing you could have done. It was an accident."

"I had my chance to listen to her. And I didn't. Because of me, that beautiful girl lost her life. My parents lost their daughter. They can't ever forgive me."

"Is that why you don't see them anymore?"

"My mother told me she never wanted to see me again. She got her wish."

"People can say horrible things when they're grieving. I'm sure enough time has passed that she'll feel differently now."

"I don't think so. They moved house last year and never gave me their new address. She hates me."

"Maybe one day they'll come around."

"Maybe," he sighed. "Do you believe in fate?"

"No."

"I didn't think I did either, but I just keep thinking about how similar Jessa is to Immy. And I wonder if maybe I was meant to come here because the universe knew that I would understand when Jessa needed someone to hear her. But still, I didn't believe her at first, and I just… ugh, I feel so bad about that."

"But you came round, you're supporting her now, and that's the important thing."

"Maybe."

"Not maybe—definitely. She's lucky to have you on her side."

"I really hope so."

46

"Are you sure you're up to it?" Mrs Baxter said, distractedly shuffling through piles of invoices, receipts and binders.

"Yeah I feel much better, don't worry."

"All right. Let me put your hair up in a bun, though, because that's what the other waiting staff will have." She turned Jessa round and pulled back her hair tightly, smoothing over her head to make sure all the flyaways were captured. She rolled a hairband off her wrist and over the round ball of hair.

"You look so cute; it's like a little tuxedo! Adorable," she beamed at her grimacing daughter. "And have you realised, this is your first job! What a big day!"

"Mrgh," Jessa poked out her tongue disapprovingly.

"Oh shush, sometimes it's okay to celebrate becoming an adult, you know."

"Yeah yeah," Jessa said, walking away.

A knock sounded at the door, and Jessa hurried to let Flynn inside.

"Flynn's here! We're going upstairs for a bit!" Jessa urged Flynn to follow her upstairs quickly before her mother had the chance to make any more comments of cuteness.

"I have a confession," Jessa said quickly, making sure her bedroom door was closed shut. "I went to Woburn Vale yesterday."

"You what? Why would you go out alone like that?"

"I had to! I needed to know more about him!"

"That was really irresponsible," Flynn suddenly looked so grown-up. "We agreed we were in this together. You know, if you'd asked, we would have gone with you."

"I know. And honestly, I wish you had been there. It got a bit crazy."

"What do you mean?"

"I'll explain later. It's a long story."

Flynn gave Jessa a disapproving glare.

"Please don't be angry at me."

"I'm not angry. I'm just disappointed you went without us. Did you at least find out anything new?"

"Well, I found out he goes there, he visits that house."

"What?!"

"I know."

"So what can we do? Can we get people from the Agency to go there and wait for him?"

"I doubt it. What are they going to do, just handcuff him and walk him out?"

"I guess not."

"I told Mr Fletcher all about it, so if there's any way we can use that information to help, he'll figure out a way."

§

The hotel ballroom was extravagant even before the ostentatious centrepieces and place settings, but all the fancy additions turned it into a grotesquerie of opulence. The ceiling dripped with crystal, and candlesticks grew out of the walls, illuminating the room in a still and expensive glow.

On the stage, red, blue and white beams of light rocketed up toward the ceiling, occasionally performing a little dance to bursts of sound that hustled in through speakers as a sound technician somewhere out of sight made sure everything was working.

Mrs Baxter clipped around the room in her best strappy heels, blurting instructions into a headset microphone while confirming place-setting names on a netpad strapped to her forearm. Her staff, in matching earpieces, hurried around the room finalising the goodie-bags, primping the flowers, straightening chairs, and all the other superficial things that suddenly become so important when someone is paying an unthinkable amount for it all

"This is so fancy," Jessa said as she and Flynn wandered the hallways of the hotel, killing time before they had to join the rest of the waiting staff. "Look at the size of these doors! These must be the mega luxury suites."

Their footsteps didn't even make a sound as the soles of their shoes pressed into the expensive plush fabric of the carpet.

"Hey, this room's open," Flynn said, peeking in through the gap.

"Let's go in," Jessa whispered back.

"We can't do that!"

"Just a quick peek! It's probably empty, anyway. I bet someone just checked out. Why else would the door be open? Come on!"

Jessa entered the suite's expansive living room. She brushed her fingers over the smooth maple of a grand piano.

"Wait," Flynn whispered. "Did you hear that?"

"Hear what?" Jessa said at her normal volume.

"I thought I heard a woman."

"There's nobody here, doofus, calm down." Jessa wandered into what turned out to be a very impressive bathroom. Flynn followed hesitantly, and they admired a ginormous whirlpool tub.

Suddenly, the suite door slammed.

Jessa and Flynn froze.

"I don't know what we can do with her," a man said angrily. "You know, I really thought my goddamn wife would have the decency to stand by me on my big night. Is that too much to ask? I can hear you struggling, Elise! I've told you, if you want me to untie you, all you have to do is play nice! But you're not interested in that, are you! Stupid bitch."

"She's not important," a second, quieter, and eerier voice replied.

"But still, it looks so much better to the voters if I can present myself as 'the family man.' That's how The Times reported me. The Family Man. What good is The Family Man without his fucking family?"

"Calm yourself," the quiet man instructed.

"I need a drink. Whisky?" he said, but the other man didn't answer. "Whisky, Mr Lynch?" the loud man offered again.

Jessa's head snapped round to face Flynn.

"Lynch?!" she mouthed.

Flynn shook his head.

"I need to see if it's him," Jessa whispered, crawling forward on her hands and knees to peer around the doorframe. Flynn lurched his body over hers and pulled her back from behind. "Don't be crazy," he whispered forcefully into her ear.

"I'm gonna take a piss and then we should head down there I suppose," the loud man said.

"Shit," Flynn whispered. "Quick, in here," he opened a door to a towel cupboard, which had just enough space at the bottom for the two of them to crouch in.

The man's shiny tailored shoes clucked on the tiled floor. Just able to see out through the slats in the door, they both recognised the man as Jameson Graves. He stood with his back to them.

Urinating with a groan, he muttered under his breath. "I'm gonna kill that bitch. She's really got it coming. That bitch." He flushed the toilet and re-zipped his trousers. "No," he said, leaning heavily on the sink and sighing at his reflection. "This is your big night, Jameson. Don't make it about her. This is the night you've been waiting for."

He splashed water on his face without washing his hands first, then held a fresh, puffy towel to his skin. He strode back out of the bathroom, and Jessa and Flynn both sighed in silent relief.

"Sounds like they'll be leaving soon. We're gonna be fine," Flynn whispered.

Jessa's toes started to tingle from crouching awkwardly.

"Shall we head downstairs?" Mr Graves invited.

"No," Mr Lynch replied.

"What? What are you talking about? We have to go downstairs."

"We do. But not yet."

"Why?"

"Mr Graves, now is probably a good time to tell you that this night isn't going to go exactly as you planned."

"What do you mean?"

"This is my night, Mr Graves. Everything we've been working on up until now, has been my plan."

"That's not true at all. This is my party. I've been campaigning for months."

"And I've been controlling you for a year."

Silence.

"What? You haven't been controlling anything! You've been my partner, but this is my party!"

"The truth, Mr Graves, is this: There is no party. There will be no vote. There is only Silas Lynch."

Jessa grabbed Flynn's hand. Neither of them noticed the sweat drenching their palms.

"I suppose I should really thank you, Mr Graves. You inadvertently set me up with this wonderful event, an audience full of people who are interested in a political shift, a modest but reasonable media presence of reporters… you've really done a stellar job," he spoke slowly, patronisingly, amusedly. "So I have two options for you. The first is that you agree to stand by my side as I address the nation tonight and inspire this great country to pursue a great new future. The second, if you prefer not to be an accomplice to my revolution, is a little more macabre."

A knock sounded at the hotel door.

"Ah, perfect," Silas said. "My newest cohort. Perhaps she can help you decide."

"Hello, Daddy."

"Cecily?" Mr Graves said. "What's going on here? I demand an explanation!"

"You've always been one for demanding, haven't you, Daddy?"

"Cecily, this doesn't concern you. I command that you leave right now."

"You command it, do you? What a surprise. Tell me, is my mother still here too? You have her tied up in the big wardrobe, I presume?"

"How did you…"

"What, how did I know that? Because I know everything, now. That's right, Daddy, I know a lot more than you've given me credit for. Here's an excellent example: I know that you have another family in Abu Dhabi, and that you send them money to keep them quiet about it. I know that you've been beating my mother for the entire duration of your marriage. And I know that you never loved me. I'm your daughter! All I ever wanted was a family who cared about me, and instead, I got you. You are a worthless, disgusting excuse for a human. And guess what, Daddy? It's about time you paid for all the things you've done."

"Cecily, listen to me. You don't know what you're saying—"

"I know exactly what I'm saying!" she said. "I'm ready, Silas. I know what I want," she sighed loudly. "Do it."

"Are you sure?" he replied.

"Absolutely. If he's not going to be any more use to you, that is."

"I wouldn't have minded our business association to continue," he said, "but I'll do whatever it takes to make you happy."

"I know that," she said. "See, Daddy. I finally found someone who can hear me. It's like my whole life I've been screaming for you to notice me, but with Silas, sometimes I don't even have to say a word. I hope you know how much pain you've caused me. I want you to think about that in your last moments. I want you to think about every wrong thing you've ever done, and I want you to know that I will never forgive you. So this is the end for you, Daddy. But don't worry, Silas insisted that in your suicide note we made you out to be quite the martyr."

"My… what?" Mr Graves stuttered.

"Do keep calm, Mr Graves," said Silas. "I was quite honest in detailing how you didn't know anything about my plan, and that it was I who tricked you. And then once you found out the truth, you simply couldn't handle it, you felt so ashamed. Unfortunately, the newspapers will say that if you hadn't consumed as much whisky, maybe you'd have been thinking more clearly and wouldn't have resorted to such a tragic way out. But of course, a drinking problem can bring down even the greatest man."

"No. You're lying! And I've only had one drink, they have ways to find out those things, you know!" Mr Graves said, scared and defiant.

"You only *remember* one, Mr Graves."

"No… This isn't happening." Mr Graves hammered at the front door of the suite when something suddenly threw him back across the room. He must have crashed into a piece of furniture, because the sound of glass smashing and his terrified yelp made Jessa and Flynn jump, grabbing each other harder as they tried not to make a sound or fall out of the cupboard.

"Don't worry," said Silas. "It's not going to hurt."

"Please don't kill me!" Mr Graves snivelled. "Please! No! Get it away from me! No! How are you doing this?" he yelled, angry, confused, petrified. "No! Please don't!"

"You can beg all you like, Daddy, but I'm afraid you're the one holding the gun."

"I…don't…want…to…" Mr Graves uttered in between gulps of crying.

"It's been an honour working with you, Mr Graves. Thank you for your assistance."

Jessa and Flynn heard the door close.

"Where are you going?" Mr Graves yelled. "Come back! Make it stop! Please, stop! Why can't I let it go?" He sobbed harder.

Jessa burst out through the bathroom before Flynn could hold her back again. She ran into the living room, where Cecily's father sat, huddled in a corner, holding a gun to his own head.

"I can't stop it… he's making me do it… he's making me…" his red, tear-ridden face blubbered the words out helplessly. His finger curled around the trigger. "I don't wanna die… I don't wanna die…"

Jessa leapt forward.

It was too late.

The sound rang through the entire room. Jessa keeled over, dry heaving. Flynn shielded her face and tried to look away from the sight himself.

"We gotta go, Jess, come on," he managed to get the words out in between his hyperventilated gasps.

47

"Mr Fletcher? Is that you? It's Jessa. Listen…" she wheezed between breaths. "Silas is here. He's here. And Cecily's with him. They killed Mr Graves."

"Wait, Jessa, what's going on? Where are you?" the teacher asked calmly enough that Jessa uttered a grunt of frustration and thrust the phone into Flynn's hand.

"Jessa's right, Mr Fletcher," Flynn had never sounded so urgent. "Silas Lynch is here. He's going to do something. We don't know what. But it's bad."

"All right, stay calm. Where exactly are you now?"

"We're in the lobby of the Rococo Hotel."

"And where did Lynch go?"

"I don't know. We didn't see."

"Okay, I'm on my way. Stay in a public area. Keep this phone with you so I can keep in contact. Don't do anything until I'm there, do you understand?"

"Yes."

Mr Fletcher hung up the phone.

"We should stay out here, he said. Somewhere public."

"We should be going after them!" Jessa retorted. "I knew Cecily was an evil bitch—I just knew it! We have to find them."

"We can't do anything by ourselves! We're not strong enough to beat him. You just saw what he's capable of."

Jessa scratched her head, not caring that she was pulling loose strands from the neat bun. "Where is he…?" she muttered, her eyes frantically searching the expansive lobby that was filled with people milling around taking canapés from silver trays; the only urgency they could fathom was when a waiter would come along tending to champagne refills.

"He's on his way."

"What? No, not Fletcher, I'm talking about Lynch. And Cecily, that witch! I always knew she was vile; I said it all along. Let's just go! We have to find them!"

"What's wrong with you?" Flynn grabbed her arm and pulled her into the corner away from the oblivious party guests. "He's probably back there brainwashing or murdering someone else, Jessa. That's what he does."

"But we need to—"

"No! Listen to me! We have to wait for the others!"

"Flynn, let go of me!"

"Only if you swear you're not going to run off. We can't do this by ourselves."

"Fine, I swear!"

A loud voice boomed through a PA system as a set of grand doors were opened ceremoniously by two attendants in top hats.

"Would all event guests kindly make their way into the ballroom and take their assigned seats. Thank you."

The crowd of well-dressed people funnelled into the ballroom, discarding their half-consumed champagne flutes onto tall tables.

"Look, there's Rachel!" Flynn said and waved her over. She scooped them into a protective double hug.

"Are you guys okay?" she smoothed Jessa's hair gently. "Hugo told me what happened."

"We're fine. We lost him, though," said Jessa.

"Don't worry, he's around somewhere. You did the right thing, calling Hugo. Felicia, over here!" Rachel said, noticing Dr Mortlock at the door.

"Come with me," Dr Mortlock instructed immediately. She walked them down a corridor adjacent to the ballroom and pulled them into a darkened room labelled Ice Vending.

"Now listen," Dr Mortlock's searing gaze alternated between the both of them. "You must tell me exactly what happened."

"Well, some of it we didn't see, but we heard it. We were in their hotel room. We didn't know it was theirs, though. I swear we only wanted to peek inside, but then we heard them talking," Jessa's words picked up speed as they tumbled out of her mouth.

"And who is 'they'?" Dr Mortlock asked stoically.

"At first, it was Silas Lynch and Mr Graves. Cecily's dad," Flynn answered. "Mr Graves was mad about something. But then Silas Lynch said that it didn't matter anyway because things weren't going to go as Mr Graves had planned, and that he was controlling Mr Graves this whole time. Silas said that he was taking over. And then Cecily was there."

"All right," Dr Mortlock frowned slightly, trying to keep up.

"Wait, where were you two while this was happening?" Rachel asked.

"Hiding in the bathroom," they said simultaneously. Rachel looked horrified.

"And she was really mad. Crazier than her normal self, and she wanted him dead. Her own father…" Jessa trailed off. "Silas made Mr Graves shoot himself."

"He made him?"

"We heard them leave the room so we went out of the bathroom and then… we saw him… he had the gun in his hand…" Flynn finished the story without finishing his sentence.

Dr Mortlock pursed her lips.

"What do you think we should do, Felicia?"

"The thing is supposed to start at 9 o'clock," said Flynn.

"Lynch said he's taking over this event," said Jessa.

"What's the time now?" asked Dr Mortlock.

"Almost 9," Rachel checked her phone.

"Well, I'm reluctant to say this, but we can't do anything unless we know what's happening. Considering we are moments away from the beginning of the event, we should go out there."

"Really?" said Rachel. "How do you know for sure he's gonna come out?"

"If these actions were indeed as deliberate as they seem, his public appearance is inevitable, and I have no reason to believe that Silas Lynch would be anything but punctual. All of you, stay close to me."

The four of them stood just inside the ballroom, backs against the wall. "8:59," Rachel whispered.

They looked out over the round tables. The room sang with the sound of clinking glasses and oblivious conversation.

Hugo Fletcher and Audrey Baxter hurled into the room. Audrey wrapped her arm around her little sister while Dr Mortlock conveyed the story so far to Hugo.

Precisely on time, the house lights went down and the red, white and blue beacons danced across the stage. Jessa looked around the room for her mother. She thought she could see her at the back of the room, but it was too dark back there to tell.

"Ladies and gentlemen," a refined voice resonated through the speakers. "Please welcome, Jameson Graves."

They applauded politely and enthusiastically, but the applause came to a sluggish halt when it was a different man who entered the stage. Jessa's spit caught at the back of her mouth. Her skin suddenly felt alight.

With a wave of his hand, the music stopped, the dancing lights stopped, the entire show stopped. The yellowy house lights re-lit the room as a few whispers sounded around tables, answered by shrugs and lightly shaken heads.

"Good evening," he said, uncomfortably softly and too far away from the microphone. "I'm afraid Mr Graves couldn't make it here today."

A wave of voices washed over the room. Questions, concerns. Jessa could see Cecily standing in the shadows of the stage wing.

"But this evening was never about Mr Graves." His slick hair shone under the lights. From the stage, his scarred skin was barely noticeable. He looked almost normal. "My name is Silas Lynch."

A few murmurs of confused recognition.

"Yes, some of you may remember me."

"Rubbish! Silas Lynch is dead!" someone called out from the audience.

"Silas Lynch is very much alive," his lips curled slightly.

"Is this a joke? Where's Jameson?" another voice called out.

"Quiet, please."

The voices grew louder.

"I'm out of here, this is nonsense," an angry man marched away from his table and toward the furthest doors.

"No," Silas raised his hands and the man flew backwards. He hit the ground with a thud that made everyone gasp. His large body slithered down the aisle, legs and arms flailing helplessly. Silas' invisible hold on the man's body ceased, allowing him to stand.

"Please return to your seat, sir."

The man gaped at Silas, shocked and scared, and scuttled back to his table.

Every door to the ballroom slammed shut with a loud bang.

"I am simply here for your time and attention," Silas said, almost pleasantly. "If the news reporters around the room with cameras would kindly come forward toward the stage."

Three wary-looking people with small cameras shuffled a little closer to him, as instructed.

"It is my hope that this moment is a turning point for humanity. An awakening. A resurrection, if you will. You are correct; I was condemned to execution a long time ago. But I did not die. In fact, I used my parapsychological ability to keep myself alive.

As long as I have lived, I felt something within me that nobody else saw. A deeper, stronger power. I imagine some of you may have felt it when you were younger, perhaps."

Scared faces, doubtful faces, curious faces watched him in silence.

"You believe your government protects you. You believe your schools train your children to be the best they can be. You're wrong. There is no parapsych in this great country that is as powerful as they can be. There are books, ancient books that teach of advanced parapsychism that could change the way we use our abilities. They were written by a small group very long ago who believed in bigger things. But over time, those beliefs gave way to fear and control. Your government controls you. And your fear controls you. Imagine what you could do, imagine what you could be, in a fearless world where parapsychism is revered as it should be."

He paused. The audience gave him no response. Jessa watched intently.

"I do not care for politics. I only care about change. I ask you to imagine a world where parapsych schools taught children how to influence plant growth, how many more people could be fed? Imagine if they were taught how to combine their parapsych energy with another's, how strong could they be? Imagine a country where parapsych education didn't end in youth, but continued into adulthood.

The people who govern you have imagined all these things, and more. And they have chosen not to act on these ideas. They have chosen to keep you all in the dark. I believe that now is the time for you, for us, to show them the light."

The ballroom audience looked to each other, some confused, some fearful. Jessa's mother had inched her way around the room and held each of her arms around each of her daughters.

Silas Lynch stood still, his dark eyes looking around at the people watching him.

Jessa's mind raced back to her visions. She'd seen him through someone else's eyes and felt the burn of his torture. Yet here, through her own eyes in the clear lights of the stage, he seemed put-together, confident, and unpretentious. He looked physically weak and relatively harmless.

"I suspected I wouldn't be able to win you over immediately with my words," he said, cocking his head slightly to the side like a curious dog waiting for a reaction from an object. "So I took the liberty of preparing a display for you. Hopefully then you'll understand, and you'll join me in a revolution. But it is not I who will show you. No. Not I. It is your children who will show you the way."

He had their attention. Mrs Baxter pulled Jessa tighter.

"I have chosen one hundred children from London and implanted them with a seed, if you will, from my own mind." His mouth twisted in a way that could only have been intended as a smile. "The seed will germinate at midnight tomorrow—approximately twenty-seven hours from now—and it will blossom into its fullest expression of power. Your children will cease their earthly lives of suffering, and they will donate to me their newly kindled energy, and then, I will reign as the most powerful parapsych in history. I will lead you all as we welcome a new era."

"Bullshit!" a woman called out from one of the furthest away tables.

"I'd prefer not to hear that kind of language, Marilyn Downton," he replied. "And perhaps you'll change your opinion tomorrow night when your daughter Polly shows you true power—"

"Don't you dare touch my daughter, you sick freak," the man next to Marilyn Downton stood up and slammed his fists on the table.

Silas smiled. "Your daughter has been chosen, Mr Downton. She has been blessed."

"I'm gonna kill you," Mr Downton raced toward Silas, who simply flipped his fingers upward and invisibly hoisted the man into the air. Men gasped, women shrieked, and Mr Downton continued yelling obscenities at an unphased Silas Lynch.

"I implore you to direct your anger to the right people, Mr Downton,' Silas spoke louder. "To the schools that don't teach your children how to embrace their power and protect themselves with it. The teachers who fail to protect your children from predators. The laterals who mock us by demanding a false equality; the parapsychs who mock us by trying to maintain the illusion of justice. The government that lies to you every single day. Your fellow countrymen who look to the ground and don't even have the gumption to question their own hearts. Mr Downton, your government let me lie in hiding and increase my own power completely undetected. I have remained alive by lying, gambling and stealing. If they could catch me, they'd call me a criminal. And yet your prime minister lies, gambles and steals from his citizens every day and you all pay him to do so."

Mr Downton held still in thin-air, arms sprawled away from his body, his eyes staring down at the man who spoke up to him. "Your daughter is a necessary sacrifice in this turning point for humanity. Citizens will march upon London and demand justice, safety, and education. This is the beginning for us all."

Mr Downton dropped from the air, crashing directly onto one of the round tables. Wine, champagne, and shattered glass sprang over the linen tablecloth and the eveningwear of shocked guests who helped him scramble down from the tabletop. One woman ran to the back of the room, hammering on the door for help. Silas ignored her.

"The children are the future," he said. "Take, for example, this young girl," he reached out toward Jessa and telekinetically moved her across the room to him. Mrs Baxter's hands covered her face, frozen in terror. Jessa felt the invisible pull and didn't try to resist it. The rubber soles of her shoes swabbed against the parquet floor as he dragged her closer. Dr Mortlock followed, holding on to Jessa's arm in case she needed to intervene.

Jessa couldn't look away from him. She recognised him so intensely that she felt nauseated by his ragged, scarred face.

"This young girl lives in a world where she is judged more highly for her face than the remarkable things she could do with her brain. But what if something happened to her face? If she were covered in scars, perhaps? Then you would pity her," he reached out and touched Jessa's skin. His fingers felt icy and lean.

"I know you dream of more," he said, looking into her eyes with a blazing intensity. "You can have everything."

"No," Dr Mortlock said.

Silas snapped his gaze from Jessa's and looked directly at Dr Mortlock. His eyes narrowed in realisation. And with Silas' hand on her face, and Dr Mortlock's grasp on her arm, Jessa heard their silent communication.

"Lissy? Is that you?"

"Not anymore, Silas. You have to stop this."

"It's only the beginning. This is the moment we've been waiting for. Come back to me."

"Let her go, please!" Mrs Baxter begged. Silas released his touch and his invisible hold on Jessa. Dr Mortlock and Hugo Fletcher pulled Jessa back away from the stage and Mrs Baxter clutched her daughter into her body.

Silas sneered. He looked back to the audience to see that many of them had risen from their seats and were approaching him, some holding the clean silver knives from their table settings. He crooked his head to the side once more and ended his speech with two cold words.

"Tomorrow. Midnight."

And he was gone. Disappeared from sight, without a sound or a trace.

1st August 1985

I've been getting to know Tegan lately. She was the one who helped choose my name when I joined. I couldn't think what to call myself, and I didn't want anything too radical, so she suggested the variation of my real name. It's fine.

Tegan was one of Silas' first followers, so she's been studying with him longer than I. She has a lot to say.

She apparently questioned Silas on his choice not to give this group a formal name. Tegan said she thought an official name would legitimise the group, but Silas thinks it would cheapen it. Silas thinks that a name would become the group's definition, and he doesn't think that his ideas can be epitomised into a name.

Tegan also thinks we should make flyers to advertise so that more people can hear about us. I probably don't need to tell you what Silas thought of that idea, but I will explain because I want this diary to be an accurate tale of how Silas and his followers will come to change the way the world views parapsychism. To be frank, he is simply not interested in advertisement. He wants people's attention to come to us organically, not simply as a result of bombardment. This isn't business. It's wholly personal, and Silas wants to keep it that way.

This all makes me think about how I came to be follower...

It was roughly a year ago that I left my hometown. I don't wish to give too many details of my life prior to this (the original followers made a choice to remain anonymous from their previous lives, and that is a tradition

I would like the honour), but I experienced a painful childhood and then escaped to a marriage when I was seventeen. Within three years, it was my marriage I was escaping, as my abusive older husband attacked me and I was powerless to defend myself. I left everything behind, ran to the train station, and with every penny I had in my purse, I managed to buy a ticket as far as here. I wasn't prepared with a place to stay, nor could I afford a hotel. I was devastated. I sat down on a park bench with my coat on top of me like a blanket, and I stayed there for probably hours, just wondering where I had gone so wrong in my life that I could end up homeless, broke, and trying to divorce my husband from afar.

I was thinking how hungry I was when a man walked by. He asked if he could sit next to me. He asked if I'd like to share a meal with him. Then he introduced himself as Silas Lynch. He told me he knew I was hungry. He told me he knew I was running away. That someone tried to hurt me. That I was ashamed that I couldn't fight back.

He told me I didn't have to run anymore. He told me he could teach me how to defend myself. How could I turn that down?

Lissy

48

"Where the hell is your father?" Mrs Baxter frantically searched the house for her husband.

"Dad, are you here?" Audrey called out.

Hugo Fletcher ushered Dr Mortlock, Rachel and Flynn into the Baxters' house. Mrs Baxter had barely finished checking all the rooms when her husband flung through the front door.

"Jean? Jessa? What on earth...?" Mrs Baxter flew into his arms and smacked a grateful kiss onto his mouth.

"We're all fine," she assured him.

"I was at the pub, and this emergency news report flashed up. Jessa was on the screen! What on Earth is going on?"

"Please sit down, Mr and Mrs Baxter," Dr Mortlock urged. "We'll explain everything we know."

"You!" Jessa said, looking directly at Dr Mortlock. "You're working with him!"

"No, that's not the case."

"Wait, what's going on?" said Hugo.

"They know each other! I heard it! He called her Lissy?!"

Dr Mortlock perched on the arm of the sofa and her face fell into her hands. "I knew him," she said sadly. "But I haven't seen him since the night they tried to execute him."

"Liar!" Jessa shouted.

Dr Mortlock shook her head. "I'm telling the truth."

"Are you telling us you were in that cult?" said Hugo.

She nodded. "I'm ashamed to say it, but yes."

"Shit, Felicia, why didn't you say anything sooner?" Rachel said. "You might have been able to help the investigation—"

"I've been working on my own time to see if anything I might know could have helped, Rachel, and I was not able to uncover anything beneficial. I hope you all understand—this was a very dark part of my past, and I couldn't simply tell you all about it. It would risk my position as headteacher, and it could put Winsbury in danger. I moved on a long time ago."

"Why were you involved with him in the first place?!" said Hugo.

"In short, because I was naive and I always saw the best in people. Believe it or not, he made some good points. He talked about teaching people how to increase their parabilities, and about making life better for parapsychs. I was young, and he was honest. He made a few turns for the worst, and I did my best to talk him out of it. Eventually, his other followers planned their mutiny, and while I tried to warn him, he wasn't willing to change, so I had to leave."

"And you really haven't seen him since?"

"Not once. It wasn't until I saw him tonight that I truly believed he could evade death. But he was right. He is just as powerful as he always claimed, and I am a fool for doubting it. I'm thoroughly ashamed."

"Would someone, anyone, please tell me *what* is going on?!" Mr Baxter grieved.

"Where do we start?" Jessa said.

§

"I don't believe it," Jean Baxter shook her head. "You're telling me that this man is some kind of supervillain?"

"I'm not saying that at all, Mrs Baxter. He's just an incredibly angry and powerful man—"

"And you exposed my teenage daughter to him? What kind of teachers are you?" her raised voiced turned to a stern yell. "We parents put our trust in you to take care of our children, and now I'm learning that the headteacher is an ex-cult member and that you've been taking my child to some nutty parapsych free-for-all where you got her involved in what, some kind of secret service? She's fourteen years old! What were you thinking?!"

"Jean, please understand—" Hugo tried to speak.

"No, you shut up and sit down!" Mrs Baxter spat back at him. "You did this. You came along with all your secrets and you upset my Audrey and you got my baby involved in all of this… this…" she broke down in tears and flopped back onto the sofa.

"They didn't do it, Mum. It was me. I insisted that I wanted to be included. I honestly didn't give them a choice."

"Mum, these people wouldn't have even known about Silas Lynch if it weren't for Jessa," Audrey added.

"It's true, Jean. Jessa's proven herself to have abilities far beyond any parapsych I've ever seen from someone her age."

"Agreed," said Dr Mortlock.

"And what good has it done?" Michael Baxter asked sadly, cradling his sobbing wife. "You knew about it, but it happened anyway? We welcomed you into this family, Hugo, and treated you like one of our own. So tell me, honestly: what good has it done?"

Hugo Fletcher opened his mouth as if to speak and then shut it promptly, looking down at the carpet. "I'm sorry," was all he could muster.

They were interrupted by the shrill ring of the house videophone.

"It's Maggie," Jessa plucked the cordless handset from the glowing blue box. "Hey."

"THERE YOU ARE!" Everyone in the room heard Maggie Turner's relieved words. "I've been trying to call you!"

"You're not the only one. We have forty-eight missed calls. Looks like there were so many calls coming in at once that nobody could even get through."

"You were on the news! *He* was there!" Maggie blurted. "What's going on? Can I come over? What should we do?"

"Maggie, hi, it's Hugo Fletcher. Don't come here. Stay inside, okay? Are your parents there?"

"Yes."

"Okay, good. Just… stay inside," he tried to sound sensible and authoritative, but Jessa had a feeling he was as worried and confused as everyone else. At least Audrey seemed calmed by his words.

"Okay, I will. Is Flynn there?"

"Yeah. His mum's on her way home from work, and she'll be here soon," Jessa answered.

"All right," Maggie sighed quietly. "Please keep in touch, my parents are flipping out. Let me know if there's anything I can do."

"We will. Love you, Mags," said Jessa.

"Love you guys," and Maggie hung up the phone leaving everyone at the Baxter house in silence again.

Mr Baxter switched on the television with a swipe of the remote control. Newsflash reports showed on every channel. Headlines ticker-taped at the bottom of each screen, words of horror that hinted at revolt and screamed of chaos.

"From Dawn 'til Doom?" Audrey scoffed. "Trust Channel 5 to come up with something sensationalist like that. Go back to BBC1, Dad."

He took his daughter's suggestion but muted the television. They all watched the unnaturally attractive young news anchor silently reiterating a tale of the evening's events as a small box in the corner played clips of footage on repeat.

Jessa realised how surreal it was to see the evening through the screen. The video showed the man called Mr Downton being lifted up into the air as if attached to invisible strings.

The camera-people had managed to get some shaky close-ups of other people in the audience, so Jessa was now able to see details she had missed in person. Husbands, wives, friends, clutching each other's hands in fright; mouths gaping in horror; people trying to subtly call the police but their phones showing an unexpected 'No Signal' message.

"This isn't helping," Rachel stood in front of the television. "They don't know anything."

"If anyone can stop Lynch," said Hugo, "it's the people in this room."

"But how?" Rachel replied.

"I'm not sure. Jessa?" he turned to face the young girl. "You've been right about everything. What do you think?"

Jessa saw the furrowed brows of her parents, and the expectant expression on Flynn's face, and the concern on Audrey's. Hugo, Dr Mortlock, and Rachel looked to Jessa imploringly.

Not long ago I had to fight to convince them Silas Lynch was alive.
Now look at them.

"Well. I think he was being honest. He told us exactly what he was going to do and why he wanted to do it."

"You think there are really one hundred kids out there who have been brainwashed into committing suicide at his command?" Flynn questioned.

"Not quite. I think there's ninety-nine left. Annora must have been one of them."

"What about the other victims, the first ones?" Flynn asked quickly.

Jessa shook her head thoughtfully. "No, those were different. I think they must have been practice attempts. Prototypes. He tried a few times before figuring it out."

"Look," Mr Baxter pointed to the television. The replaying footage from the night's event had gone away and been replaced by a reporter holding a microphone, talking directly to the camera with a crowd of people marching behind. The word "live" hung in the top corner of the screen, fixed atop a silent scene of unrest. He pinched outward on the glass remote and brought the sound of disquiet into their living room.

"…and the crowd continues to grow as more families descend upon the streets of London. You can see across the river behind me, the Houses of Parliament, where this particular march is heading right now."

The reporter's voice was slightly distorted as he spoke a little too loudly into his puffy microphone.

"I'd estimate there are roughly four, maybe five hundred people here already, with no sign of quiet yet. These people want answers, and they won't rest until they get them."

"Thank you, Aaron," the news anchor brought the attention back to himself for a moment before throwing it back out to another street reporter. "Now we're going to Peter, reporting live from 10 Downing Street, where another group of angry citizens have gathered this evening."

"That's right, Bill," said a peppy reporter who seemed cheerful enough that it might have actually been the first time he was allowed to report live. "As you can see here, there's a lot of police arriving now to keep the crowd back. A few people have thrown things at the Prime Minister's house, but so far this does seem to be a relatively peaceful protest."

The shaky camera panned across a scene of people chanting for answers and truth, as a team of riot police gathered in front of 10 Downing Street with their perspex shields and noticeable truncheons.

"And has there been any sighting of the Prime Minister himself?"

"Not yet, Bill. We've seen a few people escorted into the building, though their identity was hidden from the crowd, but this has led to speculation that the Prime Minister is inside and we can only assume that at this time, he's preparing his plan of action. Back to you in the studio."

"Thank you, Peter. And we have with us in the studio a professor of Parapsych Politics at UCL, who thinks this should be regarded as an act of terrorism, isn't that right, Professor?"

"That's exactly right. By all definitions of the word, the actions of Silas Lynch are absolutely an act of terrorism. I have no idea what—"

Mr Baxter muted the sound once more so his wife could answer the ringing telephone. She was assuring someone on the other end that she and Jessa were fine, and she urged the other person to please be the one to contact the rest of the family to tell them so.

"I'm turning the ringer off, I can't handle more calls right now," she said.

"Look, if we're going to stop him, we have to find him first," Rachel said to the group. "Jessa, any ideas?"

They all looked at her again.

"I don't know why you all suddenly think I know everything about him."

"I just mean, if anyone has any suggestions, it would be you."

"Well, I don't know!" Jessa snapped, looking back at the television screen which was once again showing the live feed of the crowd outside the Prime Minister's house. "I saw him disappear like you all did, that's as much as I know. He's been hiding for over two decades, so I'm pretty sure he's not going to be easy to find. I just need to think." She let out a frustrated grunt.

"Maybe we should go out," said Flynn. "There's nothing we can do from here, right?"

"Perhaps," said Hugo. "Given what we know, we must have the upper hand. If we can get out there, see what's really going on, maybe we can start to make sense of it and put together some kind of..." he shrugged, "some kind of plan. So let's think logically. Here's what we know: One - Silas is out there somewhere. Two - he's given us a deadline, so we know what he's planning and when."

"We don't know where, though," said Rachel. "What if we don't find out where he's going to be?"

"We'll know," Jessa said quietly. "He'll find a way to show us. He wants this to be public. But we shouldn't all go. Mum and Dad, I think you two should stay here—"

"Damn right we're staying here, and so are you, Jessa."

"No, I have to go!"

Her parents both blew up into a wild disapproval.

"You don't understand!"

"I understand fully, Jessamine," said Mr Baxter. "I understand that you're fourteen years old, and you are forbidden to leave this house."

"You can't tell me what to do, when you don't even—"

"This is my house, young lady, and I most certainly can tell you what to do. I've had enough of all this funny-business."

"But Dad—"

"No buts! You're not going out, and that's final. So if you must, you can help concoct a plan, and then your friends here can go out and execute it, but you are not going anywhere."

49

If the group of adults had any reservation about Jessa's ability to formulate a reasonable strategy, they didn't show it. They muttered among themselves but didn't interrupt her as she paced around the room, mumbling thoughts and questions to herself. None of them knew what to say. All of their faith was in her.

Mrs Baxter soothed tensions the best way she knew how—by making pots of tea and presenting the group with a selection of biscuits and a few thrown-together cheese and pickle rolls.

Jessa rewound and replayed a clip on the television. It was the moment in which Silas had summoned her to the stage. She could see herself in the clip, but her eyes, just like the eyes of her televised counterpart, were on Silas, as he vanished from sight. Rewind, play, vanish. Rewind, play, vanish.

"Rachel," Jessa spun round to the young woman whose mouth was full of cheese and bread. "You know about telelocation, right?"

"Psychokinetics, yes. I don't really know much about telelocation."

"Who does know?"

"There's a small research group that studies it, but not like that," she gestured toward the television. "Telelocation is the physical breaking down of matter and reassembling it in another location. To actually perform it on a person is crazy advanced. For someone to perform it themself? I've no idea who could know anything about that."

"Someone has to know..." Jessa said, gazing back at the paused screen.

"Professor Cyrus Arnold," said Flynn. Jessa flew around to look at him. He held up the netpad, showing her the search results. "Apparently, he developed a theory about this very thing. He called it auto-telelocation, but everyone said it was ridiculous and journals wouldn't publish it. He lives in Covent Garden."

"Write down the address. That's where we're going."

"Jessa, I told you, you're not going out there."

"Yes I am, Dad."

"Listen to me—"

"No, listen to me! Please! Listen to what's happening on the TV right now! Listen to all the things we've been talking about! This is really happening, Dad! You and Mum are always telling me to grow up and be more responsible, so here I am, taking responsibility for something!"

"You know this isn't the kind of thing we meant."

"I know that, but I didn't choose this. These abilities came to me, and now I'm just doing what I have to do. I have to go."

Jessa pulled her jacket from the coat rack. Her mother sobbed heavily. "Please, Jessa love, I really wish you wouldn't go out there! Audrey, I know you're an adult so I can't tell you what to do, but please stay and make Jessa stay too."

"Mama, don't cry," Audrey hugged her mother close. "It's going to be fine. I'll stay with her, and we'll keep her safe."

"Come on, let's go," Jessa addressed the group. She gave each of her parents a kiss on the cheek.

"Jessa, please don't do this!" Jean wailed.

"We have to go, Jean. I'm so sorry," Hugo said as he followed Audrey, Flynn, Rachel, Dr Mortlock and Jessa from the house.

"Please don't! Please!"

Jessa walked away from her mother's lament.

The streets of suburban London hadn't been so packed since the England football team had won the World Cup a decade ago. But this time, there were no celebrations in sight. Neighbours converged outside their homes, regaling the details to anyone who had not yet seen the news. Traffic moving in the direction of Central London crawled and honked, so it was somewhat fortunate that they were able to get to Covent Garden in the other direction. The journey felt even longer considering the distinct lack of conversation among the six passengers squeezed uncomfortably into the vehicle. A few times during the ride, Hugo reached over and squeezed Audrey's hand.

"It's this one, the red house," Flynn said as he followed the map on Hugo's phone. They piled out from the car, noting the equally busy streets in their new location.

"Professor Arnold! Please open the door! Professor, we need to speak to you, it's urgent!"

"Who is it?" came a voice from inside.

"My name's Jessamine Baxter. I'm the girl from the television! From the news report about Silas Lynch!"

Her words were enough to capture the wary Professor's curiosity, and the door opened up.

"Come in, quick, quick," he said, locking the door again behind them.

"I'm sorry to barge in on you, but we need your help," said Jessa.

"What could you possibly want from me?"

"You know about telelocation, don't you?" Flynn stepped forward next to his best friend.

"I'm not exactly an expert."

"We know you wrote papers about it. How does it work?"

"I don't really know how it works; my research was all theoretical."

Jessa frowned at the man's lack of immediate support, and was grateful when Flynn initiated more information. "Let me explain," he said, confidently. "We're part of a top secret agency investigating the criminal activity of Silas Lynch."

The Professor looked at them disbelievingly. Flynn continued. "You've seen on the TV that Silas can telelocate himself, and we believe that if we can track him down, we might just be able to stop him. That's why we need your help. We're trying to understand how he can do it, because then maybe we can work out where he is now."

"Is this a joke?"

"No, sir."

"But you're just kids."

"The short version of the story," said Hugo, "is that Rachel, Felicia and I are part of the security force, and we felt that the circumstances warranted an exception to the rule this time. Yes, they're young, but they did some excellent detective work independently, so we asked them for help. And now, for the same reason, we're asking for yours. Can you help us?"

"This is most unexpected, though I suppose I can try. What do you want to know?" the Professor took a seat at his kitchen table. Jessa mirrored his actions and pulled up the chair next to him.

"How far do you think he can telelocate?"

"Oh, I'm sure not very far at all. I found in my research that the laws of telelocation adhere quite strongly to a mathematical equation. We can use this particular equation to find a radius of location by using an object's mass and density, which we can then apply to physical principles of potential energy…" he noticed the scrunched faces of the two teenagers and paused. "I apologise. What I mean is, I wouldn't be able to calculate his distance of travel exactly without knowing things like his mass and having some kind of reading of his parapsychological energy—another reason my research was widely discredited, by the way. Evidently, nobody was interested in a method of quantifying parapsych abilities."

"But could you guess?" asked Jessa. "Do you think it would be, like, one mile? Two miles?"

"Oh, certainly not. A couple of hundred feet, and that would be the uppermost limit. Auto-telelocation in itself is advanced enough that this is now the only recorded incidence of it ever occurring, but to auto-telelocate more than about three hundred feet, well, that would be positively superhuman."

"So there are limits to where he could travel…" said Hugo.

"Of course!" the Professor exclaimed. "I can't reiterate enough that my research is all hypothetical, so I don't have proof of any of this (though I do believe the mathematics speaks for itself), but I'm sure there would have to be clearly planned courses of movement in order to telelocate oneself. For instance, I believe one would have to study every detail of the place to which one wishes to travel. The act requires complete control over one's physical and super-physical self. By which I mean, you would be breaking down your entire person and recreating it elsewhere, while keeping your consciousness intact. This kind of stuff, however, falls into the realm of quantum mechanics, and as far as most scientists are concerned, is impossible."

"But we know it's possible, because we all just saw it," said Jessa. "Has anyone else tried contacting you about this?"

"I wouldn't know, I don't have a telephone. You're the only people who bothered coming to my house. But honestly, I think my research has been forgotten about by now."

"Professor, how might one have a 'planned course' of travel?" Dr Mortlock asked.

"Ah, yes, well, I believe that would depend on the individual and how their memory responds to various stimuli. But my best guess is that someone could use an object or a symbol as some kind of 'anchor' to that place."

"Like in a video game when your character dies and then materialises at a checkpoint," Jessa nodded.

"I'm not entirely familiar with that analogy, but yes that sounds close enough," the older man said.

"So let me understand one thing," Audrey began, "if someone needs a very clear image in their mind's eye of the place they want to telelocate to, that means they can't just do it anywhere whenever they feel like? So Silas must have clearly planned every one of his telelocation movements."

"Exactly. So that moment he was seen disappearing in the hotel bathroom is unlikely to have been the first time. And he can't have gone far. I believe it's also worth pointing out that such an act would completely deplete someone of energy for some time, so wherever he is, he's probably still recovering."

"So maybe he just telelocated to a different room," said Flynn. "How would he get out of the hotel without being noticed, though?"

"Probably would have been easy enough in all that panic," Jessa shrugged. "Unless he knew some back way out."

"He's clearly done his research," Rachel mused. "Plus, it's a Graves hotel, and if the two of them were working together, Silas could easily learn every possible way in and out."

Jessa closed her eyes and rumpled her face deep in thought. "What about places?" she said thoughtfully. "You said it would require these anchors to locations, but is there anything about particular places that would make it easier or more difficult to telelocate?"

"Hmmm," the Professor scratched at some dry skin on the back of his hand. "That is a good question. I would guess that the type of place would vary depending on the parapsych's level of ability, personal experiences and psychological connections. For example, you know how some objects manage to absorb and retain the energy from events?"

"Like in object reading," she said.

"Yes, quite. Well, places can have the same quality. It would probably be easier to telelocate within an area to which one feels a strong emotional connection."

"Professor, based on your knowledge of the science of parapsychism, do you think he could really be strong enough to, you know, do what he's saying he's going to do?" Audrey asked. "I mean... those children..."

"Admittedly, I don't know anything about this man. I saw the BBC just going over the details of his activities from the 80s, but they're still speculating many of the whys and hows of his return. So far, I have no reason to believe that he isn't capable of doing these things."

50

"Why is it taking so long?" Jessa whined from the back seat as Hugo Fletcher's car sat in traffic despite the green light.

"Nobody's paying attention to the rules anymore," Flynn muttered, watching another driver trying to make a U-turn right in front of a no-U-turns sign. "It's madness."

The pavements milled with pedestrians. Front doors lay open as occupants spilled out from their homes to converge, discuss, and speculate.

Suddenly, the buzz turned to a veritable hubbub, as people ran out from houses, urging those outside to come in to watch something on the television. Any traffic that was moving, stopped. Car doors opened, and radios turned up. Some passengers gathered around the cars of others to listen to the update.

"There, quick," Hugo said, indicating the house closest to them, whose owner had pushed their television up toward the open window so people outside could watch. They ran over as quickly as possible, and Jessa pushed through the small crowd to get a better view.

Silas Lynch spoke directly to the camera. Soft, calculated, ominous.

"It's not the time to be afraid. It's time to embrace change. Let us begin the era of the parapsych. Let us be a people that honours and praises those among us who transcend human possibility. I survived death, and I became powerful. Let me show you the almighty energy that lies within you. Let me save you like I saved myself."

The video ended. Back to the studio, where stunned news anchors awaited their next words from their earpieces.

"What did we miss, what did he say first?" Hugo asked the onlookers who were there for the whole thing.

"Something about a symbol."

"What?"

"Oh man, he had this cut in the palm of his hand. Like an arrow or something. Or a triangle, sort of. I don't know. What a fuckin' psycho."

The phones in Jessa and Hugo's pockets buzzed as a message from Mrs Baxter arrived.

Did you see the video?

Watching now, Hugo wrote back.

"Look, they're playing it again," someone in the crowd hushed the group and they watched the video play from the beginning.

It began with Silas holding his right hand up to the camera. A fresh red incision lay in his flesh. His bony white fingers radiated outward like rays from a weird sunrise.

"This is to show you I am real. This symbol shows you that I am willing to bleed for my cause. For my people. It is not the time to be afraid…"

Jessa pulled out from the crowd, motioning for the others to join her. "I've seen that symbol before. It was written all over a book in that display at the museum."

"That's the one that Francis Jackson ordered back, he was the original owner," said Hugo.

"Wait," said Jessa. "There's a second copy at Francis Jackson's house. And… hold on, let me think," she wracked her brain. "I saw it… He said something about a book…"

"What did he say?" asked Audrey.

"If I could remember that, I would have just said it!" Jessa snapped back.

"You don't have to yell at me. I was just asking."

"Well don't!"

"Chill out, please," said Hugo. "Let's not lose our tempers."

Jessa closed her eyes tightly and pushed her brain to recall her visit to Woburn Vale. She clenched her fists atop one another in front of her chest and found herself rubbing the pendant of her necklace between her thumb and forefinger. She focused on the hissing of breath in her throat as the air came in and out.

"It still has all your scribbles on it. Why did you want it back?"

"For the same reason I have the other copy in this room. It's much easier for me to transport when I use the book. Takes a lot less energy. Now I can keep this one with me."

She recalled the book from the museum, its pages lewdly splayed, showing off all its secrets. All its symbols and memories. All Silas' symbols and memories.

Her eyes flickered open and her ears suddenly tuned back into the madness around her.

"It's his anchor," she said.

§

Any chance of driving back into the centre of London had gone from little to none since Silas's video had aired. It had also come to light that the internet had been hacked and every web page had been replaced with a link to the same video. There was no escaping it. No escaping him.

Under the darkened sky, the streets became more animated and more agitated. Jessa, Flynn, Rachel, Hugo, Audrey, and Dr Mortlock did their best to walk through the crowd that meandered frustratingly slowly, constantly distracted by conversation and consternation.

"Flynn, my mum just texted me," Jessa held out her phone. "She heard from your mum. She's safe but stuck in Battersea. The Underground is a mess, apparently."

"I believe that," he replied. "Tell her thanks for letting me know."

"She'll be all right," Jessa assured him, linking her arm with his.

"I know," he said faintly.

"I keep thinking about what he said in that video," said Audrey.

"What about it?" Dr Mortlock replied.

"He was using very specific language, saying things like 'almighty' and 'saved,' it's very reminiscent of old world religions."

"Yeah, we heard about some of that when we learned about Christianity in school this year," said Jessa. "So what, you think he's religious?"

"I think he's effectively trying to start a religion."

"How do you just start a religion?" asked Flynn.

"Well, presumably you just devote yourself to your belief and then preach it to other people. That's exactly what he seems to be doing, doesn't it?"

"He's rather brazen to think he can win people over by starting with the sacrifice of a hundred children," said Hugo.

"Speaking from experience," said Dr Mortlock, "if people are convinced enough by an argument, they'll go along with anything."

"Exactly," Audrey said gravely. "He said he's going to somehow absorb their energy, right? And make himself stronger in doing so? He's basically turning himself into some kind of all-powerful deity. And those kids, his "chosen ones" will go down in history as becoming part of a… you know, a god."

"You think people will be persuaded by that?" Flynn frowned.

"If there's one thing I've learned in all my years of psychology studies, it's that many people, deep down, are afraid. They're afraid of dying unfulfilled, and they're afraid of never finding their true purpose. Throughout history, religious fanatics have gained followers by promising salvation. And that's kind of what he's doing."

"Many people are still going to fight against it," said Rachel.

"Maybe the majority will fight against it. But my guess is that if he succeeds, he'll manage to get a few people on his side."

"Then we can't let him succeed," Rachel replied. "What's the time?"

"Eleven," said Hugo.

"We need to figure out where he is," Audrey said plainly.

"Well let's hope it's in this direction," he said as they inched their way through the crowded street. "Because otherwise we have no chance."

51

The crowd marched on, and Jessa and her friends heard Big Ben chiming midnight in the not-so-distant distance. Ding, dong, ding, dong, his unfaltering boom said, counting down to the uncertain inevitable. Twenty-four hours remained until Silas's apparent sacrifice, and as yet they had no idea where he was.

It was clear that Silas's speech at the hotel had hit home with many London citizens, who could only react by taking their anger to the streets and heading toward Westminster, home of the politics and government that they'd believed would educate them and protect them from the very things that were beginning to happen. Things they'd never even considered a possibility

They stayed connected by hand-holding and arm-linking. Anything to stop the crowd from pulling them apart.

The closer they came to the Houses of Parliament, the unrest became even more palpable.

Then suddenly, through the rumbles of human commotion came a piercing blare from seemingly all around them.

"What is that?" Audrey cringed.

People started taking phones out of their pockets, and then there were glowing screens and ear-splitting alarms quaquaversally.

CITY-WIDE CURFEW.
RETURN TO YOUR HOME AND REMAIN INDOORS UNTIL

FURTHER NOTICE.

"What the…" Jessa tried to close the message, but it wouldn't go away. All around her, fingers pushed at screens to no avail. The surrounding sound became one all-encompassing tinny wail of electronic noise.

"Use the power button!" Rachel called out. "Just turn it off!"

But just as quickly as they found relief from the electric bleats, they were shoving fingers back into their ears again under the thunderous thwack of helicopter blades spinning overhead.

"The Prime Minister has issued a city-wide curfew," cami-green officers yelled down through a gigantic megaphone. "Please return to your homes and remain indoors until told otherwise. The British Armed Forces are being deployed, and anyone who fails to comply will be liable to arrest or detainment.

Repeat: the City of London is under curfew, effective immediately."

"Boo!" came the angry replies among the maddening crowd.

"That's ridiculous, how can they possibly enforce a curfew when everyone is out like this?" Rachel enquired.

"They can't," Hugo said, wrapping his arm around Flynn as Audrey did the same to her sister. "They're clutching at straws."

"I'm trying to call John Cane, but there's no signal anymore," said Rachel. "I think the phone lines are all jammed. I thought maybe he'd be able to help, but it looks like we're on our own."

All of a sudden a toppling wave came throughout the crowd. People yelled and cursed as they tumbled into one another.

"What's happening?" Flynn grasped a petite woman to save her from falling to the ground. "Who's pushing?"

"Lift me up," Jessa said to Hugo, who crouched slightly, allowing her to climb onto his shoulders. She held tightly onto his hands to steady herself, and looked out over the sea of people.

"The police are up there!" she called down. "They're pushing everyone back! I can see their yellow jackets! Hang on, something's happening further ahead… it's too dark to make it out… whoa."

She slid down from Hugo's shoulders. "A massive group of people just charged the line of police. I mean, they literally trampled over them."

"Well that's not good," said Flynn.

Gunshots.

Everyone cowered. Some screamed. Others tried to scatter but were unable to escape through the mess of a crowd. More pushing, more rushing, more limbs of panicked citizens flailing aimlessly.

More shots rang out clearly into the air.

"Must be warning shots," said Rachel. "I can't imagine the police would open fire on a crowd. Would they?"

"In the right circumstances, I do believe they would," said Dr Mortlock.

The grumble of distant voices turned into the undeniable roar of a charge, followed by the shrill and deadly pitter-patter of bullets pouring from machine guns.

The crowd's bellow turned to terrified screams as the guns continued to fire.

"This way!" Hugo pulled them back, hands clasped together in a desperate chain as they tried to wind through the crowd that simply didn't know which way to turn. Some people scattered in directions away from the commotion, while others charged to join in the battle.

The gunshots continued.

Hugo Fletcher directed them down a side-street, where they caught their breath.

"I didn't think the police were allowed to have guns!" Flynn rested his hands on his knees to regain his composure.

"They're riot police," Hugo replied. "They can use a lot more force.'

"Hey, over here!" a gruff voice called from a doorway further down the quiet alley. The five of them followed him inside to find a well-hidden old pub. Most seats were already filled by anxious locals who had congregated there to wait out the night's events with their fellow citizens. Safety in numbers, people had said.

A buxom, tired-looking lady went behind the bar and returned with a cola for each of them and threw a few packets of crisps onto the table.

"On the house," she said without a smile.

In the booth next to them lay two sleeping children with their heads in the laps of parents cradling barely-sipped pints of lager.

Two television screens each showed a different news channel. One played Silas' video over and over, while another showed aerial footage of the riot outside Westminster, the very scene they had just escaped.

"Warning," a banner across the screen read. "Graphic violence."

52

Jessa washed her face with cold water in the pub's dingy toilet room. The smell of papery potpourri stung her senses. She rinsed out her mouth in an attempt to wash away the sugary residue left behind by the cola.

"I have those chewy toothbrush things," said Audrey. "You want one?" She opened her little shoulder bag and pulled out a box of SparkleChewz. She bit one in half and handed the other half to her sister.

"Thanks. I didn't know they still made these," Jessa said in between munches. "I've only ever seen them at service stations."

"That's where I got these!" Audrey smiled a tired smile. "I knew they'd come in handy someday." She ran a brush through her hair and tied it back into a neat ponytail. "Do you remember that one time we were driving down to Cornwall for a holiday and Mum wanted to go to McDonald's at a service station but Dad insisted on going to that bacon butty stand by the side of the motorway?"

"No?"

"I guess you were pretty young. Dad was so persistent that Mum gave in, and he ate the biggest bacon and sausage sandwich that you could imagine. And Mum didn't have anything, because she insisted she wanted McDonald's instead, and I wanted to go, too. Anyway, Dad basically spent the whole holiday with food poisoning. He didn't go to the beach once." She huffed quietly in a way that could have been a subtle laugh or a saddened sigh. "These things remind me of that holiday. I ate a Happy Meal and then asked

Mum for 50p so I could buy SparkleChewz because I hated the weird feeling on my teeth after the fizzy drink."

"I wish we could go on holiday right now," said Jessa, looking in the mirror at her cheeks that were still rosy from being dabbed with cold water.

"Yeah, that would be nice."

The pub became quieter, and people rested, hushed into turbulent naps.

"Curfew," the banners kept rolling across the screen. "Chaos."

Jessa sat in the corner of the seating booth with her arms wrapped tightly around her knees. The din outside descended from a raging war into a rumbling lullaby. Exhaustion finally got the better of her, and she fluttered her eyes closed.

53

"Huh?" Jessa felt something brush past her foot. She wiped away the wetness that had escaped from the side of her mouth, and looked down through her sore and barely focusing eyes to see a little girl.

"Sorry!" her young mouth whispered. "I didn't mean to wake you up."

"That's okay," Jessa whispered back. "What's the time?"

The young girl shrugged. "People are sleeping. Night time."

Jessa saw the televisions still revelling in horror. 4:47 am, the ticker said.

"I'm really thirsty, but I don't want to wake my mummy up," said the little girl.

"Come on, I'll help you," Jessa wriggled herself off the bench and explored the pub. There was a small kitchen in the back where she found some milk, and poured a glass for herself and another for the girl.

"Are we going to die?" the little girl asked.

"Umm. What?" Jessa was so taken aback at first that she forgot to wipe away the milk moustache. "Why would you think that?"

"I heard my mum and dad talking about someone killing children."

"Oh."

"So are you scared that you're going to die?"

"I hadn't really thought about it. But everyone has to die sometime, I suppose."

The little girl frowned and Jessa suddenly wondered if she'd said the wrong thing.

"Don't worry, you're safe in here, for sure. Your parents are here, and there are other people to look after you, too." She tried her best to sound knowledgeable and supportive, the way she imagined she was supposed to speak to a child. "We should go back in there—I don't want your parents to panic if they wake up and see you gone."

Jessa offered her hand to the child, who reached up her little fingers gratefully.

And then.

Whoosh.

The little fingers were Jessa's own, clenching hard into fists that she was desperately trying to throw at the two men holding her arms back. Visceral screams rattled through her throat but couldn't make it out through her mouth. Some invisible force held her lips shut no matter how hard she tried to open them and scream for help.

Jessa felt the child's terror, her pounding heart.

"Keep her still," Silas Lynch sneered at the two men. "You know I can't control the deflection if she keeps moving. We can't risk being seen."

The men held the girl's arms tighter. They were in the corner of a car park. From Jessa's limited awareness it seemed to be the back of a school. She could see parents walking their children to cars, listening to cheery young voices regaling lessons in colour, seasons or telling the time.

"Yes," Silas growled. "Here we go..."

Jessa felt his spindly fingertips clutching the girl's skull. She felt burning on her scalp, then pulling, then something else entirely as Silas grafted shards from his own consciousness into the pure white innocence of the girl's mind.

And then it was gone. All of it. The pain was gone, his fingers were gone, the two men, all dissipated.

Jessa watched on from someone else's vision as the girl skipped away happily.

"Mummy!" she tugged on the coat of a woman chatting away distractedly.

"Oh, there you are!" the mother said, tousling the girl's childish mess of hair.

Whoosh.

Jessa was up high. Floating, undetected. She looked out over the vastness of a hall from above. Greyish brown columns held up an elaborately painted ceiling. Gold embellishments all around reflected light that poured in through stained-glass windows.

She'd never been there before, but she'd seen this place in photographs and movies. A prestigious venue, a house of faith turned into a home for the arts. And in the centre of it all, alone, on the smooth expanse of well-maintained tile stood Silas Lynch.

"One hundred," the cavernous room carried his timid voice. "One hundred souls will feel my salvation."

He placed his hands face-down to the floor, and telekinetically pushed his body from the ground, folding his feet beneath himself into a cross-legged position. Jessa's form floated down until she found herself gazing, face-to-face with this strange and feared man.

His palms were upward and open to the ceiling, resting on his knees. Remnants of scars lay across his skin, his face ruined by time. His eyelids were closed but flickered with unease. His nostrils, filled with dark wiry hair, flared slightly with each breath. His earlobes were white and curiously shrivelled from scar tissue. The skin on his neck was bumpy and prickled with a cold that Jessa's transcendental form could not perceive. In his details, he seemed frail and wholly mortal.

Whoosh.

Hugo and Audrey shook her awake. She was back in the kitchen, and Audrey was dribbling cold water from a cup onto Jessa's sweat-glistened forehead.

"Hey," Hugo said gently. "You okay? Did you see something?"

"She's number one hundred," Jessa said, letting her pupils adjust to reality. "And I think I know where he is."

"Where?" demanded Audrey.

"St Paul's."

54

"What are we going to do, though?" Audrey asked, exasperated. Even in the earliest hours of the morning, the streets of London teemed with crowds, despite the imposition of a curfew. What would have once been a pleasantly long walk to St Paul's had become nothing short of a hike.

Many protesters had exhausted themselves for the night and were lying on the ground. People curled under jackets for warmth. Their arms hooked awkwardly into pillows under their heads. Some sat upright, holding pieces of pipe, bricks, planks of wood. Anything that could be a weapon if necessary. Just in case, they'd said. Just in case.

"You're very quiet, Felicia," said Rachel. "Are you doing okay?"

"Yes, thank you. I'm doing exactly as okay as I presume you'd expect."

Rachel placed her hand lightly on Dr Mortlock's back. "We're going to stop him."

"I dare say we'll try," said Dr Mortlock.

"We need a plan, though, don't we?" Audrey insisted once more. "It's not like we can just waltz in there and he'll see us and say 'oh darn, you got me' and all of this will stop?"

"Audrey, please calm down," said Hugo.

"Oh, I'm sorry, is my anxiety bothering everyone?"

"We don't know what to do!" Jessa snapped. "You're supposed to be the smart one, why don't you figure out a plan?"

"How am I supposed to know, evidently you're the one with the superpowers!"

"I am not!"

"Ugh!" Audrey rubbed her face hard. "I'm sorry, I didn't mean to snap at you."

Jessa sulked at the ground.

"Jessa, I apologise."

"Okay," she said quietly.

"But before we go any further, can you please just tell me that you're sure it's St Paul's you saw?"

"I'm sure, I've seen it before."

"Have you been there before?" asked Rachel.

"No, but I've seen it in movies. I've watched streaming concerts online when they have shows there. Just the other day I saw a post on HeadBread that was called something like "Top 15 Coolest Buildings in London" and St Paul's was in, like, the top five."

They were interrupted by a group of people quickly exiting a supermarket, grappling with components of computers. Through the broken glass of the windowed shop front, they could see mostly bare shelves. A few people stood in the aisles, shoving cans of food into bags or holding their sweaters out into hammocks for harbouring whatever foodstuffs they could grab.

"Come on," Hugo urged, "we should see if there's any food left."

"I don't think we should," Audrey hesitated at the door.

"Why?"

"Because it's stealing."

"Audrey, love. I know you want to do the right thing. But look around, would you?"

"Fine, but when all this is over, can we come back and pay?"

"Absolutely. You lovely, lovely nutcase."

"That's mean!" she followed him inside through the smashed door.

The food supply had been almost obliterated. The fresh produce section was completely empty. The cleaning products had all been snapped up. All the fridges and freezers were depleted of their contents.

"Did you find anything?" Hugo asked as he and Audrey met up with Jessa and Flynn in the ready-meals aisle.

"Nope," said Flynn, "everything's gone."

"I found two first-aid kits, but nothing else of note," Dr Mortlock handed the kits to Audrey, who put them in her bag.

"Hey guys, I found something!" Rachel joined them and took out four cans from the large pocket in the front of her hoodie.

"Tapioca?!" Jessa pulled a face.

"It's all that was left, just a few of these at the back of the shelf."

"Gross. You should put them back."

"Jessa, now is not the time to be fussy," Audrey scolded.

"What is tapioca?" asked Hugo. "I've never had it."

"You're lucky," said Jessa. "It's our dad's favourite pudding."

"It's not that bad," said Audrey.

"The only thing worse than no pudding, is tapioca."

"Come on, let's keep moving," Hugo ushered them all out of the supermarket.

"I actually really like tapioca," Flynn mumbled.

"Don't ever let me hear you talk like that again," said Jessa.

§

"What is that smell?!" Audrey exclaimed, hiking the neck of her shirt up over her nose. The others quickly followed suit. Dr Mortlock prudently closed her nostrils with a thumb and forefinger.

"Just don't think about it. Walking alongside the river is probably going to be the most direct and safe route to St Paul's."

"I don't think I can do it, Hugo," Rachel held her nostrils closed.

"Where is it even coming from?" Jessa whined, her mouth inside the crook of her arm. "Is it just the river?"

"I think it's less a river and more of a toilet right now," said Flynn. Jessa wondered if it was just the light or if his face was indeed a very pale shade of violet.

"People are revolting," Audrey stated. "Why can't they be decent and just find a real toilet?"

"I guess hygiene isn't a priority at this moment," Hugo replied, rubbing Audrey's back affectionately.

Flynn gagged, hocking up a massive ball of watery spit onto the pavement.

"All right, maybe we should find a different way there," said Hugo.

They speedily made their way back up through the smaller side streets, which felt less dangerous than the main roads, but still bustled with life. There was nowhere they could turn, no road they could travel, that wasn't occupied by people or fear.

Jessa kept looking up into the windows of houses and flats, noticing rooms flashing with the glare from the televisions that warned everyone to remain afraid. Occasionally she would see a person at the window, looking down to the streets below. They would share a fleeting glance.

"Hey, you!" a man's voice spoke loudly out from the hushedness. "Kid!'

The six of them turned around.

"It is you! The girl from the telly! And the woman! Hey lads, look!" A few other gruff men hung back behind him, staring at Jessa and her group with a quiet savagery. Hugo took a stride forward, pushing Jessa behind him. Dr Mortlock stood to his side, but he turned and gave her a knowing nod. She stepped back.

"Hey man, we don't want any trouble," Hugo said.

"I'm not talking to you, pretty boy. I wanna talk to the kid."

"She has nothing to say to you, so just back off, yeah?" he said gently. The men continued to step toward them.

"Do you know him, girl? Do you know Lynch?" the main man asked, as Hugo continued to shield Jessa behind him. Rachel and Flynn too, stepped forward to flank Hugo.

"I said back off," Hugo said more forcefully.

"Fuck you, ponce!" the man said, throwing a punch that landed right onto Hugo's cheek. He snapped into action, returning the punch with a surprising velocity.

The man readied his fist once again, but before he was able to land another thump, a shot rang out into the air and the man cowered.

They all recoiled, waiting for a second shot. But it didn't come. Instead, a crochety voice sounded from an upstairs window.

"Leave 'em alone, Sonny Jim." They all looked up and saw Detective John Cane standing there, pointing his loaded gun down toward the brawler.

The man and his angry cronies receded, shuffling and huffling back to the other end of the narrow street. Puffing and shrugging his shoulders in his umbrage, the main man disappeared out of sight.

"I'm buzzing you in," John called out through his open window.

"Wow, I'm happy to see you," Hugo greeted John with a hearty hug.

"Ah, you could have taken 'em," John replied buoyantly.

"Maybe so, but I'm still glad we ran into you."

"And I'm glad you did too. Come in, everyone. Make yourselves comfy."

A myriad of muffled voices grunted statically from his desk.

"What's that?" said Flynn.

"I'm listening to police radio frequencies. They're getting a lot of reported sightings of Lynch, but I suspect they're all false."

"Those reports are rubbish. He's at St Paul's," Jessa blurted.

"The Old Cathedral?"

"Yes. I saw it."

"Another of your intuitions, eh?"

"Yes, sir, the same kind of intuition that led me to figure out that Silas Lynch was behind all this a long time before you and your Agents did."

He raised an eyebrow but realised he was out of reasons to doubt Jessa anymore. "All right, so he's at St Paul's. What else?"

"That's all we know," said Hugo.

The group looked from one another. Nothing needed to be said. None of them had a plan. Nobody knew what to do next.

"It's almost 6 am, have you been up all night? You must be knackered," John Cane said as his five guests rested into his floral upholstery.

"Yep," said Hugo. "And I don't know about the others, but I could eat a horse."

"Let's rustle you up something," John pulled out a pyrex dish from the refrigerator.

"Shepherd's pie?" Jessa almost felt herself retch at the thought of eating minced beef and mashed potato at six in the morning. A small piece from the corner of the pie had already been eaten, leaving behind a gravyish residue and some leftover peas sitting on the dirty glass.

"This is all I have, sorry. We were meant to go shopping today, but then, well, this, all happened." He dished out portions for them to microwave.

"My wife, Martha, drove out of the city as soon as she could, to be with her parents in Hertfordshire. The poor old folks were petrified. But anyway, she put some things in the fridge to defrost so I'd have something to eat."

"Thank you so much," Audrey said gratefully, then glared at her sister who was poking at a wet carrot slice in her bowl.

55

"I just don't think I can."

"Of course you can. It's easy. We just walk out the door."

"No, but my parents. My whole family… They'll kill me when they find out."

"Fine, Maggie, whatever. But whether you're coming or not, I'm still going."

"Tonia!"

"I can't leave her alone in the hospital while all this is going on."

"She's not alone; she has doctors and nurses."

"I've been calling and calling, and I can't get one helpful person on the phone. Twice they picked up, but all I heard was "umm sorry we're busy." They were just watching TV! I could hear it in the background!"

"That's not their fault. Everyone's watching TV right now."

"That's not the point. Look, I need to be with her. Just in case anything happens."

"What do you think will happen? They undid it, didn't they? He's not controlling her anymore.

"I don't know. I just have to go."

"Tonia, you can't."

"If you're coming with me, let's go."

"…"

"Okay, then. Well, I'm leaving," Tonia opened the door to exit Maggie's bedroom.

"Wait. Fine," Maggie grunted a sigh of surrender and Tonia pushed the door closed. "I can't believe I'm actually agreeing to this, but fine. I'll go with you."

"Are you serious?"

"Yes. But we have to go quickly before I see sense and change my mind. Oh my goodness, I will be in so much trouble."

"Don't think about that. Think about Annora."

"Yes. We're doing it for Annora."

"That's my girl. So how should we get there?"

"We can take my brother's moped."

"Do you know how to drive it?"

"I don't have a licence, but yeah. Oh my goodness, what if I get caught by the police, driving without a license?" Maggie rubbed her eyes vigorously.

"It's okay," Tonia soothed. "We're going to be fine."

Maggie took a deep breath. "You get to work printing out directions, and I'll write my parents a note."

56

Jessa woke up between her sister and Flynn on John Cane's too-small-for-three-people-to-sleep-on-comfortably sofa. Rachel was curled up in a firm-looking armchair, and Hugo Fletcher sat on the floor in the corner, leaning onto a pillow sandwiched between the wall and his head. Dr Mortlock took the other corner, with her head neatly tipped backwards against the wall. Bleary eyed and drool-mouthed, Jessa felt relief at having been able to get some rest.

Her eyes focused on the television, muted but active, its colours dancing upon the glassy surface.

A mass of orange. And black. She blinked away the remnants of snooze and pulled herself into cognisance.

"Oh crap!" she exclaimed without thinking. Everyone woke up with a start. "Look!" She grabbed the remote control next to her and pulled the volume up.

"*…In case you're just joining us, we have breaking news that there's been an explosion at 10 Downing Street. Firefighters on the ground haven't yet been able to reach the property due to crowding in the streets, but military forces have been deployed and are fighting the blaze from the air. There is currently no word on whether the Prime Minister and his family are safe. The bomb seems to have been a homemade device, thrown by someone in the crowd…*"

Everyone stared at the screen. Before long, their surprise subsided into despondent acceptance. Nothing seemed too shocking anymore.

§

Jessa breathed in the steam from the shower. She closed her eyes and stood directly under the head, feeling the force of its hot streams spilling over her scalp and cascading down over her face. She opened her mouth and drew in long, cleansing breaths from John Cane's flowery tiled bathroom.

Patchoulied, lavendered and waterlillied, she stepped out from the shower and scrunched her clean toes into the fluffy bathmat. Her red-hot skin cooled down quickly in the fresher air outside of the shower confinement.

John had selected a few items of his wife's clothing to offer Jessa in case she wanted to change, and though she didn't feel very enthusiastic about the beige slacks, she decided that the slightly-too-big v-neck t-shirt in middle-aged-lady-lilac was better than the sweat-soaked stripy number she'd been sporting before. Disappointed that John hadn't thought to find her any clean underwear, and too embarrassed to ask for any, she turned her one pair of underpants inside out and pulled them on.

She stared into Mrs Cane's vanity mirror and took a moment to sniff all the perfumes that stood together, lined up like fragrant little soldiers. She found a relatively inoffensive body lotion and squeezed a dollop into the palm of her hand. She mindlessly smeared the cool white cream over her arms, hands and neck, letting its synthetic aroma and moisture fill her nostrils and pores. Finally, she put on her pendant, cold and metallic against her skin.

She lightly fingered the symbol, and was overcome by the memory of receiving the necklace from her parents on her first day at Winsbury.

Her parents.

She'd been trying not to think about them, but she couldn't help but wonder how they were. She imagined her mother continuously bursting into tears and her father being sensible and protective. *Everything's going to be fine and dandy,* he always said.

Jessa re-joined her colleagues in the living room, towel-squeezing the ends of her hair before they dripped onto her new old shirt.

"Nice top," Audrey nudged her sister and pointed at the roses and birds embroidered near the collar.

"Ha," Jessa narrowed her eyes. "Wait 'til you see what he picked out for you. What did I miss?"

"Nothing much, but the reward for someone turning Silas in is now a million pounds," said Flynn.

"And still no word about the Prime Minister," Hugo added. "Rachel's been checking up on satellite maps of the city. It's getting worse out there. The streets are just packed with people."

"I think it's worse than the TV is showing," Rachel said, swivelling away from the computer to face the group. "Most of the news channels are showing all these localised events, but I've set up this feed from social media that's showing me updates from all over the UK, and it's happening everywhere. There are user-uploaded photos and videos of police violence, people getting arrested all over the place, this crazy rioting. But we're only seeing on the news what's happening in London."

"How are you seeing social media?" asked Jessa. "I thought Silas took over the internet?"

"He has, mostly. But he's left the biggest social sites untouched, which of course means people can share pictures and discuss what's happening. He's letting people get riled up in the best way they know how. It's pretty genius. My Soshe feed is going insane."

"So, what you're seeing on social media isn't cohesive with what we're seeing on the news?" said Hugo.

"I'm sure that's a calculated move on the part of the news networks," Dr Mortlock said wryly.

"Agreed," Audrey said sadly. "It's probably in the networks' best interest to make it seem less... you know..."

"Apocalyptic?" Flynn suggested. "Because that's how it seems if you think that this is happening all over the country."

Jessa kept her eyes on the screen, watching the replays of footage from all the different angles from the news cameras and their voyeuristic reporting. The bang. The cowering. The smoke. The flames.

"That's it," she said. "That's what we should do."

"What?" said Flynn.

"If we're going to stop him, we need something big and powerful. Like an explosion."

"You want to blow him up?"

"What else can we do? We know where he's going to be and when. We have some time to figure out all the details and set it up. What do you think?" she turned to Hugo.

"Not the worst idea I've ever heard, in theory. I'm sure the military would be getting the SAS ready for some similar action if they knew where he was."

"But they don't."

"An explosion is so destructive," said Audrey. "What if it brings the whole building down?"

"Then the building comes down."

"It'll be full of people, though."

"Then we can try and make the blast as specific as possible, right? I'm sure I've seen them do that in movies."

"Jessa, this is real life, not Die Hard."

"I know that, but come on, Audrey! If this is happening everywhere, then in the grand scheme of things, doing a little damage to stop it all, don't you think it would be worth it?"

"For the greater good," Flynn said quietly.

"Everyone is so angry about this, though. We can't be the only people setting out to hurt him. What if there are others planning how to destroy him too?" Rachel wondered aloud. "I mean, what if other people turn up with guns or homemade bombs or something?"

Jessa shook her head. "He'll see that coming. He knows he's making a lot of people angry, so he must be expecting them to try something like that. So he must have a way to protect himself. We need an attack he doesn't expect. We need to get in there first and plant something that he can't see coming." she looked back to Hugo Fletcher.

He thought for a moment. "I think you're right, we need something big to bring him down. But logistically, it would be tricky. The first hurdle would be that we don't even have any kind of explosives."

"I have a few items in my stash, but nothing like that," John Cane added. "But actually… I might be able to get some.

"Seriously?" asked Jessa.

"Well, I do have my connections. I know people in the secret service and the military, I can try all the possible angles and see what I can do."

"Won't that be hard to do, though?" Audrey said discerningly. "I mean, surely there's paperwork involved in acquiring explosives."

"In ordinary circumstances, yes," John replied politely. "But in this situation, I'm sure people will be preoccupied enough that we could circumvent the, uh, administrative side of things. And I certainly don't have any better ideas. Anyone else?"

They all shook their heads.

"All right then, dare I say we have a plan."

57

"Wait here."

"What?" Tonia replied, but Maggie had already dashed out of the room. Tonia perched on the edge of Maggie's lacy bedspread and pursed her lips.

"Here," Maggie said upon returning. She took a kitchen knife out from the waistband of her jeans and offered it, handle first, to Tonia.

"What's that for?!"

"Just tuck it into your jeans like this," Maggie whispered loudly. "Don't look at me like that! You've seen the news—it's dangerous out there!"

"Isn't it also dangerous to have a sharp blade just hanging out near your special place?" Tonia raised her eyebrows. "Look, I'll put it here in between my jeans and my belt. Feels a bit safer."

"Suit yourself," Maggie tapped the handle of the three-inch paring knife tucked against her hip. "All right," she said into a small shoulder bag. "Phone, purse, torch, first-aid kit, tissues... anything else we might need?"

"You are such a mum right now. Let me guess - you have some snacks in there too?"

"Just a couple of cereal bars, do you think that's enough?"

"Uh. Sure."

"Let's go, then," Maggie picked up the hand-written note and placed it prominently on her bed. She smoothed out the duvet to eradicate the dip left from Tonia's seat.

Without looking back a second time, Maggie left her bedroom, with Tonia closely behind.

58

"Geez, John, are you sure it's safe up there?" Hugo called out to John, who was invisible in the darkness of the attic. Hugo and Jessa dodged a sprinkling of dust that flew out of the black and toward their faces.

"It's fine once you're up here!" John called back. "Aha! Here we go!" The dark portal above them lit up in a yellowy glow. John's face came into view from the hole. "Come on up."

Jessa took the stairs first. Her bare feet balanced precariously on each skinny rung. She poked her head in through the entrance and was pleasantly surprised at the cleanliness of the attic space.

Her family only visited their attic twice a year: once to retrieve the Christmas decorations, and then again to put them back. Dusting in the attic is a waste of time, Mr Baxter had said. But John Cane's attic, while definitely a little dusty, was nothing if not organised. Jessa swung her legs up into the loft and joined John, who was unlocking padlocks on the doors of an antique armoire.

"Don't see many locks like that anymore," Jessa admired.

"Well, I've had the electronic keys malfunction on me many times, and this cupboard contains some fairly important merchandise, so I figured I wouldn't risk anything. If it ain't broke..." John smiled.

Hugo joined them just as John removed the final padlock.

Jessa tried to say "whoa," but barely managed the w sound. It just wafted from her mouth like a short breeze.

"Nice stash," Hugo patted John heartily on the back.

They brought the loot to the living room and laid it out on the floor, under the instruction that nobody was to touch anything until given permission to do so.

Guns and ammunition and bulletproof vests and plenty of devices that Jessa couldn't even name were methodically laid out on the ground.

"Any of you ever held a gun before?" John questioned.

"I've been known to do a little weapons training in my time," said Dr Mortlock.

"Me too," said Hugo.

Audrey, Jessa and Flynn shook their heads.

"All right, then you three get the kiddie guns." John picked up three of the smaller weapons and handed one each to the inexperienced members of the team. "Semi-automatic. Nice and easy to use. Felicia, you can take this pistol. Not too heavy. Hugo, you take this one—a miniature submachine. In the military, they call it a 'Hummingbird.' If you need to use it, you'll know why they call it that."

"I don't know if I feel comfortable with this," Audrey held the gun away from her body.

"It's not loaded right now, don't worry," John Cane replied.

"But what about when it is loaded?" Flynn seemed to share Audrey's concern.

"The safety will be on until you need to fire."

"You may not even have to use it," Hugo assured them. "It's just a precaution. We don't quite know what we're getting ourselves in for, and we need to be as prepared as possible."

§

After an hour-long crash course in beginners' weaponry, the new students were pretty well-versed on loading, unloading, gun hold technique and aiming. Jessa became so focused on learning how to use the weapon that she hadn't yet considered that she might have to use it to harm another person. On the other hand, Audrey looked increasingly uncomfortable just holding the gun, let alone pointing it at a target, human or otherwise.

Rounds, chambers, magazines; vocabulary and technical instruction were repeated again and again until they were all as well-educated as possible in such a short amount of time.

John gave a sturdy thumbs up when he decided his students were ready to become soldiers.

Jessa and Flynn were kitted out with the two lightweight bulletproof vests from John's stockpile, while Hugo was helped into a high-tech garment of belts and straps on which to store armaments and other necessities for this new, strange, and most unserendipitous warfare.

Hugo and Jessa were each given a communication device that hooked uncomfortably over their right ears. It trailed a wire down underneath the backs of their shirts and into a clunky black box that clipped over the waistband of their trousers.

"What is this stuff?" Jessa enquired, straining her torso sideways to watch John fiddling with the strange device.

"Gosh, you kids really don't know how good you have it these days. This is analogue, kid! The kind of technology we used to have, in the good old days. Before all this complicated wireless and digital kind of stuff, everything was wired and reliable. Lift up your shoes."

"What?"

"Lift up your foot."

Jessa copied Hugo, who did as he was told, lifting up his foot as though he were a horse having his hooves inspected. John poked a pin into the sole of Hugo's shoe.

"This part is a little more modern, though," said John. "These pins will allow us to follow your whereabouts on the map on the computer. Rachel is going to stay here to keep an eye on you and guide you remotely."

"Does the map actually work? Considering so many web pages are down, I mean…" said Jessa.

"Yeah, don't worry," Rachel replied. "We're accessing it through a different type of server."

"Wow, how do you know how to do all this?" Jessa marvelled. "I thought you worked in physics or something."

"Psychokinetics, yes. But my undergraduate degree was in Engineering and Computer Science. Plus, the Agency keeps me on my toes, you know."

"Cool," said Flynn. "Maybe when this is all over you can help me with something I was working on for Coding Club."

"Yeah, maybe," Rachel smiled.

"Can you hear that crackle in the earpiece now?" said John.

They nodded.

"Great, then we're all good here. You'll be able to hear us through the earpieces. And if you want to talk to us, I'm putting these two walkie-talkies in the backpack. They're already configured to the right frequency, so all you have to do is press the talkback button and speak, and we'll be here to help you out. As soon as you leave, I'll work on getting you the, uh… stuff. I'll get you what you need."

"Are you sure you can get it, John?" Hugo asked. "Because if not, it's okay, but—"

"I can do it."

"How will you get it to us?" Audrey followed up.

"I don't know yet. But you just worry about getting where you need to be. Leave the rest to me."

Dr Mortlock looked at her reflection in the mirror. She untied her hair, and it tumbled down her back. It was a lot longer than Jessa had expected; she'd only ever seen it in a bun. The stark darkness of the roots transitioned into gentle waves in a slightly lighter shade of brown, which gave Dr Mortlock a more feminine touch than her usual look. She looked sadly into her own face.

"I'm sorry I called you a liar," said Jessa.

"Thank you for the apology," Dr Mortlock replied. "Though I appreciate you holding me to your usual standard of scrutiny. Given the circumstance, I know I had it coming." Her honesty gave her face a pretty glow.

"Is it weird, knowing that we're setting out to destroy someone you used to know?" Flynn asked.

"Indeed it is." Dr Mortlock swooped her hair back into a ponytail. "Part of me wishes we didn't have to resort to such measures, but I fear the alternative is considerably more destructive for a greater number of people."

"We're doing the right thing, Felicia," said Hugo.

"The sadly beautiful thing about morality is that doing the right thing doesn't always result in happiness," Dr Mortlock said. "It's always painted in shades of grey. But it's what keeps us moving forward and progressing as conscious beings."

"Progress is the best we can hope for," Hugo picked off some pieces of lint that had become marooned on the arm of his blazer. He fastened the two buttons on the front and checked in John's ostentatious mantelpiece mirror that the belt vest underneath wasn't visible enough to attract any unwanted attention. Satisfied, he turned back to the group.

"I think we're ready," he said, sounding not very ready at all.

59

Behind the living room door, Maggie and Tonia heard a smattering of voices as Maggie's family chattered over the sound of the television.

Maggie's hand hovered over the handle.

She pulled it back.

She grabbed some keys from the decorative key hook, being careful not to let them jangle, then she opened a small cupboard and took out two helmets and handed one to Tonia.

The two girls slipped out through the front door.

"Are you okay?" Tonia asked as Maggie fumbled for the moped key. The street was alive with the bustle of a neighbourhood in distress.

"Yeah," Maggie replied quietly.

"It's all right, you don't have to come."

Maggie looked at her. "You're still going, though, if I don't go with you?"

Tonia nodded.

"I can't let you travel through this by yourself," said Maggie. "I'm sure it'll be fine; we'll just head straight to the hospital, and then we'll wait with Annora until this is over. It's all going to be fine. Isn't it?"

"I hope so," said Tonia.

Maggie put the key into the ignition.

"Let's get out of here quickly before my parents notice we're gone."

60

The sheer number of people out on the streets of London was too many to estimate. The alley directly outside John's building was relatively quiet, but just looking up ahead where it met a major road, they could see a current of bodies being pushed along.

Chants and shouts greeted them as they approached the edge of the flow, and eventually they got too close that the only option left was to join it. Sink or swim. Move or be moved.

Jessa felt as though the whole world must be able to see the concealed weapon strapped underneath her jacket. Fortunately for her, everyone was too preoccupied with the goings on to either notice or care.

It wasn't a particularly warm spring day, but it didn't take long for them to be feeling uncomfortably warm and for their showers in John's clean and peaceful bathroom to seem like a very distant memory. Thousands of people, unwashed and uncontrolled, emitted their unstoppable scent into the stifling air.

What would once have been an enjoyable walk through Central London had become dangerous and wearisome. Glass from smashed shop windows crunched underfoot. Luxury homes slumped in the rapid depreciation of their locale. Worried homeowners tried desperately to hide away any treasures contained in their property by boarding up windows with anything they could find; kitchen cupboard doors nailed heavy-handedly into the window frames. Haphazard.

Rachel was able to view real-time satellite maps to guide them to St Paul's Old Cathedral via back roads and lanes. The long route.

Jessa had always hated the longest way of doing anything. As a young child, she'd quickly learned that shortcuts were almost always her preferred option, even if it meant a less desirable outcome. For example: spend less time doing homework, therefore play video games sooner, and put up with getting a B or a C in school. Skip any unnecessary girlish primping in the morning, therefore get to sleep in later, and put up with being deemed homely by the popular kids or hearing from family 'you could be so pretty if you put in a little more effort.'

The long route to St Paul's wasn't just a matter of geography—it was mentally and physically draining. Constantly aware of avoiding confrontation with any more aggravated protesters, Jessa pulled up her hood and kept her head down. She held tightly onto Audrey's hand, letting her older sister lead her through the crowd.

Jessa's stomach occasionally grumbled as an unkindly reminder that her belly had received little else than shepherd's pie and a few Christmas biscuits that John had remembered were hiding in one of his cupboards.

They took methodical sips from canisters John had prepared for them. Jessa let the saccharine substance coat her mouth before gulping it down. It wasn't unpleasant in taste, but it was too viscous to be quenching, and too limited to be savoured at all. The perfect energy source, John had said, it combatted thirst and blood sugar levels in one. Jessa had doubted him then, and she continued to doubt him with every gelatinous swig.

Thoughts of summers gone and homemade lemonade played on Jessa's mind as she, Audrey, Hugo, Flynn, and Dr Mortlock plodded on, barely saying a word to one another. Jessa wondered if they would survive another summer. She wondered if she would survive another night.

61

Maggie pulled her phone out from her jacket.

"Oh crap, my phone signal came back for a moment, and I have fifty-one missed calls from my parents. So far they've left fourteen voicemails," she sighed loudly and put down her helmet so she could more comfortably send a message. "I'm just going to text them and say we're fine and not to worry."

"Are you gonna listen to their messages?"

"No way. I don't feel like being screamed at fourteen times."

"Fair enough."

The automatic doors to the hospital entrance didn't open. Through the glass they could see plenty of doctors and nurses and hospital staff, none of whom were looking in their direction. Tonia knocked on the window and managed to catch the eye of a young male nurse.

"Uh, hello?" he opened the door slightly and stuck his head out cautiously.

"Hello, can we come in please?" Maggie asked politely.

"I'm not sure if I can let you in. We're on something of a lockdown right now, you see. What are you doing here?"

"We're here to visit our friend," said Tonia.

"Who's your friend?"

"Annora Huff," the two girls replied at the same time.

The nurse looked suspicious.

"So, the two of you, completely randomly, despite everything that's going on right now, decided to come and visit your mate?"

"Of course it wasn't random," Tonia said derisively. "We came because of what's happening. Annora's very sensitive and gets scared easily. We didn't want her to be alone."

"What's going on out here?" a buxom lady interrupted, pushing the door open wider to get a good look.

"Just talking to these two girls, Cheryl. Apparently they came to see Annora."

"Now?!"

"Please just let us in," Maggie implored. "We're really tired and quite thirsty. I swear we're not up to anything bad. We're fourteen so we both have CityID cards, you're welcome to scan them and run a check. But I promise you we're telling the truth. We're just here for Annora."

She offered her laminated identification card. The lady glanced at it but then stepped back. "Fine. But I'm only letting you in because I can't knowingly send you back out into this mad city today."

"Thank you," they said gratefully.

"Connor here will take you up to Annora's room," the lady finished and quickly went back to the huddle around the reception desk. Everyone was staring at a computer screen but Maggie and Tonia couldn't see over them enough to tell what was happening. They didn't have to.

The man called Connor escorted them hurriedly through the protected hallways. He was visibly annoyed when Maggie asked to stop at the water fountain for a moment, and as soon as they reached Annora's room, he unlocked it and departed without so much as a word.

"Hi!" Annora croaked from the bed. "Maggie! What are you doing here?"

"She's here to keep you company with me, silly," Tonia planted a light kiss onto Annora's forehead.

"Couldn't they have given you a more cozy room?" Maggie said, looking around.

"That would be nice," Annora smiled. She pulled her legs into a crossed position, making room for them to sit on the bed with her. "Please tell me what's going on, the nurses won't say. I've heard bits and bobs when people talk in the hallway, but I don't really know anything. Please tell me."

They did.

62

"How does it look?" Rachel's voice came through clearly in Jessa's earpiece.

"Crowded. Although there actually might be fewer people here than back near Westminster."

"Thank goodness," Flynn added.

They walked around the perimeter of St Paul's Old Cathedral, and could see at the rear of the building that some people had set up camp on the grassy courtyard. The building itself was still sealed.

At the front of the building again, they surveyed the steps leading up to the main entrance. A group of large men hammered at the opening. They counted to three and hurled their rugby shoulders into the giant hunk of a door. It didn't budge. Another onlooker informed them they weren't the first to try getting inside.

"How about the windows?" Rachel's voice suggested.

"No chance, they're too high up," said Hugo.

"If it stays locked like this when not in use, he must have another way of getting in and out," Jessa said, looking up at the majestic building.

"Maybe he has a key?" Audrey shrugged.

"He's not that reasonable," her sister answered definitively.

"Maybe he just telelocates himself in and out?" Flynn suggested.

"Possible," said Dr Mortlock. "But presumably, he can't simply walk up to the building and transport himself through walls. He'd be spotted instantly. There must be another route."

"Rachel," said Jessa, "can you find out if there's any way in through other buildings nearby?"

"I'll try. It's possible there were once other passages for clergymen and whatnot, but I'm sure those tunnels will have been blocked for a long time. Bear with me; I'm going to access a different view of the map here."

They whiled the moments away with more sips from their flasks. Hugo heaved off the backpack and flapped the sweat-drenched back of his jacket lightly in the breeze.

"Hey, are you guys there?" Rachel said.

"Yes," Jessa and Hugo responded quickly.

"All right. This might sound crazy, but I think you can actually get in through the Underground tunnel. I'm looking at a subterranean map right now, and it looks like there's a tunnel right off the Tube line that should lead you directly into the building. Seems like there's some kind of bunker in there."

§

Jessa pulled hard on the gates at the entrance to St Paul's underground station and let out an involuntary grunt of annoyance.

"What's your plan, Rachel?" Hugo asked their remote director.

"Hang on. The whole Tube network has been locked as a safety precaution, and I can't overwrite that, but it looks like I can access them individually. Do you see a keypad?

"Yes," said Hugo.

"Great. I can activate it from here, but you have to type in the number to open the gate. I think you'll only have a few seconds though before it locks again behind you. Ready?"

A few nearby onlookers had become curious and wandered closer to the group loitering at the entrance to the tube station.

"I don't like the look of these folks," he said quietly. "Felicia, keep an eye on them. Go ahead, Rachel."

"Zero…zero…four…nine…five…three…three…nine…zero…one."

He input the numbers as inconspicuously as possible.

The incoming gang gathered closer.

The lock buzzed.

"Go, go go!" Hugo urged, and Audrey pulled the gates apart just enough to slip through. Flynn followed, then Jessa, then Felicia Mortlock. Lastly, Hugo moved to step through the gap in the gates, but someone grabbed his rucksack and pulled him back.

"Where you goin'!" a woman's voice called.

"What you up to?" yelled someone else. "Let us in!"

Audrey and Flynn yanked on Hugo's arms as hard as they could but there were more hands grabbing at the backpack. Jessa threw herself up to the gate and, with all the force she could muster, directed energy through her hand and knocked the main perpetrator backwards with an invisible crunch to his nose.

Hugo flew through the gate. Jessa pulled it closed behind him and the lock buzzed one more time, sealing them on the inside of the tube station.

"You better watch yourself, you parapsych witch!" the angry man bellowed, rattling the gate hard with one hand and wiping away blood from his face with the other.

The tube station languished, eerily quiet. The escalators waited, motionless and unclunking. A smattering of rubbish lay strewn across the floor, obvious remnants of a hasty evacuation. Ticket barriers greeted them with their electronic vigilance, waiting for the scan of a ticket or Tuberiders' card. The sound was still and the air felt stale.

Hugo climbed over the barrier, and Jessa and Flynn copied him.

"Hold on!" Audrey called out.

"What are you doing?" Jessa said, watching Audrey fiddle to get something out of her bag.

"Found it," Audrey pulled out her wallet to scan her Tuberiders' card, then walked through the barrier that opened itself welcomingly. "Just because the station's closed doesn't mean we should deliberately break the rules," she glared at Jessa.

"We're not even getting a train," Jessa rolled her eyes.

"You still there, Rachel?" Jessa asked as they began the descent into the depths of the station.

"I'm here. You might lose me down there, though, so make a note of this. Ready? You gotta head to the eastbound track, and then enter the tunnel on your left. Walk through about a quarter of a mile and there's a way out from the side of the tunnel. It should be on the right-hand side. Follow the passageway to the end, then take another right turn. That should lead you right up to the bunker, which is directly under St Paul's. I can't see from here the exact routes out from the bunker, but hopefully that'll become clear when you're there."

Hugo scribbled down notes as Rachel spoke.

"Is there anything else you need from me?"

"Rachel, is there any word from John about the explosives?" Jessa asked.

"He's located the stuff. Right now he's working on getting it to you. But we know where you are, so we'll get it delivered to you as soon as we can."

"Okay."

"Thanks, Rachel," said Hugo.

"You're welcome. Stay safe, guys. Good luck."

63

Annora stared down at her thin blanket. Her mouth drooped, her eyes were soft and sad. She looked healthy but unwashed. She looked well but tired.

"You're going to be fine," Tonia stated.

"Thanks, Ton, but you know as well as I do what's going to happen," Annora said. "I think this is going to be it."

"You don't know that."

"I do, though. And so do you. You've seen it."

"That might not mean anything. It's psychology stuff, isn't it? Your brain might just be remembering things and acting out. Or something. I don't know."

"Ton, it's okay."

"I'm sorry, but I'm not following," Maggie interjected. "What's happening here?"

"I'm one of his chosen ones."

"You were, but they healed you, remember? At the Agency."

Annora shook her head. "I don't think so. I don't think it worked."

"Why do you say that?"

"I get these dreams," Annora said slowly.

"Pff," Maggie dismissed. "Dreams can mean so much. You experienced a trauma, and in that event, it's very likely that you'll re-live those moments in dreams. You probably just have PTSD."

"She has seizures too," Tonia added.

"That could also just be a symptom of injury. In trauma patients—"

"They're not like normal seizures, Mags," Tonia added. "They're like… I don't know. Something else."

"You didn't tell her anything?" Annora said. "She ought to be prepared."

"Maybe we should go outside first, and I'll explain in private."

"No, please stay. Don't worry about me—I can hear it."

Tonia sighed. "It's like… his power, and his voice, and his evilness are all inside her. And then it comes out in these bursts, and she's not Annora anymore, she's this thing that wants to destroy everything and everyone in the room. She becomes possessed."

Maggie's face dropped. "That's why you wanted to come here, isn't it? It's not just to keep Annora company. You know something's going to happen."

"I'm sorry," Tonia muttered. "I understand if you want to leave."

"Yes, I would love to leave!" Maggie spurted. "I would love to just go home to my family and feel safe in my house. Even better, I would love for none of this to be happening. But what am I going to do, just take the moped and leave you here? Ride back through that disaster by myself? I don't have a choice now, do I?"

"I'm really sorry, Maggie," Annora blubbed.

"Annora, please don't cry. It's not your fault," Maggie put her arm around Annora's shoulder.

"I feel bad, though, because you don't want to be here, but now you're stuck."

"It's my fault," said Tonia. "Maggie, I am sorry. I just wanted to do the right thing. The thought of not being here for her just broke my heart. I had to come. I shouldn't have got you involved. But honestly, I was scared to come by myself."

"What difference did you think I could make?!" Maggie shrugged.

"I don't know—you're Maggie! You're good at everything. You always know what to do, and you're good at staying calm. Shit, girl, you brought snacks. Who wouldn't want you around?"

"What's done is done, I suppose," Maggie said sadly. "I forgive you."

"Ton, did you hear from my parents?"

"They called me a while before I went to Maggie's, but I haven't heard anything since. I guess they're on their way."

"Wait, you're in touch with Annora's parents?"

"Yeah," Tonia said. "We kind of had an agreement, that if anything happened, we'd come here. When they saw the news, they called me. That was a while ago, though."

"I hope they're all right," Annora's voice was muffled through her arms as they held tight around her knees.

"I'm sure they're fine, Annora, it's just a bit mad outside. There are people everywhere."

"Why?" Annora replied. "What are they trying to do?"

Maggie and Tonia looked at each other and shrugged.

"I'm not sure," Maggie admitted. "I guess they're trying to do whatever people do in a crisis."

"Yeah," Tonia added. "I think they're just trying to stay together."

64

The platform was deserted. Where a hundred commuters would usually stand, there was no-one. Where scheduling announcements would usually scroll, there was nothing. Where the seemingly endless trains would be, there were none.

Jessa and the others climbed down from the platform and stood before the mouth of the impossibly dark tunnel. In normal circumstances, climbing down onto the tracks would probably require a death wish. But these were the most unnormal of circumstances. Jessa felt an undeniable apprehension as they entered the unwelcoming roundness of the tunnel.

Flynn grasped Jessa's hand.

Hugo opened the backpack and pulled out a powerful torch that lit up the tunnel a great deal. Shedding light on the shadows helped Jessa's uneasiness, but the torch's gleaming beam only reached so far, and it made the ebony darkness beyond seem even more sinister.

"What was that?" Jessa whispered suddenly, spinning around and straining her eyes to see in the darkness.

"What is it?" Audrey spun around. Hugo followed her gaze and turned the torch around quickly, shining the light back in the direction they had walked. There was nothing there. "Jessa, don't frighten me like that."

"I didn't mean to; I thought I heard something."

"The Tube is all locked up, remember?" Hugo said softly. "Nobody else can get down here, don't worry."

"And we must be almost there," said Dr Mortlock.

They walked on, taking slow steps inside the tunnel. Every step echoed. Jessa felt Flynn turn back and look over his shoulder.

"Did you hear something?" she whispered.

"I think my ears are playing tricks on me," he whispered back.

"Did it sound like footsteps?"

He made no spoken reply, but squeezed her fingers tighter and took a few steps closer to Hugo and Audrey, and that was all she needed to know that they had definitely heard the same thing.

"Hold it," a man said.

Before Jessa could react, his hands were on her throat.

Hugo shone the light onto the intruder. Jessa winced at the bright light in her eyes and the stench from the man holding her.

"What brings you fine looking folks down here, then?" he breathed his hot, putrid air into Jessa's face.

"Nothing that concerns you. Let her go, mate," Hugo's hand visibly hovered near the open edge of his jacket, and the weapons hidden beneath.

"How about this? I'll trade you for her."

"What do you want?" Audrey said defiantly, her eyes focused on the dirty hand around her sister's neck.

"How much have you got?" he snarled back.

"You want money?" Audrey huffed. "Fine!" She pulled out her wallet and threw a small pile of notes at him. They separated in the air and floated down over the tracks. She unzipped the coin pocket and turned it upside down, trinkling coins onto the ground.

"More," he said.

"That's all we have," Audrey replied firmly.

"More!" he said again, pulling out a switchblade knife from somewhere unseen.

"Hey, take it easy!" Hugo Fletcher said loudly. "Nobody has to get hurt."

Jessa felt the cool blade against her soft skin, and her first thought was how quickly she would bleed to death if he made the slice.

"Why don't you put the knife down, mate?" Hugo said.

The man gripped Jessa tighter, and she whimpered at the pressure from the blade edge on her throat. "I told you what I want!"

"You pig," Audrey scowled, dropping her smartphone onto the ground and unbuckling her watch. "That watch is the most valuable thing I have, so I hope you enjoy it."

"You rich assholes," the man said.

Dr Mortlock subtly put her hand on the back of Hugo's shoulder. Hugo's stance changed. His knees locked, his spine straightened, and his chin raised confidently.

A strained groan gurgled from the man's mouth as though he were struggling with something. Jessa felt the blade lift away from her skin, and the man released the tightness of his clamp on her as he fought to keep hold of his knife.

Audrey and Flynn raced forward to pull Jessa free. When she turned back to look at him, the knife was high in the air, with the man's arm desperately trying to keep hold of it as it slowly pulled further away from his body. He grunted as it finally moved far enough that he couldn't hold on to it any longer. His fingers loosened, he let go of the handle, and in release of his applied force, the knife shot away from him, hit the roof of the tunnel and fell to the ground.

Jessa scrambled to pick it up before he could.

She hadn't anticipated it, but wasn't surprised when,

Whoosh.

The man's hands were her own. She could feel the irritating pressure of his dirt-soaked clothing rubbing against his skin with every tiny movement. His entire head itched. The inside of his mouth tasted acidic and fermented like rotten fruit.

He held the knife in one hand and rested the blade against the filthy palm of the other.

"Show me that you bleed for me, as I bleed for you, my friends," the voice of Silas Lynch came from somewhere else.

The point of the knife pierced his skin with a sharp scratch and a bubble of bright red blood emerged. He scalpelled an angled line.

"Show me your dedication. Show me that you, too, are willing to sacrifice."

He lifted the blade and drew the other line, crossing over at the top and running down symmetrically.

"When the revolution comes, you will be rewarded for your assistance and your devotion. Brothers and sisters, hear me when I say: the revolution is coming."

Whoosh.

Jessa dropped the knife with a shudder.

The man tried to shuffle toward it again, but Hugo halted him.

"Nope," Hugo said. When the man looked up, he stared right into the barrel of Hugo's weapon. Felicia Mortlock, too, pulled her gun from concealment. Then Flynn. Then Audrey, with shaking hands, held a double grip as she pointed it directly at his face.

"I think you should leave," said Flynn.

The man's wild eyes laughed, and his mouth danced under a beard of grime and defeat. He backed away into the darkness, and his limping footsteps faded into the distance.

65

"Mummy! Dad! I missed you so much!" Annora melted into her mother's arms.

"Hello, sweetie," Mr Huff kissed his daughter on the cheek before embracing both Tonia and Maggie. "Thank you for being here with our Annora."

"Of course," they replied. "You're welcome."

"We had such trouble getting here," Carol Huff told the three girls

"It was a nightmare!" her husband added, shaking his head. "We set out in the car and then had to leave it halfway, there was just no getting through the crowd."

"So you walked the rest of the way?" Maggie exclaimed.

"Indeed, what a palaver! It's all right though, we're here now," Stanley Huff scratched his bald patch. He pulled over the mid-century armchair and grimaced at the harsh scraping sound its legs made on the floor. "Ouch," he chuckled. His wife perched on the arm of the chair, and he put his arm around her waist.

The Huffs, Maggie, Tonia and Annora sat for a moment.

"So," Stanley Huff broke the silence. "What has Annora missed at school? Anything exciting?"

"Oh yes," said Maggie. "We have end-of-year exams coming up, see. So we've finished all of the curriculum and for most subjects we're in the review period. Next week we have some more mock exams too."

"I don't think so, Mags," said Tonia.

"Why?"

"Umm, because of everything?"

Maggie's forehead wrinkled in horror. "They wouldn't close the school, though. Surely not. They can't close school, can they?"

"I think they can."

"But it's exam season!"

"I'm sure it'll be fine, dear," Carol Huff smiled gently. "Every year schools get closed for a few days when it snows. Just think about it like that."

"Winsbury never closes for snow!" Maggie shrieked. "Oh no, what if we miss our exams and have to repeat the year?"

"You have to calm down," said Tonia. "Look at me, Maggie. Seriously, look at me. Now look around this room. And now remember how we got here."

Maggie's mouth closed, then her eyes followed. For a moment, her bottom lip wavered. She inhaled loudly through her nose. "I'm sorry. I just had this moment where I almost forgot—"

"Annora?" Carol Huff jumped from her seat.

"Annora!" Tonia crawled up from the foot of the bed.

Annora's hands were over her ears, and her eyes were squeezed closed. "Make it stop!" she screamed.

"It's okay! You're okay! You're safe!" Tonia held her hands over Annora's, desperately trying to soothe her.

Annora froze, and removed her hands slowly away from the sides of her head. She stared into nothingness.

"I can hear him," she whispered. "He's talking to me."

"Lynch?" Maggie came closer. "What can you hear? What's he saying?"

"He says I've been chosen. He says I'll feel what it's like to be infinite." Suddenly she keeled forward, clutching her stomach and whining in distress. "I can see him." Her face wrinkled in pain. "I can remember when he took my mind. I remember when he stole me."

"My sweet girl," tears rolled down Mrs Huff's face as she stroked Annora's hair.

Annora's small body fell limp, away from the hands of her loved ones. She slumped into convulsions, her body cramped and ghoulish.

"Quick, put her in the recovery position," said Maggie.

Mr Huff shifted his daughter onto her side, while Tonia sat behind her, rubbing her back until the fit subsided. Mrs Huff used the sleeve of her cardigan to tenderly wipe away a string of saliva from the side of Annora's mouth.

"Mummy?" Annora wept.

"I'm here, flower. Daddy's here too. And Maggie and Tonia. We're all here."

"I'm tired."

"You can rest. We've got you."

66

Hugo shone the torch beam over the walls, and the shaft of light revealed a small metal hatch in the side of the Tube tunnel.

"This must be it," said Audrey. "I guess you open it with this wheel thing," she tapped her fingernails on the round metal structure. "Hugo, you wanna get started on this?"

He slid the giant backpack off and stepped up to the steering wheel of a handle. He grasped it forcefully, pulled the wheel with the weight of his whole body, and it slowly began to budge.

The hatch opened with a heavy clunk, revealing behind it another rounded tunnel, smaller and metaller. Jessa volunteered to go first and took the torch from Hugo, and quickly realised she couldn't quite stand at her full height. Hugo and Dr Mortlock looked particularly uncomfortable as they contorted their tallness to fit in the tunnel.

Hugo pulled the hatch door closed with a slam, and they were sealed into the next section of their journey.

Where the ground of the Tube tunnel had absorbed most of their footstep thuds, the new tunnel amplified each step with an inescapable chime. A count down. Counting down to something inevitably strange and strangely inevitable.

The tunnel came to a stark end as it opened perpendicularly into another thoroughfare. The intersection was a mixture of old and new, as the modernity of the dark metal tunnel gave way to an old brick passageway, narrower indeed but tall enough to stand in, and smelling of damp and dust and age.

"We make a right turn here," Hugo consulted his notes.

Stirring up dust with every cautious step, they all steadied their traipse by running hands along the inside of the passageway walls. They scuffled and turned, right, then left, then right, then left again, then right again, in a bubble of illumination that moved with and around them.

The brick-lined beige corridors reminded Jessa of a video game she'd played as a child; a first-person romp through Medieval times that made her feel like she was transcending worlds and time. Now she felt like she was transcending real life. Transcending. Escaping. Protecting.

Eventually, the passageway came to a welcome end and opened into the vastness of the underground bunker. They all stretched away the hunches and compression of tunnel claustrophobia.

"Whoa, this is gigantic," Flynn observed as Jessa cast the light all around. "Why is this even here?"

"A lot of bunkers like this were built in the event that people would need to be evacuated underground, like in a nuclear fallout," Audrey explained. "There's a lot more than you'd think, all over the world, actually. I'm not sure why it was built into this church specifically, though. And St Paul's predates any nuclear power, so that couldn't possibly have been a factor in its design."

"So you have no idea why this is here," Jessa scoffed.

"Well, I don't know for definite. I could hypothesise—"

"You mean you could guess. But you don't know."

"Jessa, please. Not now."

They moved curiously and carefully through the caverns of the bunker, travelling through rooms and around corners until there was only one possible way out. A skinny stairwell took them upward and outward, spiralling in steps of stone. Jessa took some solace in knowing the underground would soon be deep beneath them once again.

"It's blocked," said Flynn. "We're trapped."

Hugo tapped on the object hindering their exit, and it sounded hollow and heavy.

"Flynn, you want to help me with this?" he said.

"Really?"

"Sure, why not?"

Flynn shrugged. "I don't know. I don't often get asked to help move heavy things."

"You look perfectly strong to me," Hugo said. "Here, just do what I do. Lean into it with your body, keep your knees slightly bent, and keep your back straight. That's all there is to it. Ready? One…two…three…go!"

Hugo and Flynn pushed against the timber with all their might, and slowly it began to budge.

"Keep pushing, Flynn!"

"It's too heavy!"

Jessa handed the torch to Audrey and joined them, pressing her weight as hard as she could into the object.

It moved a little more, announcing their arrival to the other side with the conspicuous screech of heaviness pushing across bare floor.

As soon as the gap was large enough, Hugo snuck through, armed and poised, pointing the gun in any direction that someone could be lurking.

"Clear," he announced, and Jessa, Flynn, Audrey and Felicia Mortlock exited the secret passageway and joined him in a new room.

It was an old office, still equipped but lacking signs of life. They inspected other rooms along the corridor and found much of the same. Abandonment under broken lights.

"Hello?" Rachel's voice crackled in Jessa and Hugo's ears.

"Rachel!" Jessa said.

"Hey Jessa, are you all okay?"

"We're fine. We just got inside."

"I thought as much. You just appeared on my satellite map again. It looks like you're still underground, though. Are you in the main building?"

"Doesn't look like it," Hugo joined in the conversation, creeping into an empty room with a gun drawn. "These rooms look like they haven't been used for decades."

"Clear!" he called to the others.

"Over here," Flynn waved. "There are stairs leading up."

They departed the deserted corridor and ascended from the bowels of the building. Their eyes gulped at the brightness in hearty, deliberate blinks. A heavy door closed behind them with a click, locking them out of their entrance and giving them no choice but to continue.

67

Signal unavailable. Every time Maggie tried to call Jessa, the signal was unavailable. She tried sending a text, but to no avail. They were marooned from outside communication.

"How long was I asleep?" Annora rubbed her eyes.

"Only about an hour," Mrs Huff replied quietly, not wanting to disturb the napping Mr Huff. "How do you feel?"

"Tired still."

"You can sleep more if you need to."

"No, I want to be awake now. Where are Maggie and Tonia?"

The two girls stood up from their seats on the floor.

"We're here!" Tonia lay down on the bed next to Annora, who shuffled sideways to give her more room.

Mr Huff also snuffled awake. "Is anyone else getting peckish?" he said. "My tummy's rumbling."

"There's a vending machine at the end of the corridor," said Tonia.

"Let's go and get some snacks, Stan," Mrs Huff patted her husband's knee.

Annora waited until the room door had closed fully. "I think I'm going to die today."

Saliva caught in Maggie's throat.

"Don't you dare say that," Tonia scolded.

"You think it too. And my parents do. Why else are you all here?"

"To just be with you, to stay with you while all this is happening!"

"No. You heard what he said. You heard what he's going to do."

All Maggie could do was say what she was thinking. "Annora, I'm so sorry."

Annora looked at her and squeezed her lips into a half-hearted and wistful smile. "I know. I am too."

"Are you afraid?" Tonia whispered.

"I don't know. My parents always told me that death isn't something to fear, because when you live each day to the fullest, there's nothing to be scared of when it ends."

"My parents never talk about death," Maggie said thoughtfully. "Not like that, anyway."

"Have I lived every day to the fullest?"

There was nothing they could say.

"I mean, how do you know if you've made the most of your life? All I've done is go to school and then do homework. Sometimes I dance. I like to put on a playlist and dance around my room until my feet hurt. I can't do that here, though. They don't let me listen to music."

"If you could listen to anything right now, what would it be?" Maggie asked.

"Hmm," Annora thought aloud. "I don't have much energy, so maybe something classical. Something pretty."

Maggie smiled. "Good choice."

"I think you make the most of every day just by being yourself," said Tonia.

"Really? How?"

"Annora, you're my most favourite person in the whole world," Tonia replied. "You're the kindest person I've ever met. I mean, when my dad got arrested a few months ago, you made me a lasagna and went on an hour-long bus journey to bring it to me so that I'd have a real dinner. And when my charm bracelet broke and the little horse charm got lost, you spent the weekend going to every jewellery shop trying to find another one. It takes a really special person to go out of their way to help others."

"My favourite Annora Huff moment," Maggie chimed in, "was when Jessa was desperate to go to that concert. What band was it? I don't even remember. But I know she really wanted tickets, but they sold out too quickly. So you spent hours entering contests online to win tickets for her."

"It worked!" Annora smiled.

"I know! When you told her you got tickets… I don't think I've ever seen a smile that big."

Annora paused for a moment. "Do you think Jessa can stop him?"

"I don't know," Tonia admitted.

"I think she can," said Maggie. "She has Flynn, and Mr Fletcher, and Dr Mortlock, and Audrey and Rachel. That's a good team."

"I think he might be too strong for her," Annora looked down. "He might be too strong for anyone."

They were blind to the magnificent interior of St Paul's Old Cathedral.

"No sign of Lynch," Hugo sighed, frustrated.

"I don't know what I was expecting," Flynn said, "but I thought we'd see something, you know? Like something here would jump out at us. A sign."

"Mmhmm," Audrey nodded.

"This is the right place," Jessa tilted her head back, looking far up into the domed ceiling, "I can feel it." She ran her thumb over the tips of her fingers lightly as if feeling a light fabric or oily substance. "There's something in the air, like a weird energy. A heat. I can see why he likes it here."

"He always did have a taste for grandeur," Felicia said thoughtfully.

He'll need somewhere private. Where nobody can stop him.

But he'll want to see everything.

"The balcony," Jessa pointed.

"What about it?" Flynn questioned. "Did you see someone up there?"

"No, but I think that's it. That's where he'd want to be. That's where I'd want to be."

They found the spiralling stone stairwell up to the balcony and climbed, eventually coming out at the balcony edge. The intricate dome directly above tried to pull their gaze upward into its hypnotic centre, but Jessa was distracted, crouching on the ground, running her hands over the aged stone floor that had been engraved over time.

Details. Details everywhere.

The balcony itself was supported by rails of twisted metal that Jessa caressed curiously with her grimy hands.

"What is it, Jess?" Audrey asked gently. Jessa made no sign that she even heard the question, but merely grabbed a torch from the backpack and disappeared back into the narrow stairwell. The others had no choice but to follow, single file and irrefutably agog.

"Here," Jessa shone the light onto a fixed spot on the aged wall.

"I don't see anything," said Audrey.

"Come here."

Hugo stepped down. Jessa took his hand, positioned his finger against the stone and moved it side to side.

"You feel that? Like it's been scooped out a little?"

"I think so."

"Follow it up," Jessa motioned and he did as he was told.

"You see now?" she shone the light widely over the whole area. "It's the symbol. It's an anchor."

"Why here?" asked Flynn.

"Remember what Professor Arnold said about auto-telelocation? The traveller has to have a clear image of the place they're trying to locate to. I'm sure he's going to use the balcony. But it's so detailed up there, it would be a nightmare to memorise that place. But in here, there's barely anything to see."

"Not to mention safer," Hugo added. "Much less chance of accidentally being seen in here. Hey, Rachel, can you hear me?"

"I hear you," she said.

"Can you see on the 3D map how high up we are?"

"Yep, you're about 160ft above ground level. And for what it's worth, that underground area you were in when I spoke to you earlier, is several floors directly below you, and that was roughly 30ft below ground level."

"That's a difference of 190ft," said Flynn.

"The Professor said it should be possible to auto-telelocate up to a couple of hundred feet," said Hugo.

"There must be more anchors down there," said Felicia.

"Right," said Jessa. "He's set up these checkpoints that he can travel between without being detected. This is how he gets in and out. I wonder how many there are."

"I'd guess that depends on just how powerful he is," Audrey mused.

"Hey guys, sorry to interrupt," Rachel said into their earpieces, "but you should know that John liaised with Matt Allerton, and Matt's on his way to you now. I'm sending him in the same way you went, so don't be alarmed when you hear someone else coming up behind you. Just hang tight."

69

"Are there any phone charging stations in this place?" Maggie asked the others.

"I haven't seen any," Tonia shook her head.

"There's definitely none in this ward," Mrs Huff said. "They don't let the patients use anything electrical."

"My phone's almost out of battery," Maggie put the device back in her bag.

"Do you want to charge from mine?" Tonia offered. "I have the BuddyCharger app."

"Nah, that's all right. It's useless anyway with no signal. I just like the safety of having it with me."

Maggie walked around the bed to see Annora's sleeping face.

"How does she look?" Tonia asked.

"Pale."

"That's three seizures since we got here," Tonia whispered.

"I know."

"Maggie, would you mind coming to the toilets with me?"

"Not at all. Mr and Mrs Huff, we'll be back in a minute."

§

Tonia held her hands under the cold running water. "I don't think I can do this."

"What do you mean?" Maggie replied.

"I don't think I can watch her deteriorate—it's heartbreaking. I just keep thinking about what he did to her. It makes me so angry. It's like I can feel my blood getting hot." She placed her wet, cool hands over her face. "And I keep looking at the time, keeping track in my mind of this horrible countdown. And it's like she's getting worse every minute. And then I flash forward to midnight, and I wonder what or how it's going to happen…"

Maggie put her arm around Tonia. "Jessa's out there, remember. She might be able to stop him."

"But she might not. Since all this started, we've been putting all our trust in Jessa and her "intuition," even though nobody really seems to know what that is. We trusted her, then Mr Fletcher trusted her, then the Agency trusted her. And now they're all out there following her around like she's some super army general."

Tonia stared into Maggie's face in the mirror.

"What if she's not what they think she is? Or what if she's not what we think she is? What if she's just a person, with no more ability than you or me?"

"We can't afford to think like that."

"I can't help it. And it's not just Annora. I also keep thinking about what it was like on the journey from your house to here, and then imagining them out there…"

"Are you worried about Flynn?"

Tonia sighed. Her mouth turned downwards. "No. I can't think about Flynn right now."

"Why?"

"Because I can't. I mean, I'm thinking about him as part of the group that's out there. But I can't think of him as my… whatever he is."

"Your boyfriend?"

"I don't think he's actually my boyfriend yet. We haven't said that, anyway."

"He likes you a lot. A lot."

"I like him a lot too."

"Look, it's completely okay for you to think about him—"

"I should be focusing on Annora!" Tonia interrupted.

"Annora has your focus. You're here for her. But you can't make yourself feel bad for thinking about Flynn, or any of them, or anything else. Nothing you do or think right now will change Annora's situation. So just keep doing what you're doing. Just be here for her. Keep showing her how much you care and how much you love her."

"Maggie, I'm so scared," the tears finally wobbled from Tonia's eyes.

"Shh," Maggie pulled Tonia into her arms. "We'll get through it."

Tonia took a deep breath. "But maybe not all of us."

70

"Matt! Good to see you, mate!" Hugo embraced his colleague with a genuine hug.

"You too, Hugo. And all of you. I'm glad you're all okay," he placed a hefty briefcase on the ground. "I come bearing gifts. So what's the plan?"

"Well, we found his route in and out of the building," Jessa began.

"It's a pretty big distance," Hugo followed up. "What's our range?"

"Probably up to eighty feet. I could only get the cable stuff, you know?"

"Yeah, don't worry, that'll work. We can lace the stairwell and the balcony with that, no problem."

"How long will it take to set up?" Flynn asked.

"Not long, maybe an hour or two," Matt replied, patting Flynn on the shoulder. "It's getting late, though, so we should get started."

Jessa was surprised to see inside the suitcase. It mostly contained a large wire, nothing like the red sticks of dynamite she'd been expecting. The only explosive devices she'd ever seen were in movies and cartoons, and despite Matt's precursor that he had brought "the cable stuff," she still hadn't expected something so pedestrian.

"Are you sure this'll do it?" she asked, trying not to sound doubtful. "I mean, it doesn't look very powerful."

"Don't be too quick to judge. This is good stuff, I promise," Matt said. "They use this a lot in controlled demolitions. It's a really localised blast. Nice and clean."

They laid the cable along the edge of the steps and up to the balcony, positioning it all around the skirt of the balcony before trailing it back down the other side of the stairs. Matt explained that it had to be carefully pinned into place, making full contact with the receiving surface, and that it had to retain maximum tautness for the signals to travel through the wiring. He explained it all so matter-of-factly that they didn't even stop to consider what they were setting up for. Explosion. Destruction. Murder.

"I keep thinking…" Audrey said, hushedly, "should we be worried that he's around here somewhere? Right now, I mean. That he knows what we're doing, or that he can see us?"

"Doubtful," said Felicia. "I don't believe he would waste his energy coming out here prematurely. He's around, somewhere. But far enough."

Slowly, the cable was affixed. Each pin had to be knocked into the stone, which was tiring and precise work. There was only one mallet, too, which meant it was also slow progress. The weary group took the chance to rest while Matt and Hugo took turns hammering. Audrey pulled out a miniature first aid kit from the backpack and found a sanitary wipe.

"Hold still," she said.

"What is it?" Jessa asked.

"Nothing, you're just a little grubby."

Jessa looked at Audrey's face. Her skin looked less porcelain than usual. Her eyes were tired, and her lips looked dry and glossless. Audrey rubbed the wet wipe over Jessa's hands like a mother would a toddler after petting animals at the zoo. Caring, concerned, calming.

"All right, I think we're almost done," Matt stood back, admiring their work. The cable was so perfectly flush with the wall that it was almost invisible against the centuries-old interior that they were preparing to devastate.

"Now I have to assemble the important bit." He attached a few small boxes to each end of the cable, which fortunately were far enough inside the stairwell that they were completely veiled by darkness. Then he pulled out a strange laptop computer and connected it to one of the little boxes. "I just have to program it, then we'll be ready to rock."

They sat without conversation, listening to the sound of Matt's typing and tapping and humming and haaing.

"Done," he closed the mini computer, put it back in the briefcase, and took out one last object.

"Here," he offered something to Hugo. "Detonator. Hold the underneath button for five seconds to activate. Let go. Press three times to confirm activation. Then press the red button on the top when you're ready to—" he imitated a bomb going off.

They wandered away from the balcony and walked around on the ground level of St Paul's Old Cathedral, where they came across an entire wing of the building that had become a storage area for staging blocks and large structures of folded tiered seating. They pulled apart a few obstacles and crawled into a space just large enough for the six of them to sit. Protected by a giant wall of the vacant audience seats on one side, and a cold stone wall of the building on the other, they took a moment to relax, as much as relaxing was possible. Hugo and Matt both sat with loaded weapons close at hand.

"Now what?" asked Flynn. "Should we go outside?"

"No way," Matt said quickly. "It's chaos out there."

"Really?" said Audrey. "Did it get worse?"

"You wouldn't believe it," Matt answered. "Fires, riots, stabbings, gunfights. There have been a few street fights between groups of parapsychs and laterals."

"That's absurd!" Audrey burst angrily. "People need to come together in a time like this, not fight over petty differences! Why is that happening?"

"I don't really know," Matt shrugged. "Seems that there's some kind of parapsych-a-phobia catching on. Some people seem to think that every parapsych knew about Lynch and all this stuff."

"But it's not as though every parapsych is like him," said Flynn.

"Silas believes every parapsych could be as powerful as he is," said Felicia. "And he might be right. If laterals realised that, the world as we know it could change in an instant."

"But every parapsych isn't just going to suddenly be like "yeah, great, please make me powerful and evil," though," Flynn replied.

"I guess if you're a lateral then maybe you just don't really understand how it works," Matt said. "They're not thinking logically. All they know is, they now have a reason to be scared."

"But I'm a lateral and I'm not scared of parapsychs, and I know plenty of people who will be very reasonable," said Audrey.

"I hope you're right," said Matt.

71

"Help! Someone, please help!"

"Mrs Huff?" Tonia snapped to attention and raced out of the toilets.

The two girls froze in the doorway.

Carol and Stanley Huff were using all their strength to hold Annora down by her arms, but her legs continued to flail violently. Her skin looked drained, her fingers were curved and talon-like. Her mouth was open and askew, tongue flitting savagely. She groaned and snarled, animal and brutish.

"Oh… oh shit…" Tonia managed to say.

"Please help!" Stanley yelled. "Get the restraints! They're tucked under the bed!"

Maggie and Tonia ran to either side of Annora's bed and did as instructed, unleashing the chunky leather straps. Annora's parents did their best to hold down her wrists while the two girls tightened and fastened the straps into place.

They tried to grab at her legs, receiving multiple walloping kicks in the process, before finally wrestling her feet into the restraint loops.

Annora's body continued to thrash and pull and writhe. Mrs Huff held her daughter's head and spoke soothingly. But Annora was gone. In her place was a rabid wraith, boney and grotesque.

"We mark the path— We mark— " she snarled, coughing out the sentences with her twisted, wet mouth. "We mark the p—, the p—," she stammered.

Maggie dashed to the panic button on the wall and smashed her fist into it again and again. A siren began to wail and a light outside the room blazed bright red.

Tonia covered her hands with her ears. Maggie watched Mrs Huff nestling into her husband's chest, both of them in tears. Annora's growled words turned to pained groans. The groans turned to yelps, which turned to screams. Long, agonised screams. They all cowered from the sound.

Maggie continued to pound on the emergency call button.

"Please, please…" she said, pressing it over and over.

Three nurses burst into the room.

"Please help!" Carol Huff cried.

"Fucking hell," the nurse's jaw dropped when she saw Annora on the bed.

Annora continued to struggle and scream. With every movement she pulled the restraints taught, testing their limits. Her wrists and ankles were red and distressed. Her entire lower jaw and the top part of her nightgown were covered in fresh blood.

"What the—" one of the other nurses managed to say.

"Jenny," the main woman spun around, "open the seizure kit, prepare the highest dose of Clonazepam."

Jenny fumbled inside the suitcase-like box she'd brought to the room and handed up a syringe. "Cheryl! Here!" she said, thrusting it to the woman, who ran forward and slammed the needle into Annora's thigh.

Her body wrenched out a few more hefty spasms and then slumped onto the plasticky hospital sheet, motionless.

"Ugh," Jenny the nurse stepped forward, "she bit her tongue."

"What happened to her?" Cheryl exclaimed. "She's never had a seizure like that before."

"She's…" Tonia didn't know what to say. "She's one of them."

"One of who?"

"Silas Lynch… the one hundred children…"

The nurses looked at one another.

"Are you telling me this girl is affiliated with Silas Lynch?"

"No!" Maggie blurted.

"He took her and he did this to her," Mrs Huff whimpered.

The nurses shook their heads disbelievingly.

"So you're telling me," Cheryl continued, "that all this stuff we've been hearing, about Silas Lynch and those one hundred children he's supposedly "chosen," is happening right here in our ward."

Mrs Huff nodded.

"Some powerful parapsychs tried to heal her," Tonia spoke quickly, "but it didn't work. He still has control over her mind."

"And what exactly is he controlling her to do?" the nurse spat back angrily.

"Well, somehow he's going to… you know… he's going to try and kill her. All of them."

"I don't understand. He's not here?"

"Lynch isn't here, no. Of course not," said Maggie.

"But if he's controlling her, then he might as well be here," Jenny said.

"If she's one of his chosen ones, whatever that means exactly, then how is he going to get her?" Cheryl asked.

"We don't know."

"I don't like this one bit," Cheryl said. "She's dangerous."

"She's not! Not really! It's not her fault!" Tonia cried.

"Maybe not, but I can't put innocent people at risk in this facility."

"There's nowhere else for her to go," said Maggie.

"She can stay, but I'm afraid I have to initiate a quarantine protocol on this wing of the hospital."

"Why? She's restrained, look at her."

They all looked at Annora. Crumpled, pathetic, and bloody.

Cheryl shook her head. "I'm sorry. I have to seal the ward and put extra security measures in place."

"Please, miss, I think that might be unnecessary," Mr Huff stepped forward.

"It's my job to protect the other patients and staff. If this girl has a supernatural condition, I don't know what she's capable of. She could be being used as a weapon."

"Please, this is madness—"

"Have you seen the news right now? The whole country is madness!"

They couldn't argue.

"Under quarantine protocol, nobody can enter or exit the ward. If you want to leave, please come with us now."

"We're not leaving our daughter," Mrs Huff held tight onto Annora's paralysed hand.

"I can't leave her either," Tonia said, looking at Maggie. "I promised."

Maggie looked back at Tonia. She wanted nothing more than to walk out of the ward and ride home to her parents and brothers.

"You should go," Tonia nodded. "It's all right."

Maggie's gaze fell back to Annora.

"No," she said quietly. "I'm staying, too."

"Are you sure?" Cheryl asked the room again. Everyone nodded.

"Suit yourselves," she said. "Good luck."

72

The great bell at St Paul's Old Cathedral chimed Silas' deadline. They all stood, ready, waiting, and unknowing, backs to the wall and looking out at the vast interior of the still empty building.

"Maybe we were wrong," Audrey said under her breath. "Oh no, what if we're in the wrong place."

"We're not," Jessa said.

"But how do you know?"

"I just do."

Audrey frowned.

"Hey, are you guys there?" Rachel's voice suddenly came back to life. "Please be there. Can you hear me?"

"Yes, Rachel, we hear you!" Jessa responded into the walkie-talkie.

"It's happening," the words rushed out of her mouth, breathless, agitated. "It's on the news."

"What can you see?" asked Hugo.

"I... Uh... I don't..."

"Rachel, what is it?" Jessa urged.

"They're like... I don't know... they're floating."

"What? Who is?"

"The children. There's a news camera, and the children are just... floating by. I—I don't know."

"How many?" Jessa demanded.

"Two. There's two on the screen right now. Oh shit, three. Another one just kind of… rose up and joined them. People are trying to grab them but they're too high. What the fuck is happening? What the fuck…" Rachel let out a long breath. "Sorry. Sorry. What can you see where you are?"

"Nothing," Hugo replied. "This place is empty."

"Oh no, are you sure you're in the right place?"

"He'll be here," said Jessa.

Rachel turned up the volume on the television.

"Can you hear this? People are going insane."

"It just sounds like noise from here."

"That's basically all it is," Rachel muttered. "Oh geez… there's this woman pushing through the crowd, trying to pull her daughter down. I can't take it…"

"I think we need to get out of here," Audrey paced back and forth. "I know they're locked, but maybe we can break through these doors from the inside."

"No," said Jessa.

"Jess, nothing's happening here! He said midnight! But it's now past midnight and he's not here!"

"He will be! Right, Dr Mortlock?"

"I would like to think you're right, Jessa," she replied.

"Jessa, try and remember the vision you had," Hugo said gently. "Did anything about it suggest that he would be here tonight? Or just that he has been here?"

"It's going to be here! I know it is!"

"Let's try getting outside, just in case," Matt nodded to the group, and he, Audrey and Hugo ran to the doors to investigate the locks.

"Why don't you believe me?" Jessa stared at them. Nobody responded.

"I think there's a toolbox in here somewhere, I probably have a blowtorch or something," Hugo said, rummaging in the backpack. "Maybe we can bust off the locks."

"Wait, listen," said Flynn.

In the distance was the sound of a crowd. The quivering mumble of countless thousands; irate and irrational.

"There's more," Rachel said quietly into their earpieces. "Moving quicker now, I think. I'm looking at the satellite map. It looks like the whole crowd is moving in your direction."

Hugo glanced at Jessa.

"See?" she said. "They're coming here."

The distant rumble grew closer and into a roar, like an ocean wave approaching the shore. Growing, rushing, and unstoppable. Minutes flew by in seconds, and Rachel's map updates and stunted descriptions of televised horrors cast imagery and fear in their minds. They had seen it all coming. But, physically trapped inside the final destination of their foreseen fate, they couldn't see a thing.

"There's loads more now—the crowd is crushing onto Fleet Street."

"Rachel says they're on Fleet Street," Hugo relayed to the group.

"That's a straight road to here," Audrey said.

"What does it look like, Rachel? What can you see?"

"They're still just... floating. Close together. Above the crowd. And occasionally one of the kids who's in the crowd on the ground just kind of lifts up and floats along with them. How is he doing this?" Her question was rhetorical. They had no answer.

All they could do was wait and listen to the sea of chaos rolling toward them and the pittering sound of helicopter blades chugging in circles above. In a matter of moments, the sound grew exponentially as the huge wooden doors at the front of St Paul's creaked open, ripping the locks apart with an unimaginable and unseen force. The crowd poured in before Jessa and the others had time to even think. They were pushed back into a corner under the force of a thousand people rushing into the building. They grabbed at each other to try and stay together.

"We need to get closer!" Hugo shouted over the deafening roar of fear and confusion. "The detonator will be out of range!"

He snatched Audrey's hand. She held Jessa's. Jessa grabbed Flynn. Matt and Felicia brought up the rear, trying to protect the teenagers from the crush. Together they snaked through the tightness of the crowd that flooded into St Paul's. They made it to the centre of the main atrium, where the density of the crowd forced them to stop. With nowhere else to turn, the only direction for Jessa to look was up.

That's when she saw them.

Some as young as six, some perhaps as old as sixteen, but all there, dead-faced and staring. Silas' chosen hovered above the crowd that reached and pawed upwards in unsuccessful rescue. They floated, horizontal, face-down, their toes pointed to the earth, their mouths wordless and still.

Directly above Jessa's face was the face of another, about her age. Her long hair fell in a cascade around her skull. Looking up among the mass of limp hair, Jessa stared into the girl's eyes. They looked down upon her, open but unseeing.

The chosen lay in the air above the crowd, positioned uniformly apart from one another and just high enough that nobody could reach them.

Their mouths began to move. The crowd silenced to hear it.

"We mark the path for his mighty resurrection."

The sea of spectators looked upward. Helpless, fearing, and pathetic. Sobs rang out from the mouths of the bystanders.

Jessa threw her gaze to the balcony.

"Where is he?" she said under her breath.

As if in response, shadows emerged from the back of the balcony. First, the two large men stepped out and looked down onto the crowd below. Next, another familiar face came into view. Cecily Graves. Her eyes moved quickly over the sea of onlookers and the floating chosen. She held her head proudly.

And then, there he was. Silas Lynch stepped forward to the edge of the balcony, and the screams rose. Angry, chaotic, echoing, questioning. Some people closest to the balcony corner rushed to find the entrance to the stairwell up, only to be blocked by a force keeping them out. Still they tried, desperately throwing themselves at the invisible wall.

The face-down chosen continued the chant that spoke unconsciously from their mouths.

"Detonator! Do it now!" Audrey shook at Hugo's arm frantically, and he reached into his pocket for the device. He activated the detonator and held his thumb atop it. Under the chanting canopy of the chosen and surrounded by human walls of riotous noise, he pressed the red button.

73

"Huh?" Annora jerked awake. "What?" she pulled at the restraints holding her wrists down.

"Annora," Mrs Huff whispered. "Is it you?"

"Mum!" the girl wailed through the pain of her torn and swollen tongue.

"It's all right, sweetheart, we're here. You just had an episode."

"Can you untie me?"

Mrs Huff quickly started work loosening one of the wrist straps.

"Carol, wait," Mr Huff stopped her. "That might not be a good idea."

"She's fine now, Stan," Mrs Huff's eyebrows furrowed. "They gave her the medicine!"

"Daddy, please."

"I don't know… I just don't think we should."

"Please," Annora begged softly.

"I just don't want you to hurt yourself, sweetpea."

"I won't. I think… I think it's over."

"Really?" Tonia and Maggie gathered at Annora's bedside.

"Yeah. I feel different."

"Hmm. Maybe it's okay, then," her father conceded.

"Can you at least undo that one? It's a bit too tight."

"All right, we'll do the one for now and see how you get on," Mrs Huff nodded. She continued unbuckling the strap. "Hmm," she muttered under her breath, struggling with one particular buckle. "What's going on here, then? I think this bit's stuck. Oh, darn… Let me just…" she leaned in close to get a better look.

Before Carol Huff even realised what was happening, Annora slipped her hand free, grabbed the back of her mother's head, and smashed her face into the metal frame of the bed.

"Let me go!" Annora roared.

She was no longer the Annora Huff they knew. She was deranged, pulling harder on the restraints than before and bellowing nonsensically. With one tremendous pull, Annora was able to free one of her legs.

Mr Huff helped his hysterical wife to the side of the room, where they cowered from the monster that had encompassed their daughter.

Maggie and Tonia backed up against the wall. Maggie noticed the medical box the nurses had left on the floor and flung it open. Behind her, Annora tossed and hollered and thrust her head backwards again and again.

Copying the nurse as best she could, Maggie dispensed a bottle of the anticonvulsant into the syringe. She uncovered the needle and took tentative steps toward Annora's side.

"I can't get close enough! She's kicking too much!"

Tonia leapt to Annora's other side. After taking several hefty kicks to her stomach and chest, Tonia was able to grab Annora's ankle and hold it just long enough. Maggie lunged forward and sank the needle deep into Annora's flesh and pushed the plunger.

She fell back into stillness on the bed.

"Did it work?" Tonia asked.

"I think so," Maggie stepped toward Annora's head. Annora didn't move. Maggie reached out her hand toward Annora's forehead. She delicately placed her thumb over Annora's eye and lifted the lid to check her pupils.

Annora's eyes flew open and stared at Maggie, who froze in place.

"We mark… we mark the…" her whole body started shaking and rolling drunkenly, working through the effect of the drug.

She flung her arm over and grabbed Maggie's shirt and yanked her in. Annora snarled and snapped and bit at Maggie's head until Tonia could pull Maggie free.

"Quick, get more of the stuff!" Tonia gestured toward the medical kit.

Maggie threw herself onto the ground and prepared another syringe with twice the amount of the drug. She battled away Annora's free leg and again plummeted the needle into her skin. Annora took a breath as though she'd been winded, but then continued writhing more savagely than before.

"It's not doing anything," Maggie breathed. "She's fighting it off."

"Shit!" Tonia yelled, looking around the room.

"We mark the path for… We mark…"

"She can't seem to get the whole sentence out," Maggie said to Tonia. "It's like she's trying but can't quite get there."

"So?"

"So maybe he doesn't have complete control over her. Maybe the real Annora is in there somewhere, trying to stop it."

"I don't know, Mags."

Annora spat out a clot of bloody saliva. "Let me go."

"No," Maggie said, defiantly.

"Let. Me. Go." Annora barked.

"No, we're not letting you go!"

"His Grace needs me."

"He's trying to kill you!"

"He will save me."

"No, he won't! You're going to die because he's some crazy lunatic who wants to rule everyone."

"He will save us all."

"No, he'll destroy us! He's a madman! You have to fight this!"

"He is almighty."

Maggie changed her tone. "Annora, it's me, Maggie."

Annora pulled at the restraints again, growling and drooling.

"Annora, I think you can hear me! Don't let him win! Don't let him!" Maggie's throat choked up. "Please, Annora!" she sobbed.

"I think she's gone, Mags," Tonia whispered. Maggie fell to her knees.

With an immense screech, Annora pulled the restraints right out from their metal fastenings and leapt from the bed. She hunched on the floor like an animal stalking prey.

"Oh no," the words barely came out of Maggie's mouth.

"My Annora!" Mrs Huff wailed.

Annora spun round. The chain on the end of the leather strap jangled against the floor as she moved. Every step was sinister. Every jerking movement of her body was villainous. Then, she stopped. She straightened, pulling her body from that of a broken doll and into something hominine and forgivable. Something recognisable.

"Mummy?" her voice wavered.

"Annora?" a cowering Mrs Huff said.

"Mummy, it's me!"

"My flower!" she held her arms outstretched, inviting the small girl in.

Annora flew forward, throwing her arms around her mother's neck.

But it became quickly apparent that something was wrong. Very wrong. Mrs Huff's hands swiped and scraped at Annora's back. She tried to scream but nothing came out. No sound. No air.

"No!" Tonia screeched.

Mr Huff came to his senses and jumped to his wife's aid, but it was too late.

One final crack, and Annora let go. Carol Huff's body fell to the ground.

Mr Huff melted over his wife, bawling.

"Let me out," Annora said to him.

"There's no way out," he mumbled the words through hefty sobs.

She stepped closer to him. "Let me out."

Across the room, Maggie side-stepped to her bag in the corner and took out the two knives she and Tonia had carried on their journey. She handed one back to Tonia and held the other close to her.

"He's telling the truth," Maggie called. "There's no way out of here. They locked us in."

"His Grace needs me," Annora rocked back and forth and side to side, manic. "We will mark the path for him. He will show the world that he is almighty."

"He's disgusting," Mr Huff spat.

Annora roared. She picked up the corner of the bed and flipped it onto its side. Then, without blinking, she smashed her fist directly into Mr Huff's face. And again. And again.

Maggie and Tonia gaped in horror.

The sound of bone on bone pierced the room.

His cries finally stopped, and Stanley Huff joined his lifeless wife on the floor of the hospital room.

"We have to get out of here," Tonia stuttered.

Maggie pulled out the electronic key from her pocket and buzzed the door open.

They raced to the nearest exit and tried to open it with the key card. A red light told them their access was denied.

"Try again!" Tonia urged, banging her fist on the door.

"It's not working! They locked down this whole wing, remember?"

"Let's try the other way," Tonia pulled at Maggie's sleeve.

As they ran down the corridor, they could hear the scraping and banging as Annora tried to escape her room.

"Fuck!" Maggie cried. "All of these doors are locked! Shouldn't there be a fire escape or something?"

Tonia looked at her, answerless.

Maggie froze. "Tonia," she whispered.

"What?" Tonia whispered back.

"Do you hear that?"

Tonia stood still. Her face drained. She nodded.

A low, gurgling breath was clearly audible. Every few seconds, the sound of chains rattled.

Both girls took a defensive stance, holding out the knives.

Slowly, Annora dragged herself round the corner and into view.

"Let. Me. Out."

"We can't! Look!" Without turning her back, Maggie reached out and swiped the sensor. "Access denied, see! We're all trapped!"

Annora put her hands up and scraped her fingers down the wall with the desperation of someone being buried alive. One hand left fresh blood tracks on the whitewashed walls.

"Let me out!" came her frenzied caterwaul again.

"I told you, I can't!"

Annora let out the most mind-piercing of banshee screams and leapt toward Maggie, pushing her back into the wall, tearing at her face and hair.

"No!" Tonia yelled.

"Annora, stop, please!" Maggie bellowed.

But Annora couldn't hear Maggie's plea.

With all the strength she could muster, Maggie thrust the blade upward into Annora's stomach.

Annora continued thrashing at Maggie, biting at her face.

"No!" Maggie cried helplessly.

Annora's hands found their way to Maggie's throat. She squeezed. She squeezed and barraged the back of Maggie's head against the wall. Maggie's fingernails sank into Annora's bony hands.

And then she fell.

Annora collapsed, face down onto the floor, with the blade handle sticking out of her back.

74

Jessa opened her eyes and released the tension from her hunched neck as she looked up. She was still surrounded by a crowd of chaos, and the dead eyes still looked down on her from above. Flynn, Hugo, Felicia, Audrey and Matt all wore scowls on their faces. Something wasn't right. Their plan had failed. Again and again, Hugo's thumb jammed into the top of the detonator. Nothing.

"We're in range, this has to be close enough," he said desperately.

Silas remained on the balcony, looking down at the mass below. His mouth hung slightly open, breathing long breaths, taking in the sight and the sound of the madness he created.

"No!" Jessa held back tears of frustration. "This is the only plan we had! Maybe we need to be closer?"

"I just don't know," Hugo said, helpless.

Jessa seized the detonator and ran before any of them could stop her. With all her strength she pushed and squeezed through the crowd to get closer to the stairwell. Suddenly, the sound of bullets ripped through the air. Jessa cowered amid shrieks around her. Again, another round of bullets machined from the barrel of a high-powered weapon, and Jessa knew it must be the others trying a more conventional way to bring Silas down. To the amazement of the crowd, Silas didn't even flinch at the bullets. They ricocheted off the forcefield around him and scattered down below.

Jessa realised the extent to which Silas had prepared for this occasion, and at the same time realised that they could not eradicate him with their shoddy on-the-fly traps or weaponry. He was smarter than that. He was completely prepared and totally unreachable.

Finally, he spoke.

"Welcome to the revolution."

His voice not only carried through the vaulted ceiling of St Paul's, but also spoke out through the mouths of his chosen, speaking down to the onlookers like a surround sound system.

"The Age of the Parapsych begins tonight. People, citizens, realise unto me your faith in the parapsych and the unstoppable force of human evolution.'

All around, stunned faces stared and sobbed and begged for it to stop.

"Let me lead you all in this new beginning."

"Please... please, no..." the beseeching voices whispered in response.

Silas' arms rose up, as did the floating bodies above the crowd. His jaw hung low in an inhuman gasp as a deathly groan escaped the mouths of the children. Their small frames shook and shivered as Silas began to suck the life from them, pulling all the energy from their barely conscious bodies.

He shuddered. His face turned psychotically gleeful as the power took over him, running through his veins like electricity.

Then, in a second, he changed. A different expression flew over him. Shock, confusion. Jessa squinted, focusing hard on what was happening in the balcony above.

Pain. He was in pain. The children continued to tremble violently in the air, but as Silas tried to steal the life from them, his reality came crashing down.

Cecily turned her attention to him. Her face panicked, her hands gripped at Silas, trying to help him stand. Silas's other two companions looked on, flummoxed and impotent.

Silas clutched at his chest, gasping for air. Pounding at his heart with one hand, he leaned against the balcony with the other, desperately trying to hold himself up. It looked like he was trying to speak, but anything he could say was drowned out by wails and shouts from the sea of confused and fearful onlookers below, their arms outstretched to the children above.

Jessa couldn't take her eyes off Silas Lynch.

In an instant that took everyone in the room by surprise, a lightning strike of energy shot from his outreached fingertips and cracked across the expansive room. The crowd below screamed and instinctively shielded their heads. Cecily and the two men jumped back.

A silvery white beam shattered again through Silas' body and up into the ceiling, fracturing stonework that crumbled down onto the heads of people below. Jessa could only look on as Silas battled between frantic writhing and spontaneous outbursts of energy that fizzled visibly below his skin before escaping his body and violently shooting outward into the high ceiling, showering the audience with dust and stone.

The children's shuddering grew more intense, but their eyes regained a terrified focus, as each shake seemed to bring them back from the brink of death. Several of the younger and smaller children began to gasp in long, deliberate breaths, then the older ones followed suit.

Silas' movement became intermittent, though the electric bursts continued to rip from his body.

Suddenly, the children choked one giant gulp together, taking in air like they'd been rescued from underwater. They fell back down to the earth, crashing into arms and heads below that pulled them into the crowd tightly and protectively.

And in one final burst of crackling energy, Silas's form slumped over the balcony, his arms hanging down, his head dangling, his body dead and human.

The crowd roared, and many of them pushed toward the balcony entrance. The two men grabbed hold of the body and disappeared into the darkness of the stairwell. By the time the crowd rushed in, the men, Cecily Graves, and Silas' lifeless body were all gone. Vanished.

75

"Tonia?" Annora croaked.

"Annora?"

"What have I done..."

Maggie and Tonia rushed to Annora's side.

"It's really you?" Maggie said, tentative.

"He's gone."

"What?"

"I don't... I don't feel him anymore."

Annora's hospital gown was quickly becoming drenched in blood.

"Try not to talk, okay?" Tonia stroked Annora's hair. "Maggie, maybe there's something in that kit you can use? Bandages, or stitches? Anything?"

"No, please don't leave," Annora said. "Can you both stay with me? I don't have much time."

"But there's this box of medical supplies—Maggie might be able to—"

Annora coughed a glob of bright red blood.

"It's too late," she wheezed.

"I'm so sorry. I'm so, so sorry," Tonia grovelled over Annora's shivering body. "Please forgive me."

"I forgive you..." the words lurched from her throat. "You saved Maggie... I'm proud of you."

Every breath sounded wet.

"I'm proud of you, too," Tonia cradled Annora's hand in her own.

"Is there anything we can do?" Maggie asked. "Anything?"

"No, it's okay," Annora coughed again and groaned in pain. "Actually," she muttered. "Do you have music?"

"I do," Maggie couldn't help but smile a choked and sorrowful smile. "I don't have very much, though, I'm sorry. What would you like to listen to?" she tried not to let the tears overrun her.

"Something… pretty."

Maggie searched her playlist quickly.

"Ah, this one's my favourite, it's a piano sonata. Here," she placed the device near Annora so she could hear it better.

Tonia and Maggie lay down beside Annora, and each of them held one of her hands. Over the music, they could no longer hear her pained sighs and the laborious breaths from her blood-filled lungs. And there they lay, on the hospital floor, and they listened until the very last note.

76

"It was my little brother, Aiden. He was one of the chosen. He's eight. We had no idea anything had even happened to him. He didn't have any symptoms. So my family and me were all just watching TV, and Aiden was asleep in our mum's lap. And then all of a sudden he wakes up and he's possessed or mad or something, and he's running around like an animal. He bit our Dad. It was horrible. And then he went to the front door and was scraping at it but couldn't get the door unlocked. Eventually, he pulled the chain off the door and got out. We followed him into the crowd outside, and then he lifted his arms up. The next thing we knew, he was above the crowd, like he was flying."

Jessa woke up for what felt like the hundredth time, unsticking her eyelids and blinking away the blurs of desperate slumber. Her head pounded from the dehydration of too much sleep, and she could tell that her three days of rest and no shower had led her to a lazy stink. She finally pulled herself out of bed and scuffled past the tray of comfort food that had been left outside her bedroom door.

She took a cool shower and tried to gather some semblance of personness.

"Me and my mates saw it on the news after Lynch showed up at that hotel. And when he said all that about being really powerful and all, we didn't really believe it at first, we thought it was just someone having a laugh. Then when

*he used his telekinesis to actually lift that fella up, we were like what the f**k?! And then he disappeared and we was proper livid, then. Lynch was obviously a monster, but the fact that he was able to do all that stuff, and nobody knew about it? Yeah, that made us properly pissed off. That's probably the main reason we joined the march. Even by the time we got to Downing Street, though, it was already packed enough that we couldn't get close."*

Cleaner and more awake, Jessa slipped into a fresh bath robe and took a deep breath before going downstairs. As she approached the kitchen, she could hear the sound of adults talking. In the background, the television regaled first-hand tales of the recent happenings.

"I told you, Mike, I think we should leave her be."

"She's been in bed for three days, Jean. She's barely eaten; she hasn't said a word."

"She just needs to come to terms with things on her own time."

"But she has no idea what's going on at the moment. What if they come and she's not ready? Remember what they said on the news, Jean, 'resistance will not be tolerated'."

"Oh, stop that right now. Stop talking like one of them."

"But they are coming, we know that. And we know our sweet girl doesn't have a bad bone in her body, so it's all going to be fine. It's just a precaution."

Jean Baxter sighed loudly. "Precaution, yeah right. It's inhumane, Mike, that's what it is! What right do they have to do this?"

"They're just afraid."

"Of what?! Lynch was the one to be afraid of, and he's gone now. End of story."

"Sweetheart, not everyone sees it the way we do. They need to make sure this won't happen again."

"And what, treating all parapsychs like criminals is going to help? It's monstrous. I thought we as a civilised population were past this kind of judgment and barbarism."

"I just can't believe all this is happening," Audrey said sadly. "I would have always thought that an event like this would bring people together, not drive them further apart."

"At the very least," Hugo replied, "I would never have expected things to go this way."

"My husband and I live in a flat on Fleet Street. We're on the second floor, so we saw the whole thing. We were watching the news, and there was a cameraman in the crowd. So there we were, following it live, and then my husband says to me, "Janet, that's just up the road," and he was right, they were heading right for us. So we ran to the window, and sure enough, they went right past our building. It was just horrifying. People didn't know what to do. From above them, all we could see of the chosen were the backs of them as they floated along above the crowd. It was like something from a nightmare. Some people were chanting "get Lynch," and others were just screaming and crying. Eventually, the chosen passed and then it was just a mass of people in the street, climbing over cars, and others were smashing shop windows in. I don't know if they were looting or just looking for a place to hide, but we were so frightened that we barricaded our door from the inside."

"Have you heard anything about them reopening the borders?" Jean asked.

"Nope," said Hugo. "I think it's indefinite, until they get all the interviews done."

"I'm really worried about Jessa's interview," Audrey said quietly. "They're bound to find out that she knew something. Especially after what happened to Felicia Mortlock."

"Felicia's situation was different; she has a history with Lynch. Plus, they seized her possessions. That won't happen to Jessa," Hugo said quietly.

"Poor Felicia," Audrey replied. "What did they even find that was so damning?"

"I heard from John that she'd kept an old diary from back in the day, but that's all I know. I just hope she's all right."

"I doubt it," Audrey said. "We don't even know where they took her. I wonder how many others have been detained."

"What are you talking about?" Jessa entered the kitchen. "What happened to Dr Mortlock?"

"Oh, Jessa! There you are!" her mother embraced her with a tight hug that Jessa half-heartedly returned.

"What were you talking about? What's going on?"

"Sit down, love. We'll explain everything."

"I was by myself. I tried to join a peaceful protest at Westminster, but when the fights started breaking out, I ran away. Then when I saw the big march toward St Paul's, I guess I just panicked and joined them, because I didn't know what else to do. It was horrendous, but I couldn't look away. They all filled the place so quickly that by the time I got inside, I was quite far back, near the front door, but I could see clearly enough. When he came out onto the balcony, the sound from the crowd was the loudest thing I've ever heard. Then when they all started shaking, I cried. I don't even know any of the chosen, but I got so overwhelmed that I was just bawling my eyes out, and the people all around me all started holding each other's hands. It was surreal; I can't believe it actually happened. I know a lot of people are trying to figure out what happened to Silas Lynch, and I was pretty far back, so I guess I'm not the most accurate source, but it looked to me like he had a heart attack. It's like he was taking all that energy from the chosen but he couldn't handle it—his body literally just failed. I guess maybe that's a good thing, right? That there's a limit to how much power someone could have? I don't know. I just hope everything gets back to normal soon."

77

"I think mine's on too tight," Maggie fiddled with the bracelet on her wrist.

"Nah, you're just getting used to it still," Flynn said, checking the space between Maggie's bracelet and her skin. "It's fine."

"I don't get it, though. How is it supposed to measure our parabilities?" Jessa asked, stretching her legs out across the picnic blanket on the lawn.

"Something to do with electromagnetic readings," Maggie said. "It's similar to those smartwatch monitors that record heart rate and stuff."

"So it's just going to be constantly recording information about when we use our abilities?" Jessa frowned.

"I think so," Maggie shrugged.

"I don't see how it's going to help," Flynn said.

"I heard that the information it records won't be readily available," Maggie continued, "but can be accessed if necessary. The example they used on the news was if a parapsych is arrested for breaking into someone's house, then they can check the electromagnetic data for that time and see if there's an energy spike, and if there is, you'll know that person used their abilities to commit that crime."

"But that person's abilities didn't make them a criminal," Jessa snapped. "And a parapsych could still commit a crime without using their abilities."

"I know," Maggie nodded. "The whole premise is flawed. And it's a violation of human rights, so I'm sure the decision will get overturned soon."

"I'm not so sure about that," Flynn raised his eyebrows.

"Why? It has to get overturned."

"Maybe eventually, but I don't see it happening anytime soon," Flynn continued. "They seem to be going to a lot of effort to put all these things in place. I don't see why they'd go to the trouble of interviewing every parapsych and making everyone wear these things if there wasn't a long-term change in the process."

The cheerful din of electronic pop on the radio faded out, and a series of digital pellet sounds pattered in.

"It's 2 pm on Saturday the 8th of May. I'm Sandy Sanderson, and this is NewsBullet. The Home Office has once again defended its decision to roll out extreme security measures among the parapsych population. The Home Secretary said in a statement today that he is considering the recent developments an issue of national security, and is determined to find all those accountable and hold them to justice.

Caroline Hambledon, the mother of chosen teenager Lauren Hambledon, has passed away after weeks in a coma. 42-year-old Mrs Hambledon becomes the twenty-seventh victim who died after being brutally attacked by the chosen in their efforts to join the now deceased Silas Lynch—"

Jessa snapped off the radio.

"Sorry," she said quietly. "I can't listen to that."

"Do you think they'll find Cecily?" Maggie asked.

"Probably," said Flynn. "If they're really tracking down every parapsych, they'll catch up with her eventually."

Jessa sighed.

"I wonder if school will be open next term," Flynn changed the subject, running his hand gently over the tops of the blades of grass.

"I have no idea. Hugo hasn't said anything about it," Jessa shrugged. "I heard that parapsych students might just have to go to regular schools until the curriculum is reworked."

"I saw the same thing," Maggie shook her head. "I don't want to go to a comprehensive!"

"You might not have to go to a comp, there are still lateral grammar schools," Flynn reasoned.

"I can't believe we didn't get to do final exams," Maggie mourned.

"Why are you so sad? They just used our coursework for grades, and you still got As in everything," Jessa mocked.

"Yeah, but still," Maggie sulked.

"But nothing," Jessa said back, playfully nudging Maggie with her foot. "Are you okay, Flynn? You're really quiet."

He sighed. "I'm all right, I just—I heard from Tonia today."

"Really?" the girls said. "What did she say? Where is she? Is she okay?"

"Yeah. She left right after the funeral. She's staying with her aunt and uncle in Wales."

"Is she coming back?"

"I don't know. If Winsbury re-opens, then maybe. But if not, apparently she might just stay and go to school in Cardiff."

"I'm sorry," said Jessa.

Flynn poked at the ice in his cup.

"Everything's changing," Jessa said quietly.

The three teenagers sipped quietly at their drinks as each of them fell into a private contemplation. The sounds of London floated into and out of the garden on a breeze. The occasional waft of petroleum or barbeque wandered over them. Jessa Baxter stared up from the lawn at a single magpie in a tree above her. It twittered and hopped from branch to branch and then flew away out of sight, leaving Jessa there, staring up through the trees and into the vast expanse of an overcast summer sky.

Acknowledgements

The first person I need to thank is Matthew Milligan. It's taken me two years to write this book, and he's been one-hundred-percent supportive since day one. He listened to me whine when I couldn't make a scene work. He listened to my nonsensical babble as I bounced plot ideas off him, and he was even able to make sense of questions like "if you were an evil cult leader, what would you do in this situation?" or "if you were a teenage girl, what would you think if someone said this to you?" Matthew has been an integral part in the writing of this story, and I am extremely lucky and grateful to have such a supportive partner in creativity, love and life.

Thank you to my writing helpers: Kyra Challen, Manda Evans, and Missy Krufka. Even though we are all located so far away from one another, they were always hand via Facebook, text, and email, when I couldn't figure out how to get from one scene to another, or when I couldn't decide whether to use a semicolon or an em-dash.

Then we have my readers: Ken Flagg, Reagan Edmiston, and Tom Milligan. They connected the things that needed connecting. They helped me turn my raw, typo-ridden ideas into an actual, readable book.

Bonus thanks go to Arlaina Tibensky and my classmates at the Gotham Writers' Workshop, for helping me re-work the opening of the novel, and for giving such positive feedback on my writing as a whole. On days when I was generally just feeling bad about my writing ability, I would look back over the notes they made on my stories and I would remind myself: "Yes. I can do this."

And now, a shower of appreciation for all the other important people in my life. Thanks go to:

Sara Na, for being a consistent ray of sunshine in an often dark world.

Michele, Thomas, Andrew, and the extended Milligan family, for always being interested in my activities and supporting me no matter what.

Danny, Jayde, and David, for being the coolest brother, sister-in-law and nephew I could ask for.

My parents, who are no longer with us but who taught me that the world is made brighter by creativity.

Karlie Bruce, for always being on hand for coffee breaks.

Nate Roberson, for helping make a little more sense of the publishing world.

Brendan B. Brown and the entire Wheatus family, for being the hardest-working and most creative bunch of people I've ever had the pleasure of knowing.

Seth Krufka, for being an exemplary human.

Andrew Monsen, Katie Monsen, Phil Mazzullo and Laura Schmidt, for consistent fun and friendship.

Netflix, for always being there when I needed help the most.

J.K. Rowling, for Harry Potter.